Marry
PRINCE
Wedding Party Collection

Marrying the
PRINCE

Wedding Party Collection

Kate
HEWITT

Sandra
HYATT

Published in Great Britain 2017
By Mills & Boon, an imprint of HarperCollins*Publishers*
1 London Bridge Street, London, SE1 9GF

WEDDING PARTY COLLECTION: MARRYING THE PRINCE
© 2017 Harlequin Books S.A.

The Prince She Never Knew © 2013 Kate Hewitt
His Bride for the Taking © 2010 Sandra Hyatt
A Queen for the Taking? © 2014 Kate Hewitt

ISBN: 9780263930993

09-0517

Our policy is to use papers that are natural, renewable and recyclable products and made from wood grown in sustainable forests.
The logging and manufacturing processes conform to the legal environmental regulations of the country of origin.

Printed and bound in Spain
by CPI, Barcelona

THE PRINCE SHE NEVER KNEW

KATE HEWITT

Kate Hewitt discovered her first Mills & Boon romance novel on a trip to England when she was thirteen, and she's continued to read them ever since. She wrote her first story at the age of five, simply because her older brother had written one and she thought she could do it, too. That story was one sentence long – fortunately, they've become a bit more detailed as she's grown older.

She studied drama in college and shortly after graduation moved to New York City to pursue a career in theatre. This was derailed by something far better – meeting the man of her dreams, who happened also to be her older brother's childhood friend. Ten days after their wedding they moved to England, where Kate worked in a variety of different jobs – drama teacher, editorial assistant, youth worker, secretary and, finally, mother.

When her oldest daughter was one year old, Kate sold her first short story to a British magazine. Since then she has sold many stories and serials, but writing romance remains her first love – of course!

Besides writing, she enjoys reading, travelling and learning to knit – it's an on-going process and she's made a lot of scarves. After living in England for six years, she now resides in Connecticut with her husband, her three young children and, possibly one day, a dog.

Kate loves to hear from readers. You can contact her through her website, **www.kate-hewitt.com**.

CHAPTER ONE

Today was her wedding day. Alyse Barras gazed at her pale, pinched face in the mirror and decided that not all brides were radiant. As it happened, she looked as if she were on the way to the gallows.

No, she amended, not the gallows; a quick and brutal end was not to be hers, but rather a long, drawn-out life sentence: a loveless marriage to a man whom she barely knew, despite their six-year engagement. Yet even so a small kernel of hope was determined to take root in her heart, to unfurl and grow in the shallowest and poorest of soils.

Maybe he'll learn to love me...

Prince Leo Diomedi of Maldinia seemed unlikely to learn anything of the sort, yet still she hoped. She had to.

'Miss Barras? Are you ready?'

Alyse turned from her reflection to face one of the wedding coordinator's assistants who stood in the doorway of the room she'd been given in the vast royal palace in Averne, Maldinia's capital city, nestled in the foothills of the Alps.

'As ready as I'll ever be,' she replied, trying to smile, but everything in her felt fragile, breakable, and the curve of her lips seemed as if it could crack her face. Split her apart.

The assistant Marina came forward, looking her over

in the assessing and proprietary way Alyse had got used to in the three days since she'd arrived in Maldinia—or, really, the six years since she'd agreed to this engagement. She was a commodity to be bought, shaped, presented. An object of great value, to be sure, but still an object.

She'd learned to live with it, although on today of all days—her wedding day, the day most little girls dreamed about—she felt the falseness of her own role more, the sense that her life was simply something to be staged.

Marina twitched Alyse's veil this way and that, until she gave a nod of satisfaction. It billowed gauzily over her shoulders, a gossamer web edged with three-hundred-year-old lace.

'And now the dress,' Marina said, and flicked her fingers to indicate that Alyse should turn around.

Alyse moved slowly in a circle as Marina examined the yards of white satin that billowed out behind her, the lace bodice that hugged her breasts and hips and had taken eight top-secret fittings over the last six months. The dress had been the source of intense media speculation, the subject of hundreds of articles in tabloids, gossip magazines, even respected newspapers, television and radio interviews, celebrity and gossip blogs and websites.

What kind of dress would the world's real-life Cinderella—not a very creative way of typecasting her, but it had stuck—wear to marry her very own prince, her one true love?

Well, this. And Alyse had had no say in it at all. It was a beautiful dress, she allowed as she caught a glance of the billowing white satin in the full-length mirror. She could hardly complain. She might have chosen something just like it—if she'd been given a choice.

Marina's walkie-talkie crackled and she spoke into it in rapid Italian, too fast for Alyse to understand, even though she'd been learning Italian ever since she'd become engaged to Leo. It was the native language of his country, and Maldinia's queen-in-waiting should be able to speak it. Unfortunately no one spoke slowly enough for her to be able to understand.

'They're ready.' Marina twitched the dress just as she had the veil and then rummaged on the vanity table for some blusher. 'You look a bit pale,' she explained, and brushed Alyse's cheeks with blusher even though the make-up artist had already spent an hour on her face.

'Thank you,' Alyse murmured. She wished her mother were here, but the royal protocol was—and always had been, according to Queen Sophia—that the bride prepare by herself. Alyse wondered whether that was true. Queen Sophia tended to insist on doing things the way they'd 'always been done' when really it was simply the way she wanted them done. And even though Alyse's mother, Natalie, was Queen Sophia's best friend from their days together at a Swiss boarding school, she clearly didn't want Natalie getting in the way on this most important and august of occasions.

Or so Alyse assumed. She was the bride, and she felt as if she were in the way.

She wondered if she would feel so as a wife.

No. She closed her eyes as Marina next dusted her face with loose powder. She couldn't think like that, couldn't give in to the despair, not on today of all days. She had once before, and it had led only to heartache and regret. Today she wanted to hope, to believe, or at least to try to. Today was meant to be a beginning, not an end.

But if Leo hasn't learned to love me in the last six years, why should he now?

Two months ago, with media interest at a frenzied height, her mother had taken her on a weekend to Monaco. They'd sat in deck chairs and sipped frothy drinks and

Alyse had felt herself just begin to relax when Natalie had said, 'You don't have to do this if you don't want to.'

She'd tensed all over again, her drink halfway to her lips. 'Do what?'

'Marry him, Alyse. I know it's all got completely out of hand with the media, and also with the Diomedis, to be frank. But you are still your own woman and I want to make sure you're sure…' Her mother had trailed off, her eyes clouded with anxiety, and Alyse had wondered what she'd guessed.

Did she have even an inkling of how little there was between her and Leo? Few people knew; the world believed they were madly in love, and had done ever since Leo had first kissed her cheek six years ago and the resulting photograph had captured the public's imagination.

Leo's mother Sophia knew, of course, as the pretense of their grand romance had been her idea, Alyse suspected, and of course Leo's father, Alessandro, who had first broached the whole idea to her when she'd been just eighteen years old and starry-eyed over Leo. Perhaps Alexa—Leo's sister, her fiery nature so different from his own sense of cool containment—had guessed.

And, naturally, Leo knew. Leo knew he didn't love her. He just didn't know that for six years she'd been secretly, desperately, loving him.

'I'm happy, Maman,' Alyse had said quietly, and had reached over to squeeze her mother's hand. 'I admit, the media circus isn't my favourite part, but…I love Leo.' She had stumbled only slightly over this unfortunate truth.

'I want for you what your father and I have had,' Natalie had said, and Alyse had smiled wanly. Her parents' romance was something out of a fairy tale: the American heiress who had captured the heart of a wealthy French financier. Alyse had heard the story many times, how her father had seen her mother across a crowded room—they'd both been attending some important dinner—and he had made his way over to her and said, 'What are you doing with the rest of your life?'

She'd simply smiled and answered, 'Spending it with you.'

Love at first sight. And not just an ordinary, run-of-the-mill love, but of the over-the-top, utterly consuming variety.

Of course her mother wanted that for her. And Alyse would never admit to her how little she actually had, even as she still clung stubbornly to the hope that one day it might become more.

'I'm happy,' she'd repeated, and her mother had looked relieved if not entirely convinced.

Marina's walkie-talkie crackled again, and once again Alyse let the rapid-fire Italian assault her with incomprehension.

'They're waiting,' Marina announced briskly, and Alyse wondered if she imagined that slightly accusing tone. She'd felt it since she'd arrived in Maldinia, mostly from Queen Sophia: *you're not precisely what we'd have chosen for our son and heir, but you'll have to do. We have no choice, after all.*

The media—the whole world—had made sure of that. There had been no going back from that moment captured by a photographer six years ago when Leo had come to her eighteenth birthday party and brushed his lips against her cheek in a congratulatory kiss. Alyse, instinctively and helplessly, had stood on her tiptoes and clasped her hand to his face.

If she could go back in time, would she change that moment? Would she have turned her face away and stopped all the speculation, the frenzy?

No, she wouldn't have, and the knowledge was galling. At first it had been her love for Leo that had made her agree to their faked fairy tale, but as the years had passed and Leo had shown no interest in loving her—or love at all—she'd considered whether to cut her losses and break off the engagement.

She never had; she'd possessed neither the courage nor conviction to do something that would quite literally have rocked the world. And of course she'd clung to a hope that seemed naïve at best, more likely desperate: that he would learn to love her.

And yet...we get along. We're friends, of a sort. Surely that's a good foundation for marriage?

Always the hope.

'This way, Miss Barras,' Marina said, and ushered her out of the room she'd been getting dressed in and down a long, ornate corridor with marble walls and chandeliers glittering overhead every few feet.

The stiff satin folds of Alyse's dress rustled against the parquet as she followed Marina down the hallway and towards the main entrance of the palace where a dozen liveried footmen stood to attention. She would make the walk to the cathedral across the street and then the far more important walk down the aisle by herself, another Maldinian tradition.

'Wait.' Marina held up a hand and Alyse paused in front of the gilt-panelled doors that led to the front courtyard of the palace where at least a hundred reporters and photographers, probably more, waited to capture this iconic moment. Alyse had had so many iconic moments in the last six years she felt as if her entire adult life had been catalogued in the glossy pages of gossip magazines.

Marina circled her the way Alyse imagined a lion or tiger circled its prey. She was being fanciful, she knew, but her nerves were stretched to breaking point. She'd been in Maldinia for three days and she hadn't seen Leo outside of state functions once. Hadn't spoken to him alone in over a year.

And she was marrying him in approximately three minutes.

Paula, the royal family's press secretary, approached with a brisk click of heels. 'Alyse? You're ready?' she asked in accented English.

She nodded back, not trusting herself to speak.

'Excellent. Now, all you need to remember is to smile. You're Cinderella and this is your glass slipper moment, yes?' She twitched Alyse's veil just as Sophia had done, and Alyse wondered how much more pointless primping she would have to endure. As soon as she stepped outside the veil would probably blow across her face anyway. At least she had enough hair spray in her hair to prevent a single strand from so much as stirring. She felt positively shellacked.

'Cinderella,' she repeated. 'Right.' She'd been acting like Cinderella for six years. She didn't really need the reminder.

'Everyone wants to be you,' Paula continued. 'Every girl, every woman, is dreaming of walking in your shoes right now. And every man wants to be the prince. Don't forget to wave—this is about them as much as you. Include everyone in the fantasy, yes?'

'Right. Yes.' She knew that, had learned it over the years of public attention. And, truthfully, she didn't mind the attention of the crowds, of people who rather incredibly took encouragement and hope from her and her alleged fairy tale of a life. All they wanted from her was friendliness, a smile, a word. All she needed to be was herself.

It was the paparazzi she had trouble with, the constant scrutiny and sense of invasion as rabid journalists and photographers looked for cracks in the fairy-tale image, ways to shatter it completely.

'I'd better get out there before the clock strikes twelve,' she joked, trying to smile, but her mouth was so dry her lips stuck to her teeth. Paula frowned, whipping a tissue from her pocket to blot Alyse's lipstick.

'We're at thirty seconds,' Marina intoned, and Paula positioned Alyse in front of the doors. 'Twenty...'

Alyse knew she was supposed to emerge when the huge, ornate clock on one of the palace's towers chimed the first of its eleven sonorous notes. She would walk sedately, head held high, towards the cathedral as the clock continued chiming and arrive at its doors when the last chime fell into silence.

It had all been choreographed and rehearsed several times, down to the last second. Everything arranged, orchestrated, managed.

'Ten...'

Alyse took a deep breath, or as deep a breath as the tightly fitted bodice of her dress would allow. She felt dizzy, spots dancing before her eyes, although whether from lack of air or sheer nerves she didn't know.

'Five...'

Two footmen opened the doors to the courtyard with a flourish, and Alyse blinked in the sudden brilliance of the sun. The open doorway framed a dazzling blue sky, the two Gothic towers of the cathedral opposite and a huge throng of people.

'Go,' Paula whispered, and gave her a firm nudge in the small of her back.

Pushed by Paula, she moved forward, her dress snagging on her heel so she stumbled ever so slightly. Still it was enough for the paparazzi to notice, and dozens of cameras snapped frantically to capture the moment. Another iconic moment; Alyse could already picture the headlines: *First Stumble on The Road to Happiness?*

She steadied herself, lifted her head and gave the entire viewing world a brilliant smile. The answering cheer roared through the courtyard. Alyse could feel the sound reverberate through her chest, felt her spirits lift at their obvious excitement and approbation.

This was why she was marrying Leo, why the royal family of Maldinia had agreed to his engagement to a mere commoner: because everyone loved her.

Everyone but Leo.

Still smiling, raising one hand in a not-so-regal wave, Alyse started walking towards the cathedral. She heard a few snatched voices amidst the crowd, shouting her name, asking her to turn for a photo. She smiled, leaving the white carpet that had been laid from the palace to the cathedral to shake people's hands, accept posies of flowers.

She was deviating from the remote, regal script she'd been given, but then she always did. She couldn't help but respond to people's warmth and friendliness; all too often it was what strengthened her to maintain this charade that wasn't a charade at all—for her. For Leo, of course, it was.

But maybe, please God, it won't always be...

'Good luck, Alyse,' one starry-eyed teen gushed, clasping her hands tightly. 'You look so beautiful—you really are a princess!'

Alyse squeezed the girl's hands. 'Thank you,' she murmured. 'You look beautiful too, you know. You're glowing more than I am!'

She realised the clock had stopped chiming; she was late. Queen Sophia would be furious, yet it was because of moments like these she was here at all. She didn't stick to the royal family's formalised script; she wrote her own lines without even meaning to and the public loved them.

Except she didn't know what her lines would be once she was married. She had no idea what she would say to Leo when she finally faced him as his wife.

I love you.

Those were words she was afraid he'd never want to hear.

The cathedral doors loomed in front of her, the interior of the building dim and hushed. Alyse turned one last time towards the crowd and another roar went up, echoing through the ancient streets of Averne. She waved and blew them a kiss, and she heard another cheer. Perhaps the kiss was a bit over the top, but she felt in that moment strangely reckless, almost defiant. There was no going back now.

And then she turned back to the cathedral and her waiting groom.

Leo stood with his back to the doors of the cathedral, but he knew the moment when Alyse had entered. He heard the murmurs fall to an expectant hush, and the roar of approbation that she generated wherever she went had fallen to silence outside. He flexed his shoulders once and remained with his back to the door—and his bride. Maldinian princes did not turn around until the bride had reached the altar and Leo deviated from neither tradition nor duty.

The organ had started playing with sonorous grandeur, some kind of baroque march, and he knew Alyse was walking towards him. He felt a flicker of curiosity; he hadn't seen her dress, had no idea what she looked like in it. Polished, poised and as perfect as usual, he presumed. The perfect bride. The perfect love story. And of course, the perfect marriage. All of it the perfect pretense.

Nothing more.

Finally he felt the folds of her dress whisper against his legs and he turned to face her. He barely noticed the dress. Her face was pale except for two spots of blusher high on her cheekbones. She looked surprisingly nervous, he thought. For the past six years she'd been handling the intense media scrutiny of their engagement with apparent effortless ease, and her attack of nerves now surprised him. Alarmed him a bit too.

She'd agreed to all of this. It was a little late for cold feet.

Conscious of the stares of the congregation—as well as the cameras televising the ceremony live to millions of people—he smiled and took her hand, which was icy and small in his. He squeezed her fingers, an encouragement if anyone saw, but also a warning. Neither of them could make a mistake now. Too much rode on this marriage, this masquerade. She knew that; so did he. They'd both sold their souls, and willingly.

Now he watched as Alyse lifted her chin, her wide grey eyes flashing with both comprehension and spirit. Her lips curved in a tiny smile and she squeezed his hand back. He felt a flicker of admiration for her courage and poise—as well as one of relief. Crisis averted.

She turned towards the archbishop who was performing the ceremony and he saw the gleam of chestnut hair beneath the lace of her veil, the soft glimmer of a pearl in the shell-like curve of her ear. He turned to face the man as well.

Fifteen minutes later it was done. They'd said their vows and Leo had brushed his lips against Alyse's. He'd kissed her dozens, perhaps hundreds, of times during their engagement, always in front of a crowd. A camera.

He kissed her now as he always had, a firm press of lips that conveyed enthusiasm and even desire without actually feeling either. He didn't want to feel either; he wasn't about to complicate what had been a business arrangement by stirring up a hornet's nest of emotions—either in her or himself.

Although now that they were married, now that they would actually consummate this marriage, he would certainly allow himself to feel attraction at least, a natural desire. All his life he'd controlled such contrary emotions, refused to let them dictate his behaviour as they had his parents'. Refused to let them ruin his life and wreck the monarchy, as they had with his parents.

No, he had more dignity, more self-control, than that. But he certainly intended to take full advantage of his marriage vows—and his marriage bed. It didn't mean his emotions would actually be engaged.

Just his libido.

Leo lifted his head and gazed down at her, smiling slightly for the sake of their audience, and saw that Alyse was gazing at him with panic in her eyes. Her nerves clearly had not abated.

Suppressing his own annoyance, he gently wrapped his hands around hers—they were still icy—and pried them from his shoulders. 'All right?' he murmured.

She nodded, managed a rather sickly smile and turned towards the congregation for their recession down the aisle.

And now it begins, Leo thought. The rest of his life enacting this endless charade, started by a single moment six years ago.

Who could ever have known how a paparazzi photographer would catch that kiss? And not just his lips on her cheek but her hand clasped against his cheek, her face uplifted, eyes shining like silver stars.

That photo had been on the cover of every major publication in the western world. It had been named the third most influential photograph of the century, a fact which made Leo want to bark in cynical laughter. A single, *stupid* kiss influential? Important?

But it had become important, because the sight of the happiness shining from Alyse's eyes had ignited a generation, fired their hearts with faith in love and hope for the future. Some economists credited the photograph with helping to kick-start Europe's economy, a fact Leo thought entirely absurd.

Yet when the monarchy's public relations department had realised the power of that photograph, they had harnessed it for themselves. For him, his father King Alessandro and all the future Diomedis that would reign over Maldinia.

Which had led, inevitably, to this engagement and now marriage, he all the while pretending to live up to what that photograph had promised—because for the public to realise it was nothing more than a fake would be a disaster.

Hand in hand with his bride, he walked down the aisle and into a lifetime of pretending.

She was breaking up, splitting apart, all the fragile, barely held parts of her shattering into pieces. She'd held herself together for so long and now…?

She wasn't sure she could do it any more. And it was too late not to.

Somehow Alyse made it down the aisle, although everything around her—the people, the colours, the noise and light—was a blur. Everything but the look that had flashed in Leo's eyes after he'd kissed her, something bordering on impatient annoyance at her obvious unease. Her panic.

She felt Leo's arm like a band of iron beneath her hand. 'Smile as we come out of the cathedral,' he murmured, and then the crowds were upon them, their roar loud in their ears and, still feeling sick inside, she smiled for all she was worth.

The wordless roar turned into a rhythmic chant: *bacialo! Bacialo!*

The crowd wanted them to kiss. Wordlessly, Alyse turned to Leo, tilted her head up at him as he gazed down at her and stroked her cheek with a single fingertip and then, once again, brushed his lips against her in another emotionless kiss.

Even so that cool kiss touched Alyse's soul, whispered its impossible hopes into her heart. She kept her lips mostly slack beneath his, knowing after six years of such kisses he didn't want her to respond, never had. No hot, open-mouthed kisses of passion for them. Just these chaste displays of their mutual love and devotion.

He lifted his head and she smiled and waved to the crowd. It was done.

Still smiling, Leo led her to the waiting carriage, all gilt and scrollwork, like something out of a fairy tale. A Cinderella carriage for a Cinderella bride.

He helped her in and then sat next to her on the narrow leather seat, his thigh pressing against her hip, her dress billowing over his lap. The liveried coachman closed the door and they were off for a celebratory ride through the city, then back to the palace for the reception.

As soon as the door had closed, Leo's smile, his mask, dropped. There was no need for it now; no one was watching. He turned to her, a frown appearing between his brows.

'You're too pale.'

'I'm sorry,' she murmured. 'I'm tired.'

Leo's frown deepened, and then it ironed out and he sighed and raked his hands through his hair. 'It's no wonder. The last few days have been exhausting. I expect it will be good to get away.'

They were leaving tomorrow for a ten-day honeymoon: first a week on a private Caribbean island and then a whistle-stop tour through London, Paris and Rome.

Alyse's insides quaked as she thought of that first week. An entire week alone, without cameras or crowds, no one to perform for, no audience to entertain. A week completely by themselves.

She lived in both hope and fear of that week.

'Yes,' she said now, and thankfully her voice remained steady, strong. 'I expect it will.'

Leo turned to the window and waved at the crowds lining the ancient cobbled streets of Averne, and Alyse turned to her own window and waved as well. Each flutter of her fingers drained her, as if she were lifting a huge weight. Her engagement ring, an enormous emerald surrounded by pearls and diamonds, sparkled in the sun.

She didn't know why everything felt so much harder now. She'd been living this life for six years, after all. She'd come to enjoy her interactions with the public and had learned to live with the media's attention.

Yet today, on her wedding day, with nearly the last words she'd spoken having been vows before the world, before *God*…

She felt the falseness of their masquerade more than ever. They'd only been married a few minutes and already she felt how difficult, how draining, this life of play-acting was going to be. She'd been moving towards that realisation for months as the weight had dropped off and her stomach had churned with nerves, as everything had steamrolled ahead with such frightening implacability that she had known she couldn't call a halt to the proceedings even if she'd wanted to. The pretending.

And the terrible truth was, she *still* didn't want to. She'd still rather hope.

'Alyse?'

She turned from the window where she'd been blindly staring at the crowds, her hand rising and falling in a fluttering wave without even realising she was doing so. 'Yes?'

'You don't look well,' Leo said and he sounded concerned. 'Do you need a few moments to rest before we go into the reception?'

Alyse knew what the reception would entail: hours of

chatting, laughing and pretending to be in love. Of kissing Leo, squeezing his hand and laying her head on his shoulder. She'd done it all before, of course, but now it hurt more. It felt, absurdly perhaps, more fake.

'I'm fine.' She smiled and turned back to the window so he wouldn't see how her smile trembled and almost slid right off her face. 'I'm fine,' she said again, this time for herself, because she needed to believe it. She was stronger than this. She had to be stronger, because she'd chosen this life, knowing how hard it would be.

At times it might have felt as if she had no choice, with the pressure of both the media and the monarchy urging her to agree, but if she'd really wanted to break off the engagement she surely could have. She would have found the strength to.

No, she'd chosen this life, and chosen Leo; she'd believed in the duty she was performing and she'd held out for love.

She still did. Today was a beginning, she reminded herself. Today was the start of her and Leo's life together, days and nights spent with each other in a way neither of them had ever experienced before. Maybe, finally, Leo would fall in love with her.

Leo just wanted this day to be over. Although of course with its end would come a whole new, and rather interesting, complication: the night. Their wedding night.

He glanced again at Alyse; her face was turned away from him but he could still see how pale and wan she looked. And thin. The dress clung to her figure, which had already been slender but now looked rather waif-like. Clearly the strain of the heightened media attention had got to her over these last few months.

Just as it had got to him. He'd lived his life in the spotlight and he certainly should be used to it now. As a child, the play-acting for the media had confused him, but as he'd grown older he'd accepted it as the price he had to pay for the sake of his duty to the crown. At least this time, with Alyse, he'd chosen it. He'd entered this loveless marriage willingly, even happily.

Because wasn't it better to know love was a sham from the beginning, than to live in desperate yearning for it—just as he had done for the whole of his confused and unhappy childhood?

At least he and Alyse agreed on that. She'd always known he didn't love her, and he knew she didn't love him. Really, it was the perfect foundation for a marriage: agreed and emotionless expectations.

Yet he'd found the last few months of intense media speculation and interest wearying. The charade of acting as if they were in love had started to wear thin. And he'd wondered, not for the first time, just why Alyse had agreed to this marriage.

He'd never asked her, had never wanted to know. It was enough that she'd agreed, and she'd gone along with it ever since. Just as he had.

Only, unlike him, she had no incentive to please the press, no duty to repair a badly damaged monarchy and increase the tourist revenue for a small and struggling country. No need to pretend to be wildly in love. So why had she agreed all those years ago? Why had she continued to agree?

He had to assume it was because, like him, she wanted this kind of marriage. Or maybe she just wanted this kind of life—the life of a princess and one day a queen. He didn't fault her for it. She wouldn't be the first person to have her head turned by wealth and fame. In any case, she'd approached their union with a practical acceptance he admired, and she'd embraced the public as much as they'd embraced her.

Really, she was perfect. So why did he wonder? Why did he now feel a new, creeping uncertainty? The questions—and the lack of answers—annoyed him. He liked certainty and precision; he prided himself on both.

He didn't want to wonder about his bride on his wedding day. Didn't want to worry about why she looked so pale and shaky, or why her smile seemed less assured. He wanted things to be simple, straightforward, as they had been for the last six years.

There was no reason for marriage to complicate matters, he told himself.

The carriage came to a stop in front of the palace and he turned to her with a faint smile, determined to banish his brooding thoughts and keep their relationship on the courteous yet impersonal footing they'd maintained for their entire engagement.

'Shall we?' he said, one eyebrow lifted, and Alyse managed just as faint a smile back as she took his hand and allowed him to help her out of the carriage.

CHAPTER TWO

THEY WERE ALONE. Every muscle in Alyse's body ached with exhaustion, yet even so she could not keep a heart-stopping awareness of Leo from streaking through her as he closed the door behind them.

They'd retired to the tower suite, a sumptuous bed-room, bathroom and dressing-room all housed in one of the stone turrets of the ancient royal palace. A fire blazed in the hearth and a huge four-poster bed with silk cover-ings and sheets took up the main part of the room. Alyse stared at the white silk and lace negligee laid out on the bed and swallowed hard.

She and Leo had never talked about *this*.

They should have, she supposed, but then they had never really talked about anything. Their relationship— and she could only use that word loosely—had been little more than a long-term publicity stunt. Conversation had been limited to managing their appearances together.

And now they were married. It felt, at least to her, like a complete game-changer. Until now they'd only expe-rienced manufactured moments lived in the public eye; but here, for the first time, they were alone with no need for pretence.

Would *this* moment be real?

'Relax,' Leo said, coming up behind her. Alyse felt his breath on the back of her neck and she suppressed a shiver of both anticipation and nervousness. 'We've been waiting for six years; we don't need to rush things.'

'Right,' she murmured, and then he moved past her to the window. The latticed shutters were thrown open to a starlit sky. Earlier in the evening there had been fireworks all over the city; the celebrations of their marriage had gone on all day.

It was only now that the city's joy was finally subsiding, everyone heading back to his or her home—and Alyse and Leo to this honeymoon suite.

She watched as Leo loosened his black tie. He'd changed into a tuxedo for the evening party, and she into a designer gown chosen by the team of stylists hired to work on her. It was pale pink, strapless, with a frothy skirt. A Cinderella dress.

'Do you want to change?' Leo asked as he undid the top few studs of his shirt. Standing there, framed by the window, the ends of his bow-tie dangling against the crisp whiteness of his shirt, he looked unbearably handsome. His hair was a glossy midnight-black, and rumpled from where he'd carelessly driven his fingers through it.

His eyes were dark too—once Alyse had thought they were black but she'd learned long ago from having had to gaze adoringly up into them so many times they were actually a very dark blue.

And his body… She might not have seen it in all of its bare glory, but he certainly wore a suit well. Broad shoulders, trim hips, long and powerful legs, every part of him declared he was wonderfully, potently male.

Would she see that body tonight? Would she caress and kiss it, give in to the passion she knew she could feel for him if he let her?

And what about him? Would he feel it?

In the course of six years, he'd always been solicitous, considerate, unfailingly polite. She couldn't fault him, and yet she'd yearned for more. For emotion, passion and, yes, always love. She'd always been drawn to the intensity she felt pulsing latent beneath his coolness, the passion she wanted to believe could be unleashed if he ever freed himself from the bonds of duty and decorum. If he ever revealed himself to her.

Would he tonight, if just a little? Or would this part of their marriage be a masquerade as well?

'I suppose I'll change,' she said, her gaze sliding inexorably to the negligee laid out for both their perusals.

'You don't need to wear that,' Leo said, and he let out an abrupt laugh, the sound without humour. 'There's no point, really, is there?'

Wasn't there? Alyse felt a needle of hurt burrow under her skin, into her soul. What did he want her to wear, if not that?

'Why don't you take a bath?' he suggested. 'Relax. It's been a very long day.' He turned away from her, yanking off his tie, and after a moment Alyse headed to the bathroom, telling herself she was grateful for the temporary reprieve. They could both, perhaps, use a little time apart.

We've basically had six years apart.

Swallowing hard, she turned on the taps.

There were no clothes in the bathroom, something she should have realised before she got in the tub. Two sumptuous terry-cloth robes hung on the door, and after soaking in the bath for a good half-hour Alyse slipped one on, the sleeves coming past her hands and the hem nearly skimming her ankles. She tied it securely, wondering what on earth would happen now. What she wanted to happen.

For Leo to gasp at the sight of me and sweep me into his arms, admit the feelings he's been hiding all along...

Fantasies, pathetic fantasies, and she *knew* that. She wasn't expecting a lightning bolt of love to strike Leo; she just wanted to start building something, something real. And that took time.

Tonight was a *beginning*.

Taking a deep breath, stealing herself for whatever lay ahead, she opened the door.

Leo had changed out of his tuxedo and now wore a pair of navy-blue silk draw-string pyjama bottoms and nothing else. He sat sprawled in a chair by the fire, a tumbler of whisky cradled in his hands, the amber liquid glinting in the firelight.

Alyse barely noticed any of that; her gaze was ensnared by the sight of his bare chest. She'd never seen it before, not in the flesh, although there had been several paparazzi photographs of him in swimming trunks while on holiday—though not with her. They'd never actually had a holiday together in six years' engagement.

Seeing his chest now, up close and in the glorious flesh, was another thing entirely. His skin was bronzed, the fire casting long shadows on the taut flesh and sculpted muscle. She could see dark whorls of hair on his chest, veeing down to the loose waistband of his trousers slung low on his lean hips, and her heart felt as if it had flipped right over in her chest. He was just so beautiful.

He glanced up as she approached, and his lips twitched in sardonic amusement as he took in her huge robe. 'I think that one's mine.'

'Oh.' She blushed, and then as she imagined Leo attempting to wear the smaller, woman's-sized robe, a sudden bubble of nervous laughter escaped her. He arched an eyebrow and she came forward to explain. 'I was picturing you in the other robe. Mine, apparently.'

'An interesting image.' His lips twitched again in a tiny smile and her heart lightened ridiculously. All she needed was a smile. A single smile on which to build a world of dreams.

She sat in the chair opposite his and stretched her bare feet towards the fire. Neither of them spoke for several minutes, the only sound the comforting crackle and spit of the flames.

'This is strange,' Alyse finally said softly, her gaze still on the fire. She heard Leo shift in his seat.

'It's bound to be, I suppose.'

She glanced upwards and saw his face was half in darkness, the firelight casting flickering shadows over the other half. She could see the hard plane of one cheek, the dark glint of stubble on his jaw, the pouty fullness of his sculpted lips. He had the lips of a screen siren, yet he was unabashedly, arrogantly male.

She'd felt those lips on her own so many times, cool brushes of mouths when what she wanted, what she *craved*, was hot, mindless passion—tongues tangling, plunging, hands moving and groping...

She forced the images, and the resulting heat, away from her mind and body.

'Do you realise,' she said, trying to keep her tone light, and even teasing, although they'd never actually teased each other, 'we haven't actually been alone together in about a year?'

He shrugged one bare, powerful shoulder. 'That's not all that surprising, considering.'

She glanced back at the fire, tucking her now-warmed feet underneath the hem of her robe. 'Considering what?'

'Considering we've been living separate lives ever since we announced this sham of an engagement.'

Alyse swallowed. 'I know that.' Neither of them had been in a rush to get married. Leo certainly hadn't, and Alyse had already accepted a place at Durham University. Her parents hadn't wanted her to give it up for marriage at eighteen, and neither had she, although she suspected Queen Sophia could have bullied her into it.

She'd been so young then, so naïve and overwhelmed. She liked to think she'd changed, that she'd grown up, at least a bit. She hoped she had, but right now she felt as gauche as ever.

At any rate, a long engagement had fed the media frenzy, accomplishing the monarchy's purposes of keeping them in positive press for over half a decade. For the last six years she'd been living in England, completing her BA and then her MA in European history—a subject the monarchy had considered acceptable for its future queen, since it could be relevant to her rule. Alyse just loved history.

She'd wanted to have some kind of normalcy in her life, some kind of separation from Leo and the feelings he stirred up in her; from the bizarre intensity of life in the media spotlight and under the monarchy's critical eye.

University had thankfully given her a degree of that normalcy she'd craved. Out of respect, and perhaps even love for her, the paparazzi hadn't followed her too closely.

She'd had a somewhat usual university experience— or as usual as it could be, considering the jaunts to royal functions every few weeks, her carefully choreographed appearances with Leo and the constant curiosity and speculation of the other students and even some of the tutors and lecturers.

Remembering it all now brought a sudden lump to her throat. No matter how normal her life had seemed on the surface, she'd still felt the loneliness of being different from the other students. Of knowing the paltry truth of her relationship with Leo.

It was a knowledge that had sometimes led to despair, and that had once led to a foolish choice and a heartache and shame that even now could bring her to a cringing blush.

She pushed the memory away. It had no place here and now, on her wedding night.

'But we're not going to live separate lives now,' she said and Leo inclined his head in brief acknowledgement.

'I suppose we need to decide how we want to conduct our marriage, now that we'll be under the same roof.' He paused to take a long swallow of whisky, and Alyse watched the movement of the corded muscles of his throat, felt a spasm of helpless longing. 'I don't see any real reason to change things too much,' he continued. Her longing left her in a rush.

She felt the way you did when you thought there was one more step in a staircase, the jolt going right through her bones to her soul. Had she actually thought things would change that much now they were married? That Leo would? It would mean more pretending, not less. Yet how could they pretend *that* much?

'Things will have to change a bit, I imagine,' she said, trying to speak lightly. 'I mean…we're married. It's different.'

'Assuredly, but it doesn't mean we have to be different, does it?' He glanced at her, eyebrows raised, cool smile in place. 'The last six years have worked out quite well, don't you think?'

No. *No, no, no.* Yet how could she disagree with him when she'd been acting like she'd agreed with him all along? Alyse swallowed. 'I suppose, but now we have a chance to actually get to know each other…' She trailed off uncertainly, wanting him to leap in and agree. When would she learn? He wasn't going to do that. He wasn't that kind of man.

Leo frowned, then turned back to the fire. 'We've always had that chance,' he answered after a moment. 'We just chose not to take it.'

'I suppose,' Alyse managed. She tried not to let his

words hurt her; he didn't mean to be cruel; he simply had no idea of how she felt, never had. This wasn't his fault, it was hers, for agreeing to pretend for so long. For never having been honest with him about how she really felt.

'It might get a bit tedious,' she ventured. 'Pretending for so long. We'll have to appear together more often, I mean.'

'Oh, the media will get tired of us eventually,' Leo said dismissively. He gave her a quick, cool smile, his eyes hard and glinting. 'Especially once the next generation comes along.'

The next generation. Their children. Alyse felt her heart start to thud.

He put his glass down, raking both hands through his hair so Alyse's gaze was drawn to the ripple of muscles in his arms and chest, the sculpted beauty of his body. Desire twisted and writhed inside her like some desperate, untamed creature seeking its freedom.

Leo dropped his hands and gave her a measured look. 'I know tonight is bound to be awkward, at least at first.' He nodded towards the huge bed looming behind them. 'I think if we acknowledge that up front, it might be easier.'

Alyse's mouth felt like sandpaper as she stared at him. 'Yes, probably it will be.' She tried for a light tone, or at least as matter-of-fact as his. She wasn't sure she managed either. 'Much better to be upfront and honest with each other from the start.' She forced a smile, knowing her words for lies. 'We pretend enough as it is.'

'Exactly.' Leo nodded in approval. 'It's one thing to pretend to the press, but I hope we can always be honest with each other.'

She nodded back mechanically. 'That…would be good.'

'Don't look so terrified,' Leo said dryly. He nodded once more towards the bed. 'I hope we can find a little pleasure there at least.'

A little pleasure? His words stung. 'I'm not terrified,'

she told him crisply. 'It's just— It's a bit awkward, like you said; that's all.'

'Naturally. I'll do my best to alleviate that awkwardness, of course.'

She heard a thread of amusement in his voice, saw it in his cool smile, and knew that being made love to by Leo wouldn't be awkward at all. It would be wonderful.

Except it wouldn't be making love. It would be cold, emotionless sex. A physical act, a soulless transaction. 'A little pleasure', indeed. She closed her eyes, hating the thought. Hating the fact that she had to pretend, would always have to pretend, not just with the press but with him. It would be so, so much harder now. Why hadn't she realised that?

'Alyse,' Leo said, and she opened her eyes. He was leaning forward, his eyes narrowed in concern. 'If you'd rather, we can wait. We don't have to consummate our marriage tonight.'

'A reprieve?' she said, her voice sounding cynical even to her own ears.

'It might be more pleasant when we're not so tired and there are fewer expectations on us,' Leo answered with a shrug. 'And frankly, no matter what you've said, you do look terrified.'

Yes, she was, but not in the way he thought. She wasn't afraid of sex. She was afraid of it being meaningless for Leo. Did he want her at all? Was this a bore for him, a *chore*?

'I promise you, I'm not afraid,' she said when she trusted herself to speak as neutrally as he had. 'But I am tired, so perhaps this…aspect of our marriage can wait a little while.'

Leo shrugged, as if he didn't care either way, and that hurt too. 'Of course. But we should both sleep in the bed.

Staff see everything, and even palace employees have been known to gossip.'

She nodded, trying not to imagine lying next to Leo, his nearly bare body so close to hers. It was a big bed, after all. And she needed to learn how to manage this kind of situation. They would, after all, be sleeping in the same bed for the next...

Except, no; perhaps they wouldn't. Perhaps they would have separate bedrooms along with separate lives, coming together only for the cameras or to create an heir.

'That's fine,' she said. 'I'll just put some...' She trailed off, because the only clothes in the room were her ball-gown and the negligee. She didn't like either option.

Leo glanced at the lace confection spread out on the bed. 'It's a big bed,' he said dryly. 'And I think I can control myself, even if you wear that bit of nonsense.'

Alyse swallowed, nodded. Even tried to smile, though every careless word he spoke felt like a dagger thrust to her heart. She didn't want him to be able to control himself. She'd always known him to be cool, pragmatic, even ruthless. Yet she wanted him to be different with her, and she was honest enough to recognise that some stupid, school-girl part of her had secretly hoped things might change when they were finally alone.

'Fine,' she said and, rising from the chair, she went to the bed and swept the negligee from it before disappearing into the bathroom once more.

Leo stretched out on one side of the bed and waited for Alyse to emerge from the bathroom. He felt the conversation hadn't gone as well as he would have liked. Alyse had seemed brittle, almost as if he'd hurt her feelings, a possibility which exasperated him. He'd thought she was as pragmatic as he was about their union, yet this new, unexpected awkwardness clearly unnerved her—as well as him.

When had he started caring about her feelings, whether she felt nervous, awkward or afraid? The whole point of this marriage, this pretence, was that he didn't have to care. He didn't have to engage emotions he'd purposely kept dormant for so long.

And while he might be weary of pretending—he'd done enough of it in his life, God only knew—at least this marriage, this pretence, had been his choice. His decision.

He still remembered the negotiation they'd gone through after that wretched photograph had gone viral. His father had asked to see them privately.

Alyse had flown to Maldinia a few weeks after her birthday party; her mother had accompanied her. And, when she'd walked into his father's private study alone, Leo had been jolted by how young and vulnerable she looked, dressed simply in a plain skirt and schoolgirl's blouse, her dark hair held back in a ponytail.

His father hadn't minced words; he never did. Queen Sophia and her mother were friends, he told Alyse, and they'd considered a match between her and Leo. Leo knew that hadn't exactly been true; his mother had wanted someone with slightly bluer blood than Alyse's to marry her son. Leo had gone to that birthday party with only a vague and passing knowledge of Alyse's existence and it was the media hype that had turned it into something else entirely.

'In an ideal world,' King Alessandro had said with a geniality Leo knew his father did not remotely possess, *'you would have got to know each other, courted. Seen if you suited. But it's not an ideal world.'*

Alyse had simply stared.

Leo, of course, had known where this was going all along. He'd talked to his parents already, had received the assignment from on high. *You must marry her, Leo. The public adores her. Think of what it will do for your country, your kingship.*

He'd known what they really meant: what it would do for them. They'd done enough damage to Maldinia's monarchy with their lies, affairs and careless spending. He was the only one left to clean up the mess.

He'd understood all that, but Alyse hadn't. She'd just looked thunderstruck. She'd barely spoken for that whole meeting, just listened as the King went on about the benefits of a 'decided' marriage—a much more innocuous term than *arranged,* Leo had thought cynically. Or *commanded.*

She'd only spoken when she'd begun to perceive, dimly, just what kind of charade they would be perpetuating and for how long. 'You mean,' she'd said in a voice only a little above a whisper, 'we have to…to *pretend* we're in love?'

'Feelings come in time, don't they?' Alessandro had answered with that same false joviality, and Leo had looked away. *No, they didn't.* If Alessandro held up his own marriage, his own family, as an example, it showed they never came. And you couldn't trust them anyway.

But Alyse had nodded slowly, accepting, and their engagement had been announced the next day along with them posing for requisite photos.

And the rest, Leo thought now, lacing his arms above his head, was history. Repeating itself over and over again.

The door to the bathroom opened and Alyse emerged, wearing the woman's robe. Leo wondered if she'd try to sleep in that bulky thing. He supposed a little virginal shyness was natural.

He watched as she skirted the bed and then hesitated on the far side, her fingers playing with the sash of her robe. Leo reached for his bedside lamp.

'Shall I turn out the light?'

'If you like.'

Actually, he didn't like. He was suddenly rather curious as to what Alyse looked like in the skimpy negligee. He'd seen her in plenty of designer dresses and well-coordinated outfits, hair and make-up immaculately styled, always primped to perfection.

But he'd never seen her like this—wearing a bridal nightgown, her chestnut hair loose about her shoulders, grey eyes wide, about to climb into his bed. He felt an insistent stirring of arousal; it had been a long time since he'd been with a woman. A *very* long time.

He switched the light off, but the moon spilling through the open windows was enough to see by anyway, and as he lay back against the pillows he saw her slip the bulky robe from her body. Dressed as she was in only the slinky negligee, the moon gilded her slender curves in silver.

He could see the shadowy vee between her breasts, the dip of her waist, the hidden juncture of her thighs. Then she slid hurriedly under the covers and lay there, rigid and unmoving.

Leo had never felt so far from sleep and, judging by how she lay there like a board, he suspected Alyse was the same. Perhaps they should have agreed to consummate their marriage tonight. At least it would have given them something to do.

He considered talking to her, but after six years of enacting this parody of love he had nothing of consequence to say, and he didn't think she had either. Which was how he'd wanted it.

Yet in the darkness and silence of that moment he felt a sudden, surprising need for conversation, even connection. Something he'd taught himself never to crave.

And he had no idea how to go about creating it now.

'Goodnight,' he finally said, his voice coming out gruffer than he'd meant it to, and he felt Alyse tense even more next to him.

'Goodnight,' she answered back, her voice so soft and

sad that Leo felt caught between remorse and exaspera-
tion at her obvious emotion—and his.

With a barely suppressed sigh, he rolled onto his side,
his back to Alyse, and willed himself to sleep.

CHAPTER THREE

ALYSE AWOKE GRITTY-EYED and still feeling exhausted. Lying next to Leo, she hadn't slept well, conscious of his hard, powerful form just inches away from her even when she'd been falling into a restless doze.

Now as sunlight streamed through the windows she wondered what the day would bring. They were meant to fly to St Cristos, a private island in the Caribbean, that morning to begin their honeymoon. A week completely alone, without the distractions of television, telephones, computers or any other people at all. A week, she still hoped, when they could get to know one another properly, or even at all.

A knock sounded at the door and before Alyse could say or even think anything Leo was snaking his arm around her waist, drawing her close against the seductive heat of his body. Shock turned her rigid as she felt the hard contours of his chest and thigh against her backside—and then the unmistakable press of his erection against her bottom.

'*Vieni,*' he called and then murmured against her hair, 'Sorry, but the staff will gossip.'

Alyse barely took in his words. She'd never been so close to him, every part of her body in exquisite contact with his. The crisp hair on his chest tickled her bare shoulders, and the feel of his arousal pressing insistently

against her bottom sent sizzling darts of sensation shooting through her.

She shifted instinctively, although whether she was
drawing away or closer to him she didn't even know. She
felt a new, dizzying need spiral up inside her as his own
hips flexed instinctively back. Leo groaned under his
breath and his arm came even more firmly around her.
'Stop wriggling,' he whispered, 'Or I might embarrass
myself. I'm only human, you know.'

It took a few seconds for his meaning to penetrate the
fog of her dazed mind, and by that time two young serving women were wheeling in a breakfast tray, the smell
of fresh coffee and breakfast rolls on the air.

Embarrass himself? Was he actually implying that he
wanted her that much? That a mere wriggle of hips could
send him over the edge?

Leo let go of her, straightening in bed as he adjusted the
duvet over himself. *'Grazie,'* he said and the two women
giggled and blushed as they left the room, casting covert
looks at the two of them in bed. Alyse realised the strap of
her negligee had fallen off one shoulder, and her hair was
a tangled mass about her face. Did she look like a woman
who had been pleasured and loved? She felt like a mess.

She tucked her tangled hair behind her ears and willed
her heart rate to slow. Despite the obvious evidence of his
arousal, Leo now looked completely unfazed and indifferent as he slid out of bed and went to the breakfast tray
to pour them both coffee.

'Sorry about that. Basic bodily function, at least for
a man in the morning. I think we convinced the staff, at
any rate.'

Disappointment crashed through her. *Basic bodily function.* So, no, it had had nothing to do with her in particular. Of course it didn't. 'It's fine,' Alyse murmured. She

took a steadying breath and forced herself to meet his wry gaze. 'We're married, after all.'

'So we are.' He handed her a cup of coffee and sipped his own, his expression turning preoccupied over the rim of the porcelain cup. 'But I imagine all this pretending will get tiresome for both of us after a while.'

Alyse stared into the fragrant depths of her coffee. 'Like you said, the press will get bored of us now that we're married. As long as we seem happy in public, they won't really care.' It hurt to say it, to imply that that was what she wanted.

'Perhaps.' Leo nodded slowly, and Alyse imagined he was wondering just how soon he could return to his simple, solitary life.

And when he did what would she do? Over the last few months she'd bolstered her flagging spirits by reminding herself that, just like Leo, she had a duty. A role. As princess and later Queen of Maldinia she would encourage and love her people. She would involve herself in her country, its charities and industry, and in doing so bring hope to a nation.

She tried to hold onto that idea now, but it seemed like so much airy, arrogant nonsense when she considered how the majority of her days were likely to be spent: in loneliness and isolation, separated from a husband who was perfectly happy with their business arrangement.

'When do we leave for St Cristos?' she asked, not wanting either of them to dwell on the bleak future they both clearly envisioned.

'We leave the palace at eleven o'clock for a public appearance in the front courtyard. Photo opportunity and all that.' He smiled and Alyse saw the cynicism in the twist of his lips, the flatness in his navy eyes. He never used to be so cynical, she thought. Pragmatic, yes, and even cold, but he'd approached their engagement with a brisk and accepting efficiency she'd tried to match, rather than this jaded resentment.

Was he feeling as she did, that marriage had changed something between them, made it worse? Pretending *after* the vows had been said seemed a greater travesty than before, something she'd never considered as Leo's fiancée. She didn't think Leo had considered it either.

'I'll leave you to get dressed,' he said, putting down his coffee cup. 'I'll meet you downstairs in the foyer a few minutes before eleven.'

Wordlessly Alyse nodded, seeing the practicality of it yet feeling a needling disappointment anyway. Was every interaction going to involve a way to avoid each other? Would her life consist of endless awkward exchanges without any real intimacy or emotion, *ever*? Something would have to change. She couldn't live like this; she wouldn't.

Maybe, she thought with no more than a flicker of weary hope, it would change on St Cristos.

Several hours later they boarded the royal jet and Leo disappeared into a study in the rear of the plane. Alyse had been on the jet before when she'd flown between England and Maldinia, yet the opulent luxury always amazed her. Her own family was wealthy and privileged—her father had built a financial empire and her mother had been an heiress—but they weren't this kind of rich. They weren't royal.

You are now.

It still felt unreal. If she didn't actually feel like Leo's wife, how would she ever feel like a princess? Like a queen?

Pushing the thought aside, she made herself comfortable on one of the leather sofas in the main cabin of the plane. Just as planned, she and Leo had made their appearance outside the palace doors. A crowd had surrounded the palace; posies and bouquets of flowers had been piled up by the gates. Alyse had spent a few minutes chatting, smiling and laughing, while Leo had looked on, his smile faint and a little bit wooden. While the people loved the handsome, enigmatic prince, he didn't engage the crowds the way she did, and never had. This, she knew, was why Maldinia's monarchy needed her. Why Leo needed her.

Nothing else.

Now, with the crowds and reporters gone, she wondered just how she and Leo would spend their time alone. Judging by the way he'd disappeared into the jet's study, *alone* was the operative word.

She felt a sudden stab of annoyance, which at least felt stronger than the misery that had been swamping her since their marriage. No matter how fake their relationship was, Leo's determined ignoring of her was just plain rude.

Fuelled by her outrage, Alyse rose from the sofa and went to find Leo in the study. He sat at a desk, his dark head bent over a sheaf of papers. He was dressed for travel in a crisp blue button-down shirt and dark trousers, but he still looked magnificent, his muscles taut and powerful underneath the starched cotton of his shirt. He glanced up as she approached, his dark brows snapping together.

'What is it?'

'I just wondered if you intended to spend the entire time in your study,' she said, her voice coming out close to a snap, and Leo looked at her in something close to bewilderment.

'Does it matter?'

Impatience warred with hurt. 'A bit, Leo. I understand you don't want things to change between us, but a little conversation could be nice. Or are we going to spend the next week trying to avoid each other?'

He still looked flummoxed, and now also a bit annoyed. 'I'm not trying to avoid you.'

'It just comes naturally, then?'

'We've been on this plane for ten minutes,' he replied, his voice becoming so very even. 'Don't you think you can entertain yourself for a little while longer?'

Alyse shook her head impatiently. She could see how Leo might think she was being unreasonable, but it was so much more than this one journey. 'I can entertain myself just fine,' she said. 'But I don't particularly enjoy living in isolation.'

Leo's mouth thinned into a hard line. 'The plane will take off in a few minutes. I'll join you in the cabin before it does.'

His words seemed so grudgingly given, yet Alyse knew at this point it was better simply to accept them at face value. Now was not the time to force a confrontation, to confess that she didn't think she could live like this for so much as a morning, much less a lifetime. This was, after all, what she'd agreed to all those years ago when King Alessandro had spelled it out so plainly.

Feelings come in time, don't they? She'd built her hopes on that one throwaway remark, clearly meant only to appease her. She'd lived for six years believing it could be true. She might as well have built castles in the air.

Leo had already turned back to his papers, so after a second's uneasy pause Alyse turned around and went to the cabin.

He didn't come out for take-off. Her annoyance turned to a simmering anger as the staff served her sparkling water instead of the champagne left chilling in a bucket, clearly meant for the two of them to toast their marriage.

She avoided their eyes and reached for her e-reader, bitterly glad she'd filled it with newly purchased books before she'd left. Clearly she'd be getting a lot of reading done on her honeymoon.

A few hours into the flight Leo finally made an appearance. 'Sorry about that,' he said, sitting across from her. 'I had a bit of work to catch up on before we go off the grid.'

Despite his casually made apology, Alyse couldn't let go of her anger. 'If you don't want your staff to gossip, perhaps you should be a bit more attentive to your bride,' she answered tartly. 'We've only been married for one day, you know.'

Leo stared at her, nonplussed. 'Even couples wildly in love have work to do.'

'Even on their honeymoon?'

He narrowed his gaze. 'I have a duty to my country—'

'This whole marriage is about duty.' She cut him off and realised too late how shrewish and hurt she sounded. How ridiculous, considering the nature of their relationship.

'Careful,' he said softly, glancing at the closed cabin doors.

'Our whole life is going to be about being careful,' she retorted before she could stop herself. She hated how her hurt was spilling out of her. She'd kept it hidden for so long, why was she weakening now?

'And you always knew that.' The glance he gave her was repressive. 'I think we should save this conversation for another, more private time.'

'At least I have a conversation to look forward to, then.' Leo just stared at her, and Alyse looked away, trying to reclaim some of the cool composure she'd cloaked herself with during the last few years. She'd never lit into him like this, never showed him how much his indifference hurt her or how much more she wanted from him.

'What's wrong with you?' he asked after a moment and he sounded both curious and exasperated. 'You've never acted like this before.'

'We've never been alone like this before,' she answered, her face still averted. 'I just don't want you to ignore or avoid me for the entire week. I'll go crazy.'

Leo was silent for a long moment. 'I don't mean to ignore or avoid you,' he said finally. 'I'm just acting as we
always have. I thought you accepted the nature of our relationship—preferred it, as I do.'

Alyse struggled to keep her face composed, her voice
even, but his words hurt so much. Too much. 'I've accepted it,' she said carefully. 'But it feels different now.
We're married, after all, and we're going to spend more
time together. Time alone. It would be nice if we could
enjoy it, at least.'

That was so much less than she wanted, but at least it
was a start—if Leo agreed.

He didn't answer, just reached for the champagne and
poured two flutes, the bubbles fizzing and bursting against
the crystal sides. 'I suppose that's not an unreasonable request,' he said eventually, and Alyse didn't know whether
to laugh or cry at his grudging tone.

'I'm glad you think so,' she answered, and accepted a
glass of champagne.

He eyed her evenly. 'I suppose we should have discussed our expectations of what our married life would
look like beforehand.'

'Would it have made any difference?'

'Not to me, perhaps.' He raised his glass. 'To what shall
we toast?'

Alyse couldn't think of a single thing. 'To the future,'
she finally said, and heard the bleakness in her voice.
'Whatever it may hold.'

Nodding in acceptance, Leo drank.

Leo watched Alyse slowly raise the flute of champagne
to her lips. Her face was pale, her eyes wide and dark. She
looked rather unbearably sad, he thought, and he had no
idea why. What did she want from him? And why, after
so long accepting the status quo, did she seem to want
things to change?

Shifting in his seat, he turned towards the window. Outside the sky was an endless, brilliant blue. He thought of the week they were to spend on St Cristos, which was apparently the most elite honeymoon destination in the world—chosen, of course, to perpetuate the myth of their relationship. The relationship—a word he didn't even like to use—that he didn't want to change.

But it would have to change in some ways as they spent more time together, he acknowledged. Alyse had a point, even if he didn't like it.

And she seemed to want such change. Want more. Leo felt everything in him recoil at the thought. He didn't do relationships, or intimacy, or emotion, or any of it, yet it seemed Alyse expected a little of all of the above.

He could manage some conversation, he told himself. Some simple pursuits and pleasures…such as the consummation of their marriage. Perhaps he and his wife could find some sympathy with each other in bed. They certainly didn't seem to have much out of it, although he was honest enough to admit he'd never really tried.

He didn't want to get to know Alyse. He didn't want their relationship to be anything than what it was: a carefully managed façade. He never had.

Yet now it seemed she wanted something else. Something more.

Well, she wouldn't get it. He didn't have anything more to give. Suppressing a sigh, he took another sip of champagne. Why did a thought that had once comforted and strengthened him now make him only feel restless and on edge?

By the time they arrived in St Cristos, Alyse was feeling strung out and exhausted. She hated the constant tension she felt in Leo's presence; before today, they'd only seen each other for various occasions, usually formal, and always with other people around. They'd never had more than a few hours in each other's company at a time, and never more than a few minutes alone.

She had hoped that when they were alone properly things would become more natural. They would chat, get to know one another, behave like normal, civil human beings. Except civility, in Leo's world, was a cold-hearted, emotionless thing and Alyse didn't think she could take much more of it.

After their brief exchange on the jet they'd barely spoken, and they'd ridden in silence from the island's tiny airstrip to the exclusive resort. Alyse stared out of the window at the verdant hills on the horizon, the palm trees fringing the narrow track with their fronds drooping to the ground. In the distance the sea glittered under an afternoon sun; it was seven hours behind Maldinia here.

The resort came into view, a gracious grouping of thatched huts that looked both simple yet luxurious. The limo pulled to a stop and Alyse saw that all the staff was lined up outside the main hut, beaming and expectant.

She knew the resort was closed to all other guests this week in order to give her and Leo maximum privacy, yet right now she felt too tired to sparkle and charm the crowd. She wanted to curl up into herself and hide.

'Here we go,' Leo murmured, and with a rather grim smile he helped her out of the limo.

Alyse didn't remember what she said to all the people assembled; she shook hands and murmured pleasantries and Leo put his arm around her, kissing her cheek to the sighs of several chambermaids. After what felt like an hour, but was probably only a few minutes, they were led to their guest quarters in a private cove.

Alyse stood in the middle of the hut on its raised wooden platform and stared at the few, expensive furnishings: a couple of teak bureaux, a rattan chair and a huge bed with soft linen sheets. Mosquito netting was draped over the entrance, tied back now, so she had an unrestricted view of the sea lapping only a few metres away.

There were no electrical outlets, she knew, no computers, televisions, telephones or mobile reception. Nothing to keep her and Leo from spending time with one another.

Except Leo himself.

'I think I'll take a look around,' Leo said. 'Why don't you get settled?'

So much for spending time together. Alyse set about unpacking her cases, even though one of the resort staff had offered to do it for her. Right now she wanted to be alone.

Unpacking her few outfits for their week on the Caribbean island didn't take long, however, and after she'd finished she prowled restlessly around the hut, wishing Leo would return, yet half glad he hadn't. His obvious lack of interest in so much as conversing with her was hard to take.

Since Leo still wasn't around she decided to go for a swim. With a twinge of self-consciousness, she changed into one of the bikinis that had been selected for her; she had not chosen or even seen any of the clothes in her cases, not even the shorts and tee-shirts.

The bikini was a little more revealing than she would have liked but, shrugging aside any self-consciousness— she was alone, after all—she headed for the sea.

The sand was silky under her bare feet, the water lapping her toes clear and warm. Standing there, gazing out at an endless horizon, Alyse felt just a little of the tension she'd been carrying lessen and her shoulders relaxed a fraction.

Maybe when Leo returned they'd have that private conversation he'd resisted on the plane. She'd talk to him properly, explain that she didn't want to act like strangers any more. If they couldn't act as a normal husband and wife, at least they could be friends. Surely that would be more bearable than this horribly stilted awkwardness and avoidance?

Taking a deep breath, she dove into the water, kicking her feet as she swam several metres underwater, enjoying the freedom and the silence of the world below the waves.

When she surfaced, slicking her hair back from her face, she felt a jolt deep inside—for Leo was standing in the shallows, dressed only in board shorts as he gazed out at her.

'I wondered when you'd come back up for air,' he said, his eyes narrowed against the sun's glare. 'I didn't know you were such a good swimmer.'

She stood, for the water was still shallow there, and came up only to her waist. 'There's a lot we don't know about each other.'

Even from this distance she saw the heat flare in his eyes as his gaze roved over her bikini-clad body, rivulets of water coursing down her skin. She felt her own body react—muscles tautening, awareness firing through her, hope flaring. 'Yes,' he said slowly. 'So there is.'

Alyse's heart started thudding even as she strove to sound natural. This was the first time she'd ever seen desire in Leo's eyes, such blatant hunger. It thrilled her to the core, but it surprised and even scared her too, for there was something raw and untamed in Leo's gaze, something she'd never seen from him before. Something she'd craved. When she spoke her voice came out in a husky whisper. 'Do you want to have a swim?'

'I think I might.' He waded into the water, and her breath caught in her chest. He was so beautiful, his body hard, sculpted and *perfect*. He dove neatly into the sea, and she watched with mounting anticipation as he kicked through the water towards her, cutting through the waves to come to stand right next to her, the water lapping at his hips and running down his chest.

He was close enough to feel the heat coming off his skin, to touch him, and she longed to press her hand or even her mouth against his damp chest, to catch the droplets of water with her tongue and taste the saltiness of his skin...

Her heart felt as if it were pounding in her throat. 'It's lovely here, isn't it?' she commented, knowing she sounded inane. She didn't know how to act, what to say. All she could do was *feel*—this overwhelming desire and, even more frighteningly, hope coursing through her. Hope that, if he felt this for her, there could be more. There would be.

Yet now she couldn't think about the more, only about the now. About the reality of the desire kindling in his eyes; her breath went shallow as he lifted one hand as if he would touch her. He'd never touched her without an audience.

'It is lovely,' Leo agreed in a low voice. He reached out then and touched her cheek and, even though she'd been expecting it, craving it, the caress still caught her by surprise so her breath came out in a ragged shudder.

He stroked her cheek gently with one finger. 'You're lovely.' She stared at him, ensnared by the heat of his gaze, the touch of his hand. She saw something hard in his gaze, something cynical in his smile, and she still couldn't keep from wanting him. 'I wonder,' he mused softly, his finger still stroking her cheek, 'How do you make something that's been false, true? What's fake, real?'

Her heart seemed to burst within her like fireworks had gone off in her soul. The very fact that he was even asking the question gave her a hope that was painful in its intensity. 'I want to,' she whispered, her heart beating so hard now that it hurt, the thuds slamming her chest. 'I want this to be real, Leo.'

His lips twisted again, caught between a grimace and a smile. He bent his head, his lips a whisper away from hers. 'This is real enough,' he murmured, and then he kissed her.

It was as different from the chaste kisses he'd pressed upon her for the sake of the cameras and the crowds as could be, as she could possibly want.

His mouth slanted over hers with dark possession and he ran his tongue along the seam of her lips before he went deep into her mouth, and she gasped at the sensations scorching through her. Leo's touch felt so intensely pleasurable it was painful, as painful as the hope that still burst through her and lit her on fire.

Leo fastened his hands on her hips and fitted her against his arousal as he blazed a trail of kisses from her mouth to her cheek and jaw, and then down her neck to the vee between her breasts, his tongue licking the salt from her skin. Alyse shuddered and tilted her head back, allowing him greater access to her body, to everything in her.

'Leo…'

He lifted his head, gave her one of his cool smiles. 'This has all got a bit out of control, hasn't it? I don't want to have our wedding night right here in the sea.' He stepped away and Alyse felt a sudden rush of cold emptiness. 'In any case, I only came to find you and tell you dinner will be served shortly. The staff of the resort are setting up a table here on the beach.'

Alyse's mind was spinning, the hope draining out of her, leaving nothing but that aching, pulsing need. Somehow she forced herself to sound as unconcerned, as unaffected as he seemed to be. 'We could eat in the restaurant.'

'Ah, but this is more romantic.'

Alyse watched Leo swim back to the beach and with a deep, shuddering breath, willing her wayward body back under control, she dove underwater and started back towards the shore.

* * *

As soon as he reached their hut, Leo grabbed his clothes and headed for the shower. He needed a cold one. He hadn't meant lust to overtake him quite so much when he'd joined Alyse in the water, but the sight of her barely clad body had driven all rational thought from his mind. He'd been waiting a long time for his body's basic needs to be fulfilled, and the kiss he'd shared with her had been surprisingly sweet.

No, not sweet—hungry, demanding and raw. It had awakened a deeper need in him than he'd ever acknowledged before, and it had taken nearly all of his willpower to step away from her. She was surely a virgin, and he knew she deserved more than a fumbled grope on the sand. He wanted to take his time, bring them both pleasure and not just release. That was one area of their marriage where, he hoped, they could both find some kind of happiness.

Still, he didn't like how close he'd come to losing control there in the water. He never lost control, never even let it slip—and the last person he wanted to weaken him in that area was his wife.

By the time he'd spent ten minutes in an icy shower he felt his composure return and his libido calm down. He changed into a fresh pair of chinos and a dark green polo shirt, and headed back to their hut.

Alyse had already showered in a separate bathroom and was sitting in a rattan chair, her hair damp and curling about her shoulders. She wore a floaty blue sundress that brought out the blue in her eyes, her legs tanned and endless, her feet bare.

Every time he'd seen Alyse she'd been surrounded by stylists, her clothes carefully chosen, her make-up perfectly done, not a hair out of place. Now he saw her face was make-up-free and the sun had already caused a few freckles to appear on the bridge of her nose. She looked better like this, he decided. More natural. He wondered if she missed all the primping and attention, if she enjoyed the clothes, make-up and jewels.

He didn't know, and decided not to ask. He didn't need to know. He didn't want to care.

Yet even so he couldn't suppress the flicker of interest—and, yes, desire—this new, natural Alyse stirred within him.

The sun was just starting to set, sending long, golden rays across the placid surface of the sea, and Leo could see the staff already setting up their romantic table for two there on the beach. He busied himself unpacking his things while Alyse read, conscious of her nearness, the warmth and softness of her, and even the subtle floral scent of her shampoo or perfume, something he'd never even noticed before.

Even now he remembered the feel of her lips on his, the lush softness of her mouth, her breasts, the hunger of her response. His libido stirred insistently and he blew out an impatient breath. *Control.*

'Dinner's ready,' he said more brusquely than he intended, and nodded towards the table now laid for two on the sand.

Alyse looked up from her e-reader and, tossing it aside, rose from her chair. The sundress she wore clung to her figure, highlighting the small yet perfect roundness of her breasts, her tiny waist, her endless legs. Even though she was thinner than she probably should have been—no doubt due to the stress of the run-up to the wedding—she still had a lovely figure, an amazing figure, and Leo's palms itched to touch her. His body stirred again, insistent, demanding.

Tonight, he decided. They would make their marriage real tonight—real in the only way that mattered, the only way possible.

In bed.

CHAPTER FOUR

ALYSE FOLLOWED LEO out onto the beach, a violet twilight settling all around them as the sun started to slip beneath the sea.

The staff who had set up their table had all melted away, so they were alone with the flickering candlelight, a bucket on the sand with champagne chilling, the first course of crab salad already laid out on exquisite porcelain plates. It was the most romantic dinner Alyse ever could have imagined…and it felt like a minefield.

She had no idea how to act with Leo, especially after that kiss. Already she'd spent far too long reliving it—surely the most wonderful kiss she'd ever known—and thrilling to the undeniable realisation that Leo desired her.

How do you make something that's been false, true? His words had buoyed her soul at that moment, because in all her naïve hope she'd thought he meant their relationship. Their marriage.

This is real.

Watching Leo stride along the shore away from her, Alyse had known then what he'd really meant: the only real thing between them was sexual attraction.

Still, it's something, she told herself as she followed Leo out onto the twilit beach. *It might grow into more.* But only if given a chance…a chance Leo seemed determined not to take.

With a little bow, he pulled out her chair and Alyse sat down. 'Wine?' he asked, and she nodded.

He poured them both glasses and then sat across from her, sipping his wine as he gazed out at the sea, its surface now the inky violet of twilight.

He might not be willing to take that chance, she acknowledged, but she had to be. Taking a deep breath, Alyse gave him as bright a smile as she could manage. 'So, what should we do tomorrow? Snorkel? Scuba? Hike?'

His eyebrows rose, his expression freezing for a second, so she almost laughed. 'Don't look so terrified,' she said dryly, parroting his words from last night back at him. 'I might have suggested macramé.'

'Macramé? I'm not even sure what that is.'

'Weaving with knots,' Alyse explained. 'It's one of my passions. I was hoping you might share it.' Leo looked so nonplussed that this time she did laugh, and the release felt good. Even better was his answering rasp of a chuckle.

'You're having me on.' He shook his head, taking a sip of wine. 'Six years and I had no idea you had a sense of humour.'

Because he'd never had the chance to find out, or the desire. 'Well, we've never had a proper conversation before, not really,' Alyse said. She was trying for light but her voice came out quiet, almost forlorn. She'd have to do better. 'Not one about macramé, at any rate.'

'I must admit, I'm relieved it isn't one of your passions,' Leo answered. He arched an eyebrow, and she was gratified by the lightness of his expression. 'It isn't, is it?'

'No.' A smile twitched at her mouth. 'Definitely not one of them.' Leo just nodded, and despite the obvious opening Alyse knew he wasn't going to press. He would never press, never ask her about herself, what her passions or even her hobbies were. 'So, scuba, then?' she said, keeping her voice bright. 'I'm not qualified, but I read that they have instructors here who can qualify you with a day course.'

Leo made a noncommittal noise and Alyse felt the hurt and anger return, filling the empty places inside her. 'I think you'd enjoy scuba diving,' she said, and heard a new sharp note enter her voice. 'It doesn't allow for any conversation.'

'I have nothing against conversation.'

'Conversation with *me*, then?'

He shook his head, annoyance sparking in his eyes. 'Alyse...'

'I just don't see,' she pressed on in a desperate rush, knowing she needed to say it, to get it out there, 'why we can't be friends. Our marriage is unconventional, I know. I accept that. But we have to live together, Leo. We have to have a life together of some description. And I would like to do that as—as your friend.'

Silence. Leo said nothing, just eyed her over the rim of his wine glass. Why, Alyse wondered, did such a benign offer of friendship make her feel so vulnerable? So needy and demanding?

Because Leo obviously didn't need anyone, and certainly not her. Not even as a friend.

'Say something,' she finally said, just to break the awful silence.

'I don't know what I could say that you'd wish to hear.'

'At this point, anything is better than nothing,' she answered tartly.

'I'm not sure it's possible,' Leo said, each word chosen carefully, 'for us to be friends.'

'Not possible?' She stared at him in confusion. 'Why?'

'Because,' Leo replied, his voice still so terribly careful, 'I have no wish to be friends with you.'

As soon as he said the words, Leo realised how cruel

they sounded. Cruel and deliberately cold…and he hadn't meant it quite like that. Had he?

From the moment Alyse had started teasing and tempting him in turns—asking for things he didn't know how to give—he hadn't known what he meant. How he felt.

And as for the look on Alyse's face… She looked stunned for a moment, and then he saw a flash of hurt darken her eyes before she turned her face away, her expression hidden in the dark.

'Alyse…' he said, although he had no idea how to explain himself, or even if he could. In any case, he didn't get a chance.

With a small sound of distress she rose from the table and walked quickly across the beach, her slight form soon swallowed up by darkness.

Irritation mixed uncomfortably with an already increasing guilt—and a wretched sense of disappointment in himself. He should have handled that better. He should have known how.

He threw his napkin down and rose, his hands braced flat on the table. 'Where are you going?' he called, and from the twilit shadows he heard her muffled response.

'If you're worried I'm going to do something indiscreet, never fear. I just couldn't bear sitting at the table with you.'

His lips twitched with a sudden, macabre humour. 'I'm not surprised.' She didn't answer and he sighed wearily. 'I can't even see you,' he said, taking a few steps towards her. The sand was cool and silky under his bare feet. 'Where are you hiding?'

'I'm not *hiding*,' she snapped, and as he moved closer to the sound of her voice he saw she'd gone to the far side of the little cove, her back to him and the sea as she stood facing the rocky outcropping, her shoulders hunched, her arms wrapped around herself. There wasn't really anywhere else for her to go.

'I'm sorry,' he said after a moment. 'That came out wrong.'

'Was there really room for misinterpretation?'

'I only meant I think it would be easier if we didn't attempt to be friends.'

She let out a harsh bark of disbelieving laughter and turned around. 'Easier? For you, maybe.'

'Yes, for me.' He shifted his weight, his hands digging into his pockets. 'I don't think I need to remind you that this marriage was never meant to be anything but a matter of convenience, Alyse. A business deal.'

'That doesn't mean it can't become something else,' she said quietly. 'Something more.'

Something more? Even though he'd begun to suspect she harboured such hopes, the possibility still appalled him.

'Clearly you find that notion horrifying,' she continued, a hint of mockery in her voice. 'I've reduced you to silence.'

'It's unexpected,' he answered carefully. 'I've thought we've been in agreement about what our marriage would look like.'

'Considering we never discussed it, I don't know how we could be, or why you would think so.'

'Considering we both agreed to play-act at a relationship for six whole years,' he retorted, 'I'm not sure why you think it would suddenly change now, or why either of us would want it to.' He stared at her, her chin tilted in determination or maybe even defiance, her eyes sparking silver. Frustration flared within him; this was so *unexpected*. And he hated how it made him feel—cornered, angry and, damn it, uncertain. He'd been so sure about what he wanted—and what he didn't want.

Why was this woman he'd thought he knew so well—

that was, not at all—changing and, far more alarmingly, making him change?

He straightened, arms folded. 'We both got what we wanted out of this union, Alyse.'

She lifted her chin a notch. 'Which is?'

'To restore the monarchy's reputation and provide an heir.'

'Ah, an heir.' She folded her arms, mirroring his own implacable stance, and stared him down. 'And sex with you is such an appealing prospect, considering you just told me you have no interest at all in getting to know me.'

'I don't know why it would make a difference,' he answered coolly, and she let out a high, wild laugh.

'I should have known you'd say something like that.'

Leo raked a hand through his hair. He needed to perform some damage control, and quickly. 'Look, I told you, I didn't mean it quite like it sounded. I just never thought about—about friendship.'

'Actually, I think you did mean it. You just didn't mean for it to sound as brutal as it really is.' She walked past him back to their table, her dress nearly brushing his legs, and he inhaled the scent of sunshine and sea as she passed.

After a moment Leo followed her back to the table; she'd sat down and was eating her salad with a methodical diligence that suggested no enjoyment in the food at all.

Leo sat down as well, although his appetite had, annoyingly, vanished. Gazing at her pale, drawn face, he still felt guilty, as if he'd disappointed or even hurt her somehow. It was a feeling he'd experienced in varying degrees since they'd said their marriage vows, and he didn't like it.

He didn't want her to be hurt, and more to the point he didn't want to care if she was. Yet somehow he knew both were true, and he wasn't sure what to do about it.

'I honestly didn't mean to offend you,' he finally said,

his tone terse, when Alyse had ploughed through half her salad. His remained untouched.

'I suggest we be friends and you say you have no interest in such a thing,' she returned, not even looking up from her food. 'How is that not going to be offensive?'

'You took me by surprise,' he snapped, goaded into revealing a temper he'd barely known he had. 'For six years we've been as strangers to each other, and you seemed fine with that. Why should I expect anything to change now?'

'Because we're *married*.'

'It's nothing more than a promise and a piece of paper,' Leo said brutally, his temper now well and truly lit. 'It doesn't actually change anything. It doesn't have to.'

She looked up then, her face pale, her lush mouth bloodless. 'Because you don't want anything to change.'

'No, I don't.'

She shook her head slowly, biting those bloodless lips as she looked away. 'Why not?' she asked softly. 'What do you have against me?'

'Oh, for...' He sighed wearily. 'Nothing. I don't have anything against you.'

'Just women in general, then?'

Leo suppressed a curse. 'No, I have no problem with women, Alyse. I don't have a problem with anything. I simply want what I thought we'd agreed on all those years ago—a relationship of convenience, managed and manufactured for the sake of restoring the monarchy.'

'Do you really think I care about the monarchy?' she asked, her voice turning ragged with emotion, reminding him of ripped and ruined things, things torn by desire and broken by need.

He'd felt it once in himself, long ago, that endless ache of disappointment and sorrow. He intended never to feel it again, and he certainly didn't want it coming from his wife. The whole *point* of this marriage had been to avoid such messiness, such pain. That was the benefit of pretending, never mind the cost.

'I suppose you care,' Leo answered evenly. 'Since you agreed to marry me and perpetuate this charade.'

She glanced away, and in the darkness he could not make out her expression at all. 'I've never cared about the monarchy. Or being queen. Or—any of it.'

The bleakness of her tone had the hairs on the back of his neck prickling. He believed her, and he didn't want to. It would be much simpler to believe she'd agreed to their arrangement because of the material benefits she'd enjoy. *So much simpler.* 'Then why did you agree to a pretend engagement? A pretend marriage?' he asked, the words drawn from him reluctantly. It was a question he'd never asked her, never wanted to ask her. It had been enough that she'd accepted. Now, with an increasing sense of foreboding, he braced himself for her answer.

'Why?' Alyse repeated, and her voice sounded far away, her face still averted. She let out a long, shuddering breath. 'It doesn't really matter now.'

And, even though he knew that was no answer at all, Leo chose not to press. He really didn't want to know.

Neither of them spoke for a long moment, the silence strained and somehow sad. Then Alyse turned to him, her expression carefully veiled, yet Leo still felt the hurt emanating from her. It exasperated him, how much he felt now, both from her and in himself. For years he'd managed perfectly well, not feeling anything. Not wanting to.

'I still don't see how friendship will complicate things,' she said quietly. 'I would have thought it would make things easier. We're going to spend the rest of our lives together, after all. We are, God willing, going to have children—' She broke off suddenly, her voice having turned ragged again, and he could feel the need pulsing through her.

That was why friendship would complicate things—because it would open a door he'd kept firmly and forever shut. 'You knew all this before, Alyse,' he said. 'You knew what you were getting into. What you were agreeing to.'

'Knowing something and actually living it are two different things.' She shook her head slowly. 'Do you really not feel any differently, Leo? That actually being married makes a difference?'

He wanted to say no. He should say no, and nip all this talk of friendship and feelings in the bud. Yet he couldn't because, damn it, he did feel differently. He just didn't want to.

Impatiently, he tossed his napkin on the table. He'd barely touched his meal, but he wasn't hungry. 'Look,' he said flatly. 'The reason I said what I said is because I'm not sure I can even be your friend.'

'Why?'

'Because I don't— I've never really had a friend before.' That sounded so utterly pathetic, he realised furiously. He hated, *hated* that she'd driven him to such a confession.

Alyse gaped at him, her jaw dropping inelegantly. 'You've never had a friend?' she said in disbelief, and Leo felt his own jaw bunch, teeth grating.

'Not really.' He was lying, though. He'd had one friend at least—the best friend and brother whom he'd loved more than anyone else. The one person he'd been real with, the one person he'd trusted.

And look how that had turned out. The most real relationship he'd ever had had turned out to be as fake as all the others.

'Why not?' she asked and he just shrugged. She waited: a stand-off.

'When you live your life under the microscope, genuine friendship isn't easy to come by,' he finally said, his voice brusque. *When you lived your life in the spotlight.*

When the only time anyone was interested in affection or emotion was for the cameras...

He wasn't about to explain all that. How could he? He'd hated the glare of the spotlight, yet he'd chosen it for himself and his marriage. Willingly...because at least then he was in control.

Yet he didn't feel much in control at the moment. He felt as if it had been slipping away from him ever since he'd stood next to Alyse in the cathedral and said those vows.

'Even so,' she said, and he heard damnable pity in her voice. 'I would have thought there would be someone—'

'I haven't lived in complete isolation.' He cut her off, his voice coming out in something close to a snap. 'I've had acquaintances, servants, staff...'

'It's not the same.'

'Probably not. But you don't miss what you've never had.' Except he'd had it, and he knew he would miss it if he let himself—which he never did.

Alyse was silent for a long moment. Her expression had turned thoughtful, her head tilted to one side as her quiet gaze swept over him. Leo felt as if he were under a searchlight. 'Do you think,' she finally asked, 'you might be willing to try with me?'

'Try what?'

'Being my friend. Letting me be yours.'

Leo felt his jaw bunch harder and he wiped a hand over his face. 'Next we'll be painting each other's nails and doing—what was it?—macramé?'

A tiny smile hovered on Alyse's lush mouth and despite all the wretched emotion between them Leo felt his libido kick in hard. 'I promise, no weaving. Or nail varnish.'

'Right.' He tried to smile in response but somehow he couldn't. He couldn't take any more of this: not the emotion, not the honesty, not the damn intimacy. He felt as if he was going to burst out of his skin.

He turned resolutely back to his meal. 'Snorkelling sounds like a plan,' he said gruffly. Just as Alyse had said, you couldn't talk with a tube in your mouth. And, from the way her mouth turned down at the corners, Leo had a feeling she'd guessed the exact nature of his thoughts.

CHAPTER FIVE

As soon as they'd finished eating, Leo excused himself to go for a walk. Alyse watched him head down the beach into the darkness with a tired sigh. She didn't ask to join him, knew he'd had enough. Their conversation tonight had been more honest and intimate than anything they'd shared in the last six years, yet it just made her realise how little they actually had. How little they knew each other.

And yet she loved him. How could you love someone you barely knew, someone who purposely kept himself hidden from you and everyone?

It was a question she'd asked herself many times, and with no real answer, and yet she'd never been able to deny or suppress the hopeless longing he made her feel, and had done from the moment he'd come to her eighteenth birthday party. How the sight of one of his rare smiles had made her heart soar, and the barest brush of his fingers had made it leap. She didn't understand why, but she recognized the signs. Just like her parents had.

Love at first sight, and she wouldn't wish it on anyone—at least not when it wasn't returned.

Sighing again, she headed back to their hut. It was the middle of the night in Maldinian time, and she was utterly exhausted.

Yet as she lay between the cool linen sheets and waited for Leo to return, listening to the waves washing onto the sound and the soothing chirrup of the cicadas, sleep continued to elude her. Her body still felt tense, her mind still racing as it replayed tonight's conversation with Leo.

I've never really had a friend before.

Had he meant that literally? How was it possible? Yet if he'd spoken the truth—which she believed he had—then it explained so much. His cool containment, his preference for his own company. His lack of desire for anything intimate, honest or real.

Her own childhood had, in a way, been similarly lonely. She was an only child of parents who had been rather rapturously wrapped up in each other. She'd been tutored by a taciturn governess and then sent to a boarding school where she'd been too shy ever to feel as if she really fit in. At university she'd made friends, at least—*and look where that had led her.*

And then of course the last six years in the public eye... Sometimes the connection she'd experienced with the people who thronged the streets to greet her felt like the most real, honest human interaction in her life, which certainly said something about the lack of real intimacy in her own life.

Strange to think both she and Leo had experienced such loneliness, yet they'd reacted to it in completely different ways. He embraced isolation; she craved closeness.

She wondered if they would ever find a way to compromise, and if such a thing could satisfy either of them.

Leo walked as far down the beach as he could, before a jagged outcropping of rocks stopped his path. He stopped and let out a weary sigh. After the excruciating intimacy of his conversation with Alyse, he'd needed space. Escape. But, standing here looking at the rocky barrier, he knew he couldn't outrun his thoughts.

She was asking for something so little, he knew. Something so reasonable: friendship. Friendship wasn't meant to be threatening or scary. It could, in fact, make things easier, just as she'd said. Certainly getting along with one another was better than existing in cold silence, and yet...

His whole life had been about cold silence. About work and duty and *doing*, because those things didn't let you down. Didn't hurt you. They were steady, safe.

And friendship might seem innocent, innocuous, but Leo knew how opening your heart just a little could still allow the pain and need to rush in. And, in any case, he didn't even know how to be a friend. Maybe it seemed incredible and, yes, pathetic, but it was the truth.

He'd lived a solitary life for so long and he didn't want to change.

Yet already, inexorably, impossibly, he felt himself changing. Already he was wondering just how badly he'd hurt her feelings tonight, and hating that he had. Hating even more that he cared that he had.

That's not what this marriage was meant to be about.

Cursing under his breath, he whirled around and began to stride back to the hut.

By the time he returned Alyse was in bed, her slight form draped with the linen sheet. She lay flat on her back, staring at the ceiling and not moving at all.

Leo came in and sat on the edge of the bed. He felt almost unbearably tired, not just from the long flight and the jet lag but from the unexpected roller coaster of emotions they'd both ridden on since their wedding, all of it too much, more than he'd felt in years.

'Are you awake?' he asked quietly and he heard Alyse exhale.

'Funnily enough, I can't get to sleep.'

He half-turned towards her, trying to make out her expression in the moonlit darkness and unable to. 'It's not just an out-of-sync body clock, I suppose?'

She let out a little huff that almost sounded like a laugh and amazingly, absurdly, Leo felt his heart lighten. 'Unfortunately not.'

She shifted in the bed, and he saw the slinky strap of her nightgown fall from one shoulder. His gaze was drawn inexorably to the smooth skin of her neck, her shoulder, and then downwards to the warm curve of her breast. Despite the tension that still vibrated between them, he felt the insistent stirring of arousal. He forced himself to look up into her eyes, and saw she was watching him with a wary expectation.

'I'm sorry,' he said.

'For what, exactly?' He heard a thread of humour in her voice and to his surprise he found himself matching it.

'It must be really bad, if there are options. Have you compiled a list?'

'That sounds like something you would do.'

He let out a tired huff of laughter and raked his hand through his hair. 'Yours is probably a lot longer than mine.'

'Maybe not,' she said softly, and something in him twisted. Yearned.

'I'm sorry for the way I handled our conversation,' he clarified gruffly, pushing away that strange yearning. 'And the unkind things I said to you. They were neither appropriate nor necessary.'

'That's a very formal apology.'

He bristled, instinctively, helplessly. 'I don't know any other way.'

She sighed. 'It's all right, Leo. I accept your apology.' She hesitated, and he heard the gentle in and out of her breath, saw the rise and fall of her chest in the moonlight, her breasts barely covered by a scrap of silky negligee. Had she not packed *any* decent pyjamas?

Of course she hadn't. This was their honeymoon, and they were meant to be wildly in love.

'What now?' she asked after a moment, and he watched as she picked at a thread in the linen sheet with slender, elegant fingers. 'Do you think we can be friends?'

'I can try,' Leo answered, the words drawn from him reluctantly. He hated how weak he sounded. How…incapable. But the truth was trying was all he could do, and he didn't even know if he could do that very well.

Alyse glanced up at him, blinking in the moonlit darkness, a small, wry smile curving her lips. 'I can't ask for more than that.'

'I still want what I wanted before,' Leo told her gruffly, the words a warning. 'A business arrangement, a marriage of convenience.'

Her smile faltered slightly and she glanced away before she met his gaze once more. 'Business arrangements don't have to be cold-blooded. Emotionless.'

Oh yes, they did. For him. Because that was who he was, who he'd determined to be, how to act. Not to feel. Not to want. Not to be disappointed or hurt.

'They can be friendly,' Alyse continued, her voice holding a hint of humour, of hope. And he wondered just what she was hoping for. How much.

Sighing, he pulled his shirt off and reached for his pyjamas. He changed quickly, conscious of Alyse so close to him, and the fact that despite the rather abhorrent intimacy of their conversation, they still hadn't been physically intimate yet. And, hell if he knew now when they would be. Sex and emotion did *not* go together. Yet after tonight he had a feeling Alyse wouldn't be able to separate them. The last thing he needed was her wanting something more than friendship—something ridiculous, like love.

'Look,' he said as he slid between the sheets, knowing he needed to be completely clear, 'I'm not going to love you. I don't love anyone and I never have.'

She was silent for a long moment. 'Is that what you're

worried about?' she asked eventually. 'That, in becoming friends, I might fall in love with you?'

'You might convince yourself you are.'

'You make me sound deluded.'

'Anyone who believes in love is deluded,' Leo said flatly, and he felt Alyse shift next to him, turning to face him.

'Deluded? Why do you think that?'

'Because love isn't real,' Leo stated. 'It's just a hormonal urge, a feeling that changes depending on your mood. It's certainly nothing I've ever pursued or even believed in.'

She was silent for so long Leo, annoyingly, felt a little self-conscious, as if he'd said something he shouldn't have. Revealed more about himself than he'd ever wanted to.

'If you don't think love is even real,' Alyse finally said, 'then you don't need to worry about me feeling it, do you?'

He sighed, shifting away from her tempting warmth. 'I just want to be clear about our expectations. I'm willing to try and be friends, of a sort, but that's all.'

'Of a sort?' She was trying once more for humour but he heard the hurt underneath the wryness. 'What sort is that, Leo?'

He stared up at the ceiling, the ocean breeze causing the palm fronds of the hut to rustle and sway. 'I told you, I haven't had many friends. I'll do my best.'

She turned towards him, and he felt her breasts brush his shoulder. Instantly he was hard. 'That's all anybody can do, isn't it? Your best.'

He breathed in the fresh, floral scent of her and his whole body pulsed with longing. As carefully as he could he moved away from her softness. Sex, he knew, was out of the question for tonight. But soon, damn it. *Very soon.* 'As long as being friends—of a sort—is enough for you,'

he answered grudgingly and even through the darkness
he saw and felt her sad smile.

'I suppose it will have to be,' she said, and then neither
of them spoke again.

CHAPTER SIX

ALYSE WOKE TO the warm spill of sunshine and the gentle *swooshing* of the waves just metres from their bed. She turned to see Leo still asleep next to her, one hand flung over his head, the dark glint of morning stubble visible on his jaw. His lashes, surprisingly long, feathered his cheeks and those all-too-kissable lips were slightly parted. He looked gentler, somehow, in sleep. Softer, almost vulnerable, and so different from the cold, hard man he seemed when he was awake.

She let her gaze move lower and took in his bare chest, the rise and fall of it with each steady breath. Lower still, to the sheet rucked about his waist, his legs tangled beneath it.

Her mouth dried and for a few more seconds she tortured herself by drinking in the male perfection of his body without him knowing. Her gaze was lingering, longing, and completely unrestrained. How would it feel to touch that chest, to slide her hand from shoulder to hip and feel the hot satin of his skin under her seeking fingers?

Desire spiralled dizzily inside her. Never mind wanting to be friends; she just wanted him. For a brief moment she toyed with the idea of touching him. Kissing him awake. But she knew she wasn't bold enough, was too afraid of his surprise or even rejection.

Yet when would they consummate this marriage? When would friendship and desire meld, if ever?

And dared she still hope for more?

Silently she slid from the bed and reached for the robe that matched her nightgown, yet another ridiculous, silky confection. With one last look at Leo, who still seemed deeply asleep, she slipped out of the hut.

The day was already warm although Alyse suspected it wasn't much past dawn, the sun having only just risen over the horizon, its golden light pooling on the placid surface of the sea.

She sat on the beach, tucking her robe around her, and sifted the sun-warmed sand through her fingers as last night's conversation swirled through her mind: Leo's confession that he hadn't had any friends, his grudging acceptance that they might be friends—*of a sort*—and his flat and absolute statement that he would never love her.

Could she really be surprised by that bleak statement? It was no more than what she'd suspected, feared, and had tried to convince herself to believe over the years. And yet…she *had* believed in the miracle. The possibility of a miracle. She'd lied to Leo last night about that, just as she'd lied to herself over the last six years. She'd clung, stubbornly and stupidly, to the hope that he would learn to love her. That things would somehow miraculously change.

And she still clung to it now. Alyse's mouth twisted in a grim smile as she acknowledged the truth. Despite everything Leo had said, she still hoped he might come to love her in time, that physical attraction and possible friendship might deepen into the kind of love he didn't even believe in.

The smarter thing to do would be to let go of that hope, let it trickle away like water in sand, and get on with what was possible. Alyse knew she wouldn't. Couldn't. She'd keep hoping, keep believing, because thin vapour that it was, hope was all that sustained her.

And why shouldn't Leo love her? Why shouldn't it be possible, eventually, ultimately?

I'm not going to love you. I don't love anyone and I never have. The memory of his words made her both wince and wonder. Why didn't he love anyone, not even his parents or his sister? *Anyone who believes in love is deluded.* And what had made him lock up his heart so coldly and tightly that he refused even to believe love could exist, never mind flourish?

Could she—did she dare—be the one to try and unlock it?

'Good morning.'

Alyse turned to see Leo standing on the beach just a little bit away from her. He still wore only his pyjama bottoms and he looked glorious. She hoped her recent thoughts weren't visible on her face, her contrary hope reflected in her eyes.

'Good morning.'

'Did you sleep well?'

'Not particularly.'

He smiled then, a proper grin that set her heart racing. Did he know how attractive he was, how a single smile made her heart turn somersaults and then soar straight up into the sky?

'Me neither.' Leo came to sit beside her, stretching his legs out alongside hers. 'I'm not used to conversations like last night's.'

'I gathered that.'

'It was rather obvious, wasn't it?'

His wry smile tugged at her heart. 'Considering revealing anything of a personal nature seems to be akin to pulling teeth for you, I'd say yes.'

He chuckled softly and shook his head. 'Well. I tried.'

'That's all I'm asking for.'

He turned to her then, his gaze dark and searching, his smile gone. 'Is it?'

She fell silent under that searching and seemingly knowing gaze, for of course it wasn't—and it seemed he knew that, or at least suspected. Did he guess that she was in love with him? The possibility made both humiliation and hope rush through her.

She wanted him to know her feelings, wanted to stop pretending, and yet...the thought of his contempt and horror made everything inside her shrivel. She couldn't risk revealing so much. Not yet, and maybe not ever.

'So, snorkelling,' he said, and she nodded.

'Sounds fun.'

'Why don't we get dressed and go for breakfast, and then we can sort it out after?'

'All right.'

With a brisk nod Leo rose from the sand, brushing off his pyjamas, and headed back to the hut. Alyse watched him go, half-amazed that she was finally, actually going to spend an entire day in Leo's company... And still, as always, hopeful for what this day might bring.

This friendship business, Leo decided, was simple. At least so far. All he had to do was spend a little time with Alyse, *do* things with her. That suited him; he preferred having a plan, preferred action to talking. As long as they kept it to leisure activities, preferably ones that kept them from conversing, he'd be fine. Everything would be fine. The thought brought him a rush of much-needed relief.

Twenty minutes later they were both dressed and heading over to the main resort for breakfast. Alyse wore a pair of body-hugging canvas shorts that made Leo even more aware of her long, slim legs and the curve of her bottom. The tee-shirt she wore, in a pale petal-pink, seemed tight to Leo. Not obscenely so, but he kept finding his gaze being drawn to the high, firm breasts he'd seen on such provocative display in those frothy nightgowns she wore. Her hair was loose and fell down her back in shining, dark waves and her eyes sparkled silver as she fell into step beside him.

He'd always thought her pretty enough but now, seeing her looking natural rather than coiffed, styled and professionally made up, he realised she was actually quite beautiful.

And he wanted her very badly.

There was no reason, he thought, why they couldn't be friends by day and lovers by night. Really, it was the perfect solution.

As long as Alyse didn't confuse the two. As long as she didn't start wanting more.

He'd just have to make sure she didn't.

The restaurant, of course, was empty except for half a dozen staff who scurried to attention as soon as Leo and Alyse entered the pavilion that was shaded from the sun and open to the sea.

They sat at a table in the corner and soon had a pot of coffee and a pitcher of freshly squeezed orange juice in front of them.

'I'm starving,' Alyse confessed. She glanced at the buffet that was spread out along one side of the pavilion. 'I think there's plenty of food.'

Leo followed her gaze, taking in the platters of pastries and bowls of fresh fruit, the personal chef on hand to make omelettes to order and the several silver tureens of bacon, sausage and eggs. 'So it seems.'

'It's a bit of a waste, though, isn't it?' she said. 'When we're the only ones staying here.'

'I'm sure the staff will eat it. The resort is meant to be eco-friendly.'

'That's good to know.' She looked at him curiously. 'Are you very concerned about such things?'

He shrugged. 'I certainly intend to bring my country into the twenty-first century, in environmental matters as well as in others.'

He saw the curiosity flare in her eyes. 'Others? What kinds of things?'

He shrugged again, discomfited now. He wasn't used to talking about himself. He wasn't used to anyone asking. 'Technologically, Maldinia is about twenty years behind the rest of Europe. I've been drafting a proposal for broadband to be accessible to most areas.'

'Is it not now?'

'Really just in Averne and the outlying towns and tourist resorts. Admittedly, most of Maldinia is agricultural, and their methods are about a hundred years out of date, never mind twenty.'

She smiled, her eyes lightening with humour. 'But that must be good for the tourist revenue—very quaint, those farmers in traditional dress herding their sheep along with their wooden crooks.'

He acknowledged the point with a wry nod. 'They do look rather nice on a postcard. But those farmers should be able to check the weather—or the latest football scores—on the Internet when they get back home, don't you think?'

She laughed, the sound silvery and crystal-clear. It was a sound, Leo realised with a jolt, that he liked to hear, and he hadn't heard it very much over the last six years. 'Absolutely. Internet access is practically an inalienable right these days.'

'Inalienable,' he agreed solemnly, and they smiled at each other, the moment spinning out first in simple enjoyment and then in something Leo didn't quite recognise. Something that didn't just skim the surface of his feelings but dove deeper, surprising and almost hurting him with its strange poignancy.

Alyse looked away first. 'I didn't realise you were already involved in governing your country.'

Leo's mouth tightened, the moment evaporating like so much morning mist, gone with the first glare of light. *Good.* It was better that way. 'A bit,' he answered, his tone instinctively repressive.

He wasn't involved, not as much as he wanted to be. He'd been trying to prove to his father for fifteen years that he was capable of being king. That he deserved responsibility and respect. King Alessandro might not be interested in government policy—he was too absorbed in his own selfish pleasures for that—but he didn't want his son cramping his style or seizing his power.

He'd never wanted him to be king at all, and even after a decade and a half as heir Leo never forgot he was second choice. Second best.

Alyse stirred her coffee, her gaze thoughtful. 'There's so much I don't know about you,' she said, and the ensuing, expectant pause made Leo tense. Spending time together was one thing. You couldn't talk while you were snorkelling. But getting to know each other…having Alyse ask him questions…having to answer them… That was an entirely different prospect.

'Don't look so horrified,' she continued dryly. 'I'm not about to ask you for your deepest, darkest secrets.'

'I don't have any secrets. Not too many, anyway.' He tried to speak lightly, but he felt unsettled, uneasy, because for a few moments he'd enjoyed their conversation—the light banter, as well as, God help him, the deeper discussion—and *that* horrified him more than anything Alyse could ask.

Well, almost.

'So no embarrassing moments?' she quipped, a smile

on the lips Leo kept realising were incredibly lush and kissable. He remembered how they had tasted. How *she'd* tasted. Honey-sweet with a tang of salt from the sea. Amazing. 'No secret fears?'

He forced his gaze away from her mouth, up towards her eyes that sparkled with humour. How had he never noticed how silver her eyes were? They weren't grey at all. They were warm and soft, glinting with golden lights, like a moonlit, starry sky…

Good Lord. He was thinking like some sort of besotted fool. Eyes couldn't be *soft*, and he wasn't about to compare them to the night sky.

What was *happening* to him?

'Secret fears?' he repeated, forcing his attention back to the conversation. 'No, I don't have any of those.' None he was willing to share, anyway, and he wouldn't exactly call them *fears*. More like…concerns.

'Oh come on, Leo. There must be something.'

'Why don't you tell me something about you?' he suggested. 'Most embarrassing moment or secret fear or…I don't know…funny dream.'

Her mouth curved wider and she leaned forward. 'Here's something you don't know.'

'Very well.' There had to be a thousand things he didn't know about her, but he felt a sudden, sharp curiosity to hear this one and he leaned forward too.

'That kiss? The photo that started it all?'

'Yes.'

'I only clasped your cheek because I was wearing high heels for the first time and I was about to lose my balance.'

Leo stared at her for a moment, nonplussed, almost disbelieving, and then he burst into laughter. She grinned back and then she started laughing too, and from the corner of his eye he could see several members of the restaurant staff beaming in approval.

This would make a good photo.

The thought was enough to sober him up completely. 'And to think,' he said just a little too flatly, 'if you'd been wearing flats we might not even be married.'

'No,' Alyse agreed, all traces of laughter gone from her face. 'We might not be.' They stared at each other for a moment, and this time Leo felt a certain bleakness in their shared look. Their engagement—their whole lives, entwined as they were—had hinged on something so trivial. So ridiculous.

Why did the thought—which wouldn't have bothered him a bit before; hell, he'd have appreciated the irony— make him feel almost *sad* now? Sad not just for himself but for Alyse, for the way her eyes shuttered and her mouth twisted, and the warmth and ease they'd been sharing seemed to disappear completely.

He needed to put a stop to this somehow. He needed to stop wondering, stop *feeling* so damn much. The trouble was, he didn't know how to stop it. And, worse, part of him didn't even want to.

Alyse knew she shouldn't be hurt by Leo's observation. It was no more than the truth, the truth she'd known all along. Yet the reminder stung, when for the first time they'd actually seemed to be enjoying each other's company.

Not wanting Leo to see how absurdly hurt she felt, she rose from the table and headed for the buffet, filling her plate up with a variety of tempting items. Leo followed, and by the time they were both back at the table her composure was firmly restored.

'So,' she said, spearing a piece of papaya, 'your turn. Secret fear, embarrassing moment, funny dream. Take your pick.'

'I don't have any of those,' Leo answered. She watched him neatly break a croissant in two and rolled her eyes.

'Come on, Leo. You're not a robot. You're a man with feelings and thoughts, hopes and fears. You're *human*. Aren't you? Or am I going to roll over in bed one night and see a little key in the back of your neck, like that *Dr Who* episode with the creepy dolls?'

His eyebrows lifted. 'Creepy dolls?'

'Haven't you ever watched that television programme?'

'I don't watch television.'

She let out a laugh. 'You really are a robot.'

'Ah, you've discovered my one deep secret. And here I thought I hid it so well.'

She laughed again, and his answering smile made everything in her lighten and lift. They'd never, ever joked around before. Teased each other. *Enjoyed* each other. It was as heady as a drug, his smile, his light tone. She craved more, and she knew just how dangerous and foolhardy that was.

Leo had made it abundantly clear last night. *As long as it's enough for you.*

Already she knew it wasn't.

'All right, then,' she said, taking a pastry from her plate. 'No secret fears, funny dreams, or embarrassing moments. How about hobbies, then?'

'Hobbies?' he repeated in something so close to incredulity that Alyse nearly laughed.

'Yes, you have heard of them? Pleasant pastimes such as reading, gardening, stamp-collecting?' He simply stared and she supplied helpfully, 'Tennis? Golf? Pottery?'

'Pottery? I thought macramé was bad enough.'

'You must do something to unwind.'

He arched an eyebrow. 'Do I seem unwound to you?'

'Now that you mention it…maybe I should suggest something? Watercolours, perhaps?'

His lips twitched and he shook his head. 'I play chess.'

'Chess?' She smiled, felt the sweet thrill of a small victory. 'I should have been able to guess that.'

'Oh? How so?'

'Chess is a game requiring patience and precision. You have both in spades.'

'I'm not sure that was a compliment,' he answered. 'But I'll take it as one.'

'Are you very good?'

'Passable.'

Which probably meant he was amazing. She could picture him in front of a chessboard, his long, tapered fingers caressing the smooth ivory shape of the queen... A shaft of desire blazed through her. She really needed to get a grip if she was fantasising about *chess*. Well, really, about Leo.

'Do you play?' he asked.

'I'm passable, but probably not as passable as you.'

'I didn't know there were degrees of passable.'

'There is when I feel your "passable" is a gross understatement.'

'We'll have to have a match.'

'You'll trounce me, I'm sure.' Yet the thought of playing chess—really, of doing anything with him—made her spirits lift. *See?* she wanted to say. *We are friends. This is working.*

But she still wanted more.

'So.' Leo pushed his plate away and nodded to hers. 'Are you finished? I'll just speak to the staff about arranging the snorkelling.'

Alyse watched him stride away as she sipped the last of her coffee. Despite her fledgling hope, she still wished that they were a normal couple. That this was a normal honeymoon. That Leo was striding away with a spring in his step instead of a man resigned to a lifetime of duty. That they'd spent last night wrapped in each other's arms, lost in mutual pleasure, instead of lying next to each other as rigid as two cadavers in a mortuary.

She could go on and on, Alyse knew, pointlessly wishing things had been different before, were different now. She forced herself to stop. *This* was what she had to deal with, to accept and make work. And this morning had been a beginning, a hopeful one. She needed to focus on that and let it be enough, for now at least. Maybe for ever.

Half an hour later they'd changed into swimsuits underneath tee-shirts and shorts and Leo was leading the way along the beach to where a gorgeous catamaran was pulled up on the sand.

Alyse came to a stop in front of the boat. 'Are we going in that?'

'I arranged it with the staff. I thought we'd have a better time if we could go out a bit farther.' He glanced at her, his brows knitted together in a frown. 'Are you all right with boats? I know some people are afraid of open water.'

His thoughtfulness touched her, belated as it was. It really was so confoundedly easy for Leo to affect her, she thought. To make her love him. 'It's fine,' she told him. 'It's great, actually. I love sailing.'

And as Leo navigated the boat out into the sea, the sun bathing them both in warm, golden light, Alyse stretched out on the bridge deck, it *was* great. It was fantastic.

She tilted her head back so the sun bathed her face and felt herself begin to relax, the tension dropping from her shoulders, her body loosening and leaning into the sun. She'd been strung as taut as a bow for far too long; it felt good to unbend.

When they were out on the open water, the sea shimmering in every direction, Leo came and joined her on the bridge deck.

'You look like you're enjoying yourself.'

She lowered her head to smile at him, one hand shading her eyes from the dazzling sun. 'I am. It's good to be away from it all.'

He sat beside her, his long, muscular legs stretched out next to hers, his hands braced behind him. 'The media attention was a bit wild these last few months.'

'I'll say. The journalists were going through my rubbish, and my parents' rubbish, and my friends' as well.'

His mouth twisted in a grimace. 'I'm sorry.'

She shrugged in response. 'I signed up for it, didn't I? When I agreed.'

'That still doesn't make it pleasant.'

'No, but you've been living with it for your whole life, haven't you?'

His eyes narrowed, although whether just from the sun or because of what she'd said Alyse didn't know.

'I have,' he agreed without expression and then he rose from the deck. 'We're out far enough now. We can anchor soon.'

She watched him at the sails of the catamaran, the muscles of his back rippling under the tee-shirt that the wind blew taut against his body. She felt a rush of desire but also a swell of sympathy. She hadn't considered Leo's childhood all that deeply before; she knew as prince and heir he'd lived in the spotlight for most of his life.

Of course, the glare of that spotlight had intensified with their engagement. Did he resent that? Did he resent *her*, for making something he must not like worse? It was a possibility she'd never considered before, and an unwelcome one at that.

A few minutes later Leo set anchor and the catamaran bobbed amid the waves as he tossed their snorkelling equipment on the deck.

He tugged off his tee-shirt and shorts and Alyse did the same, conscious once again of the skimpiness of the string bikini she wore. She hadn't found a single modest swimming costume in her suitcases.

She looked up and there could be no mistaking the blaze of heat in his eyes. 'Your swimming costumes,' he remarked, 'are practically indecent.'

Alyse felt a prickly blush spread not just over her face but her whole body. 'Sorry. I didn't choose them.'

'No need to apologise. I quite like them.' He handed her a pair of fins and then tugged his own on. 'What do you mean, you didn't choose them?'

'All my clothes are chosen by stylists.'

He frowned. 'Don't you see them first? And get to approve them?'

Alyse shrugged. 'I suppose I could have insisted, but...' She trailed off, not wanting to admit how cowed she'd been by Queen Sophia's army of stylists and staff who had seemed to know so much more than her, and had obviously not cared about what she thought.

At eighteen, overawed and more than a little intimidated, she hadn't possessed the courage to disagree with any of them, or so much as offer her own opinion. As the years had passed, bucking the trend had just become harder, not easier.

'I didn't realise you had so little say in such matters. I suppose my mother can be quite intimidating.'

'That's a bit of an understatement,' she answered lightly, but Leo just frowned.

'You were so young when we became engaged.'

She felt herself tense uneasily, unsure what he was implying. 'Eighteen, as you know.'

'Young. And sheltered.' His frown deepened and he shook his head. 'I remember how it was, Alyse. I know my parents can be very...persuasive. And, as the media attention grew, it might have seemed like you were caught in a whirlwind you couldn't control.'

'It did feel like that sometimes,' she allowed. 'At times it was utterly overwhelming. But I knew what I was doing, Leo.' *More or less.* 'I might have only been eighteen, but I knew my own mind.' *And her own heart.* Not that she would ever tell him that. After Leo's revelations about how he didn't even believe in love, never mind actually having ever felt it, Alyse had no intention of baring her heart. Not now, and perhaps not ever.

She forced the thought away. *This is a beginning.*

'Still…' he began, and she thought how easy it would be, to let him believe she'd been railroaded into this marriage. And there was some truth in it, after all. The media attention *had* been out of control, and in those dark moments when she'd considered breaking their engagement she'd known she didn't possess the strength to go against everything and everyone—the monarchy, the media, the adoring public. It had simply been too much.

But it wasn't the whole truth and, while it might satisfy Leo as to why she'd agreed in the first place—a question she hadn't been willing to answer last night—she wouldn't perpetuate another lie.

But neither will you tell him the real reason—that you were in love with him, and still are.

With determined flippancy she adjusted her mask and put her hands on her hips. 'How do I look? I don't think anyone can be taken seriously in flippers.'

His expression lightened into a smile, and Alyse felt a rush of relief. Now she was the one avoiding conversation. Honesty.

'Probably not,' he agreed and held out one of his own flippered feet. 'But they do the job. Are you ready?'

She nodded and a moment later they were slipping over the side of the boat. When Leo put his hands on her bared waist to steady her as she slid into the water, Alyse felt her heart rate rocket. Just the touch of his hands on her flesh sent an ache of longing through her. She wanted to turn to him, to rip off their masks and stupid fins and forget anything but this need that had been building in her for so long, the need she longed to be sated. She wanted to be his lover as well as his friend.

Then he let go of her and with a splash she landed and kicked away from the boat, Leo swimming next to her.

As soon as she put her face in the sea the world seemed to open up, the ocean floor with its twists and curves of coral stretching away endlessly in every direction. Fish of every colour and size darted among the coral: schools of black-and-yellow-striped fish, one large blue fish swimming on its own and a fish that even seemed to change colours as it moved.

Overwhelmed after just a few minutes, Alyse lifted her head from the water. Leo immediately did the same, taking his mask off to gaze at her in concern. 'Are you OK?'

'Amazed,' she admitted. 'I've never seen so many fish before. They're all so beautiful.'

'The snorkelling here is supposed to be the best in the Caribbean.'

She couldn't resist teasing him. 'You sound like a tourist advert.'

'I just do my research. You want to keep going?'

'Of course.'

They snorkelled side by side for over an hour, pointing different fish out to one another, kicking in synchronicity. At one point Leo reached for her hand and pulled her after him to view an octopus nestling in a cave of coral and they grinned at each other at the sight, Leo's eyes glinting behind his mask.

Finally, hungry and tired, they returned to the boat, hauling themselves dripping onto the deck.

'I had the staff pack us a lunch,' Leo informed her. 'They should have left it on the boat.'

Alyse sat drying in the sun while Leo took a wicker basket from one of the storage compartments and began to unpack its contents.

'Champagne and strawberries?' She surveyed the contents of the basket with her eyebrows raised. 'Quite the romantic feast.'

'Did you really expect anything else?'

She watched as he laid it all out on a blanket. 'Do you ever get tired of it?' she asked quietly. 'The pretending? With me?'

His fingers stilled around the neck of the champagne bottle and then he quickly and expertly popped the cork. 'Of course, just as I imagine you do.'

'Why did you agree to it all, Leo? Was it really just to help stabilise the monarchy?'

The glance he gave her was dark and fathomless. 'Does that not seem like enough reason to you?'

'It seems like a huge sacrifice.'

'No more than you were willing to make.'

They were getting into dangerous territory, Alyse knew. She didn't want him to ask her again why she'd agreed. She didn't want to have to answer.

'Does the monarchy matter that much to you?'

'Of course it does. It's everything to me.'

Everything. That was rather all-encompassing; it didn't leave room for much else. 'I suppose you've been preparing to be king since you were born.'

Leo didn't answer for a moment and Alyse felt the tension in his suddenly stilled hands, his long, lean fingers wrapped around the neck of the champagne bottle. Then he began to pour, the bubbles fizzing and popping against the sides of the flute. 'More or less.'

Alyse surveyed him, felt instinctively he wasn't saying something, something important. Perhaps he did have secrets…just as she did.

'Another toast?' she asked as Leo handed her a glass.

'We've had quite a few toasts recently.'

'And quite a lot of champagne.'

'People can be amazingly unoriginal about what they think is romantic,' he said dryly. He eyed her thoughtfully over the rim of his glass. 'How about a toast to friendship?'

Alyse's heart lurched. 'You're coming around, then?' she said lightly, and he inclined his head in acknowledgement.

'A bit.'

'To friendship, then,' she answered, and they both drank, their eyes meeting over the rims of their glasses. Alyse felt her insides tighten and then turn over at the look of heat in Leo's navy eyes. They simmered with it, that warmth seeming to reach out and steal right through her. For such a coldly practical man, his eyes burned. *She* burned.

'So,' she offered shakily. 'What is there to eat besides strawberries?'

'Oh, lots of things,' he said lightly, glancing away from her to fill a plate with various delectable offerings. 'You won't go hungry.'

'No,' Alyse murmured. But she *was* going hungry… hungry in an entirely different, and carnal, way. She knew he wanted her, had thrilled to the taste and feel of his desire when he'd kissed her, when he'd pulled her close to that hard, hard body. Yet she still didn't quite have the confidence to act on it now, to thrust away the plate he'd given her and reach for something far more delicious: *him*.

'Try some,' Leo offered, and she saw the heat flare in his eyes, wondered if he knew the nature of her thoughts.

Wordlessly Alyse put something in her mouth; she didn't even look to see what it was. The burst of sweet flavour on her tongue surprised her and she realised she'd bitten into a plantain fried in orange juice.

'Good?' Leo asked, and now she heard the desire in his voice as well as saw it in his eyes; it poured over her like chocolate, rich and sweet. She'd never heard him sound like this before, never felt so much in herself—or from him.

Somehow she managed to eat most of what was on her plate, the rich flavours bursting on her tongue. Every heavy-lidded look and small, knowing smile from Leo made her more aware of everything: the taste of the food; the feel of the sun on her salt-slicked skin; the heat and desire coursing through her body like warmed honey.

Finally there were only the strawberries left, and the champagne.

'And this is the only way to eat these,' Leo said, dipping a strawberry in his flute of champagne and then raising it to Alyse's parted lips.

Her heart rate skittered and her breathing hitched as she opened her mouth and took a bite of the champagne-sodden fruit. The taste on her tongue was both tart and sweet, but far headier than any champagne she could drink was the look of unabashed hunger in Leo's eyes—and the answering surge she felt in herself.

Strawberry juice dribbled down her chin and Leo's expression flared hotter as he caught it with the tip of his thumb then licked the juice from his own hand.

Alyse let out an audible shudder. Then, filled with a new daring fuelled by this heady desire, she reached for a strawberry and dunked it into her own glass of champagne. Leo's narrowed gaze followed her movements and after a heartbeat's hesitation he opened his mouth.

Her fingers near to trembling, Alyse put the strawberry to his lips. Juice ran over her fingers as he bit down, his gaze hot and hard on hers. She shuddered again, her whole body singing with awareness and need. Then Leo turned his head so his lips brushed her fingers and with his tongue he caught a drip of juice from the sensitive skin of her wrist.

Alyse let out a shocked gasp at the exquisite sensation. *'Leo...'*

And then he was pushing aside the remnants of their picnic, champagne spilling and strawberries scattering, and was reaching for her, finally, *finally* reaching for her.

His hands came hard onto her shoulders and then his mouth was hard on hers, tasting both tart and sweet from the champagne and the fruit.

His tongue swept into her mouth, tasting, searching, and then finding. Pleasure burst inside her like fireworks, like sparks of the sun, heating her all over. Alyse brought her hands up to his shoulders, her palms smoothing and then clutching the hot, bared skin.

Leo's mouth moved from her lips to her jaw and then her neck, his hand cupping her breast with only the thin, damp fabric of her bikini top between the heat of his palm and her sensitive skin.

Alyse moaned aloud, the sound escaping from her, impossible to contain, and Leo drew back.

'I'm sorry,' he murmured, smoothing her hair away from her face. 'I'm rushing like a randy schoolboy and you deserve better than that.'

She blinked, still dazed by the sensations coursing through her. Leo smiled, no more than a quirk of his mouth. 'I don't want your first time to be some hasty grope on the deck of a boat. I do have that much sensitivity, Alyse.'

Alyse blinked again, his words trickling through her, leaving ice in their wake. Her first time. Hers—not *theirs*.

Leo, she realised, thought she was a virgin.

CHAPTER SEVEN

LEO SAW THE emotions flash across Alyse's face like changes in the weather, sunshine and shadows. Even more so he felt the change in her, the tensing, the slight withdrawal even though she hadn't actually moved.

'What is it?' he asked quietly. 'What's wrong?'

She gave a little shake of her head. 'Nothing.'

He didn't believe that for a moment. Gently but firmly he took her chin in his hand, forced her to look at him. 'It's not nothing.'

Her clear grey eyes met his for a moment before she let her gaze slide away. 'Nothing to talk about now,' she said, with a not-quite-there smile.

If she was trying to sound light, she'd failed. Leo let go of her chin and sat back braced on his hands to survey her thoughtfully. She still wasn't looking at him and a tendril of hair, curly from the sea air, fell against the soft paleness of her cheek.

'Are you nervous about what will happen between us?'

She looked at him then, a small spark of humour lighting her eyes. 'You sound like something out of a melodrama, Leo. You're usually more blunt than that.'

He felt his mouth curving in an answering smile. 'I'm happy to be blunt. I want you, Alyse.' He gazed at her frankly, letting the desire that still coursed unsated through his body reveal itself in his face. 'I want you very badly. I want to touch you, to kiss you, to be inside you. And I don't want to wait very long.'

He saw an answering flare of heat in her eyes, turning them to molten silver, but her lips twisted and trembled and she looked away again. *What was going on?* 'That's admirably blunt.'

'I'll be even blunter—I think you want me just as much as I want you.' Gently he tucked that curly tendril of hair behind her ear, unable to keep his fingers from lingering on the softness of her skin. He felt her tremble in response. 'Do you deny it?'

'No,' she whispered, but she wouldn't look at him.

Frustration bit into him. *What was going on?* Compelled to make her look at him, make her acknowledge the strength of the desire between them, he touched her chin and turned her to face him. She met his gaze reluctantly but unflinchingly, her eyes like two wide, grey pools Leo thought he could drown in. Lose himself completely.

'I want to make love to you,' he said quietly, each word brought up from a deep well of desire and even emotion inside him. 'But not here, on a hard deck. We have a lovely big bed on a lovely private beach and I quite like the idea of making love to you there.'

Her eyes widened even more, surprise flickering in their depths, and with a jolt he realised what he'd said. Confessed.

Making love. It was a term he'd never used, didn't even like. If love didn't exist beyond a simple hormonal fluctuation, then you couldn't make it. And sex, in his experience, had nothing to do with love. It wouldn't, even with Alyse.

Yet the words had slipped out and he knew that Alyse had noticed. What did she think was happening between them? What *was* happening between them?

Panic, icy and overwhelming, swamped him. Why the hell had he said that? Felt it? This was what happened when you let someone in just a little bit. Friendship be damned.

He dropped his fingers from her chin and rose abruptly from the deck, thankfully shattering the moment that had stretched between them. There would be no putting it together again; he'd make sure of that. 'We should head back,' he said tersely. 'In any case.'

He set sail, his back to her, and wondered just how he could get their relationship—he didn't even like calling it that—back on the impersonal and unthreatening footing he craved. Whatever it took, he vowed grimly, he would do it. He'd had enough of this *friendship*.

Alyse sat on the bridge deck and watched as Leo set sail for their private cove. His shoulders were now rigid with tension, every muscle taut, and she didn't know if it was because of her emotional withdrawal or his. She'd seen the flare of panic in his eyes when he'd said those two revealing words: making love.

But there would be no love in their physical union, just immense, intense attraction. So why had he said it? Had he meant it simply as a turn of phrase that had alarmed him when he'd heard it aloud? Or, for a moment, had he actually felt something more? That alarmed him more than any mere words ever could.

Was she ridiculous to think that little slip might signify something? She knew she had a tendency to read far too much into a smile or a look. She didn't want to make the same mistake now, yet she couldn't keep herself from wondering. From hoping.

And yet, she felt her own flare of panic. What would Leo think—and feel—when she told him, as she must do, that she wasn't a virgin?

Alyse turned to face the sea, hugging her knees to her chest even though the wind was sultry. The coldness she felt came from inside, from the knowledge she'd been hiding from for too long already.

She'd blanked out that one fumbling evening that constituted all of her sexual experience, had consigned it to a terrible, heart-rending mistake and tried to pretend it hadn't happened.

But princesses—future queens—were meant to be pure, unblemished, and she clearly was not. In this day and age, did it really matter?

It would matter, she supposed, to someone like Queen Sophia who, despite having been born into merely an upper-class family, held fast to the archaic bastions of the monarchy as if she were descended from a millennia's worth of royalty. It probably mattered to King Alessandro as well, but she didn't care about either of them. She cared about Leo.

Would it matter to him? Would he be disappointed that he wasn't her first? She had no illusions that *he* was a virgin; he surely hadn't been celibate for the six long years of their engagement, even if he'd been admirably discreet.

Anxiety danced in her belly. Worry gnawed at her mind. She didn't want to give him any reason to withdraw emotionally from her, to feel disappointed or perhaps even angry, yet she knew she would have to tell him… before tonight.

They didn't speak until the catamaran was pulled up on the beach and they were back in their private cove, and then only to talk about when they would have dinner. It was late afternoon, the sun already starting its mellow descent towards the horizon.

Alyse went to shower in the separate bathroom facilities, all sunken marble and gold taps kept in a rocky enclosure that was meant to look like a natural part of the cove.

She washed away the remnants of sea salt and sun cream and wondered what the next few hours would hold.

Something had started to grow between her and Leo, perhaps even to blossom. Friendship—and perhaps something more, until he'd had that moment of panic.

Could they recapture both the camaraderie and passion they'd felt this afternoon?

What if her admission ruined it all?

It doesn't matter, she told herself. *It shouldn't matter. He might be a prince, but Leo's still a modern man...*

Even so, she felt the pinpricks of uncertainty. Of fear.

The staff were setting up another romantic dinner on the beach when Leo came out of the shower, his hair damp and curling slightly by his neck, the sky-blue of his shirt bringing out the blue in his eyes. Alyse had chosen another dress from her stylist-selected wardrobe, this one made of lavender silk, the colour like the last vestiges of sunset. It dipped daringly low in the front and then nipped in at the waist before flaring out around her legs. She left her hair down and her feet bare and went without make-up. It seemed ridiculous to bother with eyeliner or lipstick when they were on a secluded beach and the sea wind and salt air would mess them both up anyway.

Leo seemed to agree, for he took in her appearance with no more than a slight nod, yet she still felt the strength of his response, the leashed desire.

And something else. Something she didn't like—a coolness in his expression, a reserve in his manner. He didn't speak as he took her hand and led her to the table set up on the sand.

Still she was achingly aware of him, more now than ever before: the subtle, spicy scent of his aftershave; the dry warmth of his palm as he took her hand; the latent strength of his stride as she fell into step next to him.

'What shall we do tomorrow?' she asked brightly when they'd sat down and begun their starters, slices of succulent melon fanned out with paper-thin carpaccio. She was determined not to lose any ground, not to let him retreat back into his usual silence, as much as he might seem to want to. 'Go for a hike?'

Leo's mouth tightened and he speared a slice of melon. 'I need to work tomorrow.'

'Work?' Disappointment crashed over her but with effort she kept her smile in place, her voice light. 'This is your honeymoon, Leo.'

He pinned her with a steely gaze. 'I have duties, Alyse.'

'And what will the staff think of you ignoring your bride on the second full day of our holiday?' she asked, unable to keep herself from it even though she didn't want to bring up the whole pretence of their relationship. She wanted to talk about how it was becoming more real. Or it had seemed to be, this afternoon.

'I'm sure they'll understand. Being in love doesn't mean we live in each other's pockets. The last six years have proved that. We spent most of the time apart and yet no one seemed to have any trouble believing we were wildly, passionately in love.'

That wasn't quite true, Alyse knew. When the media hadn't been celebrating their grand romance, it had been trying to create division: publishing incriminating-looking photos, composing pages and pages of speculation that she'd feared contained more than a grain of truth.

Leo looking for love with Duke's daughter Liana?

The memory still hurt.

'I realise that,' she told him when she trusted herself to speak as evenly as he had. 'But this is our honeymoon.'

'And you know just what kind of honeymoon it is.'

'What is that supposed to mean?'

'We're pretending,' he clarified, his voice cool. 'We always will be.'

'I haven't forgotten.' Alyse stared at him. His face was

as blank as it ever had been, all traces of humour and happiness completely gone.

Today had been so sweet, so wonderful and so full of hope. She hated that they'd lost so much ground so quickly.

And why? Just because of that moment on the boat, when Leo had mentioned the dreaded L-word?

Was he actually spooked? *Afraid?*

The thought seemed ridiculous; Leo was always so confident, so assured. And yet Alyse couldn't think of another reason for his sudden and utter withdrawal.

The friendship—the intimacy—that had been growing between them had him scared.

The thought almost restored her hope. Scared was better than indifferent. Still, she knew there was no point pressing the issue now. That didn't mean she was going to let him off the hook quite so easily.

'I suppose I can entertain myself easily enough for a day,' she said lightly, and saw the flicker of surprise ripple across Leo's features that she was capitulating so easily. 'What work do you have to do?' she continued, and the surprise on his face intensified into discomfort. Alyse almost smiled. 'Are you working on that proposal for broadband?'

'Some paperwork,' he answered after a pause, his voice gruff, but Alyse was determined not to let the conversation sputter out. He would let her in, one way or another. Even if he was scared.

'Will you put the proposal before the Cabinet? That's how it works, isn't it? A constitutional monarchy.'

'Yes. I hope to put it before them eventually. It's not one of my father's priorities.'

'Why not?'

Leo shrugged. 'My father has always been more interested in enjoying the benefits of being king rather than fulfilling his royal responsibilities.'

'But you're different.'

A light blazed briefly in his eyes. 'I hope so.'

'I think you are.' She spoke softly, and was gratified to see something like surprised pleasure lift the corners of Leo's mouth before he glanced away.

'I hope I can match you as queen.' She meant to sound light but the words came out in a rush of sincerity. 'I want to be a credit to you, Leo.'

'You already are. The fact that the public fell in love with you six years ago has been a huge boon to our country. You of all people must know the power of that photograph.'

She nodded slowly. 'Yes, but more than that. I want to do something more than just smile and shake hands.'

'Understandably, but don't sell a smile and a handshake short. It's more than my parents ever did.'

'Is it?'

'One of the reasons they were so keen for our engagement to go ahead is because they'd damaged the monarchy nearly beyond repair,' Leo said flatly. He speared a slice of beef with a little more vigour than necessary.

'How?'

He shrugged. 'Very public affairs, careless spending, a complete indifference to their people. It's hard to say which aspect of their lives was the most damaging.'

And he'd grown up in that environment. 'It doesn't sound like a very happy place to have your childhood,' she said quietly.

'I didn't. I went to boarding school when I was six.'

'*Six?*'

'I didn't mind.' A waiter had materialised on the edge of the beach and with a flick of his fingers Leo indicated for him to come forward. Alyse had a feeling he'd had enough of personal conversation, but at least he'd shared something. More than he ever had before.

Leo hadn't meant to say so much. Reveal so much. How did she do it? he wondered. How did she sneak beneath the defences he'd erected as a boy, had had firmly in place for so long? He never talked about his parents, or himself, or anything. He'd always preferred it that way and yet in these unguarded moments he discovered he almost enjoyed the conversation. The sharing.

So much for getting this relationship back on the footing he'd wanted: impersonal. Unthreatening.

Frustration blazed through him. No more *friendship*. No more conversation. There was only one thing he wanted from Alyse, and he would have it. Tonight.

Over the next few courses of their meal she made a few attempts at conversation and Leo answered politely enough without encouraging further talk. Still, she tried, and he had to admire her determination.

She wouldn't give up. Well, neither would he.

The moon had risen in the sky, sending its silver rays sliding over the placid surface of the sea. The waiter brought them both tiny glasses of liqueurs and a plate of petit fours and then left them alone, retreating silently back to the main resort.

All around them the night seemed very quiet, very still, the only sound the gentle lap of the waves against the sand. In the moonlit darkness, Alyse looked almost ethereal, her hair floating softly about her shoulders, her silvery eyes soft—yes, eyes could be soft, and thoughtful.

Desire tightened inside him and he took a sip of the sweet liqueur, felt its fire join the blaze already ignited in his belly. He wanted her, just as he'd told her that afternoon, and he would have her tonight.

And it wouldn't be making love.

They sat in silence for a few more moments, sipping their liqueurs, when Leo decided he'd had enough. He placed his glass on the table with deliberate precision. 'It's getting late,' he said, and Alyse's gaze widened before she swallowed audibly. Leo smiled and stood, stretching one hand out to her.

She rose and took it, her fingers slender and feeling fragile in his as he drew her from the table and across the sand to their sleeping quarters.

While they'd been eating some of the staff had prepared their hut for the night. The sheets had been turned down and candles lit on either side of the bed, the dancing flames sending flickering shadows across the polished wooden floor.

The perfect setting for romance, for *love*, but Leo pushed that thought away. He stood in front of the bed and turned her to face him; her bare shoulders were soft and warm beneath his hands.

She shivered and he couldn't tell if it was from desire or nervousness. Perhaps both. He knew he needed to go slowly, even though the hunger inside him howled for satiation and release.

He slid his hands up from her shoulders to cup her face, his thumbs tracing the line of her jaw, her skin like silk beneath his fingers. 'Don't be nervous,' he said softly, for now that they were in the moment he still wanted to reassure her, even if he didn't want to engage his emotions.

'I'm not,' she answered, but her voice choked and she looked away.

In answer he brushed a feathery kiss across her jaw before settling his mouth on hers, his tongue tracing the seam of her lips, gently urging her to part for him.

And she did, her mouth yielding to his, her arms coming around him as he drew her pliant softness against him, loving the way her body curved and melted into his.

He kissed her deeply, sliding his hands from her face to her shoulders and then her hips, drawing her close to him, fitting her against the already hard press of his arousal.

Desire shot up through him with fiery arrows of sizzling sensation and he felt her shudder in response.

Gently, slowly, he drew the thin straps of her dress down her shoulders. Alyse stood still, her gaze fastened on him as he reached behind her, and with one sensuous tug had her dress unzipped. It slithered down her body and pooled on the floor, leaving her in only a skimpy white lace bra and matching pants—honeymoon underwear, barely serving their purpose, unless it was to inflame— which it did.

Leo let his gaze travel slowly across her barely clothed body, revelling in the beauty of her, desire coiling tighter and tighter inside him.

He placed one hand on her shoulder, sliding it down to her elbow, smoothing her skin. She drew a shuddering breath.

'Are you cold?'

'No.' She shook her head and, needing to touch her more—everywhere—he slid his hand from her elbow to her breast, his palm cupping its slight fullness as he drew his thumb across the aching peak. Alyse let out a little gasp and he smiled, felt the primal triumph of making her respond.

'I know this is new for you,' he said quietly and he saw a flash of something almost like anguish in her eyes.

'Leo…' She didn't say anything more and he didn't want to waste time or energy on words. Smiling, he brushed a kiss across her forehead and then across her mouth before he unhooked her bra and slid it off her arms. He drew her to him, her bare breasts brushing the crisp cotton of his shirt, and even that sensation made him ache. He wanted her so very much.

'What about your clothes?' she asked shakily and he arched an eyebrow.

'What about mine?'

'They're on you, for starters.'

He laughed softly. 'I suppose you could do something about that.'

Her fingers shook only a little as she fumbled with the buttons of his shirt, the tips of her fingers brushing his bare chest. He stood still, everything in him dark and hot from just those tiny touches. Then she finished unbuttoning it and pulled it off his shoulders, her gaze hungry as she let it rove over him, making him darker and hotter still.

His breathing hitched as she smoothed her hands over his chest, down to his abdomen, and then with a little, mischievous smile her fingers slipped under the waistband of his trousers.

He sucked in a hard breath as with her other hand she tugged on the zip, her fingers skimming the hard length of his erection. 'Alyse...'

'Only fair,' she whispered with a trembling laugh, and Leo's voice lowered to a growl as he answered,

'I'll show you fair.'

He pulled her even closer to him so her breasts were crushed against his bare chest and kissed her with a savage passion he hadn't even known he possessed, the self-control he'd prided himself on for so long slipping away, lost in a red tide of desire.

And she responded, her arms coming up around him, her tongue tangling with his as she matched him kiss for kiss, their breathing coming in ragged gasps as the shy gentleness of their undressing turned into something raw and powerful and almost harsh in its intensity.

He'd never felt like this before. Felt so much before. He wanted and needed her too much to be alarmed or afraid by the power of her feelings—or his own.

Alyse's mind was dazed with desire as Leo drew her to the bed. Ever since he'd led her from the dinner table she'd tried to find a way to tell him the truth, that she wasn't a virgin. His obvious assumption made the need for disclosure all the more vital, yet somehow the words wouldn't come. And when Leo had kissed her, and undressed her, and touched her...

Then she'd had no words at all.

She didn't remember how they ended up lying on the bed, Leo sliding off her underwear and then his own so they were both completely naked. It had all happened so quickly, yet she felt as if she'd been waiting for this moment for ever.

And still she hadn't told him. *Maybe later*, she thought hazily as Leo bent his head to her breast and she raked his shoulders with her nails, her body arching off the bed as he flicked his tongue against her heated, over-sensitised skin. *After.* She'd tell him after.

She felt Leo's hand between her thighs, his fingers sliding deftly to the damp warmth between them and her hips arched instinctively as he found her centre.

'You're lovely,' he murmured as he touched her, brushing kisses across her mouth, her jaw, her throat. 'So lovely.'

'You are too,' Alyse answered, her voice uneven, and he laughed softly.

He slid a finger inside her and she felt her muscles instinctively clench around him. A wave of pleasure crashed over and drowned out any possible attempts at speech or thought. Leo's touch was so knowing, so assured, and her fingernails dug into the bunched muscles of his shoulders as he rolled over her, his clever fingers replaced by the hard press of his erection.

Alyse arched her hips, welcoming this glorious invasion, the sense of completeness she ached to feel with every fibre of her being.

'This might hurt just a little,' he whispered and she closed her eyes against a sudden, soul-quenching rush of shame.

She couldn't lie to him, not even by her silence. Not now, not about this.

'It won't, Leo,' she choked, her anguish all too apparent to both of them. 'I'm—I'm not a virgin.'

She felt him poised above her, could feel the heat and strength of him so close to her; another inch or two and he'd be inside her, as she so desperately wanted. She arched her hips reflexively, but he didn't move.

Alyse let out a shudder of both longing and despair. Clearly she picked her moments well.

Leo swore under his breath and eased back. 'What a time to tell me,' he said, his voice coming out in a groan.

'I didn't—didn't know how to tell you,' she whispered miserably.

Leo rolled onto his back and stared up at the woven-grass roof of the hut, his chest heaving with the effort of stopping at such a critical moment.

'Obviously it's a distressing memory,' he said after a moment, his eyes still on the roof. 'You must have been very young.'

'It was.' She took a breath, hating that they were talking about this now, in such an intimate moment, a moment that had seconds ago promised tenderness and pleasure and perhaps even the first fragile shoots of a deeper and more sacred emotion. 'And I wasn't that young. I was twenty.'

She felt Leo still next to her, every muscle in his body seeming to go rigid. Then he turned his head to stare at her, and everything in Alyse quailed at the sight of the cold blankness in his eyes. *Twenty?*

'Yes—at university.'

'You slept with someone at university?' he repeated, sounding so disbelieving that Alyse flinched.

'Yes—do we have to talk about this?'

'I don't particularly relish the conversation myself.' In one fluid movement Leo sat up and reached for his boxers.

Alyse felt her throat thicken as disappointment and frustrated desire rushed through her. 'Leo, I'm sorry. I suppose I should have told you earlier, but we never had any remotely intimate conversations, and frankly I just wanted to forget it ever happened. That's no excuse, I know.' He finished sliding on his boxers and just picked up his shirt. 'Are you—are you angry? That I'm not a virgin?'

He let out a bark of humourless laughter and turned to face her. He looked as cold and remote as he ever had— only worse, because she'd seen his face softened in sleep or with a smile, his eyes warm with laughter and then hot with desire. Now he was reverting once more to the icy stranger she knew, the man who made her despair. 'You think I'm angry that you're not a virgin?'

'Well—yes.'

He shook his head, the movement seeming one of both incredulity and contempt. 'That would be a bit of a double standard, since I'm not one.'

She swallowed, surprised. 'I know, but it's always been different for men, hasn't it? And the whole princess thing…'

'This has nothing to do with the *princess thing*,' Leo answered her shortly. 'And I don't believe in double standards. If I seem angry, Alyse, it's not because you've had sex before. It's because you had sex while you were engaged to me.'

And, before she could even process that statement, he had yanked on his trousers and was heading out into the night.

CHAPTER EIGHT

LEO STRODE ACROSS the beach, knowing that, just like last night, he had nowhere to go and hating it. Damn this island. Damn Alyse. Damn himself, for caring about what she'd done—and who she'd done it with.

He didn't feel merely betrayed, which was what made him so angry. He felt hurt.

Stupid, because it had happened years ago, and it wasn't as if they'd actually loved each other. So what if she'd loved someone else? Given herself to someone else? What did it really matter?

And yet it did.

He knew he was overreacting; knew he should be at most surprised, and a little annoyed, perhaps, by her infidelity during their engagement, but he shouldn't actually *care*.

Not like this. Never like this.

'Leo?'

He turned and saw her slender form framed in the doorway of the hut, now clothed in one of those ridiculously frothy robes, the candlelight silhouetting her slight yet still lush curves, curves he remembered the feel of under his palms. Leo turned his face away.

'Please don't storm off,' she said, the desolation in her voice reaching him in far too many ways. 'Talk to me.'

Leo didn't reply. He didn't want to talk to her, didn't

want to explain the feelings that churned inside him, the feelings he wasn't sure he understood—or wanted to understand—himself.

'Please, Leo.'

Wordlessly he stalked back to the hut, his back to Alyse and the all-too-tempting image she presented in her ridiculous robe. Fine. They would have it out. She could spill all the gritty details and then he would *never* let her close again. Not as a friend. Not as a lover. He'd take her body and use her popularity and their marriage would be exactly what he'd always wanted and intended it to be. Nothing more.

She stood by the bed, the candlelight silhouetting her figure so she might as well have been naked. He tried not to gaze at the dip of her waist, those high, pert breasts, the shadow between her thighs, but still his groin ached. He'd been unbearably close to burying himself so deep inside her he would have forgotten who he was. What he actually wanted.

'I know I should have said something, maybe this afternoon,' she continued, her voice low, her fingers toying with the sash of her robe. 'But I didn't want to bring it up, to ruin what was between us—'

'There was nothing between us,' Leo cut her off harshly, too harshly. His words were loud and ragged in the hushed stillness of the night. They were *emotional*, he thought furiously.

Alyse stared at him, her eyes wide. 'Please don't say that.'

'I knew this would happen,' he continued relentlessly, remorseless now. 'A single day of barely enjoying each other's company and you're building castles in the air. Friendship never would have been enough for you.'

He saw the hurt flash across her face but she lifted her chin and managed a small smile that touched him with its bravery; he didn't *want* to be touched. 'Maybe not,' she said quietly. 'And I admit, I have a tendency to build those kinds of castles. I've been doing it ever since I met you.'

He stilled, every nerve tautening with sudden apprehension, even alarm. 'What are you talking about?'

Alyse drew a shuddering breath. 'I've been in love with you since I met you, Leo. Since my eighteenth birthday party.'

She *really* didn't choose her moments well. Alyse saw the shock blaze in Leo's eyes, followed quickly by something that looked almost like fury.

She shouldn't have told him now, should *never* have told him. Yet how could she keep the secret of her feelings any longer? How could she make him understand what had driven her recklessly into another man's arms— if only for one unfortunate night—if he didn't know how much she loved him?

'You love me,' he repeated, and she heard derision.

'I do,' she answered steadily. 'I fell in love with you at my party...'

He arched an eyebrow, his mouth twisting unpleasantly. 'Did you fall in love with the way I danced? Or perhaps the way I drank champagne?'

'I just fell in love with you,' she answered helplessly. 'I can't explain it. Trust me, I've tried to explain it to myself many times.'

'Such a conundrum,' he drawled, his contempt evident in every taut line of his face.

He didn't believe her, Alyse realised. She hadn't expected that. Surprise, perhaps, or even horror—but incredulity? She spread her hands. 'Why do you think I agreed to the engagement? To our marriage?'

'Not because you *loved* me.'

'I couldn't imagine life without you,' Alyse blurted, the words spilling out of her. 'And I knew—of course, I've always known—you didn't love me back. But I hoped, like your father had said, that love or at least affection might come with time. That's why I kept at it, at the pretending—because I *hoped*—'

'And did that hope lead you into another man's bed, Alyse?' Leo cut her off, his voice wintry. 'Because I can do without that kind of love, thank you very much.'

'It was a mistake,' she whispered. 'A terrible mistake.'

His expression only grew colder. 'Clearly.'

She swallowed, hating that she had to rake this all up, yet knowing she needed to come clean. She'd hidden this heartache and shame for too long already. Maybe confession would help her—and Leo—to move on. 'It was one night, Leo. One awful night. That's all.'

'Is that supposed to make it more excusable?'

She felt the first flicker of anger. 'For someone who doesn't believe in double standards, you're sounding like a bit of a hypocrite.'

'A hypocrite?' He raised his eyebrows. 'How do you reckon that?'

'It's not as if you've been celibate for the last six years,' she answered, and she watched his mouth form a smile that held no humour or happiness at all.

'Haven't I?' he asked softly, his words seeming to reverberate through the room, through the stillness of the night and of her own soul. *He couldn't actually mean...?*

'But—but six *years*...' she stammered, and his smile turned hard.

'Yes, I'm well aware of how long a period of time it was.'

She shook her head slowly. 'I never thought—or expected— The engagement wasn't *real*...'

'On the contrary, our engagement has always been real. So is our marriage. It's the emotion you insist you've been feeling that isn't, Alyse. You don't love me. You don't even

know what love is. A schoolgirl crush? A shaft of desire?'
He shook his head, the movement one of both dismissal
and derision. 'That's all love ever is. And, in any case,
you don't even know me. How on earth could you think
you loved me?'

She shook her head again, drew in a shuddering breath.
She still couldn't believe he'd been celibate for so long.
For her. 'But the magazines—they said you were with
Liana Aterno.'

'You believed them? You know how they stir up gossip. You've experienced it yourself.'

'I know, but I thought— I expected you'd have some
discreet liaisons. The Queen—' She stopped abruptly and
Leo narrowed his eyes.

'The Queen,' he repeated softly. 'What did my mother
say to you?'

'Only that I shouldn't expect you to—to be faithful.'

'Only?'

Alyse gave him a watery smile. 'She did the whole
"men have needs" spiel, and how I was to turn a blind eye.'

'My mother was basing her experience on my father,'
Leo answered shortly. 'And their marriage, which has been
nothing but unpleasant and acrimonious. I wouldn't ever
listen to marriage advice from her.'

'I was only eighteen. I didn't know any better, I suppose.'

Leo nodded, his expression still cold. He hadn't softened in the least towards her, or her indiscretion, no matter what his mother might have said. 'Well, you clearly
used my mother's advice as a justification for your own
behaviour.'

'It wasn't like that, Leo.'

'I don't really want to hear.'

'And I don't want to tell you, but you've got to understand.' She was stumbling over her words in her haste to

explain, to reach him. 'It was one awful night. A friend from university. I was drunk.'

'I really don't need these details.'

She stared at him miserably. 'I know, but I just want you to understand. I'd seen a photo of you with that duke's daughter, Liana, in a magazine. There were articles all over the place about how you were dumping me for her.'

'And you never thought to ask me about it?'

'I never asked you about anything! We never talked. I didn't even have your mobile or your email address.'

'I think,' Leo said coldly, 'you could have got in touch if you'd wanted to. In any case, it doesn't even matter.'

She blinked, stared. 'It—doesn't?'

'No. Admittedly, I'm disappointed you thought so little of the agreement we'd made, the vows we would say. I know we've been pretending to be in love, Alyse, but we weren't pretending that we were going to get married. The rings on both our fingers is a testament to that.'

'I know,' she whispered. She felt the first sting of tears and blinked hard. 'I wish it had never happened.'

'Like I said, it doesn't matter. Naturally, I expect you to be faithful to me during our marriage. What happened in the past we can forget about. Thank God the press never found out.' He turned away from her, towards the bed, and Alyse watched him miserably. She'd never felt as far away from him as she did now…and it was her own fault.

'I'm sorry,' she said quietly.

'Like I said, it's in the past. Let's go to bed.' His meaning was clear as he slid beneath the sheets, his back to her: they would not be consummating their marriage tonight.

Swallowing, Alyse slid into bed next to him. They lay there silently, the only sound the ragged draw and tear of their breathing and the whoosh of the waves on the sand. She could feel the heat of his body, inhaled the scent of his aftershave, and her body still pulsed with longing. Yet she'd never felt farther away from him, or from hope, than she did in this moment.

She knew it was her own fault. She thought of that single night four years ago and closed her eyes in shame. It had been a terrible lapse of judgement, a moment of weakness she'd tried to block out since.

She'd been revising for exams and had caught sight of that awful photograph of Leo laughing with Liana, a gorgeous icy blonde, in a way he never had with her. Jealousy had sunk its razor-sharp claws into her soul, bled out her heart.

She'd been just twenty years old, engaged to Leo for two years, having seen him only a handful of times and spoken to him even less—yet firm, so firm, in the belief she loved him. And in that moment she'd felt certain he would never love her. Never even laugh with her.

It was the closest she'd ever come to breaking off the engagement, but even at her lowest point, halfway to heartbroken, she'd known she couldn't do it. Didn't possess the strength to call a halt to a romance that had captivated the world and still didn't want to.

Yet her despair at feeling that Leo would never love her, never even like her, had led her to go out with a casual friend—Matt—and get far too drunk on cheap cider.

Even now the details of the evening were fuzzy; they'd gone back to her flat and started talking. She'd been drunk enough to be honest, too honest, and she'd said something about how Leo didn't actually love her.

Matt had laughed and said that was impossible; everyone knew how they loved each other madly. Alyse had been just sober enough to keep from insisting on the truth, but she'd stared at that picture of Leo with the lovely Liana—she'd bought the magazine, if only to torture herself—and something in her had broken.

Without thinking about what she was doing, she'd

reached for Matt and kissed him clumsily. She still didn't know what had driven that impulse, perhaps just a desperate need for someone to want her.

He had responded eagerly, both alarming and gratifying her, and somehow it had all got out of control. In her drunken state she hadn't been able or even willing to stop it.

The next morning Matt had been sheepish and she'd been stricken. She'd felt ashamed and dirty, yet also strangely defiant, imagining Leo with the lovely Liana. Hating the thought of it, and hating what she'd done too.

Just as Leo hated it. He believed her one indiscretion showed her love for the flimsy fairy tale he thought it was—and lying there, wide awake and restless, she felt the first seed of doubt burrow deep into her heart, its shell cracking apart all her certainties.

What if Leo was right?

Too restless to lie still any longer, Alyse slid from the bed and headed out to the beach. The sand was cool and soft beneath her bare feet and the sky above was inky black and spangled with stars. The air was cooler now, and in only her nightdress she felt goose bumps rise on her arms.

She sat on the sand, as miserable as she'd ever been when she'd believed herself to be hopelessly in love with Leo. And this time it was because she had a sudden, sneaking fear that she wasn't, and perhaps never had been.

What did that say about her? Could she really have been so childish, so deluded, so *wrong* to convince herself she loved a man she barely knew? And to have kept believing it for so long?

Resting her chin on her knees, Alyse thought back to that first fateful night when Leo had come to her birthday party. Her mother had been almost as excited as she was, telling her that she'd been friends with Sophia in school, and how Leo was such a handsome prince... She'd reminded her too, of course, of the way she'd fallen in love with Alyse's father Henri at a party just like that one, across a crowded room…

Just like she'd convinced herself she had with Leo.

Had she wanted her parents' fairy tale for herself? Was that why she'd convinced herself of her love for Leo, because in her loneliness and uncertainty she'd longed for something more, had half-believed she could have it with Leo?

Everyone else had seemed to think she could, and in her innocence and immaturity she'd allowed a girlish attraction to become something so much bigger and deeper in her own mind and heart. And had continued to believe it, because as time went on and the media frenzy had grown, *not* to believe it took more strength and courage than she'd ever possessed.

Alyse let out a soft groan and pressed her forehead against her drawn-up knees. She didn't want to believe she'd been so deluded, didn't want to let go of her love so easily, so awfully.

And yet the derision on Leo's face had cut her to the bone, to the soul. *You don't even know me.*

No, she didn't, although she was starting to know him now. And, despite her parents' love-at-first-sight story, she wasn't sure she could believe it for her and Leo.

But that didn't mean she couldn't love him now. Learn to love him, the real him, the man she still wanted to believe hid underneath that mask, that armour of cold purpose and ruthless efficiency. He was there; she'd seen glimpses over the years and even more in the last few days. Glimpses that had stole through her soul and touched her heart.

He was there…and farther away from her than ever.

Sighing, her body cold and aching now, Alyse rose from the sand and headed back to the hut. She didn't know what

tomorrow, or any of her tomorrows, would now hold. How
Leo would feel or act. How they could get back just a little
bit of the camaraderie they'd shared.

And as for love?

Her mouth curved in a humourless smile. She didn't
dare even think about that now.

She must have slept, although she didn't remember doing
so as she'd lain next to Leo's hard body. But when she
next opened her eyes sunlight was flooding the little hut
and Leo was gone.

Alyse rose and dressed quickly, tossing the lavender
silk dress Leo had stripped from her body into one of her
cases with a wince. If only the night had ended differently
and she'd woken up in Leo's arms…

'Good morning.'

She glanced up, her heart rate skittering as he came
into the tent. He was showered and dressed and he looked
coldly impassive, no expression at all lightening the navy
of his eyes or softening those impossibly stern features.
Even so all Alyse had to do was look at him to remember
the way his lips had felt on hers, hard and soft at the same
time, and how his hands had felt on her body…tormenting
her with such exquisite pleasure.

She swallowed hard and looked away. 'Good morning.'

'Sleep well?' he queried, his voice holding a slight,
mocking edge, and Alyse shook her head.

'No.'

'Pity. Breakfast is in the pavilion again. I've already
eaten.'

'You have?' He'd turned away from her and she stared
at his broad back, the stiff set of his shoulders. 'People will
talk, you know,' she said, even though she hated using that
excuse. She didn't care what people said. She cared only
what Leo thought. What he felt…or didn't feel.

'I told them you were having a lie-in after a busy night, and made all the waitresses blush.'

'You didn't.'

'No, I didn't.' He turned around then, his eyes snapping with suppressed anger. 'I've developed a distaste for lying, even to the staff. But they assumed it anyway, so don't worry, our cover isn't blown.'

'Leo, I want to talk to you—'

'And I want to talk to you,' he cut her off coolly. 'But you might as well eat first.' And, reaching for the newspaper he'd brought from the pavilion, he settled in a chair and snapped it open, managing to ignore Alyse completely.

Without another word she left the hut.

Leo stared unseeingly at the newspaper in front of him, amazed at the amount of rage that poured through him in a scalding river. Why on earth was he so angry? He couldn't remember feeling this much emotion before, and it infuriated him—and frightened him. He was honest enough to admit that at least to himself.

No matter what he'd just told her, he wasn't about to admit it to Alyse.

And, when she returned from breakfast, he'd tell her exactly what he had in mind: a return to Maldinia and to their earlier arrangement, an arrangement that had satisfied him exactly. Their marriage would be a matter of business and convenience, nothing more. He'd been a fool to allow her to entertain ideas of friendship or affection. Both were pointless and had only raised ridiculous hopes in Alyse.

And in himself.

That annoyed and angered him most of all—that he'd actually enjoyed their time together, their banter, and of course their kisses… Just remembering how close he'd been to being inside her made Leo shift uncomfortably in his chair, a persistent ache in his groin.

He still wanted her, and he'd have her, perhaps even tonight. There was no longer any need to wait. He wasn't going to concern himself with her feelings, her fears. They'd return to the firm footing he had thought they'd been on when they'd both said those wretched vows.

To have and to hold, from this day forward...

Yes, from this day forward he would know exactly what to expect. And so would Alyse.

She returned to their sleeping quarters half an hour later and Leo glanced up as she approached, forcing himself not to notice the tender, bruised-looking skin under her eyes or the way her lush, pink mouth turned down at the corners. She wore a silky tee-shirt in pale green and a swishy skirt that blew around her long, slim legs. He yanked his gaze upwards, found it settling on the rounded curve of her breasts and determinedly moved it up to her face.

'Leo, I wanted to—'

'Let me tell you what I want to say,' he cut her off, his voice clipped. He had no wish to hear her stammered, desperate apologies or excuses. Neither mattered. 'This whole idea of friendship was a mistake,' he stated flatly. Alyse stilled, her face carefully blank so he couldn't tell at all what she was thinking or feeling.

Not that he cared.

'It was against my better judgement in the first place,' he continued. 'It just complicates matters. It was much simpler and easier before.'

'When we pretended all the time?' Alyse filled in.

'We'll always be pretending,' he answered, his tone deliberately brutal. 'The public expects to see us wildly in love—and, as I've told you before, that will never happen.'

'And here I thought you'd developed a distaste for lying.'

He had. Lord, how he had. He'd been doing it his whole life, just as his parents had been doing it with him. And he'd hated it all, hated how it hurt him, yet he'd thought with Alyse it would be different. It had been his choice and he would be in control.

And so he would. Starting now.

'Sometimes needs must,' he said brusquely. 'But at least we won't lie to each other.'

'So what exactly are you proposing, Leo? That we ignore each other for the length of our honeymoon? Our marriage?'

'Our honeymoon is over,' he answered, and he watched her pale.

'Over?'

'We head back to Maldinia this morning.'

'This morning.' Alyse stared at him, her face white. Then she rallied, a spark of challenge firing her eyes so Leo felt a reluctant surge of admiration for her spirit. 'So we had a honeymoon of all of two days. How do you think the public—the press—will react to that?'

'It's up to us, isn't it? If we return to Averne with faces like a wet weekend then, yes, they might suspect something. But if we smile and present a united front—royal duty must come first, after all—then I don't think we should have a problem.' He raised his eyebrows and smiled coolly. 'I trust that after six years your acting ability is up to the challenge.'

'And what about our scheduled visits to London? Paris? Rome?'

'We can fly from Maldinia. They're not until next week.'

Alyse just shook her head. 'Why do you want to return to Maldinia?' she asked quietly.

'Because I'd like to get our marriage on its proper footing,' Leo answered, his voice coming out in something

close to a snap. He strove to level it. 'And that doesn't involve romping around on the beach or playing at being
friends on a boat.'

Alyse gazed at him thoughtfully and it took all of his
effort not to avert his gaze, to hide from it. 'You're scared,'
she finally said, and Leo let out an abrupt, incredulous
laugh.

'Scared? Of what?'

'Of me—of what was happening between us. Intimacy.'

'Please.' He held up one hand. 'Spare me your fanciful
notions. I had enough of them last night, when you tried
to convince me you loved me.'

'I thought I loved you.'

'You've since been disabused of the notion? How convenient.' He felt a flash of hurt and suppressed it. 'I'll go
tell the staff to come fetch our bags.' And without a backward glance he stalked out of the hut.

CHAPTER NINE

ALYSE SAT ON the jet across from Leo. In the seven hours since they'd left St Cristos he hadn't spoken to her once. They'd flown overnight, sleeping in separate beds, and now it was morning with the sky hard and bright around them, and cups of coffee, a platter of croissants and fresh fruit set on the coffee table between them.

Leo was scanning some papers, his expression calm and so very collected, while she felt as if she'd swallowed a stone, her insides heavy and leaden, her eyes gritty with exhaustion, both emotional and physical.

They hadn't spoken since that awful exchange in their hut, when Leo had told her they were returning to Maldinia. She had no illusions about what would happen there; in a huge palace, with all of his royal duty beckoning, he would find it entirely easy to ignore her. They would see each other only for royal functions and occasions, and live separate lives the rest of the time.

Just like their engagement.

She swallowed, a hot lump of misery lodging in her throat. She couldn't go back to that. She couldn't live like that, not in Averne, where she wouldn't even have the comfort of her studies and her own circle of friends to bolster her, the way she'd had in Durham—a little bit, at least.

She supposed, like Leo, she could focus on her royal duty. She had a service to perform as a princess of Maldinia, a duty to the country's people, and she'd enjoyed and looked forward to that aspect of her royal life. Yet the thought of making it her entire purpose depressed her beyond measure.

She wanted more.

You've always wanted more. You gambled on this engagement, this marriage, in the hope of more—and now it looks like you'll never have it.

She felt a hot rush behind her lids and blinked hard. She would *not* cry. There had to be some way to salvage this, some way to reach Leo again, to make him understand and open up to her once more. But how?

Closing her eyes, she pictured his unyielding face, the grim set of his mouth and eyes as he'd spoken to her that morning. He'd seemed colder than he ever had before, almost as if he *hated* her.

How had it all gone so disastrously wrong so quickly? They'd been making steps—baby steps, true, but still *progress:* drawing closer to each other, enjoying each other's company. And then in one terrible moment everything had splintered apart. Everything had become worse than before because, instead of being merely indifferent to her, Leo was now angry.

Emotional.

Alyse stilled, realisation and hope trickling slowly, faintly through her. Why would Leo be so angry, so emotional, unless…?

Unless he cared?

Thoughts tumbled through her mind, a kaleidoscope of emotions and hopes. Maybe he'd enjoyed their brief time together more than he wanted to admit. Perhaps he was angry because he'd been hurt—and of course he wouldn't like that. He'd hate it.

Knowing Leo—and she was knowing him more and more every day—he'd fight against feeling anything for her. She didn't understand exactly why he resisted emotion and denied love so vehemently, but she knew there had to be a deep-seated reason, something most likely to do with his family and upbringing. And, when things got sticky, difficult and painful, of course he would revert back to his cold, haughty self. His protective persona, his only armour.

So how could she slip underneath it, touch the heart hidden beneath? How could she breach his defences, crack open his shell?

Sighing, Alyse opened her eyes and stared at the man across from her, his focus still solely on the papers in front of him.

'Leo,' she said, and reluctantly he lifted his gaze from the papers, his expression chillingly remote.

'Yes?'

'Are you really going to ignore me for the rest of this flight? For our entire lives?'

His mouth tightened and his gaze swept over her in unflinching assessment. 'Not ignore, precisely,' he answered coolly. 'I don't, for example, intend to ignore you tonight.'

Shock blazed through her, white-hot. 'Are you saying,' she asked in a low voice, 'that you intend to—to consummate our marriage tonight?'

Leo's expression didn't change at all. 'That's exactly what I'm saying.'

Alyse licked her dry lips. Even now she could not keep a tide of longing from washing over her. She still wanted him, cold and angry as he was. She would always want him. 'Even though you can barely summon the will to speak to me?' she observed and he arched an eyebrow.

'Speaking won't be involved.'

She flinched. 'Don't be crass. No matter how cold this business arrangement is, we both deserve more than that.'

An emotion—she couldn't quite tell what—flickered

across his face and he glanced away. 'As long as you realise that's exactly what this is,' he answered. 'A business arrangement.'

'Trust me,' she replied. 'I'm not likely to forget.'

Nodding in apparent satisfaction, Leo returned to his papers. Alyse sank against the sumptuous sofa, closing her eyes once more. So, she thought with a swamping sense of desolation, the only thing he wanted from her now was her body.

But what if, along with her body, she gave him her heart?

She stilled, opened her eyes and gazed blindly ahead. She'd just realised herself that she'd never actually loved him; her feelings for him had been part schoolgirl infatuation, part desperately wishful thinking. So how could she now offer this cold, proud, *hurting* man her heart?

Because that's what I want for my marriage. Because even if she hadn't loved him all of these years, she knew she could love him now. She could fall in love with him if he let her, if she got to know him as she had done over the last few days.

And that could begin tonight.

Five silent hours later they had landed in Maldinia on a balmy summer morning and returned by royal motorcade to the palace, unspeaking all the while.

The reporters had managed to get word of their early arrival and were waiting both at the airport and in front of the palace. They posed for photographs in both places, smiling and waving, Leo's arm snug around her waist. She glanced at him out of the corner of her eye and saw that, despite the white flash of his smile and his seemingly relaxed pose, his body was rigid next to her, his eyes flinty. He might be willing to pretend, but he certainly wasn't enjoying it. And neither was she.

Once they were back in the palace, Leo disappeared to his study and Alyse was shown to the bedroom she would have as her own—and it was clearly her own, not hers and Leo's; it was a feminine room in pale blues and greys, gorgeous and utterly impersonal.

She sank onto the bed, feeling lonely, lost and completely miserable. A few minutes later, still lost in her own unhappy thoughts, a knock sounded on the door and, without waiting for a response, Queen Sophia swept in.

Alyse stood up, a wary surprise stealing through her. She'd had very few interactions with her haughty mother-in-law and she preferred it that way.

Now Queen Sophia arched one severely plucked eyebrow and swept a thoroughly assessing gaze over Alyse. 'Why have you returned from the honeymoon so early?'

Alyse licked her dry lips. 'Leo— He had work to do.'

'Work? On his honeymoon?' Sophia's mouth pinched tight. 'How do you think the public will react to that? They want to see a young married couple in love, you know. They want to see you celebrating. The monarchy still depends on you.'

Alyse thought of what Leo had said about his parents: their affairs, careless spending and utter indifference to their own people. In light of all that, Sophia's insistence on royal decorum seemed hypocritical at best. 'I would think,' she answered, her voice wavering only slightly, 'the monarchy depends on you just as much.'

Sophia's mouth tightened further and her pale-blue eyes flashed ice. 'Don't be impertinent.'

'I wasn't. I was being honest.'

'I can do without your honesty. The only reason you've risen so high is because we decided it would be so.'

'And the only reason you decided it would be so is because it benefitted you,' Alyse retorted, a sudden anger and courage rising up inside her. 'With Leo and I in the spotlight, you could continue to do as you pleased—which it seems is all you've ever done.' Two spots of bright colour appeared on Sophia's high cheekbones. 'Oh, I know it grates on you,' Alyse continued, her temper now truly lit. 'To see your precious first-born married to a commoner.'

'Precious first-born?' Sophia's mouth twisted. 'Has Leo not even told you about his brother? But then I suppose he doesn't tell you anything.'

Alyse stared at her, nonplussed. 'His brother…?'

'Alessandro. His older brother. My husband disinherited him when he was twenty-one and Leo was eighteen. He would have been King.' For a second, no more, Alyse thought she heard a faint note of bitterness or even sorrow in Sophia's voice. Had she loved her son Alessandro? Loved him, perhaps, more than Leo?

'We don't talk about him,' Sophia continued flatly. 'The media stopped raking his story up over and over again years ago. But, if you wondered why the monarchy needed to be stabilised and restored, why we needed *you*, it's because of the scandal of Sandro leaving the way he did.' Sophia's eyes flashed malice. 'I'm surprised Leo never told you.'

Alyse didn't answer. She didn't sound at all surprised. Had Sophia guessed her schoolgirl feelings for Leo; had she perhaps used them against her all those years ago when she'd suggested their engagement? It seemed all too possible. She was shrewd and calculating and those ice-blue eyes missed nothing.

'Be careful,' Sophia continued softly. 'If the sorry truth of your relationship with Leo comes out now, the scandal will consume us all, including you. You might have enjoyed all the attention these last few years, but it won't be quite so pleasant when everyone starts to hate you.' Sophia's mouth curved in a cruel smile. 'Besides, you'd be no use to us then. No use to Leo.'

Alyse just stared, her mind spinning sickly, and with a click of her heels Sophia was gone, the door shutting firmly behind her.

Alyse sank back onto the bed. Had the Queen's parting shot been a threat? *No use to Leo.* If the media ever turned on her, if she became a liability to the monarchy rather than an asset, would Leo still want to be married to her?

It was a horrible question to ask herself, and even worse to answer. Knowing just what he thought of their marriage, she had a terrible feeling he wouldn't.

And what about his brother? She could hardly be surprised that Leo had never told her about Alessandro; he had told her barely anything personal about himself.

And yet, it could explain so much. She'd suspected his sense of cold detachment stemmed from his upbringing; with parents like King Alessandro and Queen Sophia, how could it not?

But a brother? A brother who had perhaps been the favourite, who had gone his own way, leaving Leo to try and make up for his absence? To prove himself through his endless royal duty?

She knew she was making assumptions, trying to understand the man who still seemed so much of an enigma to her.

The man who would come to her tonight...

She felt a shiver of anticipation for what lay ahead. Was it wrong—or perhaps just shameless—of her actually to be looking forward to tonight, at least in part? No matter how little Leo felt for her now, she still wanted him. Desperately.

Alyse didn't see Leo until that evening, when the royal family assembled for a formal dinner. He looked stunning in black tie, which was the standard dress for these cold family dinners. King Alessandro and Queen Sophia preferred this kind of rigid formality, and as she sat down across from Leo she wondered how it had affected him. How it had affected his brother.

It still surprised her that she'd never even known about him, not from Leo, not from his family, not even from any of the articles she'd read about the Maldinian royal family. *Her* family.

Her and Leo's engagement, and the accompanying scrutiny and excitement, must have taken the attention away from Leo's brother, almost as if everyone had forgotten it. Him.

Everyone but Leo. Somehow she didn't think he had forgotten his brother. She wanted to ask him about it, wanted to learn more about this man and what made him the way he was, and yet...

From the cool expression on Leo's face, he didn't want to have much conversation—not with anyone, and especially not with her.

The dinner was, as Alyse had expected, stilted and mainly silent. Alessandro and Sophia both made a few pointed references to their early return from honeymoon, but Leo was indifferent to any criticism, and Alyse just murmured something about looking forward to settling into life in the palace.

As if.

Alexa shot her an encouraging look when she made that remark, her dark-blue eyes—the same colour as Leo's—flashing both spirit and sympathy. Alyse knew Alexa was engaged to marry a sheikh of a small Middle Eastern country next year, and she had a feeling her new sister-in-law didn't relish the union. At least, Alyse thought with a sigh, Alexa hadn't had to pretend to be in love with her fiancé. As far as Alyse knew, she'd only seen him a handful of times.

By ten o'clock the dinner was finished and Sophia was

about to rise first to escort everyone out to the salon where they would have coffee and petits fours. It was another part of the formal ritual, and one Leo forestalled as he rose before his mother.

'It's been a very long day. Alyse and I will retire.'

Alyse felt herself blush even though there had been no innuendo in Leo's words, just a statement of fact. Sophia looked frostily affronted but Leo didn't even wait for her acquiescence as he took Alyse by the hand and led her from the dining room.

'Your mother doesn't like her order interrupted,' Alyse murmured as they headed upstairs. Her heart was pounding hard and her head felt weirdly light.

'My mother doesn't like anyone to do anything except what she commands,' Leo answered shortly. 'She'll have to get used to disappointment.'

They'd reached the top of the stairs and he drew her down the hallway to a wood-panelled door, opening it to reveal a luxurious and very masculine bedroom. The duvet on the canopied king-sized bed had been turned down and a fire blazed in the huge stone hearth.

Alyse swallowed in a desperate attempt to ease the dryness of her throat. 'This all looks very romantic.'

'Are you being cynical?'

'No, Leo.' She turned to him, tried to smile. She wasn't going to let this evening descend into something base and soulless, or even just physical. 'I was just stating a fact. Don't worry, I don't think you had anything do with it.'

Leo gazed at Alyse, graceful, slender and so achingly beautiful. She looked both vulnerable and strong, he thought and he felt a blaze of something like admiration for her presence, her self-possession. Then he pushed that feeling away, hardened his heart—if that was indeed the organ that was being so wayward—and said coolly, 'I certainly didn't.' She stood a few feet away from him and he beckoned her forward. 'Come here.'

'Is that a command?'

'A request.'

She let out a shaky laugh. 'Rather ungraciously made, Leo.' Yet she moved towards him, head held high, her eyes flashing with spirit.

Leo made no reply, because in truth he didn't know what to say, how to act. He didn't want sex between them to be romantic. He didn't want either of them engaging their emotions. Ever.

He wanted it to be nothing more than a necessary— and, albeit physically, pleasurable—transaction, yet he was already afraid it couldn't be. Already be realised that his feelings for Alyse had changed too much for this to be simple—or sordid.

With the tiniest, trembling smile on her lips, she took another step towards him. Leo watched her hips sway under the silky fabric of her evening dress, a halter-top style in ivory that hugged every slender curve. 'Why don't you take that off?' he said, his voice already thickening with desire.

'Oh, Leo.' She let out a soft laugh. 'Why don't you take it off me?' And, despite the sorrow in that laugh, he heard a hint of a challenge in her voice and he knew she wasn't going to make this easy for either of them. 'Just because this is necessary doesn't mean we can't enjoy the experience,' she continued quietly. 'You desire me, Leo, and I desire you. That's something.'

He didn't answer, because he couldn't. Somehow his throat had thickened; his blood pounded and his fingers itched to touch her. He'd thought at first she'd make it awkward by resisting, or at least not responding to his touch—a show of defiance.

Compliance, he realised then, was far more dangerous. Still he tried to keep himself emotionally distant, if physically close, knowing how difficult a task it was that he'd set himself.

Wordlessly he reached behind her and undid the halter tie of her dress. The garment slithered off her shoulders, and with one sinuous shrug it slid from her body and pooled at her feet. She gazed at him steadily, a faint blush tingeing her cheeks pink even as she kept her head held high.

She was magnificent. He'd seen her naked before but tonight it was different; tonight it was more. She wore a strapless lacy bra and matching pants, both skimpy items highlighting the lithe perfection of her body.

'I don't think I'm the only one who's meant to be naked,' Alyse said, and he heard both a smile and a tremble in her voice. She reached for the buttons on his shirt and, mesmerised, Leo watched as she undid them, her fingers long and elegant. Her hands smoothed over the already heated skin of his chest and shoulders as she pulled the tie and then the shirt off him.

She'd undressed him last night, had unbuttoned his shirt just like this and, while it had inflamed him then, it moved him now. Touched him in ways he wasn't prepared for, didn't want.

He pushed the emotion away and reached for her, needing to obliterate his thoughts—his *feelings*—with the purely physical. And at first the taste and touch of her lips against his was enough to accomplish his goal. He plundered her mouth, slid his hands through the luxuriant softness of her hair, brought her nearly naked body in achingly exquisite contact with his. All of it was enough to stop the unwanted feeling, the impossible emotion.

Almost.

Her response undid him. She wasn't just unresisting, she was more than compliant. She answered him kiss for kiss, touch for touch, and he could feel the surrender in her supple body, the giving of herself. The offering.

With Alyse sex would never be a soulless transaction. Already it was something else, something he couldn't want and yet desperately needed. He deepened the kiss.

Alyse matched him, her body molding and melting into his, her head tilted back as she emitted a low moan from deep in her throat, the sound swallowed by his own mouth. Desire consumed him in a white-hot flame; thoughts and feelings blurred and coalesced into one.

He was barely aware of unhooking her bra, sliding off her pants; distantly he felt her hands fumble boldly at his zip and then his trousers sliding down his legs. He kicked them off in one abrupt, impatient movement and, sweeping her up in his arms, her skin silken against his, he brought her to the bed.

Even now he fought against all he was feeling. She lay back on the pillows, arms spread, thighs splayed, everything about her open and giving. She gazed up at him without embarrassment or fear; even her gaze was open to him, open and trusting. Kneeling before her, his own body naked and vulnerable, his desire on obvious and proud display, Leo felt humbled.

Humbled and ashamed that he had been attempting something he now knew was impossible: emotionless sex with Alyse. With his wife.

She held out her arms to him. 'Make love to me, Leo,' she said softly, and he let out a sound that was something between a near-sob and a laugh. How had this woman reached him—reached him and felled him—so easily? His jaded cynicism fell away and his cold, hard heart warmed and softened into pliant yielding as he came to her, enfolded her body into his and buried his face in the warm, silken curve of her neck.

In response she curled around him, arching her body

into his, giving him everything she had. Leo took it as his mouth claimed hers and his hands explored her warm, supple curves; then his body found hers as he slid inside and they joined as one—one flesh, one person. It felt holy and sacred, infinitely pleasurable, and so much more than he'd ever expected or thought he wanted.

His last cold reserve broke on the sweetness of her response as he drove into her again and again, losing himself, blending into her until he didn't know where he ended and she began. And, even more amazingly and importantly, such a distinction no longer mattered.

Alyse lay back on the pillows, her whole body thrumming with pleasure. Leo had rolled onto his back next to her, one arm thrown over his face. As her heart rate began to slow from a thud she felt the perspiration cooling on her skin, the slight chill of the night air from the open windows…and the fact that she couldn't see Leo's expression. She had no idea what he was thinking or feeling at all.

Just moments ago when he'd been touching her—been *inside* her—she'd felt so close to him, in such glorious union that all of her fears and doubts had been blown away, scattered like so much cold ash.

Now they returned, settling inside her, unwelcome embers fanning into painful flame.

She'd given everything to Leo in that moment, everything she had in her to give… But perhaps even now he'd turn away from her, slide off the bed and stalk to the bathroom, as coldly indifferent as ever. Even as she braced herself for it she knew she couldn't keep herself from being hurt, or even devastated. She might not love him—yet—but she'd still given more to this man than to any other.

She felt Leo stir next to her and still she was afraid to say anything, to break whatever delicate bond held them together in this moment, the remnants of their lovemaking. Words would, she feared, sound like challenges to Leo, perhaps accusations or even ultimatums. For once she wanted simply to let this moment be whatever it was, and not demand or yearn for more.

Slowly he moved his arm from covering his face and swung up so he was sitting on the edge of the bed, his feet on the floor, his back to her.

'I'll get us something to drink,' he said and, slipping on his boxer shorts, he went to the *en suite* dressing room.

Alyse lay there for a moment, increasingly conscious with every cooling second of her own nakedness, yet she was loath to cover herself, to leave the intimacy of what had just happened behind—or, worse, pretend it had never happened... Just as Leo, perhaps, was pretending.

Or maybe he wasn't pretending. Maybe, for him, it had been just sex and she was the one, as always, who was constructing castles in the air—castles made of nothing, as insubstantial as smoke or mist, dissipating just as quickly.

He returned a few minutes later while she still lay there on the bed, naked and fighting against feeling exposed. She pushed her hair away from her eyes and struggled to a sitting position, still resisting the urge to cover herself. She'd promised herself—and, without his knowledge, Leo—that she would be open to him tonight. That she wouldn't dissemble, guard or prevaricate. Not even now, when every instinct she possessed screamed for self-protection.

'Here.' His voice sounded alarmingly brusque as he pressed a bottle of water into her hands.

'Where—?'

'There's a mini-fridge in the dressing room.' The corner of his mouth quirked in what Alyse couldn't be sure was a smile. 'They put champagne in there as well, but I thought we'd had enough of that.'

'Ah. Yes.' *Because this wasn't a champagne-worthy moment?* She took a sip of the chilled water.

Leo drained half of his own before he lowered it from his lips, twisting the bottle around in his hands, his gaze averted from hers. Alyse just waited, sensing he intended to say something, but having no idea what it was.

Finally he lifted his gaze to meet hers, and even then she couldn't gauge his mood, couldn't fathom what he intended to say, or how he felt at all. He took a deep breath and let it out slowly. Alyse braced herself.

'I don't know,' he began haltingly, 'how much I have to give.'

Ayse just stared at him, his words slowly penetrating the dazed fog of her mind. *I don't know how much I have to give.* She felt a smile spread across her face—a ridiculously huge smile, considering what he'd said was a far, far cry from a declaration of love.

And yet it was something. It was a lot, for a man like Leo, because he was saying—at least, she hoped he was saying—that he still had *something* to give. And, more importantly, that he wanted to give it.

'That's okay,' she said softly and Leo glanced away.

'I'm sorry,' he said after a moment. 'For treating our marriage—our relationship—like an imposition.'

'That's what it was for you,' Alyse answered. She didn't add what everything inside her was hoping, singing: *until now.*

'I've never tried a real relationship before,' he continued, his gaze still averted. 'At least, not for a long while.'

'Neither have I.'

He glanced at her then, a slow smile curving his mouth. 'Then that makes two of us.'

She smiled back, her hopes soaring straight to the sky. 'I suppose it does.'

Neither of them spoke for a few moments and Alyse

couldn't keep the lightness, the giddy relief, from swooping through her. She tried to tell herself that really this was very little, that she wasn't even sure what Leo was saying or offering. Yet still, the hope. The joy. She couldn't keep herself from feeling them, from wanting to feel them.

Eventually Leo took her half-empty water bottle as well as his own and put them away. Alyse slipped to the bathroom and returned to find him in bed, the firelight flickering over his bronzed body, his arms above his head. She hesitated on the threshold, still unsure how to act, and then Leo pulled aside the duvet and patted the bed.

'Come here,' he said softly and, smiling, she came.

She slid into the bed and felt her heart lurch with unexpected joy once again when he gently pulled her to him and cradled her body against his own, her head pillowed on his arm. She breathed in the scent of him, a woodsy aftershave and clean soap, and listened to the crackle of the logs in the fireplace and the steady beat of his heart against her cheek. She felt almost perfectly content.

Neither of them spoke, but the silence wasn't tense, strained or even awkward at all. It was a silence of new understanding. And, instead of pressing and longing for more, Alyse let this be enough. Lying in Leo's arms, it felt like everything.

CHAPTER TEN

WHEN SHE WOKE Leo was still stretched out beside her, a slight smile curving his mouth and softening his features. Alyse gazed at him unreservedly for a moment and then, feeling bold, brushed a kiss against that smiling mouth.

Leo's eyes fluttered open and his hands came up to her shoulders, holding her there against him.

'That's a rather nice way to wake up,' he said, and before she could respond he shifted her body so she was lying fully on top of him, the press of his arousal against her belly.

'I think you might have an even nicer way in mind,' she murmured as Leo slid his hand from her shoulder to her breast, his palm cupping its fullness.

'I certainly do,' he said, and neither of them spoke for a little while after that.

Later, when they'd showered and dressed and were eating breakfast in a private dining room, Alyse asked him what his plans were for the day. Despite their morning love-making, in the bright light of day she felt some of her old uncertainties steal back. Perhaps Leo was content to enjoy their intimacy at night while still keeping himself apart during the day, consumed with work and royal duty.

Sitting across from him, sneaking glances at his stern profile, she was conscious of how little he'd said last night.

I don't know how much I have to give. Really, in most relationships—if they even *had* a relationship—that would have been a warning, or at least a disclaimer. Not the promise she, in her naïvely and ridiculous hope, had believed it to be.

Leo considered her question. 'I have a meeting this morning with some Cabinet members about a new energy bill. But I'm free this afternoon. I thought—perhaps—I could give you a tour of the palace? You haven't actually seen much of it.'

Alyse felt a smile bloom across her face and some of those uncertainties scattered. Some, not all. Leo smiled back, a look of boyish uncertainty on his face.

'That sounds wonderful,' she said, and his smile widened, just as hers did.

They talked about other things then, a conversation that was wonderfully relaxed and yet also strangely new, exchanging views on films and books; relating anecdotes they'd never thought to share in the last six years. Simply getting to know one another.

After breakfast Leo excused himself to get ready for his meeting and Alyse went upstairs to unpack. She spent the morning in her room, catching up on correspondence and tidying her things before she went down to lunch.

Sophia had gone out for the day, thankfully, and Alessandro was otherwise occupied, so it was just her, Leo and Alexa at the lunch table.

'So how is married life, you two?' Alexa asked after the footman had served them all and retired. 'Bliss?'

Leo smiled faintly and shook his head. 'Don't be cynical, Lex.'

'*You're* telling *me* not to be cynical?'

'Wonders never cease,' Leo answered dryly, and Alexa raised her eyebrows.

'So marriage has changed you.'

Alyse held her breath as Leo took a sip of his water, his face thoughtful and yet also frustratingly blank. 'A bit,' he finally answered, not meeting anyone's gaze. Although she knew she shouldn't be, Alyse felt a rush of disappointment.

She took a steadying breath and focused on her own lunch. She knew she needed to be patient. Last night had changed things, but it was all still so new. She had to give it—*him, them*—time to strengthen and grow. Time for Leo truly to believe he *could* change.

Believe he could love.

After lunch Leo took her on a grand tour of the palace. They wandered through a dozen sun-dappled salons, empty and ornate, their footsteps echoing on the marble floors.

'This must have been great for hide and seek,' Alyse commented as they stood in one huge room decorated with portraits of his ancestors and huge pieces of gilt furniture. She tried to picture two dark-haired, solemn-eyed brothers playing in the room. Had Leo and his brother Alessandro been close? Had he missed him when he'd left? She had so many questions, but she knew Leo wasn't ready for her to ask them.

'I didn't really play in these rooms,' Leo answered, his hands shoved into his pockets, his gaze distant as he let it rove around the room. 'We were mostly confined to the nursery.'

'We?' Alyse prompted, and his expression didn't even flicker.

'The children. And of course, as I told you before, I went to boarding school when I was six.'

'That's rather young, isn't it? To go away.'

He shrugged. 'It was what my parents wanted.'

She thought of the remote King, the haughty Queen. Not the most loving of parents. 'Did you miss them?'

'No. You don't miss what you've never had.' She didn't

think he was going to say anything more, but then he took a deep breath and continued, his gaze focused on the sunshine spilling through the window. 'If you've ever wondered how my parents got the idea of having us pretend to be in love, it's because that's all they've ever done. They were only interested in me or my— Or any of us when someone was watching.' His mouth twisted. 'A photo opportunity to show how much they loved us. As soon as it passed, they moved on.'

'But…' Alyse hesitated, mentally reviewing all the magazine inserts and commemorative books she'd seen about Maldinian's golden royal family: the posed portraits, the candid shots on the beach or while skiing. Everyone smiling, laughing.

Playing at happy families.

Was Leo really saying that his whole family life had been as much a masquerade as their engagement? She knew she shouldn't be surprised, yet she was. It was so unbearably soulless, so terribly cold.

No wonder Leo didn't believe in love.

Her heart ached for Leo as a boy, lonely and ignored. 'That sounds very lonely,' she said and he just shrugged.

'I'm not sure I know what loneliness is. It was simply what I was used to.' Yet she didn't believe that; she couldn't. What child didn't long for love and affection, cuddles and laughter? It was innate, impossible to ignore.

But not to suppress. Which was what it seemed Leo had done for his whole life, she thought sadly. Now her heart ached not just for Leo as a boy, but for the man he'd become, determined not to need anyone. Not to love anyone or want to be loved back—only to be let down.

'Anyway.' He turned from the window to face her, eyebrows raised. 'What about you? You're an only child. Did you ever want siblings?'

She recognised the attempt to steer the conversation

away from himself and accepted it. He'd already revealed more than she'd ever anticipated or even hoped for. 'Yes, I did,' she admitted. 'But my parents made it clear there wouldn't be any more from a rather early age.'

'Why was that? Did they have trouble conceiving?'

'No. They just didn't want any more.' She saw the flicker of surprise cross his face and explained, 'They were happy with me—and mainly with each other. They were a real love match, you know. They may not be royalty, but they've still been featured in magazines. Their romance was a fairy tale.' Her voice came out a little flat, and Leo noticed.

'Your mother's some kind of American heiress, isn't she?'

'Her father owned a chain of successful hotels. My uncle runs it now, but my mother was called the Brearley Heiress before she married.'

'And your father?'

'A French financier. They met at a ball in Paris—saw each other across a crowded room and that was it.' She gave him a rather crooked smile. 'You might not believe in love at first sight, but that's how it was for them.'

Leo didn't speak for a moment and when he finally did it was to ask, 'And growing up in the shadow of that… how was it for you?'

And with that telling question he'd gone right to the heart of the matter. 'Hard, sometimes,' Alyse confessed quietly. 'I love my parents, and I have no doubts whatsoever that they love me. But…it was always the two of them and the one of me, if that makes sense. They've always been wrapped up in each other, which is how it should be…'

She trailed off, realising belatedly how whingy she must sound, complaining about how much her parents loved each other. Leo had grown up in a household of bitterness and play-acting, and here she was saying her own home had had too much love? She felt ridiculous and ashamed.

'But it was lonely,' Leo finished softly. 'Or so I imagine, for a little girl on her own.'

'Sometimes,' she whispered. She felt a lump rise in her throat and swallowed hard. Leo reached for her hand, threading her fingers with his, and the simple contact touched her deep inside.

'Strange, how we grew up in two such different families and homes,' he murmured. 'Yet perhaps, in an odd way, our experience was just a little bit the same.'

'I can't complain, not really.'

'You weren't complaining. I asked a question and you answered it.' He drew her towards him, his one hand still linked with hers while the other tangled itself in her hair. 'But perhaps now we can put our families behind us. We'll start our own family, one day.' His smile was knowing and teasingly lascivious as he brushed her lips against his. 'Maybe today.'

'Maybe,' Alyse whispered shakily. They hadn't used birth control, hadn't even discussed it—and why should they? An heir was part of the package, part of her responsibility as Leo's bride and Maldinia's future queen.

Leo's baby.

She wanted it: him, the promise of a new family, a family created by love. Leo broke the kiss. *Patience.* This was still so new, still just a beginning.

But a wonderful one, and with a smile still on her lips she leaned forward and kissed him back.

Alyse gazed at her reflection in the mirror, smoothing the silver gown she was to wear for tonight's reception in one of London's most exclusive clubs. It had been four days since they'd returned from St Cristos, four wonderful days—and nights.

She still had to guard herself from leaping ahead, from longing for more than Leo was ready to offer. *I don't know how much I have to give.* And yet he *was* giving, and trying, and with every new conversation, every shared joke or smile, every utterly amazing night, she knew she was falling in love with him. Falling in love with the real him, the Leo she'd never even known.

She loved discovering that man, learning his habits, preferences and his funny little quirks, like the fact that he had to read the *entire* page of a newspaper, even the adverts, before turning to another; or that he liked chess but hated draughts.

And she loved learning the taut map of his body and hearing the shudder of pleasure that ripped through him when she kissed or touched him in certain places...

Just remembering made longing sweep through her body in a heated wave.

It hadn't all been perfect, of course. The strictures of palace life, of their royal appearances, had created moments of unspoken tension and Leo's inevitable emotional withdrawal. Just that morning they'd appeared in front of the palace to fly to London, and at the sight of the cheering crowds they'd both frozen before Alyse had started forward, smiling and waving.

'How is married life?' one young woman had asked her.

'More than I'd ever hoped for,' she'd answered.

The woman had beamed and Alyse had moved on, but she'd caught a glimpse of Leo out of the corner of her eye and uneasily noted his stony expression.

They didn't talk until they were in the royal jet, flying to London. Leo had snapped open his newspaper and, scanning the headlines, had remarked, 'More than you'd ever hoped, eh?'

Alyse had blushed. 'Well...'

'Somehow I think you hope for a bit more,' he'd said

softly, and her blush had intensified. She was trying so hard to be patient and accepting, but everything in her yearned for more. For love. Leo had glanced away. 'I don't know why,' he said, 'but the pretending feels harder now. More like a lie.'

Alyse understood what he meant. The deception cut deeper, now that there was actually something between them. Pretending you were in love when you felt nothing, as Leo had, was easier than when you felt just a little. She had a feeling their pretence was making Leo realise how little he still felt, and that wasn't a revelation she felt like discussing.

Sighing now, she turned away from the mirror. *Patience.*

A knock sounded on the door of her bedroom. Despite their honeymoon status, she and Leo had been given a royal suite with two bedrooms in the hotel where they were staying, and their luggage had been delivered to separate rooms. They'd dressed for the reception separately, Alyse with her small army of stylists hired by Queen Sophia and flown in from Paris.

'Are you ready?' Leo called from behind the door. 'The car is here.'

'Yes, I'm coming.' She opened the door, her breath catching at the sight of Leo at his most debonair and dignified in a white tie and tails. Then she saw the lines of tension bracketed from nose to mouth and fanning from his eyes. She couldn't ignore the stiltedness that had developed between them since they'd stepped back into the spotlight, and she didn't know how to overcome it. Everything between them felt too new and fragile to be tested like this.

Leo nodded in the direction of her fitted gown of silver satin; from a diamanté-encrusted halter-top it skimmed her breasts and hips and then flared out around her knees to fall in sparkly swirls to the floor. 'That's quite a gown. The stylists chose well.'

'I suppose they felt I needed to make a splash, since this is our first public appearance as husband and wife.'

'Yes, I have a feeling tonight will have us both firmly in the spotlight.' Leo's mouth tightened and Alyse tried to smile.

'We did get a whole week away from it,' she said. 'And it's only one evening, after all.'

'One of many.' Leo slid his arm through hers. 'We should go. There are reporters outside.'

Once again flashbulbs went off in front of her as they stepped out of the hotel. Their car was waiting with several security guards to shepherd them from one door to another, but they paused on the threshold to smile and wave at the blurred faces in front of them. Leo's arm felt like a steel band under hers, his muscles corded with tension.

As they slid into the darkened sanctuary of the car, she felt him relax marginally, his breath coming out in a tiny sigh of relief.

'How have you stood it for so long?' she asked as she adjusted the folds of her dress around her. They were slippery to hold, and glittered even in the dim light of the car's interior.

'Stood what?'

'Being on display.'

He shrugged. 'It's all I've ever known.'

'But you don't like it.'

'I suppose I'm getting tired of it,' he allowed. 'It's been going on for a long time.'

'Since you were a child?'

'More or less.' He turned away from her then, so she could only see the shadowy profile of his cheek and jaw as he stared out of the window.

She couldn't imagine living like that for so long. The

last six years had been challenging enough, with her intermittent public appearances, and she at least had had the escape of university and a relatively normal life. Leo never had, had never experienced anything really normal—or perhaps even real.

'We're here.'

The car had pulled up in front of one of London's exclusive clubs on Pall Mall, and another contingent of photographers and journalists waited by the doors.

They didn't pose for photographs or answer questions as the security hustled them from the car to the door, and then inside to the hushed foyer of the club. Yet even inside that hallowed place Alyse was conscious of a different kind of scrutiny: the hundred or so privileged guests who mingled in the club's ballroom were eyeing them with discreet but still noticeable curiosity. The Prince and his Cinderella bride; of course people were curious. Even alone in Durham she'd received those kinds of looks, had seen herself on the covers of magazines. She'd tried not to let it bother her, had made herself shrug it off and focus on the positives, on engaging with the public in as real a way as she could.

Yet she felt different now, and it wasn't because of the looks or the photos or the endless attention and publicity. It was because of Leo. She watched him out of the corner of her eye as he fetched them both champagne, talking and nodding with some important person, a stuffy-looking man with greying hair and a paunch. Alyse thought he looked vaguely familiar, but she didn't know his name.

And Leo... Leo looked remarkably at ease, the tension he'd shown earlier firmly masked and hidden away. He put his arm around her waist, and even as she thrilled to his touch, as always, Alyse felt a chill creep into her soul because how on earth could she actually tell when her husband was being real?

Perhaps the last week had been as much about pretending as tonight. Perhaps Leo didn't even know *how* to be real.

'You need to smile,' Leo murmured, his own face set into easy, relaxed lines. 'You're looking tense.'

'Sorry.' Alyse tried to smile. This was so hard now, so much harder than it had ever been before. She was sick to death of pretending, sick of all this fear and uncertainty. Sick of wondering just what Leo felt for her, if anything.

'Now you look terrified,' Leo remarked in a low voice and she felt his arm tense around her waist. 'What's wrong? We've done this before.'

'It feels different now,' Alyse whispered. *She* felt different. But she had no idea if Leo did.

'It shouldn't,' he answered shortly, and steered her towards a crowd of speculative socialites. She forced herself to widen her wobbly smile, feeling more heartsick and uncertain than ever.

Leo fought the urge to tear off his white tie and stride from the club without a backward glance. Every second of this evening had been interminable, and the falseness of his and Alyse's behavior rubbed him horribly raw. He'd never minded before or, if he had, he'd shrugged it off. He'd had to. He'd *always* had to.

Yet now… Now the pretence irritated and even sickened him. The last week had been difficult at times, uncomfortable at others, but it had been real—or at least as real as he knew anything to be. The days and nights he'd spent with Alyse had fed something in him, a hunger he'd never known he had. He wanted more even as he doubted whether he should—or could.

He glanced again at Alyse, her eyes troubled even as she smiled at someone, and he desired nothing more in this moment than to take her in his arms and strip that shimmery gown from her body, let it slide into a silver puddle at her feet…

Her smile, he thought, looked decidedly wooden. Why was it so hard to pretend to be in love, when they'd been getting along better than ever? It should have been easier, but it wasn't. Friendship *had* complicated things, he thought darkly, just as he'd predicted. The parody of head-over-heels emotion they were enacting now only made their real relationship—whatever that was—seem paltry in comparison…and he had a feeling Alyse knew it.

I don't know how much I have to give. The words had come from him with sudden, startling honesty, because in that moment after they'd first made love he hadn't known what he was going to say, only that everything had changed.

But perhaps it hadn't changed. Perhaps even that had been nothing more than a mirage, a fantasy, just as tonight was. Everything in his life—every emotion, every caress, kiss or loving touch—had been faked. How on earth could he expect this to be real?

He didn't even know what real was.

Two hours later they were back in the car, speeding towards their hotel in Mayfair. All around them the lights of the city glittered under a midsummer drizzle, the pavement slick and gleaming with rain. Alyse hadn't spoken since they'd got into the car and Leo eyed her now, her face averted from him so he could only see the soft, sweet curve of her cheek, the surprising strength of her jaw. He longed to touch her.

He didn't.

This was their life now, he reminded himself. This pretending. No matter what might be developing between them, neither of them could escape the grim reality that every time they stepped outside of the palace they would be pretending to feel something else.

A simple, emotionless business arrangement would really be easier.

Yet, even as he told himself that, he couldn't keep from reaching for her as soon as they were back in their suite. She came willingly, her dress whispering against his legs, but he saw shadows in her eyes and her lip trembled before she bit it. He wanted to banish it all: the party, the pretence, the doubt and fear he felt in her now—and in himself. He wanted to make her smile, and the only way he knew of doing that was to kiss her, so he did.

Gently at first, but then he felt the softness of her mouth, the surrender of her sigh, and he drove his fingers into her hair, scattering all the diamond-tipped pins, as he pressed her against the wall of the foyer and devoured her with his kiss.

Alyse responded in kind and he felt a raw desperation in both of their need, a hunger to forget all the play-acting tonight and simply lose themselves in this—perhaps the only real thing they shared.

And lose himself he did, sliding his hands under the slippery satin of her gown, bunching it heedlessly about her hips as she wrapped her legs around his waist and he drove into her, lost himself inside her, his face buried in the warm curve of her neck as her body shook with pleasure.

They didn't speak afterwards and silently Leo led her from the foyer, leaving the hair pins and her shoes scattered on the floor. He peeled the dress from her body and shrugged off his own clothes before he drew her to the bed, wrapped his body around her and tried to shut out the world.

He woke several hours later, the room still swathed in darkness, and a glance at the clock told him it was an hour or so before dawn. He felt relentlessly awake and silently he slipped from Alyse's embrace, leaving her sleeping in his bed.

In the sitting room he powered up his laptop, determined to do a few hours' work before Alyse woke. They had engagements planned all day today, and they flew to Paris tonight for yet another reception, another full day tomorrow, yet another day of pretending. He pushed the thought away.

He would focus on work, the one thing that gave him satisfaction, a sense of purpose. He still needed to work on the wording of the bill for parliament regarding improvements to Maldinia's technological infrastructure, something his father had never remotely cared about.

He opened an Internet browser on his laptop to check his email and stopped dead when he saw that morning's news headline blaring across the screen:

Cinderella's Secret Lover Tells All.

Slowly he clicked on the article and scanned the first paragraph.

Prince Leo and his bride have always been the stuff of a fairy tale, and perhaps that's all it has been— for Matthew Cray, a student with the new princess at Durham University, has confessed to having a secret love affair with Alyse...

The game was up, Leo thought numbly. Everyone would know their relationship was fake, just as every relationship he'd ever had was fake. Sickened, he sat back in his chair. His mind spun with the implications of the article, the damage control that would need to be done—and quickly. But underneath the practicalities he felt something he hated to feel, didn't want to acknowledge now— the pain of hurt, the agonising ache of betrayal. He knew it wasn't fair; he'd forgiven Alyse, and it had been a long time ago anyway.

But seeing it all there on the page, knowing she'd convinced herself she loved him when she really hadn't...why should now be any different?

There's no such thing as love, he reminded himself brutally. *You've been playing at it this last week, but it's not real. It can't be.* And, swearing under his breath, he clicked on another glaring headline and began to read.

CHAPTER ELEVEN

'Leo?'

Alyse stood in the doorway of the bedroom, her gaze fastened on her husband and the stricken look on his face. He was staring blankly at the screen of his laptop, but as he heard her call his name he turned to her, his expression ironing out.

'What are you doing awake?'

'What are you?' She bit her lip. 'I woke up and wondered where you were.'

He gestured to his computer. 'Just getting a little work done. I couldn't sleep.'

Alyse took a step closer. Although Leo's face was implacable and bland now, she sensed the disquiet underneath. Something was wrong. 'What's happened?' she asked quietly.

'Nothing.'

'What were you looking at on the computer?'

'Just work—' He stopped, raking a hand through his hair. 'I suppose I'll have to tell you,' he said after a moment. 'We'll both have to deal with the damage control.'

Her stomach plunged icily. 'Damage control?'

Sighing, he clicked on the mouse and pointed to the screen. Alyse read the headline, everything in her freezing.

Cinderella's Secret Lover Tells All.

'Oh no,' she whispered. 'Oh no. How could he?'

'I imagine he was offered a great deal of money.'

'But it was years ago.' She stopped, swallowing hard, nausea rising in a roiling tide within her. She could just glimpse snatches of the awful article, phrases like 'drunken passion' and—heaven forbid—'marriage masquerade'.

She leaned forward, her eyes darting over the damning words.

According to Cray, Alyse and Prince Leonardo of Maldinia have simply been pretending to be in love to satisfy the public.

They knew. The whole world knew the truth about her and Leo. She stumbled back, one fist pressed to her lips, and Leo closed the laptop.

'I'm sorry,' she whispered and he shrugged.

'It was years ago. You have nothing to feel sorry for now.'

'But if I hadn't—'

'We'll deal with it,' he cut her off flatly. 'You should get dressed. I imagine we'll have to go back to Maldinia this morning to talk to the press office. We want a united front about how to handle this.'

He turned away and Alyse felt her insides twist with anxious misery. This was all her fault. And, while she accepted that Leo had forgiven her for her indiscretion from so many years ago, she feared their fragile relationship would not survive this ordeal.

With an icy pang of dread she remembered Queen Sophia's words: no use to Leo.

The worst had happened. She was a liability—to the monarchy and to Leo. And, if he didn't really feel anything for her, did he even want to stay married to her? What would be the point?

Miserably she went to shower and dress, her heart like lead inside her, weighing her down. The media frenzy would be excruciating, she knew. Who else would come forward to pick apart her university years? She might only have had that one lamentable experience, but she knew how the media worked, how people were tempted. Other stories would be made up; she could be depicted as a heartless, conniving slut.

And what about Leo? Her heart ached then not for herself, but for him. He'd have to deal with the shame and humiliation of being seen as the betrayed lover, the duped prince. She closed her eyes, forced the tears back. Recriminations would not serve either of them now.

Several grim-faced stylists were waiting when she emerged from the shower and they launched into a description of their strategy before she'd even taken the towel from her hair.

'You want to look muted and modest today, but not ashamed. Not like you have something to hide.'

'I don't have anything to hide,' Alyse answered before she could stop herself. 'Not any more.'

The stylists exchanged glances and ignored what she said. 'Subtle make-up, hair in a loose knot—earrings?'

'Pearl studs,' the other one answered firmly, and numbly Alyse let them go to work.

Forty-five minutes later she emerged into the sitting room where Leo was dressed in a charcoal-grey suit and talking on his mobile, his voice terse. Nervously Alyse fiddled with her earrings, her heart seeming to continually lurch up into her throat. She'd always managed to handle the press before, but then they'd always been on her side. How hard was it, really, to smile and wave for people who seemed to adore you?

Today would be different. She'd turned on the television while the stylists were organising her outfit and had seen that Matt's interview was breaking news even on the major networks. Ridiculous, perhaps, but still true. They'd managed to dig up a photo of her walking to lectures with him and, innocent as it had been then, it looked damning. She had her hand on his arm and her head was tilted back as she laughed. She didn't even remember the moment; she'd only walked with him a couple of times. They hadn't even been that good friends, she thought miserably, but who would believe that now? The media was implying she'd indulged in a long, sordid affair.

'No need for that,' one stylist, Aimee, had said crisply, and turned off the TV. 'Let's get you dressed.'

Now as she waited for Leo to finish his call—he was speaking in rapid Italian too fast for her to understand—Alyse smoothed the muted blue silk of her modest, high-collared dress, a satin band of deeper blue nipping in her waist. 'Virgin blue', the colour was apparently called. How unfitting.

Finally Leo disconnected the call and turned to her, his brows snapping together. 'A good choice,' he said, nodding towards her dress. 'The jet is waiting.'

'The jet? Where are we going? What's—what's going to happen?'

'We're heading back to Maldinia. I considered keeping our heads high and honouring the rest of our engagements in Paris and Rome, but I don't think that's the best course of action now.'

'You don't?'

Leo shook his head, the movement brisk and decisive. 'No. I think the best thing is to come clean. Admit what happened and that I've forgiven you. Keep it firmly in the past.'

'And how…?'

'I've arranged for us to do a television interview.'

'A television interview?' Alyse repeated sickly. She might have been on the cover of dozens of magazines, but she'd never actually been on TV. The thought of being on it now, a public confessional, made her head spin and her nerves strain to breaking. 'But—'

'I'll explain it all on the plane,' Leo said. 'We need to get going.'

The outside of the hotel was mobbed with paparazzi and the security guards had to fight their way through to get to them as they waited at the door.

Alyse ducked her head as she came out, Leo's arm around her, flashbulbs exploding in her face, questions hammering her heart.

'Did you ever love Leo, Alyse?'

'How long were you seeing Matthew Cray?'

'Have there been others?'

'Was it for money or fame, this marriage masquerade?'

'Do you have any conscience at all?'

She closed her eyes, her heart like a stone inside her as Leo and the security guard guided her into the waiting limo. As soon as the doors had closed she let out a shaky sigh of relief, halfway to a sob.

'That was awful.'

Leo turned away from the window, his face expressionless. 'It will get worse.'

'I know.' She took a deep breath, let it fill her lungs before releasing it slowly. She still felt shaky from her first encounter with a malevolent press—one of many, she had no doubt. 'Leo, I'm so sorry this has happened. I know it's my fault.'

'As far as I can tell, it's Matthew Cray's fault.'

'But if I hadn't—'

'Alyse, you can beat yourself up all you like about what

happened years ago, but it doesn't change things now, so really there's no point.' His expression didn't soften as he added, 'And I don't want you to. I know you're sorry. I understand you regret it.'

'But—but do you forgive me?'

'There's nothing to forgive.'

She should have been comforted by his words, but she wasn't. He spoke them so emotionlessly, his face so terribly bland; any intimacy they'd once shared seemed utterly lost in that moment. Cold, stern, unyielding Leo was back, and she had no idea how to find the man she'd begun to fall in love with. Perhaps he didn't exist any more; perhaps he'd never existed.

Weary and heartsick, Alyse leaned her head back against the seat and closed her eyes.

Leo gazed at Alyse, her face pale, her eyes closed, and felt a needling of guilt mixed with an unexpected pang of sympathy. After being adored by the press for six years, it had to be hard to be cast as the villain.

Not that *he'd* ever cared what the media thought of him one way or the other. Perhaps Alyse didn't care either. Perhaps it was simply guilt that made her look so tired and wretched.

Leo knew he should have tried harder to comfort her. He probably should have held her and told her not to worry, that they'd get through this together. That none of it mattered. He hadn't done any of that; he hadn't thought of doing it until now, when it felt too late. He simply didn't have it in him.

I don't know how much I have to give. No, he sure as hell didn't. Ever since the news of Alyse's indiscretion had broken he'd felt his fragile emotions shutting down, the familiar retreat into cold silence. It was safer, easier,

and it was what he knew. And he also knew it was hurting
Alyse. He supposed that was a step in the right direction;
at least he was aware he was hurting her.

But he still didn't have the ability, or perhaps just the
strength, to stop it.

Alyse opened her eyes, her gaze arrowing in on him.
'Tell me about this television interview,' she said and Leo
nodded, glad to escape his thoughts.

'It's with Larissa Pozzi,' he said and Alyse blanched.

'But she's—'

'Broadcast on all the major networks. We need the publicity.' Alyse just shook her head, and Leo knew what she
wasn't saying. Larissa relished scandal and melodrama,
was always handing her guests tissues with her overly
made-up face in a moue of false sympathy. Being inter-
viewed by her was a necessary evil; he had chosen it because it would get their message across to the most people
most quickly.

'And what are we meant to say?' Alyse asked.

'That we'd had a fight and you were foolish. You've regretted it deeply ever since and I've known all along and
forgave you ages ago.' He spoke tonelessly, hating every
lie that he'd come up with with the approval of the royal
press office. Hating that, even in telling a bit of the truth,
they were still perpetuating a lie. And he was sick to the
death of pretending. Of lies.

He could not imagine saying them on live television.
Every word would stick in his throat like a jagged glass
shard. He wanted to be done with deception, with pretence,
for ever, even as he recognised how impossible it was.

Alyse's face had gone chalk-white and she glanced
away. 'I see,' she murmured, and he knew she did: more
lies. More pretending. They would never be done with
them, never have the opportunity to be real.

So how on earth could they have any kind of real relationship in that toxic environment, never mind love?

Not that he loved her. He didn't even know what love was.

Did he?

The question reverberated through him. The last week had been one of the sweetest of his life, he had to admit. The memory of Alyse's smile, the sweet slide of her lips against his, how he'd felt when he'd been buried inside her...

If that wasn't love, it was something he'd never experienced before. It was intense and overwhelming, addictive and, hell, frightening.

But was it love?

Did it even matter?

'Why don't you get some rest?' Leo said brusquely. 'You look completely washed out, and we'll be there in another hour.'

And, putting those troubling questions firmly to the back of his mind, he reached for his attaché and some paperwork that needed his attention.

Alyse's stomach clenched as they stepped off the royal jet and were ushered quickly into the waiting limo with its accompanying motorcade of security. They were to go directly to the palace for a press briefing, and then the television interview that would take place in one of the palace's private apartments. Alyse dreaded both events. She dreaded the condemnation she'd see on everyone's faces, from King Alessandro to Queen Sophia to the cloying Larissa Pozzi...to Leo.

He'd said there was nothing to forgive, but his stony face told otherwise. She had no idea what he was really thinking or feeling, and she was desperately afraid to ask. That was how fragile and untried their feelings for each other were, she acknowledged with a wry despair. It couldn't face up to a moment's honesty, never mind any hardship or scrutiny.

The press secretary, along with the Queen, were waiting for them as soon as they stepped into the palace. Alyse's stomach plunged straight to her toes as they entered one of the smaller receiving rooms. Queen Sophia stood at one end in all of her icy, regal splendour.

'Mother.' Leo's voice was toneless as he went forward to kiss his mother's cheek. She didn't offer any affection back or even move, and despite the nerves jangling inside her Alyse felt a kind of sorrowful curiosity at the dynamic between mother and son.

Queen Sophia swung her cold blue gaze to Alyse. 'This is a disaster,' she said, 'as I'm sure you're aware. A complete disaster.'

'It's under control—' Leo began tightly, but his mother cut across him.

'Do you really think so, Leo?' Her voice rang out scornfully but Leo didn't react. 'People will believe what they want to believe.'

'They've always wanted to believe in Alyse,' he answered quietly. 'They've always loved her.'

'And they'll be just as quick to hate her,' Sophia snapped. 'That's the nature of it, of publicity.'

'Then I have to wonder why we've always been so quick to court it,' Leo responded coolly. 'Oh, I remember now—because you needed the positive press. You've needed Alyse, to make up for all the selfish choices you and Father have made over the years.'

'How dare you?' Sophia breathed.

'I dare,' Leo answered, 'because you've been using me and then Alyse—using everyone you can—to make up for your own deficiencies. I won't have you blaming

us for them now. We'll handle this, Mother, and you need
not concern yourself at all.'

Sophia's eyes glinted malice. 'And what happens when
they hate her, Leo? What happens when it all falls apart?'

Ice slid down Alyse's spine. *When they had no use
for her.*

'We'll deal with that possibility when and if it happens,'
Leo answered, and turned away.

Sophia whirled away from them both. 'I'll send Paula
in,' she said tightly, and with a slam of the doors she was
gone.

'Thank you,' Alyse said quietly, 'for defending me.
Even if I don't deserve it.'

'You do deserve it. Enough with the *mea culpa* bit,
Alyse.'

'I'm sorry.'

'You're still doing it.'

She smiled wanly. 'Habit, I guess.'

'I'm not angry,' Leo said after a moment. 'At least,
not at you. I might be harbouring a little rage for the paparazzi, but I can't really blame them either. They're just
doing their job and we've been feeding their frenzy for
years now.'

'And you're sick of it.'

'Yes.' He lapsed into silence, his forehead furrowed
into a frown as he gazed out of the palace windows at
acres of manicured lawn. Alyse watched him warily, for
she sensed some conflict in him, something he wanted to
say—but did she want to hear it?

'Alyse...' he began, but before he could say any more
Paula bustled in with a sheaf of papers in one manicured
hand.

'Now, we need to go over just what you'll say.'

'It's under control,' Leo said shortly. 'I know what I'm
going to say.'

Paula looked surprised, a little insulted. 'But I'm meant to brief—'

'Consider us briefed,' Leo answered. 'We're ready.'

Alyse fought down nausea. She didn't feel remotely ready, and frankly she could use a little help from Paula. 'What are we going to say?' she whispered as they headed towards the suite where the interview would take place. 'I could use—'

'Leave it to me.'

'But—'

'Let's go in,' he said, and ushered her into the reception room with its cameras and lights already set up. 'They're waiting.'

The interview, at least at first, was a blur to Alyse. She shook Larissa Pozzi's hand and the woman, all glossy nails and too-white teeth, gushed over the two of them.

'Really, we're doing this for you,' she said, laying a hand on Alyse's arm, her long, curved nails digging into her skin. 'The world wants to hear your side of the story.'

'My side,' Alyse repeated numbly. It didn't sound good—that there were already sides, battle lines clearly drawn.

Assistants prepped them both for make-up and hair as they sat on a sofa facing Larissa and the cameras. Alyse could feel the tension coming off Leo in waves and, though he managed to convey an air of relaxation, chatting easily with Larissa, she knew he was beyond tense.

She *knew* him. She knew him now more than ever before, and that was both comforting and thrilling—that this man was no longer a stranger but someone she knew and—*loved*?

Did she love him? Had she fallen in love that quickly, that easily? And yet nothing about the last week or so had been easy. It had been wonderful, yes, but also painful, emotional, tense and fraught. And still the best time of her life.

She just prayed it wasn't over, that this wasn't the beginning of the end. Glancing at Leo's profile, his jaw taut even as he smiled, she had no idea if that was the case.

'We're just about ready,' Larissa told them both as she positioned herself in her chair, and if anything Alyse felt Leo become even tenser, although his position didn't change.

Three, two, one…

'So, Prince Leo, we're so thrilled to have you on the show,' Larissa began in her gushing voice. Alyse felt her smile already become a rictus, her hands clenched tightly together in her lap and a bead of sweat formed at her hairline under the glare of the lights and cameras. 'And of course everyone is dying to hear your side of the story…as well as your bride's.' The talk show hostess's gaze moved speculatively to Alyse, and she didn't think she was imagining the glint of malice in those over-wide eyes. No matter how Larissa gushed to Leo, Alyse knew she'd still be cast as the scarlet woman. It made for a juicy story.

'Well, it's really rather simple, Larissa,' Leo began in a calm, even voice. He had one arm stretched along the back of the sofa, his fingers grazing Alyse's shoulder. 'When that photograph was taken all those years ago—and you know the photo I mean, of course.'

'Of *course.*'

'Alyse and I barely knew each other. We'd only just met that very evening, actually.'

'But you looked so in love,' Larissa said, eyes widening even more. She glanced rather accusingly at Alyse, who only just managed to keep her smile in place. Nothing about that photo, she thought, had been deliberately faked. It was, perhaps, the one honest moment the press had actually captured between her and Leo.

Leo lifted a shoulder in a 'what can I say?' shrug and Larissa let out a breathy sigh. 'But it was love at first sight, Prince Leo, wasn't it? You haven't actually been faking your engagement all these years, as people are so cruelly suggesting?'

Smiling, he held up one hand, his wedding ring glinting on his finger. 'Does that look fake to you?'

'But your *feelings*...'

'Alyse's and my marriage was always one of convenience,' Leo said and Alyse stiffened in shock. She had a feeling this would not have been part of Paula's brief.

Larissa drew back in exaggerated shock. 'Convenience? No! Not the prince and his Cinderella bride?'

Leo just smiled and shrugged. 'Royal marriages often are.'

'But you've been portrayed as being so in love, an inspiration to couples—as well as singles—everywhere.'

'And we are in love,' Leo replied steadily. 'Now.' A moment of silence spun out as Larissa stared at him; Alyse stared at him. *What was he saying?*

'It took a long time for those feelings to come, especially on my part,' he continued in that same steady voice. 'But they have come, and that's really the important thing, don't you think? Not what happened—or didn't happen—before.' He let this sink in for a moment before continuing. 'The main thing—the beautiful thing—is that I love Alyse now. I've fallen in love with my wife.'

And then he turned to her, while Alyse tried not to gape like a fish, and gave her a smile that felt both private and tender, and was being broadcast to a billion people around the world.

A smile that was surely a lie...wasn't it? Wasn't he just pretending, as always?

'Alyse, you look surprised,' Larissa said and, blinking, Alyse tried to focus on the talk-show hostess rather than her husband.

'Not surprised so much as thrilled,' she managed, barely aware of what she was saying. 'And so happy. I admit, it's been a rocky road to get to where we are. Leo and I have always been committed to marriage, but love isn't something you can force.'

Larissa pursed her lips. 'Let's talk about Matthew Cray.'

'Let's not,' Leo interjected swiftly. 'Whatever happened was a single moment many years ago, and not worth our time or discussion. As I've said before, what matters is now—and our future.' Again he smiled at Alyse, but this time she looked into his eyes. They looked dark and hard and her heart quailed within her. He didn't look like a man in love. She could feel the tension thrumming through him and her insides roiled. He was faking; of course he was. This was just another part of the pretence, and she was a fool for thinking otherwise even for a second.

She didn't remember the rest of the interview; her mind was spinning too much and Leo did most of the talking.

After an interminable half-hour they were done and Larissa and her crew were packing up. Leo ushered her from the filming area, one hand firmly on her elbow.

'Hopefully that did the trick,' he said, and that last frail hope died.

'A very clever way to spin it,' she managed and Leo gave her a sudden, penetrating look.

'Is that how you saw it?'

She stared at him, longing to ask him what he meant, but so afraid to. Afraid to trust his feelings, or even hers. *What was real?* 'I…I don't know.'

'Prince Leo… Your Highness.' Leo turned and Alyse saw one of his father's aides hurrying towards him.

'Yes?'

'Your father requests your presence in his private study immediately.'

Leo frowned. 'Is something wrong?'

The aide looked uncomfortable as he answered, 'Prince Alessandro has arrived at the palace.'

Leo went completely still, his face draining of colour, and Alyse felt shock blaze through him. Prince Alessandro...Leo's brother. He'd returned.

Leo swallowed and then his expression ironed out. 'I'm coming,' he said shortly, and walked away from Alyse.

CHAPTER TWELVE

SANDRO WAS HERE. Leo blinked, still finding it hard to believe his brother was here, just a room away. He'd come home. After fifteen years away—a decade and a half of complete silence—he'd returned, the prodigal son. Leo could not untangle the knot of emotions that had lodged inside him, rose in his throat. Fear, anger, confusion, disbelief…and, yes, love and joy.

Too much.

He was tired of feeling so damn much. After years of schooling himself not to feel anything, not to care or want or allow himself to be hurt, it was all coming out—just like it had during that interview.

I've fallen in love with my wife.

What on earth had made him say such a thing? Made him confess it—if it were even true? The words had spilled out of him, needing to be said, burning within him. Now he fought against such an admission, attempting, quite desperately, to claw back some self-protection. Some armour.

And now Sandro.

'Leo…' Alyse hurried after him. 'Why is Sandro here?'

He turned to stare at her. 'You know about Sandro?'

'Your mother told me a few days ago.'

He shook his head, unable to untangle his emotions enough to know how he felt about Alyse knowing and not saying a word. This was intimacy? Honesty?

'Let's not talk about this here,' he said. 'My father is expecting me.' She followed him to his father's study but he barred her at the door. 'This meeting is private, Alyse. I'll talk to you after.' He knew he sounded cold and remote, but he couldn't help it. That was who he was. Everything else had been an aberration. A mistake.

A mistake he would miss.

'I'll see you later.'

She bit her lip, her eyes wide with fear and uncertainty, but then she slowly nodded. 'Okay,' she whispered, and slowly walked down the hall.

Leo knocked once and then opened the door to his father's most sacred room, his private study, and stared directly into the face of his older brother.

Alessandro. Sandro. The only person he'd ever felt was a true friend, who understood him, accepted him. Loved him. He looked the same, and yet of course so much older. His unruly dark hair had a few silver threads, the strands catching the light and matching the grey glint of his eyes. He was taller and leaner than Leo, possessing a sinewy, charismatic grace, just as he had at twenty-one when Leo had last seen him.

Don't go, Sandro. Don't leave me alone. Please.

He'd begged and Sandro had gone.

'Leo.' Sandro nodded once, his expression veiled, and Leo nodded back. Quite the emotional reunion, then.

'I've summoned Alessandro back to Maldinia,' King Alessandro said with the air of someone who trusted his innate authority.

'So I see.' Leo cleared his throat. 'It's been a long time, Sandro.'

'Fifteen years,' his brother agreed. His silver gaze swept over him, telling him nothing. 'You look well.'

'As do you.' And then they lapsed into silence, these brothers who had once, despite the six years' difference in their ages, been nearly inseparable—compatriots as children, banding together as they had determinedly tried to ignore their parents' vicious fights and sudden, insensible moments of staged affection.

Later they'd gone to the same boys' boarding school and Sandro had become Leo's champion, his hero, a sixth former to his first year, cricket star and straight-A pupil. Yet always with the time, patience and affection for his quieter, shyer younger brother. Until he'd decided to leave all of it—and him—behind.

Childish memories, Leo told himself now. Infantile thoughts. Whatever hero worship he'd had for his brother, he'd long since lost it. He didn't care any more, hadn't for years. The damnable lump in his throat was simply annoying.

'Alessandro has agreed to return to his rightful place,' his father said and Leo's gaze swung slowly to the King.

'His rightful place,' he repeated. 'You mean…?'

'When I am gone, he will be King.'

Leo didn't react. He made sure not to. He kept completely still, not even blinking, even as inside he felt as if he'd staggered back from a near-fatal blow. In one swoop his father had taken his inheritance, his *reason*, away from him. For fifteen years he'd worked hard to prove he was worthy, that he would be a good king. He'd sacrificed desire for duty, had shaped his life to become the next monarch of Maldinia.

And just like that, on his father's whim, he wouldn't be. He turned to Sandro, saw his brother's lips twist in a grimace of a smile.

'So you're off the hook, Leo.'

'Indeed.' Of course his brother would see it that way. His brother had never wanted to be king, had walked away from it all, hating both the artifice and the pretension of royal life. He'd forged his own path in California; had started a highly successful IT firm, or so Leo's Internet searches had told him. And now he was leaving that all behind to return, to take Leo's place?

And leave Leo with…nothing?

Not even a wife. There was, he realised hollowly, no reason at all for him and Alyse to be married. To stay married. A week or so of fragile feeling surely didn't justify a life sentence. She would want to be free and so would he.

He *did*. He would.

He turned back to his father, unable to miss the cold glitter of triumph in the King's eyes. 'So how did this come to pass?' he asked in as neutral a tone as he could manage.

'I've always wanted Alessandro to be King,' his father answered shortly. 'It is his birthright, his destiny. You've known that.'

Of course he had, just as he'd known he was a poor second choice. He'd simply thought he'd proved himself enough in the last fifteen years to make up for the deficiency of being born second.

'And after this latest debacle…' King Alessandro continued, his lips twisting in contempt. 'All the work we've done has been destroyed in one careless moment, Leo.'

The work we've *done?* Leo wanted to answer. *To shout.*

His father had done nothing, *nothing* to restore the damn monarchy. He'd let his son—his second son—do all the work, shoulder all the responsibility. He said nothing. He knew there was no point.

The King drew himself up. 'Bringing Alessandro back will restore the monarchy and its reputation, its place at the head of society. New blood, Leo, fresh air. And we can forget about what happened with you and Alyse.'

Forget them both, tidy them away just as his father had done with Alessandro all those years ago. Move onto the next chapter in this damnable book.

But he didn't want to move on. He wouldn't have his life—his love—treated as no more than an unfortunate mistake. He didn't care so much about being king, Leo realised with shock, as being Alyse's husband. *I've fallen in love with my wife.* And it didn't matter any more.

Alyse didn't love him, not really. She might have convinced herself once, and she'd probably do so again, but it wasn't real. It wouldn't last, just as nothing had been real or lasting in his life.

Why should he trust this? Her? Or even himself, his own feelings that might vanish tomorrow?

'The matter is finished,' King Alessandro stated. 'Alessandro has accepted his birthright. He will return to live in Maldinia and take up his royal duties.'

Without waiting for a reply, the King left the room, left the two brothers alone as a silence stretched on between them.

'He's still the same,' Sandro said after a moment, his voice flat and almost uninterested. 'Nothing's really changed.'

Everything's changed. Everything has just changed for me. Leo swallowed the words, the anger. He didn't want to feel it; there was no point. He wouldn't be king; he had no wife. 'I suppose,' he said.

'I'll need you, if you're willing,' Sandro said. 'You can pick whatever post you want. Cabinet minister?' He smiled, and for the first time Leo saw warmth in his brother's face, lighting his eyes. 'I've missed you, Leo.'

Not enough to visit, or even write. But then, he hadn't either. First he'd been forbidden, and then later he'd told himself he didn't care.

Now grief for all he'd lost rushed through him and he turned his face away, afraid Sandro would see all he felt in his eyes. 'Welcome back, Sandro,' he said when he trusted himself to speak and then he left the room.

* * *

Alyse paced the sitting room of the apartment they'd been given in one wing of the palace, her hands clenched, her stomach clenched, everything inside her taut with nerves. Her worries and uncertainties about the TV interview, and what Leo had said, had been replaced with the fear of what Sandro's return would mean for Leo—and her.

For she'd had a terrible certainty, as she'd watched Leo head for his father's study like a man on his way to the gallows, that everything had changed.

The door opened and she whirled around.

'Leo.'

His mouth twisted in what Alyse suspected was meant to be a smile but didn't remotely come close. 'It seems,' he said, striding towards the window, 'that we're both off the hook.'

'Off the *hook*? What do you mean? What's happened, Leo? Why has Sandro come back?'

'My father summoned him.'

Alyse stared at him, saw the terrible coldness, almost indifference, on his face. 'Why did he leave in the first place?'

Leo shrugged and turned away. 'He hated royal life. Hated the way we always pretended and hated the burden of becoming king. He went to university, and when he received his diploma he decided to trade it all in for a life of freedom in the States.'

There was something that Leo wasn't saying, Alyse knew. Many things. He spoke tonelessly, but she felt his bitterness, his rage and even his hurt. She took a step closer to him. 'And why were you never in touch?'

'My parents forbade it. You don't walk away from royalty, especially not when you've been groomed to be king for your entire life.'

Shock blazed coldly through her as she realised what he was saying. 'So when he walked away, you were the heir.'

'Were,' Leo repeated. 'Yes.'

His voice was toneless, yet to Alyse he still sounded so bleak. She knew this man, knew when he was angry or happy or hurt. And right now she wanted to help him... if only she knew how. 'Leo, talk to me. Turn around and look at me, please. What's happened? Why are you so...?'

'I'm not anything,' he answered, and he turned around to look at her, his face as blank as his voice. 'I told you, Alyse, we're both off the hook.'

'I don't understand why you're saying that. What it means.'

'I'm off the hook for becoming king,' Leo explained slowly, as if she were a dim-witted child. 'And you're off the hook for being married to me.'

As if her wits were truly affected, it took her a few seconds to realise what he meant. 'What does your brother have to do with our marriage?' she whispered.

'Everything and nothing. Admittedly, I doubt he even knew I was married, but since he's accepted his birthright once more I'm no longer heir to the throne. Our marriage was a royal alliance, admittedly a forced one due to all the media attention. But there are no more reasons, Alyse.' He spread his hands wide, eyebrows raised in expectation. 'The media has sussed us out, and I'm not even going to be king in the first place. So it doesn't matter what either of us do.'

'And just what is it,' Alyse asked, her voice shaking, 'that you *want* to do?'

He lowered his brows, his expression flattening out. 'I see no reason for either of us to stay in a sham of a marriage.'

A sham of a marriage. She thought of what he'd said on air, how it had filled her for a few moments with a wary hope. A hope she hadn't quite been able to let go of, even now. *I've fallen in love with my wife*. Obviously he'd been spinning more lies to Larissa Pozzi, just as everything had been lies, perhaps even this last week or so.

'So you're suggesting a divorce,' she said flatly and for a moment Leo didn't respond.

'It seems sensible,' he finally said and a sudden, choking rage filled her, made her unable to speak.

'You bastard,' she finally managed, her voice thick with tears. 'Have you meant *anything* you've ever said? Do you even know how to be real or honest or *anything*?'

'Probably not.'

Alyse pressed her fists to her eyes and drew a shuddering breath. Now was not the time for tears. She'd have plenty of time, endless amounts, later to weep, to mourn. 'Leo.' She dropped her hands and forced herself to meet his cold, blank gaze. 'What about these last few weeks? What about how things changed between us, about how you said—'

'How I didn't know how much I had to give?' he filled in, a mocking edge to his voice. 'Well, now I do, and it turns out it's not all that much.'

'Why are you doing this?' she whispered. 'When just last night—'

'That was last night.' He swung around sharply, his hands jammed in his pockets as he stared out the window once more.

'And the fact that you won't be king changes your feelings towards me?' Alyse asked helplessly. 'I don't understand how that happens—'

'It was a *week*, Alyse. Ten days at most.' His voice echoed through the room with the sharp report of a rifle as he turned back to face her. 'A single bloody week. And yes, there were very nice parts, and the intensity made both of us think it could turn into more, which is understandable. We were looking at a marriage, after all, and trying to find a way to make it work.'

'We're still looking at a marriage—'

'No,' he answered flatly, 'we're not.'

It was like hammering on an iron door, she thought hopelessly, battering her fists and her heart against a stone wall. There was simply no way inside him, no way to understand what was going on behind that cold mask.

'Don't do this, Leo,' she whispered, her voice breaking. 'Please.' He gave no answer, not even a flicker of emotion in his eyes or a grimacing twist of his mouth. 'So what is meant to happen now?' she asked, her voice turning to raw demand. 'Am I just meant to…leave? Are you kicking me out?'

'Of course not. You may stay in the palace as long as you like. I'll leave.'

'Where will you—'

'It hardly signifies. I'll send you the paperwork.'

Alyse stared at him, those stern, hard features she'd come to know so well. Those mobile lips she'd kissed, the body she'd touched…*the heart she loved.*

She loved him, she knew that now, felt it inside her like a shining gold light, and Leo was doing his damnedest to extinguish it. They'd been married for ten days.

'Please,' she said one last time, and he didn't reply. Didn't move, didn't even blink. Taking a deep, shuddering breath, Alyse slowly turned and walked out of the room.

She walked down the corridor with its crystal chandeliers and sumptuous carpet, barely aware of her surroundings, or the liveried footmen standing to attention as she came to the top of the double staircase that led down into the palace's entrance hall. Her mind was spinning and she tasted acid in her mouth. Swallowing hard, she sank onto a spindly little gilt bench, her head in her hands.

'Your Highness—' One of the footmen started forward in concern.

'Just leave me,' she whispered, her head still in her hands. 'Please.' The footman stepped back. Alyse tried to marshal her thoughts. What would she do now? Where would she go? Her entire life, since she was eighteen years old and little more than a naïve child, had been oriented towards being Leo's wife, Maldinia's queen, and now that was taken away from her she was left spinning in a void of uncertainty.

Why was he doing this? Why didn't he believe their marriage was worth saving, that she loved him?

Just like you loved him when you were eighteen? When you told him you loved him, and then took it back? And haven't told him since, haven't trusted that any of this is real?

Could she really blame Leo for doubting not just his feelings, but her own? *She'd* doubted them. She'd insisted she was in love with him once, only for him to prove her disastrously wrong. Was it any wonder he doubted? His whole life people had been telling him they loved him— his parents, his brother, and they'd all, in their own way, been liars.

Why should he think she was any different?

She straightened, her gaze unseeing as thoughts tumbled through her mind. Did she love him now, a real, strong love, not the girlish fancy of before? She felt the answer in her heart, beating with strong, sure certainty.

Yes.

And she'd never told him. She'd begged him to change his mind, had acted as if it was all up to him, when she was the one who needed to take control. Who could be strong.

Her legs felt shaky as she stood up and walked slowly back to the apartment where she knew Leo waited. Where her heart, her whole life, waited.

Taking a deep breath, letting the air buoy her lungs, she opened the door and stepped into the room.

Leo sat on the bed, his elbows braced on his knees, his head lowered. Alyse's heart ached at the sight of his wretchedness even as new hope flickered to life within her heart. This wasn't a man unaffected by what just happened, the man who had coldly stared her down and almost—almost—won.

'Leo.'

He looked up, blinking as if she were an apparition. Alyse saw grief etched in the lines of his face before he deliberately blanked his expression. She knew how he did that now. She was starting to understand why. 'What are you doing here?'

'I want to finish our conversation.'

'I think our conversation is quite finished, Alyse. There's nothing more to say.'

'I have something more to say.'

'Oh?' He arched one eyebrow, coldly skeptical, but Alyse knew it was only a mask. At least, she hoped it was only a mask, that underneath the stern coldness beat the heart of the warm, generous man she'd come to know—and love. Yet even now fear and doubt skittered along her spine, crept into her mind. She forced them back.

'You told me once you wanted there to be no lies or pretence between us.' He jerked his head in a tiny nod, and Alyse made herself continue despite the fear coursing through her veins. 'And I don't want there to be either. So if you're going to dissolve our marriage, ask for a divorce, then you need to give me the real reason.'

'I did give you the real reason.'

'I don't think you did.'

His mouth tightened. 'That's not my problem, Alyse.'

'No, it's mine. Because I haven't been honest either. I've been so afraid—afraid of losing you by pushing too

hard or asking for too much. And afraid of my own feelings, if I could trust them.' He didn't respond, but she saw
a wary alertness in his eyes and knew he was listening.
Emboldened, she took a step forward. 'I really did believe
I loved you all those years ago, you know,' she said softly.
'And then when I started to get to know you properly, I
began to doubt the feelings I'd had…just as you doubted
them.' She hesitated, wanting to be honest yet needing to
search for the words. 'It was a terrible feeling, to realise
I'd fooled myself for so long. It made me wonder if I could
ever trust my feelings—my own heart—again. Or if anyone else could. Like you.'

Still nothing from him, but Alyse kept on. She sat next
to him on the bed, her thigh nudging his, needing his
touch, his warmth. 'I've come to understand just a little
how you must have endured the same thing. Your parents
telling you they love you, but only for the cameras. Not
really meaning it.' She waited, but he didn't answer. 'And
your brother too—leaving you like that. You were close,
weren't you?'

His throat worked and he glanced away. 'Yes,' he said,
and his voice choked.

She laid a hand on his arm. 'For your whole life people
have been letting you down, Leo, pretending they love you
and then doing something else. Is it any wonder you're
afraid of relationships, of love, now? I'm afraid and I didn't
have that experience.'

'I'm not afraid—'

'Don't lie to me. Love is scary, even when you don't
have the kind of emotional baggage you do. Or I do, for
that matter. Pretending we're in love for six years didn't
do either of us any favours.'

'That's why I want this marriage to end. No more pretending. No more lies.'

Alyse drew a deep breath. 'So you'd be telling the truth

if you said you didn't feel anything for me?' No answer, but at least a vigorous *yes* hadn't sprung to his lips. 'Because I wouldn't. I do feel something for you, Leo. Something I didn't trust at first because of everything that had gone before. And maybe I'm still not exactly sure what love is, what it feels like, but with every moment I'm with you I believe I feel it for you.' She took another breath and let it out slowly. 'I love you, Leo.'

He let out a short, hard laugh. 'I've heard that before.'

'I know, which is why I've been so afraid of saying it again. What I felt for you before was a schoolgirl crush, a childish fancy. I was overwhelmed by how everything had moved so quickly, by the attention of the press, and the way my parents were thrilled—the whole world was thrilled. I wanted the fairy tale, and so I bought into it.' She reached for his hand, laced her fingers through his. He didn't, at least, pull away or even resist. 'But this last week has shown me that love isn't a fairy tale, Leo. It's hard and painful and messy. It hurts. And yet it's also wonderful, because when I'm with you there's nowhere else I'd rather be.' Still no words from him, but she felt him squeeze her fingers slightly, and hope began to unfurl inside her. 'I love seeing you smile, hearing you laugh, feeling you inside me. And I love the fact that I've come to know you, that I can tell when you're amused or annoyed or angry or hurt. That I recognise the way you try to veil your expression and hide your pain. That I know when you're reading something that bores you in the newspaper but you keep reading anyway because you just *have* to finish the page.'

Leo's lips twitched in an almost-smile and Alyse laughed softly, no more than a breath of sound. 'Loving someone is knowing them,' she continued quietly. 'I didn't understand that at first. I thought it was a lightning bolt, or an undeniable rush of feeling. But it's more than that. It's *understanding* a person inside and out. I can't pretend

I understand you completely, but I think I'm beginning to. I'm starting to see how a childhood of pretending—a lifetime of pretending—has made you not just doubt other people's feelings, but your own. You told me you loved me when we were on television, and I was afraid to believe you. I think you were afraid to believe yourself. That's why you tried to deny it afterwards. It's why I didn't press the matter. All out of fear.'

He gazed down at their intertwined hands, his thumb sliding over her fingers. 'You did say love was scary,' he said in a low voice.

'Absolutely. It's terrifying. But I also think it's worth it—it's worth the risk of being hurt. Loneliness might be easier, but it's bleak too.' She squeezed his fingers, imbuing him with her strength. Her hope. 'I don't expect you to love me yet. I know we both need time to learn to trust each other. To know each other. But I'm asking you, Leo—I'm begging you, give us that chance. Don't turn away from our marriage just because you're not going to be king. I never cared about you being king. I was scared of being queen. I just want to be with you.'

'That's not why I turned away.'

She stilled, her fingers frozen in his. 'No?'

He took a deep breath. 'I turned away because I was afraid. Because I've learned it's easier to be the first one to pull away, before you're pushed.'

'And you thought I'd...I'd push you? Because you weren't king?'

'I don't know what I thought, to be honest.' He glanced up, his gaze hooded, his eyes dark with pain. 'I was acting on instinct, shutting down, closing up. It's what I've always done, and I knew I had to do it with you. You've had more power to hurt me than anyone else, Alyse. Do you know how utterly terrifying that is?'

She managed a shaky smile, felt the sting of tears

behind her lids. 'Yes,' she answered. 'As a matter of fact, I do.'

'You're wrong, you know. I don't need time to learn to love you, or know you. I already do. I didn't mean to say that on television—the words just spilled out. It was as if I couldn't *keep* from saying them. I had to be honest about how I felt, not just to you, but to the whole world.'

Alyse felt her mouth curve in an understanding smile. 'And then as soon as you were, you wanted to take it all back.'

'Self-protection, just a little too late.'

'This is hard, no question.'

'As soon as you left the room I wanted to run after you. Take it all back. Beg—just like I used to beg my mother to spend time with me, to *love* me, or my brother not to leave.' He was quiet for a moment, his gaze still on their twined hands. 'He was a hero to me, you know. I adored him. He always looked out for me at school, he felt like the only person who really knew me—'

'And he left,' Alyse finished softly. 'He left you.'

'I can't really blame him. The atmosphere in the palace has always been toxic, and he had it worse than I did, buried under my parents' expectations.' Leo sighed and shook his head. 'But yes, he left, and it hurt. A lot. I told myself I'd never be like that again, needing someone so much, begging them to stay.'

Her heart ached and she blinked back tears. 'I'm sorry.'

'I don't know what kind of relationship we can have, now that he's back.'

'You'll find a way. Love endures, Leo. And you still love him.'

He nodded slowly. 'Yes, I suppose I do.'

It was, she knew, a big admission for him to make. And yet she needed more; *they* needed more. 'And what about us, Leo?' Alyse touched his cheek, forced him to meet her soft gaze. 'What kind of relationship can we have?'

His navy gaze bored into hers, searching for answers, and then his mouth softened in a slight smile. 'A good one, I hope. A marriage…a real marriage. If you'll have me.'

'You know I will.'

He turned his head so his lips brushed her fingers. 'I'm not saying I won't make mistakes. I will, I'm sure of it. This still terrifies me, now more than ever. I've never loved anyone before, not like this.'

'Me neither,' Alyse whispered.

'I don't want to hurt you,' he continued, his voice turning ragged. 'I love you, Alyse, so much, but I'm afraid—afraid that I will—'

'That's part of loving someone,' she answered, her voice clogged with tears, tears of happiness, of hope and relief and pure emotion, rather than sorrow. 'The joy and the pain. I'll take both, Leo, with you.'

Yet as his arms came around her and his lips found hers in a soft and unending promise, Alyse knew only joy. The joy, the wondrous joy, of being known and loved.

* * * * *

HIS BRIDE FOR
THE TAKING

SANDRA HYATT

After completing a business degree, travelling and then settling into a career in marketing, **Sandra Hyatt** was relieved to experience one of life's *Eureka*! moments while on maternity leave, she discovered that writing books, although a lot slower, was just as much fun as reading them.

She knows life doesn't always hand out happy endings and thinks that's why books ought to. She loves being along for the journey with her characters as they work around, over and through the obstacles standing in their way.

Sandra has lived in both the U.S. and England and currently lives near the coast in New Zealand with her school sweetheart and their two children.

You can visit her at **www.sandrahyatt.com**.

One

Glancing at her watch, Lexie Wyndham Jones hurried from the stables and through a back entrance of her family's Massachusetts home. The ride had taken longer than she'd intended, but she still had time to prepare herself.

Dropping onto the seat just inside the door, she began wrestling one of her riding boots off. At the sound of someone clearing his throat, she looked up to see their butler standing close, watching her. "May I be of assistance, miss?"

He had his stoic expression on, all droopy gray eyebrows and even droopier jowls. "No. I'm fine. Thank you, Stanley." He always offered. She always refused. It had been their routine since Lexie had first learned to ride. The boot came free in her hands and she dropped it to the floor.

When Stanley altered the routine by not then moving away, she glanced up.

"Your mother has been looking for you."

Sighing, Lexie turned her attention to her unyielding second boot. "What have I done now?"

"Your…prince has come."

For a second, Lexie froze. And Stanley, against every fiber of his butler being, allowed his disapproval to show. He hadn't said, he never would, but he thought she and her mother were making a mistake. She redoubled her efforts on her boot, hiding her surge of elation. The boot came free in her hands and she dropped it beside the first and stood. "He's early." Perhaps he had been so eager to see her that—

"I believe with the changeover of your mother's secretary there has been some confusion about the times. The prince was of the impression that you would be accompanying him back to San Philippe this afternoon."

"But the dinner?"

"Precisely."

"Mother has explained?"

"Of course. You'll be leaving in the morning as planned."

"Oh, dear." She didn't suppose it was good practice to thwart a prince's expectations, but it couldn't be any worse than thwarting her mother's.

"Precisely." The merest twinkle glinted in Stanley's gray eyes, and she got the feeling there was something he wasn't telling her. No doubt she'd find out soon enough.

"Where are they now?"

"The croquet lawn."

"I'd better get out there." She turned, but stopped at the sound of Stanley again clearing his throat.

"Perhaps you would like to freshen up first?"

Lexie scanned her mud-splattered jodhpurs and laughed. "Holy—" She stopped herself in time and winked. "Good heavens, yes." She mimicked her mother's cultured tones. "Thank you, Stanley."

He inclined his head.

Thirty minutes later, Lexie, now wearing a demure—and clean—sundress, lowered herself into the chair in the arbor. A dark jacket lay draped over the arm of the chair next to her. Drawn to touch it, Lexie trailed her fingers over the sun-warmed leather and the exquisitely soft silk of the lining.

Pulling her hand to her lap, she took in the croquet game that looked close to ending. There were only two people on the lawn: broad-shouldered Adam, his back to her, lining up a shot, and her fiercely slender mother. It was easy to tell from the rigid set to her mother's shoulders and the too-bright society laugh that drifted across the lawn that Antonia was losing. A result that didn't bode well. Her mother didn't quite have the power of the Queen of Hearts—no one would lose their head. Not literally. But...

Lexie watched with surprise as Adam swung his mallet and played a merciless shot, sending her mother's ball careening miles from where she'd want it. While she wouldn't expect him to throw a game, she would have thought he'd be more tactful. He was renowned as a master diplomat, and he usually managed to charm her mother. The tinkling laughter that followed his shot was anything but charmed, and Lexie cringed.

Adam straightened and turned, and her heart beat a little faster in anticipation. Then she caught his profile, and her breath stalled in her chest as she looked and, disbelieving, looked again.

Not Adam Marconi, crown prince of San Philippe.

But his brother, Rafe.

A heated flush swept up her face.

As if sensing her scrutiny, Rafe turned fully. Across half the lawn his gaze caught hers. Slowly, he inclined his head, almost as Stanley did, but with Stanley the gesture, though it could convey a dozen nuanced meanings, was usually genial or at least respectful. Rafe's nod, the stiff little bow, even from this distance, communicated displeasure.

Which made two of them. She did *not* want to see Rafe.

Fighting for composure, Lexie had to remind herself, as her mother so often did, that she, too, had royal bloodlines, her ancestors having once ruled the small European principality that Rafe's father was sovereign of. A Wyndham Jones was cool and self-possessed at all times. Supposedly.

Lexie wasn't a particularly good example of the name, but she tried. As the shock of seeing Rafe ebbed, it was replaced by disappointment and chagrin. Adam, her prince, hadn't come himself, but rather his profligate brother. The Playboy Prince, as the press called him. Or, as Lexie secretly thought of him, the Frog Prince. Nothing to do with his looks—he was Adonis personified. Even on the croquet lawn his fluid athleticism was obvious. Michelangelo's David come to life. The confidence that came from the unique combination of his position in the world and his looks pervaded everything about him.

Her mother, following Rafe's gaze, saw Lexie and abandoned the game to glide across the lawn, probably convincing herself she'd been about to win. Rafe strolled in her wake. And though he appeared relaxed, she couldn't help but feel he was zeroing in on her like an Armani-clad, heat-seeking missile. She watched him through narrowed eyes. Her mother crossed into her line of vision and scanned Lexie critically from head to toe, her expression a dire warning to behave herself.

Lexie's jaw clenched tighter, but as they neared her she forced her lips into a smile and extended her hand. Rafe reached for it, closed strong fingers around hers and then lifted her knuckles to his lips and pressed the gentlest of kisses there.

For as long as his touch lasted, confusion reigned. And in her surprise, Lexie forgot her anger, forgot her plans for her future, forgot her mother, even. She was aware only of being simultaneously swamped and stilled by sensation, warm lips and gentle fingers and the strange shiver of heat that coursed through her. Rafe lifted his head and she felt at close range the burning connection of his gaze from dark, honey-colored eyes.

As he released her fingers, her presence of mind

returned and she remembered everything, recognized his tactic as some kind of power play. "It's a pleasure to meet you again, Your Highness," she said through her most practiced smile.

He returned a smile that hid the irritation she'd glimpsed earlier. "Rafe will do. Unless you'd also prefer me to call you Miss Wyndham Jones."

"No." Lexie shook her head.

"In that case, Alexia, the pleasure is all mine. It's been too long."

She bit down on the word *liar* that wanted to escape her lips, partly because it would be so terribly impolite, but mainly because she, too, had lied. Nothing about this meeting was the pleasure it should have been. "And such a surprise, too. I must confess, I was expecting Adam." Thoughtful, gentlemanly, mature Adam.

One corner of Rafe's lips lifted in a mocking smile. "You usually are, as I recall."

Lexie felt her face pale. How dare he? One mistake. Four years ago. A mistake she'd fervently hoped he'd forgotten. After all, to a man like him it was an event that could barely have registered. It should have been nothing to him. It *was* nothing, she reminded herself. An accident, a misunderstanding.

At a glittering masquerade ball, if you had just turned eighteen, it was easy to confuse one masked prince's identity with another's, particularly when their hair and builds were so similar. And if that prince waltzed you to a quiet corner behind a fluted marble column and kissed you, gently at first and then as though you were ambrosia itself, coaxing an unguarded response in return, then when he unmasked you and realized who you were, staggered backward, cursing under his breath...

"I'm afraid I must apologize on my brother's behalf." Rafe's tone, though still formal, had softened, and he sounded almost sincere. Of course, he, too, would regret that it wasn't Adam here instead of him. "Royal duties prevented him coming to escort you back to San Philippe. He is, however, greatly looking forward to your arrival."

It took an effort of will not to roll her eyes. Greatly looking forward to? Could he be any more formal? And still the word *liar* simmered in her consciousness. Because despite the fact that she'd had a crush on Adam for almost as long as she could remember, and that she knew Adam *liked* her, and that for years the possibility of a match between them had been promoted by their respective parents, their correspondence was hardly much more than friendly.

But things were about to change. Adam hadn't seen her in four years. He was about to meet the new, improved, grown-up Alexia Wyndham Jones.

"In the meantime, unfortunately," Rafe said, "you'll have to make do with me."

"Oh, not unfortunate at all," her mother interjected before Lexie could respond. Under Rafe's questioning gaze, Lexie swallowed her retort. Probably for the best. This man, as well as potentially being her brother-in-law, was apparently her pathway to her future, and she would do what needed to be done to ensure nothing went wrong now. Not when she was this close to setting her life on its proper course.

Rafe was no more than a temporary inconvenience.

"Alexia was reminiscing just yesterday about her last visit to San Philippe," said her mother. "I don't believe you were there at the time."

"I was gone for most of it, but I did arrive back in time for her final evening and the masquerade ball." A hint of amusement and challenge laced his voice.

One stupid, mistaken kiss. Why did he have to be so intent on reminding her of it?

"The ball. I'd almost forgotten about that." Lexie smiled sweetly. "It was so overshadowed by everything else I saw and did while I was there."

Rafe's lips stretched into a grin, and a roguish gleam lit those dark eyes. "I shall have to see if I can remind you, seeing as it's all we shared of that visit. I recall your gown in particular, a deep burgundy, and it had—"

Lexie laughed, sounding scarily like her mother, but at least cutting short anything further Rafe might have said. The gown had featured a daringly low back. When they'd danced, his fingertips had caressed her skin, trailing sparks of heat. "I can scarcely remember what I wore yesterday, let alone four years ago. As for reminding me of that last visit, there's no need. I'm sure I'll make enough new memories in the future." She looked pointedly at him.

Her words, or her glance, seemed to recall Rafe to his purpose here. Not to discomfit her by reminding her of a kiss that was best forgotten because it should never have happened, but to escort her to his country so she could get to know his brother better and more important, for Adam to get to know her better. *Courtship* was the word her mother had used—but only once, because apparently Lexie had found it "inappropriately amusing."

Rafe straightened and took a step back. The gleam in his eyes disappeared, his expression hardening into regal arrogance.

"Dinner will be served at eight," her mother said, oblivious to the tension and displeasure arcing between them. "I've invited a few close friends, and some of your countrymen."

It promised to be a tedious, stuffy affair. Lexie could almost have pitied him if she hadn't been so annoyed and if he weren't so far above needing that sentiment from her. He was the one who would be on display tonight, not only for his countrymen but for friends of her mother's eager to be able to boast of their dinner with European royalty. Lexie, on the other hand, would be able to slip away relatively early.

"I look forward to it," Rafe said, sounding as though he meant it.

Liar.

Rafe tossed his dinner jacket over the back of the armchair in his room. He'd attended more boring dinners in his life than he could possibly count, but tonight's ranked among the worst. If it hadn't been for the presence of Tony, an old school friend, now a high-powered Boston attorney, the evening would have been unbearable.

Out of curiosity, he'd closely watched the woman who

hoped to snare herself a prince—his brother's would-be bride—throughout the evening. She had shown scarcely any reaction as her mother, none too subtly, toasted her success in her forthcoming travels. His observation of her served only to confirm that she was a perfect match for Adam. Demure, respectable, quiet and a gracious hostess. In a word, boring.

Even the dress she'd worn, a silvery high-necked thing that she'd teamed with pearls, had been boring. She had a passable figure, curves where they should be, yet she did nothing to accentuate her assets. She wore her glossy auburn hair swept back from her face into a sleek—boring—knot. He had seen no trace of the spark he'd imagined in her moss-green eyes this afternoon as she'd tried to challenge him.

She'd clearly been irritated that it was he who'd come for her. Tough luck. If she wanted to be Adam's wife, she'd have to learn to hide that flash of her eyes that revealed those emotions. And if she wanted to marry into his family, she'd do well to learn that more often than not royal considerations overrode personal ones. His presence here was a case in point. If it had been up to him, he would have spent the day playing polo and the evening dancing with the charming divorcée he'd met at a charity gala last week.

But Rafe's father, Prince Henri Augustus Marconi, claiming failing health and impatient to secure the family line, had, in a fit of regal autocracy, decreed that it was Adam's duty to marry—and marry well and soon—and that the heiress Alexia Wyndham Jones was the perfect candidate.

Rafe had at first thought the announcement a joke. His sister, Rebecca, had been shocked at their father's methods, though not his choice. She liked Alexia. Adam, being Adam, had let nothing of his thoughts show, except to say he wasn't able to get away from San Philippe. And somehow Rafe, still atoning for his latest scandal, and possibly his burst of laughter, had ended up here playing babysitter and escort.

Not long after the dinner was finished Alexia had claimed a headache and excused herself, leaving him without even the distraction of watching her as he made conversation with one after another of her mother's guests. He'd almost wished he could use the same excuse as she had just to get away from the endless pretension.

At the throaty rumble of an engine, he looked out his window to see a Harley Davidson carrying two leather-clad riders disappear into the night.

He removed his cufflinks, dropping them onto the antique dresser, and flicked a glance at his watch. The other good thing about catching up with Tony was that his friend had been able to fill him in on the best Boston night spots. If he couldn't be in his own country, he could as least make the most of being here.

Ten minutes later he slid behind the wheel of the car that had been arranged for him and pulled out of the garage and onto the Wyndham Joneses' driveway.

And a mere thirty minutes later, Rafe stood by Tony on the mezzanine level of the recommended club, watching the throng on the dance floor below him and wondering if coming here hadn't been a mistake. He could have been in any one of a dozen exclusive nightclubs around the world. Here, conversation was near impossible. One a.m. and the place heaved with dancers and the beat of the music. Artificial smoke swirled about the dance floor, colored lights cast eerie illumination on the faces, bodies and limbs of the dancers.

There was only one thing—one person—who piqued his curiosity. His attention kept returning to her, and he couldn't figure out why. She was familiar and yet not. Black hair, cut into a precise bob, swayed around her face as she moved to the music. The haircut and her darkly made-up eyes brought to mind Cleopatra. She danced opposite a tall, brawny man, dark hair, dark skin, possibly South American, who moved almost as well as she did. And yet, with her eyes often closed and her partner continuously scanning the crowd, she looked more as if she were dancing alone.

There was something entrancing, an innate sensuality, about the way she seemed aware of only the music and her own body—a svelte body sheathed in a subtly shimmering black dress that was almost nunlike compared to some of the outfits here tonight. But though it revealed little skin other than that of her graceful arms and a generous but still disappointing portion of her long legs, it molded lovingly to her curves and her slender waist.

Rafe wasn't the only one who noticed. From his elevated position he could see that she drew more than her share of admiring—drooling—glances.

"Who's that?" He almost had to shout in Tony's ear to be heard.

Tony followed his gaze. "The blonde? An actress, I think. Or maybe a singer? Wasn't she on the cover of the tabloids last week? The press are always after her."

Rafe saw the woman Tony meant, a Barbie doll clone. "No. Cleopatra. Over to the right a little."

Tony frowned. "Don't know. I've seen her here a couple of times. Asked her to dance once. She turned me down flat, then turned her back on me. Seems to prefer them six foot four and burly."

Rafe watched as a man with the loudest red shirt he had ever seen tried to cut in with Cleopatra. Tall and Brawny looked at his partner and she gave her head the faintest shake. He said something to Red Shirt, who scowled and then turned back to his cluster of laughing, and clearly inebriated, friends.

Rafe kept his gaze on the woman. There was something tantalizingly familiar about her. He had a good memory for faces and yet he couldn't place her.

"It happened just like that for me, too," Tony said dolefully.

Rafe laughed. "It's all in the execution."

"You think she'll dance with you? You're good, buddy, but you're not that good. She's different. Not interested."

Rafe seldom turned down a challenge, and after the boredom of the evening and the potential boredom of tomorrow, a day spent babysitting "Precious," he relished the fillip of Tony's unspoken dare even more. "Watch and learn, my friend. Watch and learn."

On the dance floor, he scarcely noticed the patrons parting to let him through. He fixed his gaze on

Cleopatra as he approached her from the side. Slender, toned arms were raised above her head. Her eyes were closed. Dark, curling lashes kissed her cheeks. A small, secretive smile played about her cherry-colored lips. She managed to look both vulnerable and untouchable.

Naturally making him want to touch.

Intrigued and appreciative, he felt an undeniable pull of attraction. She *would* dance with him, she had to. He wanted to learn how she would move when they danced together, he wanted to know the color of her eyes, he wanted to know the fullness of that smile. He wanted—

Like a bucket of cold water over his wants, recognition slammed through him.

Alexia.

Followed by denial. It couldn't be. Demure, boring Alexia was at home in bed with a headache.

He moved closer. She turned away, obscuring his view. But it was her. He knew it with absolute certainty. The porcelain skin, the almost stubborn jaw, and that something else, something hidden that he couldn't define.

He now also knew Tall and Brawny's role. Bodyguard. What he didn't know was what the hell she was doing here and, more important, what he should do about it. Did he leave her or get her out of here? She wasn't his responsibility. Yet. And chances were she'd get through the evening without a scandal.

Another of Red Shirt's group staggered her way.

Rafe flicked a glance at her partner, saw recognition of him dawn in Tall and Brawny's eyes. He signaled with a tilt of his head for the bodyguard to take care of Alexia's next would-be dance partner. The larger man nodded and stepped aside.

Two

Trying not to clench his jaw, Rafe watched Alexia dance. This woman who moved so sinuously and sensuously, lost in the music, was not the same bland woman who'd sat demurely through dinner.

She was playing some kind of game with them all.

He had no time for women who played games, women who pretended to be one thing when they were something else altogether. He was still dealing with the fallout from his last encounter with such a woman.

He was standing, arms folded, when Alexia finally opened her eyes. Her gaze alighted first on his chest, then snapped to his face. He caught the flash of horror, watched the horror schooled into a bright, false smile. "Sorry, I don't dance with other men." As if she might still get away with it. Without waiting for his response, she turned and slipped into the swirling crowd.

She didn't get far. He caught up with her at the edge of the dance floor as she tried to get past a cluster of tipsy women, one of them wearing a bridal veil, all of them shrieking with laughter.

He stilled Alexia with a hand on her slender, heated shoulder.

She spun around. "Go away," she said with a force that surprised him.

He'd lowered his hand as she turned, sliding it down the skin of her arm so that it now cupped her elbow. He leaned closer so she'd hear him over the music. "No." She stiffened at his refusal. "You're asking for trouble being in this place. My responsibility is to get you safely back to my country. The demure Alexia Wyndham Jones whom the people will love. Possibly their future princess. Someone they can look up to, bearing in mind that they're more conservative than you Americans. Not someone who dresses like, like…"

He faltered under the indignant heat of her gaze.

"Like what?" Her hands went to her hips, shaking off his touch. A mutinous expression tightened her lips. In truth there was nothing anyone could object to in what she was wearing. Anyone, apparently, except him. He couldn't put his finger on just what it was that bothered him. But it did bother him, and that was good enough for him. "Surely you don't need me to spell it out for you?" Damn, he sounded like his father. Master of the guilt trip.

Sudden resignation sagged through her body, and

he almost felt bad for it. After all, he'd been known on more than one occasion to skip out on official duties to have a little fun. And he knew what it was like to get busted.

But that was different.

Alexia was only twenty-two, and as well as being an heiress to millions, she might one day sit on the throne beside his brother. From what he knew of her, she'd led a cloistered existence. There was no end of trouble she could get into here. Very public trouble. The world was too full of predators, the press too greedy for gossip. Part of the reason her candidacy as a partner for Adam had been approved was her perceived innocence. Rafe glanced at the bodyguard hovering near her side. "Alexia and I need to have a little chat. A private chat."

The bodyguard looked at Alexia, she lifted her shoulders in a shrug. "It's okay, Mario. I may as well get this over with."

As the bodyguard moved a little farther off, Rafe leaned closer. "What exactly are you doing here?"

"Pardon?"

She'd heard him; she was just looking to delay answering, subtly challenging his right to even ask.

He leaned closer still—another millimeter and his body would be pressed against hers. Those lush, cherry-colored lips were clamped together. He caught her scent, something with an underlying zing of fresh citrus, and he felt the heat of her body radiating from her. Pushing a lock of the ridiculous dark hair—nowhere near as attractive as her natural auburn—behind her delicate ear, he put his lips close. "We'll talk in my car."

She tensed. "We don't need to talk."

Another patron passed too close, knocking into Rafe, who knocked into Alexia. His grip tightened around her.

Suddenly, flashes went off, blinding in their brightness. Rafe pulled Alexia hard against his chest, shielding her face and turning so his back was to the continuing pop of the flashes.

Damn. The paparazzi were supposed to be banned from this place. Tony had assured him of the impenetrable security.

He glanced back over his shoulder. There the leeches were, three guys with cameras pointing them in the direction of the blonde actress. Unfortunately, Alexia and he, although behind the actress, were in their line of sight.

"Clearly, we do need to talk."

Only moments too late, the club's bouncers strode through the crowd toward the cameramen. Barbie and her entourage were shrieking in outrage, but Rafe got the feeling the outrage was as much an act as her last Oscar-nominated role.

Rafe looked down into wide green eyes belatedly filled with concern. He felt the press of breasts against his chest, felt Alexia's slender fragility within the circle of his arms. She was smaller than he'd realized, and shorter, even with her death-defying heels. The top of her head was tucked neatly beneath his chin.

He felt other things, things he shouldn't feel for his brother's proposed bride. The protectiveness was okay, it was the pleasure and possessiveness that bothered him. He told himself that they were almost automatic responses when he held a woman in his arms. It didn't mean anything except that he had to let her go. He loosed his hold on her, putting a safer distance between them.

One of the actress's party made a lunge for a photographer's camera. A punch was thrown, then another.

Rafe shepherded Alexia away from the tussle. Worry creased her forehead even as the bouncers quickly separated the opponents and dragged the guy who'd thrown the first punch away with the photographers.

"Do you think we're in the shots?" She bit her bottom lip.

At least she realized how it would look if pictures of the two of them in a nightclub, standing close, got into the papers at home. Or if they were implicated in the brawl, which, given the way the press liked to play with the truth, wouldn't surprise him in the least. The public of San Philippe would be curious. Adam would be furious. And if anything happened to jeopardize his father's plans, Rafe would be in the firing line. He just needed to get this one simple job done. Get Alexia back to San Philippe—without a scandal—and wash his hands of her. How hard could it be?

He shook his head. "I'm scarcely known here, and you, fortunately, hardly look like yourself. Even if we're in the background, they weren't after us. We'll be cropped out."

"Fortunately?"

"Don't sound offended. You deliberately tried to

disguise yourself. For good reason. So, yes, fortunately."
He didn't add that in other respects it was most *un*fortunate. The figure-hugging dress, her long legs, the satiny skin of her arms, the curl of her lashes, her scent. All most unfortunate. Where was the boring—safe—Alexia? "How did you get here?" His question sounded harsher than he meant it to.

"Motorbike," she answered, with a glimmer of defiance.

He hid his surprise. "You rode?" That had been her on the bike?

Her chin lifted. "With Mario."

"In that dress?" He had a sudden vision of the dress riding high up a creamy expanse of thigh.

"I changed at a friend's apartment."

He looked at Mario. The other man moved closer. "Take the bike home."

Mario nodded.

"Where'd you get him, anyway?" he asked as they watched Mario's departing back.

"He's one of our drivers. He also has security, bodyguard-type training. And he's the best dancer of the firm's drivers."

Rafe glared at her. "Undoubtedly a reliable way to choose your security for the evening." He silently counted the hours—eighteen—till they'd be safely back in San Philippe and he'd be done with her.

Lexie sat quietly as they drove in the muted silence of Rafe's Aston Martin to the Wyndham Joneses' estate. Why him? She'd encountered good friends at the nightclub before who'd failed to recognize her. And yet Rafe, whom she'd met only a handful of times, had known her.

The purpose and urgency that had infused him as he'd all but picked her up and bundled her into his car had gone. He drove the powerful machine with relaxed effortlessness, his hands curled lightly around the distinctive three-spoked steering wheel. But she sensed his underlying tension, and it was in her interests to placate him. She wanted him to see that she really was suitable for his brother. Serene, regal, dignified.

"Nice car." She smoothed her palms over the soft black leather of her seat.

He said nothing.

"It's a Vantage, isn't it? A V12?" She exhausted her knowledge of the car.

"I wouldn't know." His usually undetectable accent, foreign and vaguely French, colored his words.

So much for getting him to relax by complimenting his car. It worked on most men she knew. His dismissiveness needled her. He'd clearly made up his mind not to engage with her. "A real playboy car."

That drew her a scornful look, at least.

"How'd you get it, anyway?"

"My secretary arranged it. Ask him."

Lexie gave up trying to either soothe or bait him and looked out her window at the city and then countryside sliding by. Gone. Soon she'd be gone from here and the narrow confines of her life.

As the estate gates closed behind them, he pulled off

the driveway into a wooded area. The house was still half a mile away.

"Why are we stopping here?"

"Because if I don't stop till we're in front of the house someone will doubtless come out and find me with my hands wrapped around your neck. And while I'm sure whoever it is will sympathize with me, it'd still be frowned upon, bound to cause a diplomatic fracas. And worse, I'll be interrupted."

He'd had a hand around the back of her neck once four years ago as he'd kissed her senseless. Which was not what she should be remembering now. She called up righteous anger. "You're assuming you'll get the chance to wrap your hands around my neck. If you'd read my background information—" which of course the Playboy Prince wouldn't have "—you'd know I have a black belt in karate. Second dan." She was tired of him thinking he could push her around. "Perhaps it'd be my hands around *your* neck."

Unfortunately, a contrary image sprang to mind of the two of them in the car with their hands all over each other in a very different way. Shocked at herself, she banished the image. It had only happened because he reminded her of Adam and they were confined in the intimacy of his car, faces and bodies close, emotions running high. The scent of his cologne, masculine and appealing, wasn't helping, either.

He laughed, low and deep. "I did read the information. My secretary handed it to me as I boarded the jet, and unfortunately there was nothing else on board to read. It mentioned years of ballet dancing, sailing and show jumping to a nationally competitive level, and musical accomplishments including flute and, rather more surprising, the saxophone. Sadly, they must have left off the karate. Though it's entirely possible that the ballet training will help in the execution of a passable roundhouse kick."

Lexie knew when to quit. He clearly wasn't going to fall for that one. Even if she had learned karate. Once. A long time ago. A secret rebellion cut short.

He turned off the engine. And though she'd scarcely heard the car's low purr before, the silence of the night settled over them like a heavy, uncomfortable blanket.

Now it was just her and Rafe.

He turned, filling the space in the suddenly too-small car from floor to ceiling, his presence surrounding her. Just enough light washed in from the closest of the lamps dotted along the driveway to make out his features, the dark brows drawn together, the strong nose, surprisingly full lips and the stubborn, stubborn jaw. And the eyes that raked disrespectfully over her. Adam would never have looked at her like that.

"Your headache is better, I take it?"

"Much, thank you." She chose to ignore the drawled sarcasm. And the lie of her fabricated illness.

"You often pull stunts like that, Precious?"

"I don't pull stunts. I wanted to go out tonight. I wanted to dance. There's no crime in it."

"It was a stunt. And it was stupid."

"It was not stupid. I was careful. I took Mario with me." Her life was about to change; all she'd wanted was one night of anonymity. It wasn't so much to ask. She'd been to the nightclub before. Many times. And in all that time she'd never been recognized.

"And look what happened."

"Nothing happened." He'd said himself they wouldn't turn up in those shots.

"Do you have any idea— Damn." He sat back in his seat.

"What?"

"I sound like my father." His hand clenched into a fist. "I can't believe it."

That concept apparently bothered him almost as much as the nightclub debacle had because he lapsed into silence. "How did you know I was at the nightclub?" she asked. "Did you follow me?"

"No. A happy coincidence."

"Not my definition of happy." At that he smiled. "So you were there, too," she accused, "for the same reason as me, and yet I'm the one in the wrong?"

"I'm not the one who left dinner early because—" he touched blunt fingertips to his temple and blinked several times, a parody of a woman fluttering her eyelashes "—I had a headache."

"I did have a headache. That dinner would have given a saint one. I never said what I was going to do about it. If you assumed I was retiring quietly to my bed, that's not my fault."

"If you want to be wife to the crown prince, you're going to need a little more fortitude. It'll be your job to stay at dinners like that till the bitter end. You weren't the only one who wanted to leave that dinner tonight. Some of us managed to tough it out."

"That's it?" She smiled with a sudden flash of insight. "You're sore that I got to leave earlier than you?"

"That's not what I said. The problem wasn't with you leaving the dinner, headache or not. It lies more in you out with other men, dancing the way you were."

"There was nothing wrong with the way I danced."

"No? Every man in the place enjoyed it."

She felt the stab of his criticism. "You are being so unfair."

Rafe turned back to stare out the windshield. "Maybe. But you need to learn how very important appearances are. How very seriously people—like Adam—take them."

The worst of it was that he was right. She'd been brought up to always consider how anything she did, said, wore might look. Her mother was as hyperaware of appearances as anyone Lexie had ever met. Which made her occasional forays to the nightclub so liberating. So exhilarating.

She hadn't planned on Adam ever knowing. "It might have been my last chance," she said quietly, leaning back in her seat, and that was the truth of it.

"You're right about that. But no one's forcing you to come to San Philippe."

She said nothing.

"Are they?"

She met his steady gaze. "No." This was her choice. She'd dreamed of it for so long.

"This arrangement is far from a done deal, Alexia," he said quietly. "I'll be watching you, and if I find out you're using Adam, that on your side the relationship is a pretence, I'll hustle your duplicitous derriere back home so fast you won't know what hit you."

"*Duplicitous derriere* sounds so much better than *my lying ass.* Or *hypocrite.*" She gave the last word emphasis because it could apply just as well to him. "You won't catch me out because there's nothing to catch me out in." She turned to stare out the window at the darker silhouettes of trees shadowing the night. "How sweet for Adam to have you coming to his assistance."

"Adam doesn't know women the way I do."

"I wouldn't choose to have any kind of a relationship with him if he did." Adam was serious and constant as well as kind. Nothing like the man sitting a hand span away from her radiating cynicism and testosterone.

"He doesn't look for subterfuge."

"But you do?" She almost felt sorry for him. "Must make for interesting relationships for you. Ever heard of trust?"

"All I'm saying is that if Adam and San Philippe are what you really want, don't screw it up."

"Don't screw it up?" Lexie's knee bumped against the gear stick as she pivoted in her seat. "That's a little rich coming from you, isn't it? I thought you were the 'Prince of Screw-Ups.'" One tabloid had, in fact, tried to pin that label on Rafe. It hadn't stuck, but Lexie suspected that was only because it lacked originality or alliteration.

"Don't try to make this about me." His voice was cold, as though she'd hit a nerve.

"Well, don't try to sully the relationship Adam and I have."

A look of scorn passed across his face. "A few letters and e-mails do not constitute a relationship."

"They constitute more of a relationship than gratuitous sex, which if the stories about you are to be believed—"

"They're not."

His vehemence silenced her.

"And even if they were, the difference, Precious, is that my business is no concern of yours. Whereas your business is my concern. At least until I get you back to San Philippe and offload you onto Adam."

"Offload me?"

"Wrong word, sorry." His offhand apology only incensed her further.

"No, it wasn't. Offload me is exactly what you meant. I'll save you the trouble for tonight." She'd had more than enough of his company for one evening. Opening her door, she climbed out and stalked down the driveway. The cool night air was the perfect antidote to the tension in the car, and she forced herself to take deep, calming breaths. Behind her, a car door shut. Moments later, the engine purred to life, the car eased alongside her, and the window slid down. "Get in. I'll drive you."

"I'm walking, so you may as well stop following me. Consider me offloaded."

"Don't be ridiculous."

"Ridiculous?"

He made no pretence this time that he'd used the wrong word. "Yes. Childishly ridiculous."

Lexie clenched her jaw and walked faster, then stumbled in the high strappy sandals, which were fine for the smooth dance floor, but definitely weren't made for striding on driveways. The low rumble of masculine laughter sounded from within the car.

She stopped and whirled to face him, then bent to take off her shoes, tossing them one at a time through the car window and onto the seat beside him. She pulled off the wig too, and it followed her shoes into his car.

As her hair unfurled around her shoulders, his smile suddenly disappeared. She turned and, ignoring his call to her, darted into the lightly wooded area bordering the driveway. She'd grown up here, had played, whenever she'd been allowed to escape, amongst these very trees. Some of those times of escape had even been at night. A girl took her freedom where she could. She scarcely needed the occasional shafts of light that filtered through from the driveway lamps.

She caught a sound behind her and stilled, alert and listening, her senses heightened. "Alexia." Her name sounded on the night, low and clear. "Cut this out and come back to the car. Now."

He was not happy. Lexie smiled. "Or what? You'll make me? I don't think so, Rafe."

His silence was ominous.

Lexie's heart beat faster. "I'm fine." She slipped behind a tree. "You drive. I'll make my own way." She darted for another tree, stopped and listened again.

She heard nothing, but caught the faintest trace of his cologne. He was close. She waited in the deepest shadows she could find, her shoulder pressed against the roughened bark of an ancient oak, and held herself perfectly still, kept her breathing quiet and even.

From behind, a strong hand clamped around her arm, and without thought a scream started in the back of her throat. The hand swept up to gently cover her mouth, cutting off the incipient sound. She was pulled back against a broad chest. "Do not scream." The softened command was spoken clearly into her ear. "It's only me—" his breath was warm on her skin "—and the very last thing we need tonight is for security to come."

She swallowed and nodded. The hand lowered from her mouth, but she was still clamped against that broad chest. It was the second time in the space of an hour she'd been pressed against its hard contours. It didn't feel like the body she would have expected from the profligate prince. Sure, he was tall and lean. She'd figured that build, combined with the occasional gym workout and exceptional tailoring, was enough to give the fine line to the clothes he wore. But the chest and the arms about her spoke of sinew and strength and an intimidating elemental toughness that was eons away from the high life he lived.

"How did you find me?"

"I've done my share of nighttime operations." His arms loosened and he stepped away from her. "You, Precious, were a piece of cake."

Of course. All men in San Philippe, including the princes, served two years in the armed forces. Rafe, from memory, had served even longer, spending time in each of the three military services.

"Now we're going back to the car." She heard the carefully reined-in temper beneath his quiet words. "And we're going to the house."

She nodded again. It was definitely time to get the willful streak she'd worked so hard to conquer back under control. She was achieving nothing letting Rafe goad her. "I was going anyway. Once I'd cooled off." Which she'd done now, emotionally and physically. She suppressed a shiver.

As they turned for the car, a jacket, warmed with the heat of Rafe's body and imbued with his subtle masculine scent, came to rest on her shoulders. The silk lining caressed the bare skin of her arms.

"Covering me up?"

"Warming you up. I personally have no problem with a little skin. But I will have a problem with my father and my brother if I take you back sick."

"Chivalrous to the end."

Unexpected, Rafe's rich, deep chuckle sounded on the air, eroding her resentment and warming her, against her will, as much as his jacket.

But the resentment was back in full force by the time Lexie reached her bedroom. She shut the door, leaned against it for a second, then crossed to a window and looked out along the shadowy driveway. The driveway, which, after insisting she come back to his car, Rafe had made her walk down. Well, not "make" exactly, but he'd somehow made it seem the only option for her pride. Another besetting sin to add to her list.

He'd idled along beside her, occasionally offering her a ride. She'd refused with the line about not getting into cars with strange men, which had drawn out that unexpected laughter again. In reality the only strange thing about him was the heat—the temper—he ignited in her. He'd talked a little about the car, the ergonomic design, the comfort of the heated leather seats, proving either that he'd lied when he pretended to know nothing about it or that he was lying now as he made up features.

As soon as she reached the house, she'd gone in, leaving him to drive around to the garage and make his own way. Army boy should have no problems with that. Unfortunately.

She sat in front of her dresser and brushed out her hair. Apparently, the hundred strokes a night that Maria, her live-in nanny for the first ten years of her life, had insisted on had been disproved as doing any real good, but sometimes it was just so therapeutic. Lexie caught her flushed reflection in the mirror and made herself take a deep, slow breath.

If only it had been Adam who'd come for her, this mess wouldn't be unraveling in her hands. She'd be the woman she was supposed to be. She would have stayed by his side for the dinner. She would have stayed in for the night. She would have had nothing to do with Rafe.

Twenty-seven, twenty-eight. Of all people, why Rafe? *Twenty- nine, thirty.* Why had he come to that same nightclub? Why had he recognized her? And more important, why did she let him make her feel so inept and inadequate and infuriated? "The arrogant, inconsiderate, hypocritical, condescending…prude."

A shape moved in the mirror behind her and she whirled to face it, her hairbrush raised. Rafe stood a few feet away, eyeing her choice of weapon with scarcely concealed amusement. "I did knock. You were talking so loudly you didn't hear me." She lowered the brush, turned back to the mirror and started brushing again. *Thirty-one, thirty-two.*

"I've definitely had arrogant and inconsiderate before," he said thoughtfully, moving a little closer. "I don't *think* I've been called hypocritical or condescending, at least not to my face. But I'm absolutely positive I've never been called a prude."

Lexie studied his reflection. His white shirt lay open at the collar, revealing a vee of tanned skin and reminding her that she still wore his jacket, the too-long sleeves pushed carelessly up. Stubble darkened his jaw. Her sandals dangled from one hand, looking ridiculously flimsy in his grip. In the other hand he held her wig. Behind him, her big bed, the covers turned back, her lacy nightgown laid out, filled the background.

She dragged her gaze away from him, focusing on her own reflection and brushing her hair. "Look at what you're wearing," she said, mimicking his voice. "The people of San Philippe are very conservative, Alexia." She spoke to him in her mirror. "And the way you dance. Sounded prudish to me."

A smile, not in the least prudish, played about his lips and eyes, threatening to distract her. "So? Prudish?" She nodded. "And hypocritical?"

She held tight to her anger, wouldn't let herself be beguiled by the charm he could wield. "I've read about you on the Internet. Seen pictures." She knew about his latest, brief affair. He shifted uncomfortably, his expression clouding. "I'm practically Amish in comparison to you. And I've been to San Philippe more than once—it's not that different from here in terms of conservatism." She waited for his response.

"Finished? You don't want to expound on arrogant and inconsiderate?"

"Self-explanatory, I would have thought." She wanted to point out just how inconsiderate he'd been, making her walk, but that had kind of been her fault. Still, she was paying for it now; the soles of her feet were stinging. She'd probably have been better off keeping the four-inch heels on.

"I can accept some of your points."

Not used to the people in her life admitting mistakes, she hid her surprise.

"And you're right, not everyone in San Philippe is conservative. But I'll tell you one person who most definitely is."

She sighed and put her brush down. "Adam?"

He nodded.

"It's one of the things I like about him. It seems sweet and noble." Unlike his brother, there had never been a hint of scandal attached to Adam.

"He's noble. He's not sweet." Rafe walked closer. The description seemed to fit him just as well. There was nobility in his bearing, his aristocratic features, and nothing sweet about the hard glaze to his eyes. He stopped at her side, heat radiating from him as he lowered her wig to the dresser. It lay like a small, sleek animal. His fingers, large and blunt, traced the length of the dark hair. And for a second she recalled how those fingers had felt the time he had plunged them into her hair. How he had cradled her head for the erotic assault of his kiss. She quickly turned her eyes back to the mirror.

He dropped her shoes to the carpet. And still he stood there, making it difficult for her to breathe normally.

"We want the same thing here, Alexia." His gaze tracked to her hair, her real hair. He lifted his hand and ran his thumb and forefinger down the length of a lock before frowning, clenching his hand into a fist and lowering it to his side. "We both want to get you to San Philippe as soon as possible. And without any scandal. Don't we?"

"Yes, of course." Lexie swallowed. "Can I point out that you being in my room at 3:00 a.m. is probably not the best way to go about that?"

"Probably not."

She waited for him to move. And waited. "If you're finished, I guess you can go."

"One more thing."

Surprising her for the second time that night, even more than the first, he crouched before her and, wrapping his fingers around her ankle, picked up her foot, lifting it so he could see the sole. He ran his forefinger along the arch. "How is it?"

Ignoring the response to his touch that seemed to slither from her sole and up along her leg, Lexie swallowed. "Fine."

A corner of Rafe's mouth quirked up. "I don't suppose it is. But you'll live." He placed her foot carefully back down on the plush carpet, picked up her other foot and, after running his thumb along the sensitive underside of that one, too, placed it back beside the first.

Lexie stood as he straightened and turned to go. "Your jacket." If she got rid of that there would be no link between them from tonight.

He moved behind her. As she shrugged the jacket from her shoulders he slipped his hands beneath her hair to grasp the collar, his knuckles skimming her neck. Her eyes met his in the mirror as he drew the garment down her arms. For a second their gazes locked. It was as though he was undressing her and she was allowing it. Sudden heat suffused her, coalescing deep inside her. Lexie closed her eyes so he wouldn't be able to read her response, part confusion and part desire.

Three

Lexie paused with her cup of strong black coffee halfway to her lips as Rafe strolled onto the terrace where her mother and the dozen or so guests who'd stayed over last night had gathered for breakfast. She put her cup down and followed his progress. He was immaculate, gorgeous. Even the sun seemed to brighten with his entrance, sparkling on the nearby lake.

It shouldn't annoy her that he looked so good and so relaxed. But it did.

He approached their table. Lexie's only comfort was that the four seats were already taken. "Antonia." He smiled at her mother, a flash of white perfect teeth, warmth in his eyes. "Clayton, Jackson," he greeted the two elderly oilmen already at her table.

Finally, deliberately, his gaze found hers. "Alexia." He

dipped his head, no trace of remembrance of that other gaze, the one that had heated her very being. No wonder women fell over themselves for him, she'd thought as she'd lain in bed, sleep slowly claiming her.

"Rafe." She nodded back, found a smile in her repertoire, hoped it was both gracious and remote.

Lexie returned her attention to Clayton. But still she was aware of Rafe as he strolled to the side table where breakfast was laid out and picked up a plate. She'd expected, hoped, he would sleep in. Wasn't that what indolent playboy princes did? Except she was having a difficult time seeing him fit so neatly into that role anymore. There was something about the ease with which he'd found her in the darkness and the steel of the body she'd twice been pressed against, the uncompromising strength of the arms that had held her. Something about the standards he wanted her to uphold, and his discomfort and displeasure when she'd mentioned his scandals.

Clayton wiped his mouth with his napkin. "I'll thank you lovely ladies for your hospitality." He addressed both her and her mother.

"You're not going?" Lexie asked, appalled.

"I'm afraid so." He smiled as he pushed back his chair, flattered by her clear disappointment.

Jackson stood too. "Likewise, ma'am."

"Surely you'll have another cup of coffee." Lexie tried to keep the desperation from her voice. She wasn't ready to face Rafe again, and if there were vacant seats at her table she just knew he'd sit there.

"Love to," Clayton said, "but the doc's told me to cut

back. Thanks again." And then they were both gone, and the housekeeper, always efficient, swept in and cleared away their plates.

Lexie, atoning for her early exit from dinner, had promised her mother she'd stay till all the guests had breakfasted. Otherwise she would have been hot on Clayton's and Jackson's heels.

She looked down at her barely touched bowl of fruit salad and yogurt and began a mental countdown. *Ten, nine...* almost exactly as she hit zero the chair opposite her was drawn out. By the time she'd readied herself and looked up, Rafe was seated and watching her.

"How was your run?" her mother asked him.

He'd been for a run already? Lexie hid her surprise. She often ran in the mornings herself, but not when she'd had only a few hours' sleep. This morning she had barely dragged herself out of bed in time to dress properly for breakfast, and had done it only because it was so important to her mother. She stabbed a cube of melon in her bowl. *Who's the indolent one now?* a little voice taunted.

"Pleasant," he said in that deep, cultured voice. "You have lovely grounds, especially that wooded area that the driveway cuts through."

He was looking at her mother, but Lexie couldn't pull her gaze from him. What was he going to say next? Why bring up the scene of their midnight cat-and-mouse game? An incident that now, in the broad light of day, seemed almost surreal.

"Thank you. And you slept well last night?"

Lexie held her breath. Would he feel compelled out of

a misplaced sense of either responsibility or mischief to mention what had happened last night, how and where he'd found her? She was leaving today. She didn't need a lecture from her mother as a parting gift.

Rafe's knowing gaze met hers before transferring back to her mother. "Deeply."

But briefly, she thought, as she let her breath out on a sigh of relief and begrudging gratitude. She took aim at a strawberry with her fork. Even without going for a run, she'd managed only a few hours' sleep. In response to the thought, her jaw tensed with the beginnings of a yawn.

"I'm afraid you must find our country ways quite dull?" Antonia smiled at Rafe, and Lexie cringed. If only her mother would stop fishing for compliments.

Lexie looked up and caught the gleam in his dark eyes, and the urge to yawn disappeared. The fork stilled in her hand as she waited for his answer.

"On the contrary," he said easily, just as her mother would have expected. "Last night was fascinating. Far more interesting than I could have anticipated." Double meaning laced his words, and Lexie waited for her mother to pick up on it and probe further.

If only she would go and chat with some of the other guests. Lexie hadn't thought that after last night she could want to be alone with Rafe, but it would undoubtedly be better than this agony of trepidation.

"I'm delighted you thought so. I do have a reputation for the best dinner parties." Fortunately, her mother, while socially astute, could also be shallow. And for once Lexie found herself grateful for that fact. Her mother had no idea that Rafe could be talking about anything other than the dinner party and truly had no idea how dull the dinner had been in the first place. If people complimented her, which they always did, it was usually because of her wealth and status. She had to know that, it was how she thought, too. Her mother just couldn't quite believe it worked in reverse.

Lexie took a bite of her strawberry and forced herself to chew, pretending to concentrate on a breakfast that she was too anxious and too tired to really be interested in. She watched with something like envy and a little irritation as Rafe started on a plate of bacon and eggs.

She ate enough that it wouldn't look as if she was running from him before she pushed her bowl away a little. She was about to stand when her mother beat her to it, saying, "I really must have a word with Bill before he leaves, I've been sadly ignoring him." And then she was gone. Lexie could hardly go now, too, and leave Rafe sitting alone at the table. Gritting her teeth, she reached for her orange juice.

"Don't stay on my account, Precious," he murmured, apparently aware of her conflict. His knowing eyes watched her over the rim of his coffee cup. A hint of a grin taunted her.

Lexie folded her hands in her lap. "Thank you for not mentioning the nightclub to my mother."

He sat back a little. "You didn't seriously think I would? What you do or don't tell your mother is no concern of mine."

"Thank you anyway."

As he shrugged off her thanks his cell phone rang.

He pulled it from his pocket and, frowning, glanced at the caller ID. "Excuse me. It's my brother. I need to take it." He stood and strolled off the terrace.

What she told her mother might be no concern of his, but what he told his brother was surely an entirely different matter. She hadn't done anything to be ashamed of, but it would still be better if she was the one to mention it to Adam.

If it needed mentioning at all.

She could hear nothing of his conversation as he walked away. He passed Stanley, who stood to one side of the terrace overseeing the proceedings, and disappeared from sight behind a manicured hedge.

Grasping what was possibly her last opportunity to talk to her old friend, she picked up her coffee cup and made her way over to the butler. If she was also closer to Rafe, it was purely coincidence.

"Pleasant evening last night, miss?" he asked, a twinkle in his eye.

"Not you, too?" Stanley was the only one in the household who knew about her love of dancing and her occasional nightclub escapes.

"Meaning?"

"I got busted."

"By?" His concern showed in that single syllable.

"The Frog Prince."

The concern deepened. "He wasn't impressed?"

"Ah, no, that's not how I'd describe his reaction."

As Stanley allowed a smile, her mother's laughter reached them, and they both looked in her direction.

"Clearly, he didn't feel obliged to mention it to your mother."

"No. Thankfully. At least not yet, anyway."

"I'm sure he's the last person who would."

Stanley, too, knew of Rafe's reputation. But despite Rafe's assurances, and his own not infrequent misdemeanors, Lexie wasn't one hundred percent certain that Rafe wouldn't use his information to her detriment if he felt it served his purpose, either here or in San Philippe. "You're probably right," she said, at least partially to reassure herself.

"One other thing," Stanley said.

"Yes?"

"You might want to stop calling him the Frog Prince, if he's to become your brother-in-law."

"I know," she said on a sigh.

"You don't have to go."

Lexie looked back at the breakfast table, the assembled guests, her mother presiding over it all, and quashed her own doubts. "I know you think what I'm doing is crazy. And sometimes I think that, too, because it doesn't always make sense. But I want to go. I love San Philippe. I can't explain why, but I've always felt welcome and at home there. And of course there's Adam." Maybe he shouldn't have been last on that list.

"Dammit, Adam," Rafe's voice carried suddenly to her. "Shouldn't you be the one to do that with her?" His pacing had brought him to the other side of the topiaried hedge. She couldn't see him because the hedge made a dense screen, but it was far from soundproof. "Logically, yes, but—" He walked a little farther off. "I have a life to get back to." Lexie still heard his words, and she was fairly sure she was the topic of conversation. "I have better things to do with my time than babysitting or running your errands for you." Now she was definitely sure, and a weight settled in her stomach. "This whole situation is ludicrous." Rafe's disdain for her was clear. "I can't imagine what sort of scheming or hopelessly naive woman would—"

Stanley cleared his throat. "On the other hand," he said, talking over Rafe's voice, "the Frog Prince has a certain ring to it."

Lexie laughed, but the sound was brittle. That was the closest she'd ever heard Stanley come to criticizing anyone, and she knew he'd done it for her.

She shouldn't let anything Rafe said cut her; he was surely the last person whose approval she needed or wanted, but still, his words, and the contempt in them, had hurt. Had sullied her dream.

A few overheard words and suddenly she was questioning not just her plans, but her very nature. Scheming or naive? Was that how Rafe and perhaps Adam saw her? Could she be either of those things? She knew she was idealistic—but that didn't make her naive, did it? And she was halfway in love with Adam, and wanted to fall the rest of the way and to have him fall in love with her—did that make her scheming?

She looked again in Rafe's direction. He'd walked round the edge of the hedge. His brows were drawn together, as though in hearing her laughter he'd perhaps realized that he, too, could be heard. He turned away, and Lexie watched his departing back as, phone still pressed to his ear, he strode in the opposite direction.

With the sun beating down on him, Rafe waited by the limousine and flicked a glance at his watch. Ten minutes late. Her bags were already in the trunk of the car; it was just Precious herself who was missing. It was hot out here, and though he could wait in the relative comfort of either the house or the car, he had no desire to be cooped up any longer than he had to be. He looked again at the wide stairs to the house and finally, finally, the door opened and the butler walked out. The butler, but no Alexia. Rafe curbed his frustration. "Where is she?"

"Not in the house, sir." The butler had been well trained; his voice revealed absolutely nothing.

"Then where?"

"Most likely out riding. I checked with the stables and one of her horses is gone, though no one actually saw her leave. I'm afraid she sometimes loses track of time when she's riding."

Rafe shrugged out of his jacket and tossed it into the limo. "Show me these stables."

"You can go now." Rafe dismissed the groom who'd accompanied him this far, then urged his mount toward the woman sitting, hands linked around her knees, on a log at the shore of the lake. Behind her, a tethered bay mare cropped the grass. With the sunlight catching on her hair, she made a picture as beautiful as any he'd seen at any of the hundreds of galleries he'd opened or visited. But something about the stillness with which she held herself and the droop to her shoulders filled him with foreboding. She looked alone and weighted with worry, or sorrow…or regret?

As he'd ridden he'd been prepared to tear strips off her when he found her. But at the sight of her his anger dissipated. He'd never been any good at holding on to that particular emotion anyway. Life was for living and was too short to waste being angry.

Leaving his horse tethered near hers, he sat beside her on the log, their shoulders almost touching. He looked at her booted feet, recalled their slender vulnerability as he'd touched them last night.

"I'm sorry," she said quietly. Her fingers were so tightly interlaced they were white.

"Don't worry. This isn't the first time I've been kept waiting by a woman." Though he knew that wasn't what her heartfelt apology had been for. "The third, I think. Although both of the others were by my sister." A curtain of auburn hair, lusher even than he'd realized last night, partially obscured her face, but he caught a rewarding glimmer of a smile before it vanished. "It doesn't matter. Private jet. It's hardly going to go without us."

"I can't go."

His foreboding deepened and settled heavily in his stomach. He had to get her back to San Philippe. "Of course you can. Everything's ready. Your cases are in the car. The pilot's one of our best. Hardly ever crashes." He tucked her hair behind her ear and searched for her smile, but found nothing.

"You were right. This whole situation is ludicrous. No normal person would have agreed to it. I've just been so caught up in the dream I never really stopped to think about it."

Ahh. So she had heard that. "Alexia, I seldom take anything seriously, so you shouldn't take anything I say seriously, either." Certainly his family knew better than to do that. "You've had a crush on Adam for years, right?"

She nodded. "Since I was twelve."

"Wow." He hadn't thought it had been that long. He'd realized the night four years ago when she'd kissed him with that odd combination of passion and melting innocence, thinking he was Adam, that she'd imagined she had feelings for his brother.

"Stupid, huh?"

Privately, he agreed with the sentiment. Adam had at the time been much taken by the ambassador's daughter, a woman of sultry beauty with ten years on Alexia in age and a lifetime in sophistication. And even now, as far as Rafe could tell, his brother was agreeing to this "courtship" primarily out of a sense of duty. "You can't help what you feel."

"Although I think it might even have started when I was eight and you threw that frog in my lap, and Adam caught it and took it away."

Rafe smiled. "Arthur."

"Arthur?"

"The frog."

She turned her face to him, curious. "He was a pet?"

Fourteen years later and he could probably still tell

her a dozen facts about Arthur and his kind. She'd
certainly be more receptive to them now than she was
when she was eight, particularly given how eager she
was not to have the discussion they should be having.
"Let's get back to Adam, your knight in shining armor.
Saving the damsel in distress. Rescuing you from evil
amphibians."

"He doesn't feel anything for me."

"*Now* this is bothering you?" That earned him a
small, sheepish smile. "Give him a chance. He doesn't
know you. I think he'll like you." He didn't add that his
father had practically ordered it.

"Do you really?" She turned toward him, all ear-
nestness.

He looked at her pale, beautiful face, hair that begged
a man to sink his hands into it, a figure he could still
recall the imprint of against him.

Something of his thoughts must have shown. "I'm
talking personalities here," she added. A twinkle of
mischief lit her eyes.

She had strength and humor to go with her beauty.
"Yes, I do think he'll like you. You might even still like
him once you get to know him. But neither of you will
know unless you give yourselves a chance. You'll regret
it if you don't go. And if it doesn't work, you haven't lost
anything."

If he went back to San Philippe without her, the
blame would be laid squarely at his feet. And the likely
punishment would be fighting off his own wedding.
Heaven only knew who his father had in mind for him,

though he'd undoubtedly have someone. He hadn't asked—that would only encourage the old man.

"Except maybe a little bit of pride."

"Pride, schmide, there's more than enough of that to go round."

"I do always enjoy visiting San Philippe. It's funny, but I feel at home there, I get a kind of déjà vu, like it's where I belong. More so than here even."

"That settles it then. Let's go." He was about to stand when she stilled him with her delicate hand on his forearm.

"Thank you. I'm not usually indecisive. It helped. Talking to you."

Unaccountably aware of her touch, wanting to take that hand in his own and lift it again to his lips, he instead stood. "Don't thank me, Alexia. I'm looking out for my interests as much as yours. There'd be no end of drama if I went home without you."

"Thank you anyway. It helped."

Rafe shrugged off her gratitude. "Anytime." Unlike with Adam, people didn't often turn to him for advice. And he didn't often dispense it. Didn't want that responsibility. But if he'd helped her he was glad of it. It meant he was one step closer to getting rid of her.

She looked at him, her green eyes bright and innocent and hopeful. "My friends call me Lexie."

Sexy Lexie. The epithet slid into his head. And she was sexy, in a way she seemed totally unaware of. It was her hair and those smiling, softly parted lips. And that was without even starting on her body. For the first time he could remember, Rafe almost envied Adam.

Oh, yeah. He definitely needed to get rid of her.

Experiencing his own sense of déjà vu, Rafe waited by the limousine. She'd said she needed just twenty minutes to change and be ready. Rafe knew a woman's twenty minutes, and he was prepared to wait. He looked up at the double front doors just as Alexia—he wouldn't let himself think of her as Lexie, because he couldn't help but rhyme it with "sexy"—stepped out, the family's butler at her side. Together they descended the stairs. She was doing the boring thing again, with her hair drawn back from her face, its auburn lushness fiercely constrained. She wore a cream suit with a beige top beneath the buttoned-up jacket and a single strand of pearls around her neck.

She stopped at his side. "Let's go, then."

"Your mother?" Who knew how long she'd be or what kind of production she'd make over her daughter's leaving.

"She's at a luncheon for the Historical Society."

Who knew indeed? Apparently, no production at all, or none more than the touching speech at dinner last night. One he'd thought at the time seemed more for the benefit of the guests than Alexia herself. Rafe understood duty and commitments better than most, but he would have thought…. It didn't matter. It was no business of his.

"We said goodbye earlier," she explained, and he

wasn't sure if the explanation was for his benefit or her own.

Their driver held open the door of the dark Bentley. Rafe waited for her to get in. Instead, she turned and enveloped the butler in a fierce hug.

"Take care, miss," the man murmured.

"I will, Stanley. You, too."

"Of course."

As Alexia was planting her neat behind in the car, Stanley turned to Rafe. "Look after her. Please."

Never in his life had he been given a command by a butler, and despite the added "please" it most definitely had been a command. But the moisture in the older man's eyes persuaded Rafe to let it pass. "Of course." Given the absence of her mother, he was glad she at least had someone who seemed to care about her.

Rafe eased into the limo, picked up the newspaper that lay on the seat between them, and scanned the headlines. Alexia was silent as the car eased along the driveway, silent as they passed the wooded area he'd found her in last night, silent as the gates swung closed behind them.

Finally, he looked at her, expecting to see a resurgence of her regret, prepared, this time, to bury his nose in the paper. She was here now and couldn't back out. Instead, the look of exhilaration on her face stole his breath away. She turned and caught him staring. If anything, her wide smile broadened.

"No more second thoughts, I take it."

"If I'm going, then I'm going to enjoy it. No point doing something halfheartedly." She glanced back over her shoulder. "Besides, you have no idea of the sense of freedom those gates shutting behind me for the last time gives me."

"Clearly."

She was still smiling. "Okay, maybe you do. But still."

"You were free to come and go, weren't you?"

"Yes. More or less. It's just different. I wouldn't expect you to understand."

"It may not be my place to break it to you, but if you're expecting freedom in signing up to join a royal family, you're sadly mistaken."

"But if..."

He waited.

"If it does work out with Adam, I'll be with a wonderful man, I'll be mistress of my own house, my own life."

It didn't escape him that she'd omitted to mention she'd also be married to the heir apparent to the San Philippe throne. How much did the cachet of that role weigh with her? "I guess," he said. "But have you seen the schedule arranged for you? From memory there are banquets, state dinners, garden shows, the anniversary parade and fireworks, a christening. The list goes on and on." She'd be on the go from the minute they touched down.

"Yes. I've seen it." She shrugged. "I like to be busy."

Which reminded him of the first amendment to that schedule. "By the way. You know we're not heading straight to San Philippe?"

"Yes."

"Adam spoke to you?"

"Just after he spoke to you, I believe."

After he'd been so tactless and careless as to allow her to overhear him. "And you're...okay with that?"

"Stopping in London, or—"

"I meant the jewelry thing." Somehow, he was taking Adam's prospective fiancée jewelry shopping for the earrings Adam wanted to give her, or that Adam's advisers had suggested he give her.

"It's sweet that Adam wants me to pick something out."

Sweet. Right. "And you don't mind that—"

"What?"

"Nothing." It was none of his business.

"That he's making you do it with me?"

If Rafe wanted to give a woman jewelry, especially a woman like Alexia, he'd pick something out himself, something with emeralds that sparkled like her eyes, or amber burnished with gold, like her hair, something a little unusual, unique even. A fire opal, lit from within. "It's no skin off my nose."

"I'm sure it is. And naturally I don't want to be an imposition to you. I understand that...you've got a life to live, but other than that—" again the smile, unfettered, joyous "—I couldn't be happier. Besides, I love London."

"We won't be there long. Just a few hours."

"And then you can offload me onto Adam." She said it with such a smile that he knew she wasn't still upset by his words, though the faux pas still irked him. He was better than that. Usually. It was just this whole thing with Alexia. He wanted no part of it.

Her gaze stayed on him, innocent and curious. "Do you have a girlfriend?"

The question, coming out of the blue, caught him by surprise. "No."

"What about—"

She was about to refer to the fiasco with his ex, Delilah. "That's over. It was over from the moment I found out she was married. Unfortunately, that was the moment I read it in the papers."

"You hadn't known?"

"She and her husband were having a trial separation. She neglected to mention his existence." Rafe was still angered by her deception, and even more annoyed at himself for being taken in by it. The media had had a field day with the story. Delilah had made a killing from selling her version of events to a prominent women's magazine.

"Did you love her?"

Rafe smiled. "No. Of course not."

"Oh."

She sounded so disappointed he almost laughed. "I don't do love. I don't even do serious. In case anyone else gets to thinking it's love."

He could see disappointment in her eyes. Her kind of naivety was exactly why he preferred to date older women. Women who knew the score. She had so much to learn, and there was a good chance she was going to get hurt in the process.

And he'd been the one to talk her into it.

Four

Lexie stood staring absently out the window at the fog shrouded London skyline. The fog lent the city an ethereal beauty, but it had closed the airport, necessitating an overnight stay.

A door shutting in the adjoining room alerted her to Rafe's return. The staff in his family's London apartments closed doors soundlessly, so it had to be him. He'd disappeared while the jewelers were still with her, leaving no indication of where he'd gone or when he'd be back. One of the staff had enquired as to whether she had any preferences for dinner and she had asked him to wait awhile. She'd been going to give Rafe another five minutes and then see about dinner for just herself, because she was ravenous. And if he didn't have the decency to tell her when, or even if, he was coming back, why should she wait?

She took a deep breath. Her emotions were all over the place—she knew that—fuelled by tiredness and anxiety. Her best course of action, she'd decided, was to remain aloof from him. Tomorrow they'd be in San Philippe and she would, she was certain, see very little of him. He, after all, had a life to live. A life she was currently interrupting.

And yet, for a few minutes as they'd sat together on the log yesterday morning, she'd imagined a connection with him. She realized now he'd just been doing what he deemed necessary to get her to come with him.

She turned as he entered the room, his long stride halting abruptly. The aura of tension that had shrouded him when he'd left had diminished, but not by much. He still radiated a barely contained, frustrated energy. It was there in the tightness of his jaw and shoulders, there in the depths of his eyes.

He didn't want to be stuck here. "The fog isn't my fault," she said in her defense. And more specifically he didn't want to be stuck here with *her*.

That much was clear from the way he tensed up around her. It would have been obvious even if she hadn't heard his phone call with Adam. He was watching her now, his steady gaze unreadable and disconcerting. "I'll be just as glad as you when we're on our way again. But in the meantime it'd certainly be a lot nicer if we could find a way to get along. And I know you don't owe me anything, but I'd appreciate it if you'd at least let me know whether or not to expect you back when you go out. So I know whether or not to eat without you."

The tension around his eyes had eased as she spoke, changing into surprised amusement. "Are you done?"

Amusement hadn't been the reaction she expected, and she sighed, realizing how petulant she'd sounded. Not in the least aloof. She had to fight not to respond to that warming humor in his eyes. "Yes," she said feeling more than a little foolish.

"And are you hungry?" he asked, a half grin lifting one corner of his lips.

"Yes." Her stomach grumbled audibly, confirming her answer. "And sometimes," she admitted, "I get a little cranky when I'm hungry."

"You don't say?" He was still trying to quell his grin. "And do you like pizza?"

Just the mention of her favorite fast food had her imagining she could smell it. "I love it," she said with possibly more enthusiasm than was appropriate, given the surprise that registered on Rafe's face. "Did that dossier on me go into that much detail?"

"What? About you getting cranky when you're hungry?" He was still grinning.

"No. About the pizza."

"No. Just asking. Hoping, actually."

At that moment, a liveried servant walked into the room carrying an incongruous-looking large, flat, cardboard box in his white-gloved hands. "The usual, sir?"

Rafe nodded.

Quickly, Rafe and the servant rearranged furniture so that two of the ornate and probably priceless dining chairs were placed in front of the wide window Lexie had recently been staring out of. An ottoman was set in front of the chairs and a side table between them.

The cardboard box, linen napkins, a bottle of pinot noir and two crystal goblets were placed on the side table.

As the servant left, Lexie glanced from the box to Rafe, and her stomach grumbled again. "Is that…?" The aroma of tomato and basil permeated the air.

Rafe smiled properly, looking inordinately proud of himself. "Sure is. The uncle of a friend of mine has a place not too far from here. He makes the best pizza outside of Italy." Rafe crossed to the table and folded back the lid of the box. "It's simple, but exquisite. And we don't have time for much else."

He gave a small bow and a theatrical sweep of his arm. "Take a seat, and help yourself."

They sat, feet almost touching on the ottoman, snow-white linen napkins on their laps, and ate looking out at the glowing lights of the fog-shrouded city.

For the first time in days the tension seeped from Lexie's shoulders and her breath slowed. She didn't speak until she'd finished her second slice of pizza. "Thank you. That was divine, and just what I needed."

"I figured it's going to be banquets from here on in till the end of the anniversary celebrations and that this might be…nice."

"It was better than nice. It was perfect."

The chimes of Big Ben rang out, carrying on the night air. Lexie took a sip of the pinot noir. "What did you mean, we don't have time for much else?"

Rafe glanced at his watch as he finished a mouthful

of pizza. From an inside pocket of his blazer he pulled a slip of paper and held it out to Lexie.

"What is it?"

"Look at it and find out."

She wiped her fingertips and took the paper, eyeing both Rafe and it suspiciously.

"Tickets," she ascertained quickly, then read the print, and then read it again. "Shakespeare. At the Globe." She stood, her napkin falling to the floor, and hugged the tickets to her chest. "I can't believe it. I didn't think there'd be any chance. I never even thought to ask."

"Royalty, even foreign and relatively minor, carries a certain amount of weight."

Lexie laughed with delight. "Thank you."

"Don't. I did it for both of us. It beats staying cooped up in these apartments all evening."

There was nothing *cooped up* about the expansive suites. But maybe to a prince? "Thank you, anyway. You have no idea how thrilled I am. I studied Shakespeare."

"At Vassar. I know."

Wow. He really had read, and paid attention to, whatever background information he'd been given on her. "So you can guess what this means to me."

"What it means is that I don't have to worry about you donning a wig and climbing out the window to go clubbing."

"I didn't bring my wig." She still clutched the tickets in her hand. "I've left my clubbing days behind."

The look Rafe cast her told her clearly he didn't believe her.

"I'm going to be a model of respectability."

His gaze swept her from head to toe. And though she knew there was no fault he could find with what she wore—it was all designed for the image she needed to project, elegant and stylish—still she sensed something close to disapproval in his frowning assessment.

"So, you didn't even bring the shimmery little dress from the other night?"

"I left it behind with instructions for it to be taken to a charity shop."

"Pity."

"Are you absolutely determined to bait me?" She knew he didn't like the dress; he'd as good as told her. "If you want an argument, just say so. I'll happily give you one." She was still smiling, content and looking forward to the Shakespeare, but she meant what she said.

Something in the vehemence of her response actually seemed to please him. "Just get ready to go out, Precious. We're leaving in fifteen minutes."

As the actors took their final bow after a stunning performance of *A Midsummer Night's Dream,* a tale of love most definitely not running smoothly, Lexie sat back and sighed with pure pleasure.

She glanced at Rafe beside her in their private box. He turned to her, affecting bored indifference. She wasn't going to let him diminish her enjoyment. "That was wonderful. Amazing. Fantastic."

"Rapturous?"

"Yes."

"I'm glad you enjoyed it," he said.

"You enjoyed it, too, didn't you?" She was fairly sure the distant superiority was an act.

"Of course."

"You were laughing." She'd heard him several times throughout the performance. He had a laugh so low and deep and rich it seemed at times to wrap itself around her.

"I said I enjoyed it."

"Then what's with the grumpy act? Did you see one of your girlfriends in the audience, out with another man?"

"No. Let's just go." He stood.

Lexie was loath to leave. "Wasn't Puck fabulous? And this theater…" She looked round the wooden, open-roofed facility, a replica of the one used in Shakespeare's time that had burned down when a prop cannon misfired.

"Save it for Adam," he said, not unkindly. "He's the Shakespeare buff."

"I know. It's just one of the things we have in common."

He rolled his eyes in a most unprincely gesture. "Are you ready yet?" He held out his hand.

"It was really sweet of you to bring me here tonight, when you don't love it."

"Sweet?"

"Yes." He clearly wasn't used to being called sweet, and clearly didn't like it. She took the hand he was still holding out for her, felt his strong fingers fold around hers and, still floating from the performance, stood.

He'd averted his face, was in fact studying the audience as though there was something or someone of the utmost importance out there. He needed to loosen up. Not something she'd ever thought she'd think about Rafe. Whether he'd enjoyed the performance or not, she'd been enraptured, and she was more grateful than he could know that he'd brought her here. On impulse, Lexie leaned forward to kiss his cheek.

At that moment he turned.

For a second, maybe two or three, her lips touched his, warm and soft. And for that sublime second, or two, or three, that simplest of kisses consumed her. Stopped the world around her, stilled everything within her, and then threatened to buckle her knees as heat shot through her.

The rapture of the play was nothing compared to this.

Strong fingers wrapped around her upper arms and set her away from him.

Lifting her hands to her lips, she met his gaze, saw the mirror of her own shock in his darkened eyes. "I'm *so* sorry." She stepped back. "That was not what I meant to happen. I was aiming for your cheek." Lexie pointed at the cheek in question, as though to reinforce her statement. And still he said nothing, didn't laugh or brush off the incident. Surely he realized it *was* unintentional. "You turned." It hadn't even been entirely her fault. Beneath his unflinching scrutiny she faltered. "It was an accident. I've said I'm sorry." He didn't so much as blink. "Say something. Please."

He opened his mouth. It was several seconds before

the words came out. "I guess we're even. Let's go." He pushed aside the curtain behind them and held open the door.

Ten minutes later in the car, as their driver negotiated the London streets, Lexie stared through the window. She'd give anything for the kiss not to have happened. To not have the fact that it did happen hanging between them. Besides, it was a nothing kiss, chaste, and as she'd pointed out, accidental. He couldn't know of the strange heat it had ignited. The heat that had flared further when he'd wrapped his fingers around her arms, when for an instant she had seen fire in his eyes. Fire that she realized now was anger.

Rafe had scarcely spoken since they'd left the theater. They were nearly back at the apartments, and she didn't want the strained silence to go on any longer. He sat leaning back against the seat, as far from her as the confines of the Bentley allowed, head tipped back on the soft leather, eyes closed. But she knew he wasn't sleeping.

Lexie pivoted in her seat to face him. "We're not even."

The eyes opened halfway, the head turned slowly toward her. From beneath his hooded lids, he studied her.

"When you said we were even, were you referring to the time you kissed me at the masquerade ball?"

His response was the barest nod.

"Then I have to disagree."

The angle of his head changed. His eyes widened ever so slightly. It was enough of a reaction that she interpreted it as curiosity, or at least tacit permission to continue.

"There was no tongue in mine." His kiss had been shockingly erotic, igniting her strange, forbidden desires. She sat back in her seat.

There was a moment of surprise, and then the deep rumble of his laughter rolled through the interior of the vehicle, pleasing her inordinately. "Only because I knew who I was kissing this time."

Five

Despite telling herself to forget about it, Lexie was still troubled by that kiss as the royal jet cruised over Europe. Twice now she and Rafe had kissed. Both times accidentally. And both times, for no good reason, their kiss had left her tossing through the night, tormented by darkly erotic dreams. Dreams that took the kiss as a starting point.

Her only consolation was that if a kiss from Rafe, a man she mostly didn't like, could have that effect on her, kissing Adam was going to be knee-weakeningly devastating.

Fortunately, once they got off this plane she'd have little more to do with Rafe and the provocation of his presence. But for now, he sat a short way away from her, stretched out on a sumptuous cream leather couch and seemingly engrossed in a book. One he'd opened immediately after seating himself. The book was, she suspected, his way of avoiding her. But it also gave her leave to study him. His sentiments showed clearly as he read, occasionally frowning, sometimes almost smiling. Though she wouldn't allow herself to look properly at his lips.

He read fast, turning the pages rapidly, his deft fingers ready in anticipation of the next page moments after turning the last. He had nice hands. Was she allowed to think that about Adam's brother?

He glanced up and caught her watching him.

"Good book?" she asked, trying to cover the fact that she'd been staring.

"Yes." He tilted it up so she could see the cover of the political thriller before returning his attention back to it, clearly shutting her out.

That was a good thing. They didn't need to be chatting. Still, Lexie had to make herself look away from him. Had to stop wondering what really went on inside his head.

She'd tried reading, too, first a book and then a glossy magazine, but she couldn't even concentrate on that. She was too anxious, and it wasn't, she told herself, just because of the inadvertent kiss, because soon that memory would fade. It had to. It was in the past.

And it wasn't because of the irrelevant question prompted by his retort in the limo—that the kiss had gone no further because he'd known who he was kissing. Did that mean he didn't find her attractive? Or that he did, but knew he shouldn't?

Neither answer would be ideal.

Turning away from Rafe, she looked out her window. What ought to concern her now was the future. Her future. She should be thinking about Adam, whom she was about to meet again. Not as an eighteen-year-old, and not through the medium of e-mail, but as a woman, and in person. She was about to truly begin the next phase of her life.

A stunningly beautiful hostess removed the remnants of their lunch from the coffee table between them and informed them they were beginning their descent. Lexie only half heard her.

It remained to be seen whether she ended up staying, falling the rest of the way in love from the halfway state she'd been in for almost as long as she could remember. And convincing Adam to fall in love with her, and eventually, or maybe even soon, marry her, was another thing entirely.

But whatever happened, she'd left her old self and her old life behind.

"You'll see San Philippe to the east in a few minutes."

Rafe's voice startled her. She'd been staring out the window, but she'd scarcely been taking anything in. Far below, the cities and mountains of Europe spread out. Features of the landscape became clearer.

"You can usually catch a glimpse of the palace, as well," he said a few minutes later.

"I see it." She felt excitement rising as the jet lowered and she glimpsed distant turrets.

She would be seeing Adam again soon. She could stop thinking about Rafe.

Miniature horses dotted a field below. "Will Adam be playing polo in the cup match next weekend? Or is his rotator cuff still bothering him?" She was eager to see Adam again, but had to admit she was a little apprehensive, too.

Rafe lifted an eyebrow in enquiry. "You know about his shoulder injury?"

She shrugged. "Ten years is a long while to have... an interest in someone." She wasn't going to say the word *crush,* because it sounded so immature, but that's admittedly what her relationship—again, probably the wrong word—had started out as. "A girl can do a lot of research in that time. I can give you the whole history of it."

"Ever heard of *stalking?*"

He said the word with a bored smile, but Lexie bristled. "It's not like that." At least not anymore. She'd long ago thrown out the embarrassing scrapbook she'd kept as a young teenager, filled with photos of Adam playing polo or attending functions. "I've looked at the odd Web site." No need to give Rafe numbers. But because he was one of the world's most eligible bachelors, plenty of sites followed Adam. "And I've studied the history of San Philippe because it's part of my heritage." And because it was potentially part of her future. "I like to think of it as being well-informed."

"Uh-huh." How did he make those two syllables sound so condescending?

"We have mutual acquaintances, as well."

"Don't feel you have to justify yourself to me."

"I'm not justifying myself, I just think you should be clear on where I stand."

"I think I'm clear." He returned his attention to his book, trying to dismiss her.

She wasn't that easy to dismiss. "And I don't think you are."

He sighed and flipped over a page.

"I'm not obsessive about Adam." He should know that. "I've dated other men. I even imagined myself in love once."

That snagged his attention. He looked back at her. "And?"

She shrugged. "It didn't work out. And not because of anything to do with Adam," she added quickly. Well, not directly, although it was possible that Paul had suffered in comparison. "I've grown and matured, and become my own woman."

"I'm sure you have."

Lexie could think of no witty or even sarcastic retort so she tried for a disdainful look before turning to her window to watch her destiny draw closer, savoring the sense of anticipation as the wheels lowered into position for landing. Rafe didn't understand. She was her own woman and knew her own mind. She just hoped—and had, in fact, planned—that she was the type of woman who appealed to Adam. And his father. Because she'd have to have Prince Henri's blessing. And probably also the approval of palace advisers. And even the public of San Philippe. Which was what was sending her heart into overdrive. Despite her mother's assurances and training, she didn't know if she was cut out for that much scrutiny, for the prospect of such a public failure. What if this was a colossal mistake?

No. Time to stop the negative self-talk. She could do this.

"Talking to yourself?" She looked across to see Rafe watching her, a smile tugging at his lips.

Had she been? "No, of course not." Against her will that smile drew her own out, making it impossible to stay mad at him. "Maybe. I've just realized what a very public spectacle I could make of myself here."

"The palace will be working to keep everything low-key. It won't be too public."

"But still a spectacle?"

"That part's up to you."

The plane touched down, decelerating rapidly. She looked out the window at a waving crowd standing behind a cordoned-off area. "So that crowd out there is normal?"

"There are always a few people with nothing better to do than hang out at the airport when the royal jet flies in."

"That many?"

He followed her gaze and she saw a flash of surprise in his eyes, but he leaned back in his seat. "Give or take a few."

"Wow."

"Don't overthink things."

"What do you mean?" She thought she knew, but talking to him, listening to his deep, calm voice, his soft accent, helped distract her.

"Worrying ahead of time about what people will think or what might go wrong. You'll step off this plane, see Adam and take it from there. One moment at a time."

"Of course we'll be taking things slowly, but controlling my thoughts and anxiety is easier said than done."

"No. It's exactly as easy to say as it is to do. In fact, your thoughts are one of the few things in life you do have control over. And thinking things over and over and round and round in your head, things you can't possibly have any control over—that's not easy. It's also a hell of a waste of mental energy."

"You could be right. But I don't think you really understand."

"I know I'm right." He pulled a business card from his pocket, flipped it over and wrote on the back before handing it to her.

She looked at the cell phone number scrawled elegantly across the card.

"I may not see that much of you around the palace. That's my private number," he said on a sigh. "In case."

"In case what?"

"In case you don't know which fork to use. I don't know. Just in case. Only a couple of people have it, so if you call, I'll answer it."

"Thank you." It struck her then that with their time in Massachusetts, London and on the plane she'd now spent more consecutive time in Rafe's company than she ever had in Adam's.

"Abuse it and I'll change the number."

Lexie smiled and lapsed into silence. She looked away from the window and at the hands clasped in her lap. After agonizing over what to wear, she'd settled on a skirt and short, tailored jacket. But maybe she should have worn the shift dress. It was probably hot out there. She glanced at Rafe. He wore an open-necked white linen shirt and cream-colored pants. He looked fantastic, as if he'd just stepped off a yacht in the Mediterranean. She chewed her bottom lip.

He sighed. "What are you worried about now?"

She hadn't thought he'd been aware of her. She swallowed. "Would calling you to ask a really stupid question be considered abusing the privilege?"

"A really stupid question like what?"

"Like, do I look okay?"

His gaze swept over her. "Fine."

"What's wrong with it?"

"I said it was fine."

"I know. So what's wrong with it?"

He shook his head. "Nothing. Adam will love it. You look very…regal. Quite proper. The pearls are a great touch."

"But you don't like it?"

He lifted a shoulder. "I'm shallower than Adam. The regal look's not my thing. Give me a short, shimmery black dress anyday."

She smiled. "I hope someday you find a tramp who'll make you very happy."

He smiled back. Finally. His first real smile of the day. A smile a person could almost grow to depend upon, bringing with it a little jolt to her insides, stronger even than that first cup of coffee in the morning. "I intend to search the world over till I find her."

Stairs were wheeled to the jet and the crew opened the door.

"Right, then, Alexia, let's get this show on the road."

Rafe stood, ready to walk with her to the exit and thank the pilot and crew who stood waiting by the door. Ready to hand her over to Adam and put her from his mind. She slipped his card into her purse and stood, too. Glancing at the door, then back at him, she placed a tentative hand on his arm. "Will you call me Lexie?"

He hesitated.

"I need one person here who does."

He nodded. Reluctantly. "Lexie," he sighed her name. Her grateful smile was pure innocence, and all he could think was sexy, sexy, Lexie. What he'd like to say to her and do with her were eons away from innocence. It had been torment enough just sitting so close beside her in the theater last night. Her rapturous sighs, her delighted laughter. And then that kiss. Damn that stupid kiss, that taste of temptation, that taste of the forbidden. He hadn't been joking when he'd said the only reason there was no tongue in it was because he knew who she was. That was also the only reason he hadn't kept her in that box and gone on kissing her. They wouldn't have been disturbed. He could have slid his hands up her legs, pulled her against him. He could have— *Stop.* He had to stop this. He'd call the sophisticated and available divorcée he'd met last week as soon as he handed Lexie—Alexia, dammit—over.

There would be two cars at the airport. He and Adam seldom traveled together. It wouldn't do to have both male heirs wiped out at once in the event of either an accident or an act of terrorism. He'd be on his own at last. Away from her smile, away from her scent. Away from her hopeful, idealistic naivety.

He'd hand her to Adam, he'd see the two of them together and cement it in his mind that she belonged with his brother, her knight in shining armor. The most she could ever be to him was his sister-in-law.

Security staff escorted them to the terminal. Alexia walked close to him. There was tension in the rigid set to her shoulders, in the stiffly held neck. He wanted to take her hand, in a brotherly fashion, he tried to tell himself. Reassuring. But far too open to misinterpretation. So instead he turned to Joseph, the family's head of security. "This is quite a crowd." Because despite what he'd said to Alexia, the crowd was considerably larger than he'd expected.

"The forthcoming anniversary celebrations. There's been something of an upsurge of interest in all things royal. It's been building for some time."

Had it? He hadn't noticed.

"And of course there's the young lady herself."

She didn't turn her head, but Rafe knew she'd heard. She really would make a good royal. He asked on her behalf. "Alexia? Why?"

"The people know she's a Wyndham. They know the families are close. There's been some speculation."

Speculation that because her family once had a claim to the throne that a union now between the two families would somehow complete a circle.

Lexie did glance at him then, her face a little paler than before. He winked. "Just smile and wave, babe. Smile and wave."

She winked back, a twinkle in her moss-green eyes, then did exactly as he'd suggested. A cheer went up in the crowd along with hundreds of fluttering San Philippe flags.

Minutes later, Rafe leaned against a pillar and watched her from across the royal lounge in the terminal building. Prince Henri, looking far too pleased with himself, had formally welcomed her. Rafe had been surprised to see his father here, revealing just how much importance he was placing on this venture succeeding. Then his sister, Rebecca, had hugged her, and last but by no means least, she had turned to Adam.

And now Lexie—no, Alexia—stood talking to his older brother, pleasure shining in her face.

Adam smiled back at her, his charismatic best. Rafe could discern none of the resentment he would have felt if he was meeting a woman he'd been told he was going to marry.

Of course, Adam was better than that. He was both diplomatic and charming. It was easy to see why Alexia, Alexia, Alexia—he'd say it over to himself a hundred times if he had to—fancied herself half in love with him. He just hoped Adam valued what he was getting. Because though he could be diplomatic and charming— that was part of his job description—he could also be self-absorbed, distant and, well, boring. And though Rafe had originally thought Alexia boring, too, he'd realized the conservatism was a front. A charade, even if she believed it, for the role she wanted to play.

Rafe watched as Adam touched her arm and smiled. Alexia laughed. Demurely.

Mission accomplished. He was free to forget about her and get on with his own life. Rafe turned and slipped away.

Six

Lexie tried to concentrate. Her dinner companion, a senior San Philippe politician, his chest weighted down with medals, whose name she had already forgotten, was explaining the evolution of the country's political system. Sadly, the throbbing in her head and the complexities of the system combined to leave her floundering. The enthusiastic playing of the band wasn't helping her efforts. She could only hope that her smiles and nods at least convinced her companion that she was both following and interested in his discourse, and not secretly wondering whether it was too soon to leave. He paused to reach across the table for a profiterole.

At first the state dinner had been exciting, the long tables set with so much silver cutlery and crystal that beneath the light of the chandeliers they gleamed with

the brilliance of diamonds. Then there were the guests,
the elite and powerful of San Philippe, the beautiful
of San Philippe. But after a while it had become just
another dinner spent having to make conversation with
people she didn't know.

Which wouldn't have been so bad if it hadn't been
for her steadily worsening headache. A maid had styled
her hair. Lexie loved the elegant twist—it was perfect
for a formal dinner, but she hadn't realized quite how
tightly her hair had been pulled until the aching in her
head began.

She found herself yearning for pizza eaten in silence
while she looked out over city lights at nighttime, her
feet resting on an ottoman.

Massaging her temple, Lexie looked at the head
table, where Adam sat deep in conversation with an
elder statesman. He had explained that it would be best
for them not to be seated together tonight. No point in
adding fire to the already circulating rumors just yet.
She completely understood and agreed. Already she felt
as if she were under a microscope.

Looking around she caught sight of Rafe, farther up
her table and on the opposite side, watching her. She
couldn't fathom the expression in his dark eyes and
couldn't quite explain the effect it had on her, causing a
strange discomfort. He raised his wineglass in a mock
salute, then turned to the voluptuous, sophisticated
blonde at his side.

Lexie's companion finished his profiterole, wiped
cream from his fingers onto his linen napkin and
invited her to dance. As far as she could see, she had

no choice but to accept. Taking her arm, he escorted her to the dance floor and pulled her into a formal and rigid clasp for the waltz. Lexie looked over his shoulder to avoid staring at the droplet of cream caught in his moustache.

As they danced, he continued talking politics. Specifically, his rise through parliament, and the problems with the younger politicians who thought they knew everything. Who knew one song could last so long?

Finally, the music slowed and quieted, but then segued immediately into another melody. "By the time I was elected for my third term," he said, giving her no opportunity to decline another dance.

Rafe appeared behind his shoulder and tapped it. "Mind if I cut in, Humphrey?"

Humphrey, that was his name.

Humphrey released her, took a step back, bowed slightly, then bowed again to Rafe. "Of course not, sir." He moved aside.

Rafe stepped in front of her. His gaze swept the length of her beaded, ice-blue gown; his undisguised masculine approval warmed her. Gentle yet sure, he took her hand in his, placed his other hand at the curve of her waist. "Thank you," she said, when what she really wanted to do was hug him in sheer gratitude.

"Dancing with Humphrey after being seated next to him for the last two hours seemed a little too much to have to put up with. Even for a woman who wants to marry Adam."

"That almost sounds chivalrous. And definitely thoughtful."

"Hmm. I suppose it was," he said, sounding surprised. They danced a few steps. "Ironic, really, isn't it?"

"What is?" She rested her left hand on the broad strength of his shoulder, felt the power beneath her touch.

"That tonight you really do have a headache," he said as they began to waltz, "but don't feel you can leave."

She hadn't thought she'd given it away, or that Rafe had been watching her closely enough to notice. "My penance, I guess. Though I have to admit I was wondering about the protocol for leaving."

He grinned and said nothing further. They danced in silence, his movements altogether more fluid and easy than Humphrey's as he led her around the room. When the band next stopped, he dropped his hand from her waist and shifted to stand beside her, keeping her right hand held in his. "This way," he said. They were on the far side of the dance floor and he began leading her, not back to her seat, but in the opposite direction.

"Where are we going?"

"You want to leave, don't you?"

She hesitated. "I shouldn't."

He led her onward. "Why not? You've had a long day, and you're jet-lagged."

"Same as you."

"Which is why I'm leaving."

"Really?"

He stopped and turned to face her. "There are some

things I don't joke about. Besides, you have a headache. A real one this time."

Leave her first official dinner early? Wouldn't that be bad form? "You said yourself that I'd have to sit through these things till the bitter end."

"You will have to stay. Once you become princess."

"If."

"If. Whatever. But now? Now you have a valid excuse. Now you're under the radar, just. Now might be your only chance."

She glanced at the head table.

"Adam won't mind." He read her thoughts, and mercifully didn't add that Adam likely wouldn't notice. They'd had a lovely but brief meeting this afternoon. He had shown her round some of the palace's enormous manicured gardens, including the renowned labyrinth.

As they'd walked arm in arm in the sunshine, he had explained the gardeners' efforts at conservation of his country's native flora. He was knowledgeable and gentlemanly, and alert to her fatigue. It had been a relief to be in the company of someone easy to be with, not like Rafe, who always seemed to be watching her and whose presence filled Lexie with a strange tension.

She and Adam had parted to prepare for this evening. But throughout the meal, he had only once looked her way and had nodded—almost paternally—at her before returning to his conversation.

Rafe, on the other hand, had caught her out more than once looking at him.

"He asked me to keep an eye on you."

She smiled. "What did you say?" She couldn't imagine he would have been pleased to have his babysitting duties extended.

"I said yes."

"Just yes?"

He smiled back, real warmth in his eyes. "Of course, just yes."

"Liar."

His smile widened. "Come on, Lexie."

Escaping with Rafe held infinitely more appeal than staying. But it was his use of her name that swayed her. Reminded her that he was her friend. Because only her friends called her Lexie.

None of the staff seemed surprised to see them as they slipped through a kitchen the size of a house. She couldn't suppress a gurgle of laughter as Rafe grasped her hand to lead her around counters and past the sous-chefs and kitchen hands, most of whom seemed to be shouting at each other.

"Rupert." Rafe acknowledged the man who stood, arms folded, surveying the entire kitchen.

Rupert, impressive gray sideburns showing from beneath his chef's hat, glanced at his watch. "You lasted well tonight, sir."

"By the time I'm your age, I expect I'll be able to last a whole evening."

"I'm sure everyone looks forward to that day."

"Everyone except me," Rafe said on a smile, not breaking his stride.

"I take it you do this often?" Lexie asked.

"Since the very first state dinner I attended. Rupert

was on dishes back then. He helped me find my way out of this maze."

"Couldn't we just have gone out the doors we came in?"

"Far less attention drawn to us this way. Too many people watch the doors."

"It's only because of my headache that I'm leaving. I have a valid reason. I don't need to be sneaking about." Although, oddly, from the moment she'd decided to leave, the headache had begun to diminish.

"So if I told you about a nightclub not too far away, where they play the most amazing music?"

"I wouldn't be even remotely tempted." Though she couldn't help but wonder what it would be like to dance with Rafe. Truly dance. And to watch the way he moved. Not like their earlier formal waltz, which she now recognized as merely a part of his escape plan.

They passed through another door and stepped into an empty, dimly lit corridor. As the door swung shut behind them, the chaos and noise of the kitchen ceased. Silence swamped them. He stopped and turned to face her, blocking her way. "Liar," he said in a whisper. "You'd be tempted."

And suddenly she wasn't sure what temptation he was referring to. The temptation of dancing or the temptation of him? The memory of the kiss that shouldn't have happened came back to her, flooding her with warmth. And she remembered, too, the even earlier kiss. One that back then had hinted at things she'd only guessed at.

Lexie couldn't speak, couldn't move.

Abruptly Rafe stepped back and turned to keep walking. Lexie clenched her fists at her side. She just needed to get away from here, away from him. She needed to spend time with Adam.

They continued in silence, along corridors, past opulent room after opulent room, climbed broad, sweeping staircases, till finally he stopped in front of a door she recognized as her own.

Lexie pushed open the door and turned back to face Rafe, keeping one hand on the handle. "Thank you."

He was looking over her shoulder and she followed his gaze, saw her nightgown, green and flimsy, laid out on her turned-back bed. Then she looked in the region of Rafe's too-broad chest. "Good night."

Gentle fingers under her chin tipped her head up so that short of closing her eyes she had to meet his gaze. She couldn't interpret what she saw in his dark eyes. It was close to anger, and yet not. "Good night, Lexie." He stood close, radiating heat.

For a second neither of them moved. She felt as powerless as she had outside the kitchen, as though he somehow sapped her strength, diverted her will. In a way that was all wrong and exhilaratingly right.

All wrong. She focused on that thought. She was here to get to know Adam, not the Frog Prince. She wanted Adam to look at her with something of what was in Rafe's gaze. She wanted to feel with Adam that same yearning she felt now to lean into Rafe, to slide her arms around him.

She was lonely. That's all it was. She was away from her home, her country, and despite her years of contact with Adam, the last few days with Rafe meant it was him she knew best. It was only natural that she wanted to turn to him. Once she'd spent more time with Adam, that would change.

Her breath caught as Rafe lifted his hand to her hair. She felt quick deft movements and then her hair tumbled down around her shoulders. "Better," he murmured, and she wasn't sure whether it was a statement or a question. He ran his fingers down a lock, then lifted her hand, turned it over, uncurled her fist and dropped her clips into her palm.

"Go to bed, Lexie."

Rafe tried to concentrate on his father's words as the prince made his speech for the official opening of the anniversary-week celebrations. The proximity of the woman seated on his left between him and his brother made the task almost impossible. The woman who'd been nothing but trouble since that first day in Boston. Big trouble—no matter how placid and regal she looked in her rose-colored dress with her beautiful hair pulled up into a twist at the back of her head.

When he'd convinced her that coming here was the right thing to do, he'd thought that that would be his reprieve. Showed how wrong he was.

At least now she wasn't his problem. Her relationship with Adam was progressing. They'd spent most of the two days she'd been here together. The fact that she was seated at Adam's right was significant. Did she know that little tidbit, and what it signaled, would have the royal-watchers all aflutter and would be all over the newspapers by tomorrow morning?

She was getting her wish, her dream come true.

He'd been observing—watching and listening to Adam. His brother was solicitous toward Lexie, charming. Smiling and handsome. They looked good together. They made the perfect couple. That fact should please Rafe.

But it didn't.

He didn't know why he was so fascinated with Lexie. Possibly it was only because he couldn't have her. Couldn't *ever* have her. Maybe he needed to date even more. Find someone like her. No. Not like her. Because he didn't want serious. The problem with Lexie was that she confused him, somehow tied him up in knots, made him forget the principles that let him comfortably live his life.

Suddenly she laughed, along with the crowd, at one of his father's jokes, the sound a delight.

As soon as the speeches were done—there would be several more after this one—he was getting out of here. He needed to be somewhere, anywhere else. Maybe even a different country, if he could arrange it.

Lexie glanced at him, her face alight with her recent laughter, her eyes sparkling.

She leaned closer and started to speak.

"Lexie, listen to my father." He cut off whatever she'd been about to say.

Lush, rose-colored lips shut together.

He hadn't done it to stop her talking, although that was probably a good thing, but he'd realized his father had started telling a story about Marie, Rafe's mother, something he'd seldom done in the years since her death, preferring to keep his memories private. And he was discussing his hopes and dreams, something he never did, either, because he didn't believe in them, believing in facts and work and duty.

Henri turned to the side of the dais and Lexie's mother, Antonia, walked in, looking both serene and smug as she made her way to stand beside Rafe's father.

They both looked at Adam and Lexie. It meant only one thing. Rafe followed their gazes, saw Lexie's surprise and confusion. Adam wasn't confused, Adam knew precisely what was happening, though Rafe was guessing Adam hadn't sanctioned it because he saw the infinitesimal shake of Adam's head, the subtle glare at their father.

"We are so pleased," his father said, "to announce tonight that we have each given our permission for my son and Alexia Wyndham Jones to become engaged. And our blessing to the future joining of the Wyndham and Marconi families."

The crowd erupted in a joyous roar. Beside Rafe, Lexie gasped and stiffened. Adam grasped her hand. The gesture looked affectionate, but Rafe suspected that his brother was also keeping her in her seat, because she looked ready to flee. Over the rousing applause, he couldn't hear what Adam whispered to a suddenly pale Lexie. Flashlights burst in a prolonged bright explosion.

Just days ago on the plane Lexie had told him that

she and his brother were going to take things slowly and quietly. And he'd told her the palace would be working to keep things low-key. Clearly he'd forgotten to factor his father's desire for a royal wedding into the equation.

Good old Dad. The family motto should be changed from Honor and Valor to Make It Happen—However You Can.

As the applause died away and his father finished speaking, Rafe leaned in to Lexie, his soon-to-be sister-in-law. "Congratulations."

She turned, and for a second he saw a plea in her wide eyes. Then it was gone and she smiled, a polite, brittle smile. "Thank you."

"Didn't know this was coming?"

She kept that smile fixed in place. "I'll admit it's something of a surprise." The smile wobbled a little. "I don't... I'm not..."

She couldn't look for support from him. "You must be thrilled. You've got your wish, your happily-ever-after."

The smile firmed. "Yes. Yes, I have. But your father only said he's given his permission. We're not actually engaged."

Yet. Clearly she didn't have a complete grasp on how things worked in his father's world. Adam may not have slipped a ring on her finger, but that part was now merely a formality. His gaze dropped to her temporarily unadorned fingers where they lay curled white-knuckled in her lap. "You should unclench your hands."

Adam stood to speak and walked to the lectern to the sound of rapturous applause. "Did Adam know about Dad's permission being granted and announced tonight?" Rafe asked. Because Adam, if unchecked, could be a little like their father. Once he'd committed to a course of action he had a way of making people fall in with him. Rafe didn't want to have to intervene.

"Apparently, your father raised it as a possibility yesterday. But he'd said he didn't think it was a good idea. That we weren't ready."

"Dad being ready and the timing being right are the only things that matter."

"Anyway, it'll be easier now. Adam and I can legitimately spend more time together. I can accompany him publicly." She'd tensed up again, her shoulders rigid, as she repeated what sounded like his brother's words.

"I wish you all the best."

"Thank you." Her hands clenched back into fists.

"You do make a nice couple."

"I know."

"The photos of the two of you at the orchestra were very fetching."

"Adam says that's largely why your father announced it. The photos, the speculation."

Unfortunately, that announcement now meant that Rafe couldn't leave the country as he'd planned. His leaving might be misinterpreted, or worse, might be correctly interpreted. "Dad has the very best PR advisers guiding him," he said. "Not to mention a will of steel. He's also shrewd and wily. And he most definitely likes to stay a step ahead of the press. They have kind of a love-hate relationship. He's misled them more than once, and though they resent it, they respect him for it, too."

She smiled. "I like him. Your father."

"By and large, so do I."

She blinked her surprise.

"He also has some unlikable qualities, but we usually ignore those." His father was grinning broadly at Lexie from his seat behind the lectern. "He likes you, too. He always has. But that doesn't mean he won't use you to suit his own purposes. In the nicest possible way."

"To suit his purposes? What does it matter to him if Adam and I get engaged or not?"

Rafe felt a sudden, cold stillness within him. She didn't know. No one had told her that Adam had more or less been instructed to marry her. And rather more than less. Rafe certainly wasn't the one to break that news to her, at least not here and not now. That was a job for someone far more tactful than he. Someone who loved her and could convince her of that.

Lexie was silent for a few steps. "Anyway, I'm used to dealing with people who like to get their own way," she glanced at her mother. "And I'm not quite the pushover I seem."

"Good for you."

The hunted look left her eyes to be replaced by the strength he'd seen in the States. "This won't happen unless I'm certain it's what I want."

Good. That meant he didn't have to worry about protecting anyone from anyone. Not Adam from Lexie or Lexie from Adam. Apparently, they both knew what they wanted and how to get it.

Two mornings later, Lexie slipped through the hushed corridors of the palace. This early in the morning there was little activity, only the occasional servant walking quietly but purposefully. Other than a respectful nod, they paid her no attention, showed no reaction to her attire. The palace was old, its layout confusing, but despite a few wrong turns she made it to the basement level and the door to the private gymnasium. She needed to work off some of the confusion and uncertainty that plagued her. She'd told Rafe the engagement wouldn't happen unless she was certain it was what she wanted. The trouble was, she still wasn't certain. Adam was lovely, everything she knew him to be, and she really liked him, but...she had too many buts.

She also needed to shut out, for a time, awareness of the building public expectation. Already this morning's papers were filled with photos of her and Adam. Some commentators were even discussing possible wedding dates.

A wave of rock music hit her as she pushed open the door and stepped inside.

Only one other person was in here, long muscular legs striding powerfully on a treadmill. He glanced over his shoulder as she came in, and if he hadn't seen her she would have backed quickly out. But Rafe, the man she wanted to stop thinking about, had already punched the buttons to slow his pace. She hadn't seen him yesterday, and had been secretly glad of the reprieve. He wiped his face with a small towel, then lowered the volume on the music. "Morning."

"Morning." The word came out far too husky, on account of being the first word she'd spoken since getting up not long ago. She hung her sweatshirt from a hook next to the much bigger sweatshirt already there and turned.

He smiled. A flash of white, perfect teeth. A gleam of knowledge and amusement in his eyes. "Running, rowing, weights or stairs? Though hardly anyone ever uses the stairs. There are enough of them throughout the palace." He ran easily as he spoke, arms swinging at his sides. His gaze slid over her, took in her hair tied back into a high ponytail, dropped to her racer-back top, lowered to her Lycra shorts and her legs, which were bare except for her trainers.

Her insides tightened and heated. She cleared her throat. "Running." That was what she'd sought out the gym for. She'd wanted to be alone with her thoughts, and running usually helped her clarify things. Already she knew that Rafe's presence would make that all but impossible because he was at least half the reason her thoughts needed clarifying in the first place. Him and the reactions he stirred, sometimes irritation, sometimes companionship, but more often than not longing and desire. Those last two were not what she wanted to feel for him. She wanted to feel them for Adam. And yet when she'd had dinner with Adam last night, she'd felt… friendship and companionship. Important qualities—a good foundation. But she wanted more and didn't know whether that was unreasonable, or just too soon.

Lexie crossed to the second treadmill, a few feet from Rafe, stood on its platform and considered the array of buttons and readouts in front of her that looked like they belonged on the Starship *Enterprise*.

"Bridge to McCoy?" Rafe got off his treadmill.

She grinned. "Exactly what I was thinking." And exactly the sort of thought—so in tune with hers—that added to her confusion.

He stepped onto the stationary edge of her treadmill. "What do you want? Tell me."

Oh, boy, there was a loaded question, when this vision of masculinity stood so close, radiating heat, his tanned skin glistening with the sheen of sweat. He'd brought his water bottle over with him and tipped it to his mouth. Lexie watched the slide of his Adam's apple as he swallowed. "I like to start off slow."

He flicked her a glance that tripped her train of thought. The glance returned, his gaze held hers, a laughing question in his dark eyes, but something else, too, something deep, something light years away from amusement.

No way could she now say, *and to build to harder and faster,* which in her naivety had been the rest of her intended sentence. She cleared her throat, hoped he wouldn't notice the heat building in her face. "I thought I'd do about forty minutes, with a few hills."

He reached past her, his chest close to her shoulder, pushed a few buttons and her treadmill began to move, slowly at first, its speed gradually increasing. Her walk morphed into a jog. And still Rafe stood there. Close. Managing to smell enticing, masculine. "You're up early."

"So are you."

"Sleep well?" he asked.

"Yes," she lied. She didn't tell him of her dreams.

"It can take a while to adjust to the time difference,"

he said, apparently seeing through her lie if not the reason for it.

Rafe stepped away, then came back a few seconds later to deposit a bottle of chilled water in her bottle holder.

"Thanks."

He returned to his treadmill, brought it back up to speed. "How was dinner last night?"

"Amazing."

"Adam took you up the San Philippe tower?"

"Yes. The view over the city at night was incredible." They'd had an entire level of the revolving restaurant to themselves. "And the food was divine." The evening had been really…nice. Adam had been a little tired, and so had she. But she at least had managed to stay awake during the ride back to the palace.

Rafe pressed a button on his treadmill and ran faster. "So, the engagement's going well? Adam's living up to your expectations?"

"I like him. He's really…nice." There was that word again.

Rafe shot her a look. "Damned with faint praise."

"It wasn't faint praise. Just because no one's ever called you nice."

"Not the women I've dated, anyway."

She wondered just what they did call him. Charming? Suave? Passionate? Electric? Till it ended, because from what Adam had told her yesterday and last night, Rafe's relationships never lasted long. Things ended before they got to the stage of him bringing anyone home to "meet Dad." "And do they call you the same sorts of things after you've dumped them as they do when you're dating?"

His bark of laughter sounded loud in the gym. "No, they don't. But I'm not always the one doing the dumping."

"No. I understand that sometimes you orchestrate it so that they dump you." His theory apparently being that if he never stayed the night, and never brought a woman to his own bed, his intentions, or lack of them, were obvious. "Or they let go because they realize you really have no intention of settling down, but mostly they never wanted anything serious, either, because that's the type of woman you look for."

"My, you did do your research on the Marconi family."

"And Adam and Rebecca have both talked to me about you. I think they worry about you."

"I think they're jealous of me."

"That wasn't the feeling I got."

He ran a few more seconds before adding, "At least the women I like don't call me *nice*. And I take that omission as a compliment."

"I wouldn't. Because when I said Adam was nice I meant it as a compliment. He's considerate, and he has an understated humor that can be really funny, and we have lots in common."

"I'm thrilled to hear it." Rafe increased the volume of the music, upped his speed again, and without breaking his stride pulled his T-shirt over his head and tossed it onto the floor.

Now seemed like a good time to stop talking, stop glancing at him and focus solely on her running.

They ran in unison, Lexie finally finding her rhythm, channeling her energy into her stride. Droplets of sweat ran down her face, trickled between her breasts. She was sure it wasn't princesslike, scarcely even ladylike. Her mother had a saying about horses sweating, men perspiring, and ladies only glowing. If that was the case, she was glowing fit to light up the whole gymnasium.

At about the same time they slowed their machines to a cool-down jog and then a walk before stopping. They stretched hamstrings and calves in silence. Crossing the floor, she followed Rafe's example, dropping her towel into the wicker hamper.

"What about you, Rafe? You've never fallen in love? Never met anyone you want to settle down with?"

He laughed as he turned to lift their sweatshirts from the hooks by the door. His back and shoulders glistened. His skin would taste salty. Lexie quashed the errant thoughts about the taste of Rafe, about her lips on his skin. Thoughts that had no place in her head.

"That's like asking if I've ever met anyone I want to climb Mount Everest with," he said as he tossed her sweatshirt to her, "when I have no desire to climb Mount Everest in the first place." Finally, he pulled his sweatshirt over his head, covering the too-distracting expanse of masculine skin and muscle.

"Everyone wants to find someone to share their life with." Lexie pushed her arms into the sleeves of her sweatshirt, shrugged it onto her shoulders and turned her attention to the zip.

Rafe's eyes tracked the movement of her zipper as she pulled it up. "Why do so many people assume that?" He turned away and held open the door. "I've met mountaineers who assume everyone, even if only secretly, wants to climb Mount Everest."

She stopped in front of him, not prepared to let him so easily dismiss the conversation. "Imagine the sense of achievement and satisfaction."

"You want to summit Everest?" He studied her face, his own thoughtful and serious.

"Well, no," she admitted, trying to ignore the building heat that had nothing to do with the exertion of her run and everything to do with standing close to Rafe. This was the reaction she wanted when she was with Adam. Hard to achieve when given the opportunity of private time, like last night in the car, he fell asleep. There was nothing sleepy about Rafe: he was vitality and masculinity personified. "But just imagine." She tried to keep her own imaginings on topic. Mount Everest. They were talking about Mount Everest.

"I'd rather not. And ditto for the settling down. I'm a happy man, Lexie. Happier than most men I know. Including the married ones." There was a warning in his words, in his eyes.

"You do have a zest for life. I think it's probably what some women—" if she said "some women" she was clearly exempting herself "—find attractive." She took the steps that carried her past him. "Like the woman with the long black hair?"

Rafe frowned, a good impersonation of incomprehension. But Lexie knew better. She'd seen the two of them with her own eyes.

"I saw you. Yesterday. As Adam and I were going to dinner. He was on the phone and I was looking out the window. He'd wanted to show me the old part of the city." They'd driven over cobbled streets with ornate, gracious old buildings that came right to the street front. "You were standing on the path, and she was there, in an open doorway. She was very beautiful." Lexie had seen that much as the woman had looked smilingly, perhaps adoringly, up at Rafe before stepping aside to let him in.

Rafe's brow cleared. He studied Lexie long enough to make her uncomfortable, a smile tilting one corner of his lips. "Yes, Adelaide is beautiful," he finally said.

"That's it?"

"You want more?"

"No. It's none of my business."

"You're right. It's not. But I'll tell you this much. She's not my Everest. Not even a foothill."

"Does she know that?"

"Of course."

"I didn't mention her to Adam."

He cut her another look, but didn't respond.

Activity in the halls, particularly on the lower levels, had increased from when she'd made her way down. And this time she did draw glances. Although given that the most lingering glances were from the female staff, she was assuming they were lingering on Rafe, not on her. She didn't blame them. Her gaze wanted to linger, too. She kept it focused straight ahead.

Her steps slowed as they reached her corridor. "Apparently, all of your friends are bachelors. And when they find partners and marry, your contact generally dies off."

"Not true," he said at her side. "I have friends who are married. I must have." They stopped outside her door, Rafe silent and thinking. "Mark and Karen," he announced proudly. "They're married, they even have a baby. I'm going to become its godfather at the christening in a few days. Though it has to be said, Mark's not as much fun as he used to be. Which is what happens when people marry. They get caught up in each other. Two's company and what have you."

"Can't you see you're shutting yourself off from even the possibility of happiness?"

"Can't you see that I *am* happy?"

"Adam says you feel uncomfortable around couples. It makes you realize the emptiness of your lifestyle."

Rafe laughed. "Perhaps Adam's transferring his feelings to me, because, Precious, that's not what I feel." They were standing close. "But surely you and Adam had better things to talk about than me?" His words were low and curious and teasing. "Otherwise I'd suggest you and Adam have problems."

She didn't step back, didn't want to reveal how unsettling his proximity was. She lifted her chin. "Don't flatter yourself. Of course we talked about other things. You were one brief snippet in the whole evening." She didn't detail the other topics, affairs of state, diplomatic considerations, the upcoming anniversary celebrations. Sadly, Rafe had for Lexie been the most interesting topic of conversation. She'd tried to draw Adam out about himself, but it wasn't till she'd lain in bed that night thinking over her evening that she realized how skillfully evasive he'd been.

"Today we're going to the Royal Garden Show, and tonight we're attending the orchestra."

"You didn't suggest a nightclub? Some dancing?"

"Do you think he'd like it?" she asked, hopefully. It hadn't occurred to her. She didn't think Adam was the type.

"No. He'd hate it. Pressing crowds, loud music."

"Just like the orchestra?"

He laughed but quickly sobered. "How much of yourself are you willing to sacrifice for him?"

Lexie lifted her chin. "He's not asking me to sacrifice anything."

"Because he doesn't know you. Doesn't know that he's not meeting the real you."

"I have more than one side to my personality. He is meeting the real me. He already knows me better than you ever will."

Rafe raised his eyebrows. "Sure." Not believing her any more than she believed herself. Rafe seemed to see a part of her she didn't even acknowledge she had.

He reached past her, turned the handle of her door and pushed it open. Then he turned her with his hands on her shoulders. His voice was close to her ear, his body close behind her. "Go have a shower, Lexie. Make yourself look regal. Your prince is waiting."

Seven

There were just three of them, and too much food, left at the shady outdoor table. The scent of roses drifted on the breeze. Adam sat with his phone pressed to his ear, and though Lexie wasn't actively listening she couldn't help hearing him patiently placating whoever was on the other end.

They had spent a pleasant afternoon together yesterday. She was slowly getting used to the concept of their engagement, and she certainly felt comfortable with Adam. They talked easily about so many subjects: Shakespeare, gardening, his charities, his work with the government. And when there were silences, they were companionable. They didn't thrum with tension and anticipation. Not like—

She glanced at Rafe, the other person at the table,

leaning back easily in his chair, his meal half-eaten, watching both her and Adam. He'd come late to the lunch. A shaggy gray dog, close to the size of a small horse, lay at his side, its eyes following Rafe's every movement.

"The dog's yours?"

"I've moved on from frogs."

She met his smile, felt the curious warmth it inevitably stirred. "What's his name?"

"Duke."

"What breed?"

"Irish wolfhound."

And there was that silence again. Even with Adam beside her talking, the short distance, the width of a table between her and Rafe was filled with the tension of thoughts and words not spoken. Of mistaken touches. Why did he fascinate her so, and how did she stop it?

He lifted his glass in a silent, almost insolent, toast to her.

"I apologize, Alexia." Adam disconnected his call. "Only half a dozen people have my private number. And they only call if it's important."

He hadn't given the number to her. Not like— She cut off that thought. "It's okay, I understand. There must be incredible demands on your time."

"There are, and there always will be—" he covered her hand with his "—but they're not so important that I wouldn't rather spend my time with a beautiful woman."

He was talking about her? He meant well, but probably had no idea how rehearsed and...insincere he sounded.

Adam turned to his suddenly coughing brother and thumped him lightly on the back. He didn't see the unholy amusement dancing in Rafe's eyes.

Lexie focused on Adam. "Are you still okay for riding the palace grounds this afternoon?"

"Absolutely. I have a couple more phone calls to make first. We'll meet in an hour."

Time together, doing something she loved and that Adam had assured her he, too, enjoyed, would surely be good.

"And tonight, I've planned a dinner. It'll be just the two of us." He smiled, real warmth in his eyes. Eyes that weren't the same dark honey as Rafe's, didn't have the simmering depths or the hint of cynicism or mystery about them, or even that sporadic amusement. But nice eyes.

His phone rang again. He looked at her. "I really am sorry about this, Alexia."

"Please, it's okay. I'll go get changed."

She stood as Adam answered his call. Both men stood, as well, a courtesy she still wasn't used to. Her gaze went to Rafe's, to eyes that saw too much. His gaze was carefully neutral now.

Rafe watched his brother as he finished his third call and turned to him. "No," he said, before Adam could ask.

It didn't stop him. "Take Alexia for the ride through the grounds for me, Rafe? Please."

Rafe dipped a chunk of bread in extra-virgin olive oil, pressed from the palace's olive grove. "Take her yourself."

"I can't. You heard that phone call."

"She could walk the labyrinth." That was a nice, solitary, time-consuming activity.

"She's walked it already."

"Then get Rebecca to take her riding. They get along well. It'll be nice for both of them."

"Rebecca's spending the afternoon with Alexia's mother. Dad's in Paris. You're the only one of us even close to available. It will only take a couple of hours."

"She's here to get to know you, not me."

"We spent all yesterday together." Adam at least had the grace to sound defensive.

"Ah, yes, the inner workings of the museum, dark, dusty corridors. You really know how to show a girl a good time."

"Alexia enjoyed the museum. She has a keen interest in history. Particularly the history of San Philippe."

Alexia. Lexie. Sexy Lexie, whom he'd been doing his best to avoid without being obvious about it. Sexy Lexie, whose hair he wanted to unpin and plunge his fingers into. Whose neck he wanted to kiss. Whose laughter he wanted to hear. Whose lips— Mustn't think about that. The same mantra he'd repeated silently whenever he was in her company and too often even when he wasn't. "Are you sure she enjoyed it? She's polite. She even managed to look interested when Humphrey was haranguing her at the dinner the other night."

"He wasn't, was he?"

"He was. Which you would have known if you'd been paying attention."

"Some of us have other demands on our attention."

Rafe let the implication that he had no demands on his pass. "Which is why you should *make* the time to ride the grounds with her."

"Fine. I will. You take my place as the chair of the meeting on the Global Garden. There's an updated dossier you'll need to read. Martin can brief you, as well. It should only take an hour, two at the most, to bring you up to speed. And the meeting itself, if you keep dissent under control, will be another two. Just be careful to keep a lid firmly on the diplomatic fracas threatening to blow up in our faces. Our so-called ambassador has been treading on toes again."

"Okay, you win. I think I'll put her on Rebecca's gray mare." Martyrdom had only so much to recommend it. Though he knew he was letting himself in for an altogether different kind of torture.

Adam smiled, looking suspiciously like their father. "You don't think Specter might be a little jittery for her?"

"Lexie's a good rider. Specter will be just perfect." And if he chose the most restive of his own horses, then he'd have enough to think about other than Sexy Lexie. "But are you sure you can trust me? She's a beautiful woman."

Adam laughed. "Neither of us has ever broken the pact. You're hardly about to start now."

Years ago, it had become apparent to the young princes that many of the women they went out with just wanted to date, and possibly marry, a prince. Any prince. If it didn't work out with Adam they made up to Rafe, and vice versa. One wine-sodden evening, the brothers had made a pact to never date a woman the other had dated first. The pact had outlived any and all relationships. So far.

"Besides, she's too serious and too intellectual to interest you." It was as if they were talking about different women. Rafe saw her serious intellectual side, but he also saw the playful, impulsive woman she was, the side she hid from Adam because she didn't think it was regal enough.

"And," Adam announced with the triumph of someone playing a trump card, "she's too young for you."

Rafe just looked at his older brother.

"Spare me the look. I realize that you're closer in age to her. But unlike you, I usually date women younger than me."

"You're right." At least in theory. "But I like her, Adam. And she really wants this to work with you."

"I want it to work, too."

"Then spend some time with her."

"As soon as I can. If Dad hadn't been so hell-bent on getting this under way, it could have been properly scheduled."

Rafe stared at his brother in incomprehension. Properly scheduled? If it was scheduled, you missed the chance of seeing her dancing with her eyes closed, oblivious to the crowd around her, missed seeing her in the moonlight beneath an oak, eyes glittering in the dark, missed the illicit thrill of hearing her laughter as you ran away from a royal dinner with her, missed the surreptitious glances at her as she ran beside you in the gym, ponytail swinging, a droplet of sweat trickling down her chest between her breasts. Instead, his brother wanted to schedule things. Properly.

He studied Adam, could see his mind already weighing solutions to the impending diplomatic problem. "You will do right by her, won't you?"

Adam's eyes widened. "That's a little rich, coming from you, but yes, of course I will. I've planned a dinner for tonight. Something special. Candles, soft music. I'll propose properly, give her the engagement ring I've had made."

Rafe tamped down on a flare of something suspiciously close to jealousy. He'd never felt the emotion before, never thought he'd feel it for Adam, whose life he was only grateful he'd escaped.

"And tonight I'll stay awake for the drive home."

Rafe sat forward. "You'll what? Are you saying you—"

"Fell asleep in the limo on the way back from dinner the other night. Hey," he said with a shrug, as he took in Rafe's stunned expression. "I was tired. It had been a long day."

"You fell asleep?" How did a man fall asleep in Lexie's presence when her proximity had every sense leaping to attention?

"I won't be so tired tonight," Adam said.

Trying to banish thoughts of Adam—not tired—with Lexie, Rafe left.

* * *

Dappled sunlight filtered through the forest canopy. The wooded trail widened, allowing Rafe to urge his mount forward and draw abreast of Lexie. Duke trotted alongside them. Rafe had thought initially that staying behind her, where they wouldn't be able to talk, where he wouldn't see her smile or her green, green eyes, was the better option. But he'd quickly realized that the flare of her hips and the curve of her derriere were a different and possibly worse distraction. He shifted in his saddle.

"This meeting Adam had to go to?" the woman who might one day be his sister-in-law asked. They'd been riding for nearly an hour, and this was the first time she'd brought up Adam's absence, the first time she'd asked anything other than polite questions about the land around them and the flora and fauna of San Philippe.

Her hair was gathered into a lush ponytail that hung down her back. It swept over her shoulder blades when she turned.

"The Global Garden. Someone's bright idea for the anniversary celebrations that has not surprisingly turned into a diplomatic nightmare. Adam has been involved—albeit reluctantly—since its inception. Trust me, he'd much rather be here than there." All three of them would have been happier with that. Particularly Lexie.

"I'd have been happy to ride on my own, or to put it off. Adam has said he'll definitely be free tomorrow." She confirmed his suspicion.

She held the reins lightly in her small, deft hands. Hands a man could imagine touching him. He cleared his throat. "Rain and thunderstorms are predicted for tomorrow."

"Oh."

For a while the only sound was the soft fall of their horses' hooves on the forest floor. She sat so well on Rebecca's gray, moved so in tune with it, that horse and rider looked almost to be one. And he was torturing himself with thoughts of her, thoughts that teetered on the brink of inappropriate or occasionally slipped over that edge. Thoughts that urged him to act. The torture was exquisite and unbearable. Distance. He needed distance.

"I hope it's not too much of an interruption to your day." There was a bite to her tone.

"No," he said evenly. "I ride most days when I'm home."

"So do I," she said with a glimmer of wistfulness and no trace of acerbity.

"You're not sorry you came, are you?" Perhaps she'd go back. He couldn't fathom whether he'd be more relieved or disappointed.

"No, definitely not. I love it here. I just don't want to be in the way." She slid him a look rich with meaning.

"You're not in the way."

"I hear the frustration in your voice."

And if only she knew its real cause. "Don't assume it's because of you."

"You have other sources of frustration?"

"I have sources of frustration you wouldn't believe. Duke," he called back the dog, who had disappeared into the undergrowth.

"What would you have been doing if Adam hadn't asked you to babysit me?" The question was laced with challenge.

"You're far from a baby, Lexie." Far, far from it. "And being with you is not a chore." Except for all the work it entailed in keeping his thoughts in order.

"You're forgetting I heard you use almost exactly those words."

"I was annoyed with Adam at the time. It was nothing to do with you." Which was a lie; it was a lot to do with her, because even back then he'd known that spending time with her was a bad thing for him to do, that there was something different, almost dangerous about her and the way she affected him.

"So, what would you be doing if you weren't filling in for Adam?"

"Nothing," he said casually.

"That's funny, because I saw you in your office earlier."

"When?" He certainly hadn't seen her this morning.

She shrugged. "The middle of the morning. I was on my way back to my room and I passed your office."

"And?"

"And you were inside. At your desk. Talking on the phone and writing something down at the same time. You sounded busy." She shot him a look. "And serious and authoritative even. The glasses were a nice touch, too, very sexy in a scholarly way." She stopped speaking and frowned. "If you like that sort of thing," she added.

Rafe ignored the glasses comment; otherwise he might be tempted to ride back to the palace for a pair. It was true, though, that he'd had dozens of phone calls to make this morning. "Appearances can be deceptive. Maybe I was doodling."

"Doodling?" It was worth it to see her smile like that. "Anyway," she said, "I appreciate you taking time out for me like this."

"You or phone calls and paperwork. It wasn't a difficult choice." It also wasn't a safe choice.

"Was it for the zoo or for the children's ward at the hospital?"

He looked at her.

"I've been trying to find out a little about the work you do. All of you."

"How?"

"I've been talking to Adam's secretary, Martin. He was quite helpful. He told me about the different charities and foundations you all head or are patrons of. The list was massive. He also talked about your personal project to raise money for a hospital gymnasium. And about how you coach and sponsor the polo team you started for the children of palace staff. His son loves it, by the way."

"Martin Junior's one of the best and the keenest players. The kid's always there ahead of time, waiting. No matter how early I get there." Rafe smiled at the thought. "He's all restless energy till you seat him on a horse."

But he didn't want to be talking to this woman about

himself. Didn't want to see or appreciate the warmth of her approval.

He did what he did for his own reasons, lived by his own code as much as that was possible for someone in his position. He'd long since stopped placing importance on anyone else's good opinion. That way he didn't have to worry about disappointing others or being disappointed in return.

"I'd love to come and watch them train." There was a question in her statement.

The fact that he wanted to show her the kids, to show her how good they'd gotten, warned him against that very course of action. "Have Adam bring you along sometime."

She tried to hide her surprise at the rebuff he'd meant to be subtle.

"We each have our charities and other duties." He kept talking to soften the slight. She had to know it was for the best. Unless he was the only one fighting inappropriate thoughts and longings? "I get to choose the fun ones. Adam's duties, as next in line to the throne, tend to be more political than mine."

"He's very diplomatic, isn't he?"

"Yes. And the Global Garden is one he just can't avoid. It's too time sensitive as well as ridiculously politically sensitive. Adam knows all the intricacies and, more important, knows how to calm the waters."

"I understand that. But do you think you could try to explain it to me? In case the workings and considerations involved are the sort of thing I should understand, if, you know…"

If—when—she married Adam and became crown princess. "It's almost incomprehensible to think that it all began two years ago. But that's the way with these things."

She looked at him, her green eyes bright and curious.

"No. I can't explain it." He didn't want her hanging off his words, even if it was for the benefit of his brother. Adam could tell her himself. He could have her looking at him like that. He at least would be able to do something about it. He at least could touch that skin, taste those lips.

"Can't?" Her face clouded over.

"Don't want to." He'd done it again. Proving he wasn't half the diplomat his brother was. He was too blunt, didn't have time for couching messages carefully so that people understood what he meant without upsetting delicate sensibilities. "It's deathly boring." That was as much of a softening as he'd give her. "If you really want to know about it, ask Adam himself. He'll be thrilled that you're interested. Or Martin. I'd only bore us both."

"Maybe I want to be bored."

He hoped Adam appreciated the sacrifices she was making for him. "Maybe I don't want to be the one boring you."

The trail widened further as the forest gave way to a grassy valley. He needed to get some distance and perspective here. If he was going to have to spend time with her, then it would be on his terms.

"Come on." He urged his horse to a canter as

Duke raced ahead. Rafe heard the sound of Lexie's horse behind him, and even more rewarding, a burst of her laughter. She pulled alongside, her expression exhilarated. Surely this was better than boring her. He urged Captain on faster still, up the gentle rise. Lexie stayed by his side. At the top they reined back to a walk. For three hundred and sixty degrees around and below them the palace grounds—forest and farmland—spread out, and beyond that the country of San Philippe itself. On the rise ahead of them stood what remained of an ancient stone church. And now that he had the chance to look behind them, he saw the gathering clouds that the forest canopy had obscured.

Lexie twisted in her saddle to take in the view. "Look. You can see the castle turrets over the treetops. It's all so beautiful. Magical, almost."

So was the glow in her cheeks and eyes. Nothing boring there. "Forecast was out. It's going to rain a whole lot sooner than tomorrow."

She didn't let his pronouncement dampen her enthusiasm. "I love the rain."

She was in some faraway fantasy land. "Even when it's soaking you to your skin?"

She looked at him then. "Not so much then. Unless a warm bath is waiting."

Did she do that deliberately? Conjure up those erotic images? Though in truth, the soaked-to-the-skin one, clothes and hair plastered to her body, blouse all but see-through, was his vision alone. But the bath—the bath image—she was responsible for. He could too easily picture her stepping—bare, slender leg lifted, toes pointed—into a deep, bubble-filled bath, sinking low, letting the heated water rise up her body, over the gentle curve of hips and waist, caressing her breasts.

"Rafe?" she asked, and he got the feeling it might have been the second, if not the third time she'd spoken his name.

He cleared his throat. "Sorry, I was thinking." About you naked. Bad, unbrotherly thoughts about a woman whose only thoughts were about his brother. The twisted mess was surely some kind of divine retribution for earlier misdemeanors.

The first fat drop of rain fell on his hand. It was followed quickly by more. Lexie lifted her face up and closed her eyes, just as she had on the nightclub dance floor, drinking in the pure sensory experience. Would she do that when she made love?

"Come on, we'd better turn back."

"We could shelter in that old church over there."

He followed her gaze to the church. "No. Roof's mostly missing." In truth he didn't think sheltering there alone with Lexie was a good idea. Being alone anywhere with Lexie didn't seem like a good idea. He had to keep his distance and get her back to the palace. No matter what. She was going to dinner with Adam tonight. She wanted to marry Adam. "We're better off heading back. This will blow through quickly enough."

The rain fell more heavily. They were going to get wet. Soaked to the skin, even. It seemed the lesser of two evils.

Rafe urged his horse forward, not looking to see that she followed.

Back at the palace, Rafe led Lexie across the courtyard. Duke's nails clicked quietly on the wet cobbles as he walked beside them. Rafe was almost ready to breathe a sigh of relief. He'd done it. The ordeal was almost over.

Needing to change into dry clothes, they'd left their horses in the care of grooms. The rain had been light and brief. Partially sheltered by the forest canopy, they'd gotten wet, but not soaked. Fortunately.

Or not, depending on your perspective.

Rafe kept his gaze straight ahead as they made their way into the palace, taking a back route to their suites. The fabric of Lexie's blouse wasn't so thin that it was plastered to her body, but it clung in certain places. And it wasn't transparent…precisely. But he knew her bra was pale blue, possibly with white polka dots.

"It must have been fun growing up here," Lexie said as they started up a sweeping staircase. She ran her fingers along the carved, curving balustrade. A caress, almost.

A muted noise that Rafe couldn't quite place sounded somewhere above them. "I guess. Though I didn't always appreciate it." He looked up to the second floor. The art gallery was up there.

"Naturally. You need perspective for that. And you can't get perspective till you've lived somewhere else. Experienced somewhere different."

Like she was changing his perspective on women. Or perhaps the women he'd known before made him appreciate Lexie.

"Did you ever run away?"

"A couple of times. It was pretty difficult. The security staff kept the challenge interesting. You?"

"A few times. I used to hide in the woods. You know, the ones—"

"Yeah. I know." Those same woods he'd found her in. "My specialty was hiding within the palace."

"Really?"

"You don't believe me?"

"You just seem a little…conspicuous."

"Maybe not so conspicuous when I was ten. And parts of this palace are hundreds of years old. There are hiding places galore. Or just places to avoid notice. There's a room at the top of the south turret with views forever, and even to this day it's almost never used." He patted a gleaming suit of armour at the top of the staircase. "The armour was too hard to get into without help. And even if you managed it, you were stuck in it."

"But you tried?"

"Makes an unbelievable racket when you fall over."

Lexie laughed, but Rafe finally placed the other sound he'd been hearing coming from the gallery and growing louder. He muttered a curse.

"What?"

"Schoolchildren. Blasted anniversary. It was in this morning's briefing, but I'd forgotten. Come on." He grabbed her hand, headed along the hallway, past the stern gazes of the portraits hanging on the walls.

Lexie was laughing still. "I didn't know children scared you so much."

"It's not just the children, it's their cameras." His gaze

dipped to her breasts. "I don't think this is the look the royal brand needs right now." And no one else needed to know her bra was pale blue. With white dots.

Her gaze followed his and her eyes widened. "Oh, help. I hadn't realized." Her giggles grew louder.

Duke still at their side, they ran the last few steps to the door he wanted. Rafe reached for the handle just as he heard a high-pitched shout of "Look!" and pulled her into the room, shutting the door behind them. Lexie leaned back against the door, her slender frame shaking with laughter.

Rafe was laughing, too, as his hands slid up, gripping her arms. "Shh." They were making too much noise.

"I'm sorry," she gasped, her mirth brimming over.

His hands reached her shoulders, curved round them. She had no idea what she did to him. How hard he fought her.

"I'm trying." She laughed harder, her eyes dancing. "Really I am."

And Rafe caved in. He stepped closer and covered those laughing lips with his and absorbed her delight as he drank in the taste of her.

Lexie stilled beneath him. A strange, hesitant pause, and then she was kissing him back, swept along with him. Rafe tasted the joy of her. His hands cupped her jaw, fingers sliding into her damp hair, as his tongue learned the sweet, hot ecstasy of her mouth. He felt her growing hunger. A hunger the echo of his own. Felt the heat and fire that was pure Lexie.

It had happened like this at the masquerade ball. The

kiss gathering a life of its own, turning heat to glowing embers to blistering flames in an instant.

He'd known he desired her, but he'd denied it. What he hadn't known enough to even refute was the fathomless depth of that desire. There was no denying it now.

The final shreds of rational thought deserted him as the damp breasts that had tormented him for the last and longest twenty minutes of his life were finally pressed against his chest. The supple length of her molded and moved against him.

He closed his eyes, lost in intoxicating sensation. Hunger and need swamped him as he drowned in the feel of her. Never had anyone's mouth, anyone's body fit so perfectly against his. Never had any woman enflamed his desire as she did. His hunger had him craving. He could kiss her forever and ever and still want to go on tasting and learning her sweet perfection.

His woman. He wanted her. And no one else.

He slid his thigh between hers, felt the exquisite and needy pressure of her as she bore down on him. Rocked, just a little. He slipped his hand beneath her blouse. The cold skin of his palm touched the damp heated curve of her waist. She gasped and froze.

The hands that had been gripping his shoulders suddenly flattened and pushed.

Too late, Rafe remembered with sickening clarity precisely who he was with.

He pulled back, breathing hard. He swallowed, and for once was lost for words. What was he supposed to say? This kiss, unlike their others, had been no accident.

There had been no masks. He'd known precisely who she was as he lowered his mouth to hers.

There had been no thoughts of a peck on the cheek. He'd aimed for her lips.

Officially, only to silence her laughter. But unofficially…that had been an excuse. He'd wanted her kiss. And the instant his lips had touched hers he'd wanted everything from her. All of her.

His brother's woman.

Damn.

Her blouse had slipped from one shoulder, and through his shock he saw that the dots were in fact tiny white daisies. So innocent. A woman who wanted a fairy tale. Which made him the evil villain. He turned away from the distress in her eyes, and away from the reproach in Duke's. And realized he'd led her to a bedroom. That part at least had been unintentional. He strode past the bed to look out the window, giving himself time to gather his thoughts, giving Lexie time to right her blouse and gather her words for the verbal lashing he deserved.

The silence stretched on. Outside, a team of gardeners shoveled mulch around the rose garden. "Lexie, that shouldn't have happened. I shouldn't have done that. I'm sorry."

"So am I." Her quiet voice carried to him. Not angry as she should have been, but distressed. He turned in time to see her striding through the doorway, her blouse hanging loose and untucked at one side.

"Lexie."

She didn't turn, didn't so much as pause or even slow.

Eight

Lexie's hat did little to shade her from the sun beating down on the San Philippe anniversary parade. The cheering, flag-waving crowd, most dressed in the national colors, many in traditional costume, lined both sides of the street.

Feeling like the ultimate fraud, she made her way carefully along the open-topped, double-decker bus that crawled at a snail's pace, bringing up the rear of the parade. The bus carried the royal family and senior dignitaries and a few other guests. But not her mother, who had left early this morning after Lexie's brief conversation with her.

She'd sat beside Adam at the front of the bus for a while, but there was something she had to do, and in public seemed like the safest place.

Her gaze was on the dark head of her quarry as she slid into the empty seat beside Rafe. She hadn't seen or spoken to him since that kiss. He didn't move, though he had to know someone was there. And she figured the very fact that he didn't turn around meant he knew it was her. He just kept waving at an adoring public. Maybe it would be easier to say what she had to if he wasn't looking at her, if she wasn't reading contempt in his eyes. She took a deep breath. "I'm not leaving."

"Seat's free," he said after several seconds. "Doesn't bother me if you sit in it."

Lexie gritted her teeth and then tried again. "I meant I'm not leaving San Philippe."

Rafe glanced over his shoulder at her. "I gathered that much."

"I told Adam about…"

Rafe lifted a hand and waved at the cheering crowds. "I know," he said without looking at her. "So did I."

"He wants me to stay. And I've agreed." She leaned forward to better see his profile. And still knew no more than when she couldn't see his face. He had on his public face, the smiling, pleasant expression he wore in all his publicity shots. The shots that missed the fire and depth of his eyes, and the smile that was a mix of knowledge and temptation.

Maybe his lack of reaction to her news was for the best, because she didn't know whether she wanted him to be pleased or displeased that she wasn't leaving. She didn't, she admitted, know anything at all when it came to Rafe.

His gaze dropped to the unadorned hands in her

lap. She offered no explanation for the lack of a ring. Adam had, in fact, wanted her to have and wear his ring. Lexie hadn't been able to carry the deception that far. But for his sake, though their engagement was off, she'd agreed to stay and be seen with him for one more week. There were joint appearances, like this parade and tomorrow night's Veterans' dinner and dance, that they were committed to, that they would be expected to be seen at.

She'd also agreed to keep their...arrangement a secret. Even from his family. Even from Rafe.

After she left, the news would be released.

A cheer went up somewhere ahead of the bus. The most devoted of the public had waited hours to see this, staking out the positions lining the streets well before the parade began. And prior to the bus's appearance, they'd waited through forty-five minutes' worth of floats and bands and dancers.

Trying to get caught up in the enthusiasm of the waving crowd, and trying to look like she belonged, Lexie waved back. A proper wave, her whole arm moving, none of this sedate hand lifting and twisting of the wrist that most of the royal party thought passed for a wave.

"I fell into your trap. You made your point." She needed Rafe to at least know that she knew what he'd been up to.

"*My* trap?" For the first time he turned and looked at her properly, a frown creasing his brow.

"You said at the outset you'd be watching me, that if you thought I wasn't worthy of Adam you'd do what you could to send me packing. You were trying to prove that

I don't love Adam." In reality he'd only helped speed the decision she would have made anyway.

"We don't need to discuss it," he said sharply.

But she hadn't got to the important bit. She kept her voice low. "I just wanted to say I was sorry."

"*You're* sorry?" He stopped waving and turned to look at her again, those dark brows drawn together.

Fighting the urge to cower beneath the fierceness of his expression, Lexie instead sat straighter. "Yes. I'm apologizing for my part in it."

He shook his head and looked back out at the crowd. "Enough. The fault wasn't yours."

"The weakness was."

"The weakness was mine." He stood, towering over her before he stepped past her. "I've seen someone I need to speak to."

As he walked away, Lexie sagged back into her seat. It was over.

Rafe stood staring absently out one of the ballroom's velvet-curtained, floor-to-ceiling windows. He'd thought his trials were over. He was wrong.

He needed something to take his mind off this test. Because that's clearly what it was. His brother, called into yet another unexpected and unavoidable meeting, had enlisted him to teach Lexie the folk dance, watching him closely for his reaction as he made his request.

Things had, understandably, been strained between Adam and him since he'd kissed Lexie. Though when Rafe had fronted up to Adam about it he'd been surprised at the lack of fire in Adam's annoyance. If their situations had been reversed, he wouldn't have been anywhere near as understanding as his brother.

Of course, Adam, too, thought Rafe had planned and executed the kiss, but in Adam's case he thought it was to teach *him* a lesson. The only consensus they'd reached was in his assurance to Adam that it wouldn't happen again.

But Rafe could do nothing to stop the kiss from replaying itself in his dreams as he slept at night, the touch of her lips to his, the press of her body against his.

It might be easier if either or both Lexie and Adam looked happier. He'd been watching them since Lexie first got here, smiling and doing their best to look like a devoted couple.

Rafe had seen a few devoted couples in his time, and Adam and Lexie didn't even come close. Something wasn't right. Though fortunately the press were buying it. Today's papers had again been filled with photos of Adam and Lexie together. Just one renowned gossip columnist had hinted that she, too, thought their relationship lacked spark.

And now this.

The folk dance might to all appearances be nothing more than a quaint number, but it had its intricacies and its intimacies, and the princes and their partners had to dance it slightly differently from anyone else at the anniversary gala. Or at least that was the story Adam and Rafe had told their respective girlfriends.

And the two of them had, in their day, enjoyed teaching the dance to their dates far too much. They both knew how seductive the held eye contact, the gentle palm-to-palm touches and the story the dance invoked could be.

And now Adam wanted him to teach the dance to Alexia and Rafe had to not seduce or be seduced by her in the process. Wittingly or unwittingly.

Of course it was also possible that Adam was trying to show that he trusted them. Either way, it would still be a trial for Rafe, dancing with the sweet Lexie who was to marry his brother. A man shouldn't have to test his fiancée or his brother, but if Adam needed this, just this, then Rafe would give him that proof. And perhaps he needed it, too.

He turned as Lexie entered the ballroom. Her hair was tied up again—he preferred it that way, it didn't tempt him the way it did when it sat softly over her shoulders, begging to be touched, so that his fingers itched to know the feel of it. She wore a simple silk blouse and a skirt that skimmed the flare of her hips and floated around her calves.

Her hands—her fingers—were still unadorned. Where was Adam's ring? If she were wearing it, that would help; it would be another sign, and he needed all the signs, all the help he could get, to remind him that this woman was not for him.

But for as long as she didn't wear a ring the possible reasons for that lack would taunt and tempt him.

She walked carefully, and Rafe could see in her bearing, her erect posture, her graceful steps, the years of ballet training. He could also see her reluctance to be here with him. "I'm sorry, you have to do this," she said, looking around the cavernous ballroom. "I know you're busy."

"Don't be sorry. I'm not," he lied. No point in her feeling bad, too.

"Yes, you are."

The smile she delivered her accusation with reminded him of the Lexie he'd met that first day in Massachusetts, full of sass. And he realized that his glimpses of that woman were becoming fewer and fewer. Her fault or his?

She was right, of course, about him not wanting to do this, but not for the reasons she suspected. At least he hoped she didn't know the temptation he fought and would go on fighting with every breath he took.

He already had the music for the dance on a loop on the sound system—a flute melody that changed from jaunty to rousing to haunting as it told the story of the two lovers credited with founding the nation of San Philippe and the battles fought between and because of them.

"You know the basic steps?" he asked.

"I learned them as a child, and I found a tutorial on the Internet, but it's not the same as actually dancing it with a partner."

"It's not the same, but it's a simple dance. This won't take long."

She was standing in the center of the ballroom. Sunlight slanted in from the high windows, seeking her out, burnishing her hair. His chosen one.

Rafe banished the thought as he approached her. She stood taller and her hands flexed and clenched at her sides, as though this was some kind of test for her, too.

"And you know the story that the music and the dance tell."

"It used to be my favorite bedtime reading."

He allowed himself a secret sigh of relief. He didn't want to speak to her of the man and woman, at first distrustful of each other, who ended up as lovers meeting clandestinely against their family's wishes, and of how as their families fought, they ran away together, escaping over the Alps and journeying to this land.

"We begin the usual way." Rafe circled her while she stood still, looking straight ahead. The second time he circled her she followed him with her eyes, and the third time, as his shoulder drew level with hers, he held up his palm in a stop gesture and she did the same, touching her palm to his.

That simple touch ricocheted through him. Only, he told himself, because touching her from now on, in any way other than the most formal, was forbidden. *Sister-in-law, sister-in-law,* he repeated the mantra as they moved through the steps, Rafe instructing her, giving her pointers where necessary, keeping his touch as brief as possible.

"You've pretty much got it," he said after ten torturous minutes. "Let's run through it one more time." Just once. He could do that. *Sister-in-law, sister-in-law.* Once and then they'd leave. Then he wouldn't see her or the image of the two of them together reflected in the mirrors on the ballroom walls.

They began again. Holding eye contact they turned

together. Rafe shut down his mind. He just had to get through this. It was a simple dance. Get through it and then get out of here.

Maybe asking him to teach Lexie the dance was neither a test nor a sign of trust, but a punishment. Adam knew Rafe would let nothing happen and he wanted to rub his nose in it.

As the beat of the music changed, they lowered their arms and turned to each other, and he took both of Lexie's hands in his, leaning out, relying on each other for a full rotation. He pulled her closer and then they each stepped back out again. She moved so well, she was so in control of her body. The pale vee of skin at her neckline looked so soft. The curve of her waist, the flare of her hip so tempting. *Sister-in-law, sister-in-law.* He would not be tempted. For a second she closed her eyes, and she could have no idea how that affected him. He'd imagined her, eyes closed, moving with him in a very different way. *Sister-in-law, sister-in-law.* This had to pass. Either that or he'd have to leave the country. Maybe New York? Somewhere he could lose himself. Speculation be dammed.

"Both hands on my shoulders now. And look at me as we step to your left."

He placed his hands at the curve of her waist. Her eyes flew open again and a flush bloomed in her cheeks.

She had eyes of the deepest green. He could lose himself there if he wasn't careful. Two steps to the left. Or Vienna? He could go there. He'd always liked the Austrian capital.

Her foot caught on his as she moved right instead of

left and she stumbled. He tightened his hold reflexively, and for a breath-stealing second the length of her was pressed against him.

They jumped apart and, gazes averted, came warily back together again.

"Sorry," she said, "I wasn't thinking."

"An easy mistake. You've done perfectly otherwise."

"Thank you," she said, her voice as strained and formal as his sounded.

Then silence, except for the delicate teasing music. He could do this—dance with her and not hold her properly, dance with her and not kiss her, dance with her and not want to make love with her.

They were almost finished. Thirty seconds and he'd made it.

He twirled her out and back again so that she finished at his side within the shelter of his arm. As they made the small, courtly bow that signaled the end he sent up a prayer of thanks that this was over.

"We're done?" she asked, her relief palpable.

"Yes. The old soldiers will love you." He stepped away from her, headed for the door.

She passed by him as he held the door for her. This is where he'd say goodbye. And if he could get himself on a plane in a few hours' time, it would be best for all. But if he was leaving, then he only had these few minutes with her.

Being with her was torture, and yet it was better than being without her. And so he walked with her through the palace. Too soon they reached the door to her suite.

All he had to do now was walk away. And he would; he was strong enough for that.

He looked down at her. She was so beautiful it unnerved him. Which was why he was leaving.

A small smile, almost sad, played about her lips, but her eyes drank him in. He recognized that hunger—it was the echo of his own. "Don't look at me like that. I'm only human, Lexie."

She backed away, crossed her arms as she shook her head. "I wasn't looking at you…like that."

"Yes, you were. You want me."

Her jaw dropped open.

"It's nothing more than the truth. And if you're looking at me like that, why are you marrying my brother?" The brother who liked and respected her, but who didn't love her, not with the kind of love she deserved, the love she'd dreamed of for so many years.

She paused, didn't quite meet his gaze. "Adam is a good, kind, honorable man," she said, not quite answering his question.

"You forgot noble and sweet."

"You're right. Noble and sweet."

"And nice."

"Yes. Nice."

"So, why do you think about me?"

"I don't."

"Yes, you do. You watch me and you think about me. You think about me touching you." He lifted his hand, touched fingertips to her jaw. A tremor shivered over his skin and her eyelids fluttered closed. With a gasp, she turned her head and stepped away from his touch.

"You're the last man on earth I'd think about."

Who did she think she was fooling? Rafe took a step closer. She took another away from him, stopping as her back pressed against her door.

A sliver of air separated them, and it hummed with his need for her. "First and last, and all the ones in between."

"No." She whispered her denial through softly parted lips.

"Marrying Adam is a mistake. For you. For him." He could see the rise and fall of her breasts as she drew in shallow, ragged breaths. "Don't do it."

"No. I'm not," she whispered.

Her response didn't quite make sense, but the pull of her overwhelmed him. He was leaving. For forever if he had to. But heaven help him he was going to kiss her.

Just once more.

One kiss to prove she shouldn't marry his brother, one kiss to prove he was as depraved as the tabloids painted him.

He lowered his head, his face so close to hers that her breath caressed his lips. Whatever happened, whether he kissed her or not, he couldn't win; he would regret the decision for the rest of his life.

Lexie closed her eyes. So young. So innocent.

Calling on reserves of strength he didn't know he had, Rafe pulled away.

Her eyes flew open, locked on his for a timeless second. He tried and failed to back away. "I'm not marrying Adam." Her words rushed out. And suddenly it was her hands in his hair, pulling him down, and Lexie rising up to him, pressing her lips to his.

Her mouth fitted perfectly against his. She tasted of sweetness and sunshine. For long, exquisite moments there was just that simple joining, lips to lips and somehow soul to soul.

He broke the kiss. "Say that again." He needed the words that made sense of everything.

"I'm not marrying Adam. We broke it off." She reached for him again and her kiss was everything he needed and wanted in the world. She was his perfection.

Still kissing her, he moved with her into her room, shut the door behind them. Lexie sighed against him as she melted into him, an echo of his own surrender.

And he lost himself in her kiss.

Thought deserted him, overwhelmed by sensation.

"When?" he finally asked, minutes later.

"After I kissed you the last time. I knew then that—"

He pulled her against him, hip-to-hip, her yielding softness against his hardness. His hands desperately learning her shape, sliding beneath the silk of her blouse, touching heated skin smoother than the silk, tracing her contours, the flare of her hips, the curve of her waist, filling himself with the feel of her, her taste, her scent. Imprinting her against him, within him.

Her tongue danced with his, an erotic twining as they each teased and explored. Nothing sweet, all heated desire. He cupped the soft weight of her breast, his thumb caressing the lace-covered nipple.

"Why?" He heard his own doubt. Felt his desperation.

She hesitated. "Because I don't love him. I can't love him. Not the way I want to."

Could it be the insanity telling him he heard the words he needed to hear? The relentless grip of his ungovernable need for her? He undid the top button of her blouse.

"He was very gracious about it."

Showed what a fool his brother could be.

"I think he was secretly relieved."

Not half as relieved as Rafe was. He undid the second delicate button. "Why are you still here?"

"For Adam."

He frowned, his fingers stilling on the third button. "You do still have feelings for him?"

"No. I told him I'd stay and attend any engagements I'm expected at. If I left so soon it wouldn't look good. There would be all sorts of speculation. I leave after the christening."

Rafe's hands resumed their exploring.

"It turns out he was mainly going through with this to please your father and the country. Apparently, a wedding, any royal wedding, will be good for the country's morale. Funny how no one thought to mention that to me."

"You're not angry with him?"

She shrugged and he felt the movement beneath his fingertips. "I was hardly in a position to take the moral high ground."

He undid the fourth and final button and, with a

profound sense of achievement and victory, pushed apart the sides of her blouse, revealing a strip of creamy skin and partially uncovering the swell of lace-covered breasts.

His breath caught in his throat.

He arranged the blouse to his liking and traced a finger along the edge of the lace. "Why didn't you tell me sooner?"

"Because I didn't want this to happen."

He paused. "Why are you telling me now?"

"Because now…now I want this to happen. I can't bear it any longer. The wanting you. I didn't break up with him because of you. We're supposed to be keeping it a secret, but…"

He didn't need buts. She wasn't engaged to his brother, and the realization filled him with euphoria, swamped any other thought.

He cupped her sweet face in his hands and kissed her again. He could no more have stopped himself than he could from taking his next breath. He wanted to know her, every inch of her.

She wasn't marrying Adam. She didn't love his brother. His brother didn't love her. That was all he needed to know.

Wrapping his arms around her, he held her to him, drowning in the sensation of her, in the shape of her and how she fit against him, body and mouth and soul.

Her hands slid from his shoulders to his head, her fingers threading through his hair, her touch becoming fevered.

He kissed her lips, her eyes, her jaw, her throat. His

hands learned the exquisite shape of her body as he led her to the broad bed in the center of the room. He eased the sides of her blouse farther open, kissed her breast above the lace of her bra, moved lower till his lips covered the nipple beneath the lace.

Sweet Lexie arched into him.

He pushed her blouse from her shoulders. Her skin was so pale, so beautiful. He found the single button at the back of her skirt, a short zip, and the fabric slithered to the floor. She stood before him in delicate scraps of lace and her shoes.

Almost perfect.

He unpinned her hair, let it cascade over his hands as it came loose. He undid the clasp of her bra and her breasts spilled free. He tossed the lace aside and then drew her panties down her legs. Breathless, he looked at her, his fantasy complete.

Now she was perfect.

And Rafe was both honored and humbled.

Her lips curved into a slow, sensuous smile. With just a touch of hesitancy she reached for his belt. Urgency replaced the hesitancy as she worked the buckle and then the button and zipper behind it.

He pulled his top off, stepped out of his shoes and the pants she'd pushed down his legs. He held himself still while those pale, delicate hands of hers explored his torso, lighting sparks with her curious, reverent touch.

Demure Lexie was his siren. Bold, beautiful. Smiling. Her hair whispering over her shoulders.

He could bear it no longer. He scooped her up and lowered her down onto the bed. Where he'd wanted this woman from the moment he saw her dancing in the nightclub. He raised her arms above her head, captured her wrists in one hand so that his other was free to caress and slide and cover and tease. And to claim. Every inch. Sliding his hand up one pale thigh to her apex, he covered her and she arched into his hand. She closed her eyes, as he'd imagined, as he'd dreamed.

He found her center and took delight in her pleasure and her growing need till her head swung from side to side, her breathing ragged.

The only thing he wanted was to give her pleasure.

He covered her lips again with his and moved his body over hers. She parted beneath him, welcomed him as he slid slowly into the depth of her, sheathing himself in her heat. She opened her eyes then, and her gaze locked on his as he began to move within her.

Slowly. He should take it slowly, but she moved beneath him, urging him faster, her hips rising to meet his thrusts, the hands he'd freed now clasping his hips, pulling him in deeper.

Little moans and mewls of pleasure escaped her, driving him out of his mind with need for her. Along with the spiraling need, a rhythm that was theirs alone grew and hastened. All the world narrowed down to this one joining. Her with him.

As she cried out his name, he lost himself in her.

Afterward, she lay within the circle of his arms, her hair auburn and beautiful spilling over the pillow, across his shoulder, its faint floral scent teasing his senses. As Rafe watched her, a strange sense of bliss settled over him.

Nine

Lexie stood between Adam and Rebecca in the royal enclosure, trying to enjoy the anniversary fireworks display. As per their arrangement, she'd stayed at Adam's side through yet another formal dinner and for the last half hour out here. And still she'd been constantly aware of Rafe.

Rafe, whom she'd slept with.

She watched a series of starbursts of color and noise. As dandelions blossomed in the night sky, she heard the oohs and ahhs of the gathered crowd. But from the corner of her eye she watched Rafe. More riveting than the fireworks.

Among the royal guests were the young teens from Rafe's polo team, whom he'd promised this treat to if they won their last match. They had. Convincingly.

He was great with the kids and they clearly idolized him, the boys and girls alike. They listened avidly to what he said and tried hard to impress him. And he seemed to give them just the right amount of attention and encouragement back. Not too much, not too little. For someone who didn't want a relationship, he'd make a great dad. And that was not a thought she should be having.

As he crouched to speak with an older man in a wheelchair, her thoughts began to wander.

She hadn't seen him since she'd left her bed yesterday afternoon to shower.

Sanity had returned after the desperation of their lovemaking. They'd agreed, as they'd lain together, legs entwined, Rafe stroking her hair, touching her face, that it couldn't be allowed to happen again. That, in fact, they'd pretend that it had never happened in the first place.

It was the only sensible course of action. No matter how hollow the decision had made her feel.

A failed engagement with Adam was bad enough. A relationship with Rafe, the Playboy Prince, even if it never became public, could only be catastrophic, on so many levels.

He'd been gone by the time she came back out from her shower. Today she'd had back-to-back engagements. Mostly with Adam. During all of which she had thought about Rafe.

And missed him.

Rafe, who'd made no attempt to contact her. She knew he wouldn't, because they'd agreed that was best.

And the fact that she'd wanted him to only made her a fool.

She'd half hoped, as she gave herself to him, that he would be a disappointment. Because there was no future in a relationship with Rafe. They wanted different things.

But he hadn't been a disappointment. He'd been a revelation. An insanity. Ecstasy and bliss. He'd been overwhelming passion. Infinitely more than her meager imagination had conjured.

"How are things going with Adam?" Rebecca asked.

"Fine," she said hesitantly. Not wanting to discuss Adam with Rebecca. Not wanting to carry the deception any further than she had to. "Who's Rafe talking to?"

Rebecca followed her gaze and smiled. "Malcolm. He was our head groundsman for decades. Such a lovely man. It's so hard to see him like this. He and Rafe had a really special bond. Rafe was so active, always needing to be doing something, and Malcolm had the patience to teach him practical skills as well as a love of the outdoors to share. It all started with the tadpoles and frogs he used to find for Rafe in the lily pond."

Lexie smiled at the thought. "I used to call Rafe the Frog Prince. Ever since that time I was eight and he threw a frog at me."

Rebecca laughed. "Rafe went through such a phase with them. And turtles. That particular frog was one of the last generation in a long line of frogs he'd had since he was a little kid. He even had a name for it. Arnold or something."

"Arthur."

"That's it. Dad had told us to think of something nice for you on that visit. That frog was the best Rafe could think of. He wanted to show it to you. Thought that an eight-year-old girl would have been as interested as he'd been when he was eight. Adam and I tried to tell him it wasn't the thing, but he wasn't having it. Then Adam knocked him and it fell into your lap."

"Adam knocked him? I thought Rafe threw it."

Rebecca was still smiling. "I remember the pandemonium. Us all on our hands and knees searching for it. Dad had a fit. Rafe had to put it out in the pond after that. In fact, he was banned from frogs thereafter."

Lexie had to rewrite the entire incident in her head. Her Frog Prince. It had been a small thing, but pivotal in her admiration of Adam and her dislike of Rafe. For an eight-year-old, she'd been able to hold a powerful grudge.

And she'd had it all wrong.

He hadn't been trying to torment her. He should have been the one with the grudge. Because of her, he'd lost his pet. Though she couldn't help thinking Duke was a vast improvement.

Rebecca looked back in Rafe's direction. "It's so nice that Adelaide, Malcolm's granddaughter, is home for the summer now, to help look after him. She got back just a couple of days ago."

Lexie looked at the woman behind Malcolm. She was the same woman she'd seen Rafe talking to in a doorway just a few nights ago. Her heart sank. This was the woman she'd more or less implied he was having an illicit relationship with. Adelaide lifted her sunglasses from her eyes and Lexie realized just how young she was, still a teenager. A handsome youth approached and slung his arm around Adelaide's shoulders and the girl blushed. And Lexie was racked with yet more guilt. She'd all but accused Rafe of having an affair with the young woman, thinking herself worldly as she did so. She was as bad as the tabloids. And Rafe had done almost nothing to defend himself or correct her assumption. He'd said there was nothing going on and she hadn't believed him.

She'd done him such a disservice, thinking the worst of him, believing his tabloid reputation when she should have known better. There was so much more to him than the picture the press liked to paint of him. He let people believe the worst of him, when clearly he was so much better than that.

And here in public, with camera lenses trained on the whole royal party, she couldn't go to him and apologize. Nor could she go to him in private. The risk there was entirely different and far graver.

She couldn't go to him at all. It was her only option.

Lexie looked in horror from the newspapers spread out on her bed, to the card in her hand, to the phone beside her and then back to the papers.

Staying away from Rafe was not an option now. She had to do this. Taking a deep breath, she reached for the phone and slowly dialed the number.

Three rings. It was too early to be calling. But she

couldn't leave it and risk missing him. Four rings. One more and she'd hang up.

"Rafe." A single rough syllable.

Her throat dried up.

"Who's there?" he asked, a little more gently, but still with a husky, sleep-filled inflection. "Lex?"

"I'm sorry. I didn't mean to wake you. I can call again later." She tried not to recall the image of him sprawled and slumberous in this very bed.

"I'm awake now. What's wrong?"

"Aside from the fact that we slept together?" She looked again at the pictures in the papers.

Silence.

"Can I see you? It's the papers."

"To which you should pay no attention."

"Please? You should see this. I don't know what to do about it. I mean, I know I have to tell Adam, but I thought you should see it first. That was all."

A ray of sunlight slanted through her window, highlighting the very picture she needed to show him. Outside, she heard the notes of the mockingbird whose bachelor's song had disrupted her sleep throughout the night.

"You know where my office is?"

"Yes." His office was relatively neutral territory, nice and official, not tempting.

"Can you be there in twenty minutes?"

"Yes. Thank you."

When she got there, she waited outside the door to Rafe's office and forced herself to stand still. She'd pulled on the first clothes to hand, jeans and a white blouse, and come straight here. She was at least five minutes early, undoubtedly a mistake because now she was loitering in the corridor where any of the staff or family, if they were up, could see her and wonder what she was doing, why she was waiting for Rafe. Had gossip already spread through the castle? As far as she knew no one had seen them, but…

She clutched this morning's San Philippe paper and yesterday's American paper in her hands. Both had been delivered early to her room, as they had been every day she'd been here. The first had caused her to spill her coffee, the second to forget her coffee altogether. She'd only looked at each once before quickly closing them. And she hadn't yet dared check the Internet.

Her first panicked impulse had been to call Rafe. Not only because her predicament involved him, but because he'd know what to do. He'd dealt with scandals before, and for the first time she could see some benefit in that.

And like her, he didn't want his brother to be hurt.

She was on the verge of walking away, planning to come back shortly, when Rafe strode down the corridor. His hair was damp, and his white linen shirt revealed a vee of tanned skin. He wore black jeans and he looked masculine and earthy. The sort of man her mother had warned her about. She should have listened. But more important, she told herself, he looked calm and capable. Some of her anxiety eased. She'd made the right decision. He'd know what to do, how she should handle this.

"Lex," he said by way of a greeting. She wasn't sure

whether she imagined the same longing in his voice that she was unable to quell. For all the lectures she'd given herself, she still thought about him, dreamed about him.

His gaze traveled leisurely over her, and she had to hide the physical reaction, the leap of her pulse, that his presence inevitably caused. His eyes seemed to linger on her hair, which because of her distraction still lay loose around her shoulders. A frown creased Rafe's brow and he swallowed. Clearly she should have taken the time to put it up. She remembered too well how much he loved her hair, how he had run his fingers through it, arranged it over her shoulders, her chest.

"I'm sorry about this," she said, clutching the papers tighter. "I didn't want to bother you. I just didn't know who else to ask for advice. And you did give me your phone number and say to call. This isn't about a fork or anything, but it concerns you, too."

He turned from her and tapped a code into the keypad by the door. After pushing it open he stood aside for her to enter. "You can call me anytime, Lex. You don't need to apologize."

She stepped past him. She'd seen his office once before, a glance as she'd passed by, but she hadn't had a good look at it, partly because her attention had been caught by the man who'd occupied it.

She looked now. It was a beautiful room, dominated by a massive, intricately carved desk, its surface clear of anything. The paperwork that had covered it the time she'd seen him in here working was nowhere in sight.

The walls were lined with floor-to-ceiling book-filled shelves. Plush carpet cushioned her footsteps as she crossed to the window she knew to be bulletproof. A view over the palace grounds and beyond to the rolling farmland and forest greeted her. And in the distance, golden sunlight bathed mountaintops still capped with snow.

"How bad is this situation?" he asked. "Do I need to close the door?"

Lexie turned at the reluctance in his voice. He still stood by the door, watching her. She hesitated. "No. I don't think so." A closed door would be bad. That would suggest she—they—had something to hide. And it could also too easily lead to temptation.

"Sit down—" he gestured to one of the leather chairs in front of his desk "—and tell me what's wrong."

As he spoke he crossed to his desk and sat behind it. He looked remote and strained, not the friend she'd thought she had in him. But remote was good. Remote worked for her. She could have friendship with Adam and Rebecca. For now all she needed was to let Rafe know what had happened and get his opinion and his advice.

She'd be gone from here soon. He, on the other hand, would have to stay and deal with the fallout. Lexie put the newspapers on the desk. He smoothed out the creases her clutching had caused. And she remembered those hands on her body. To distract herself, she turned over the first page of the San Philippe Times. Rafe raised his eyes to hers briefly before scanning the page before him.

It was covered almost entirely in the story of her

supposed engagement to Adam. There was one picture of her unadorned left hand and some speculation as to the possible reason for the delay in the appearance of a ring.

"This was expected," he said. "There'll be more when the news that you're going home—permanently—breaks, but then that, too, will pass. Something bigger always eventually comes along."

As bothered as she was by all the talk of an engagement that no longer existed, that wasn't why she was here. "Bottom right photo. The one of you."

His gaze tracked to the photo in question.

"And...me. Together." It had been taken in the nightclub in Boston. And it looked like he was holding her to him. His lips were close to her ear. It looked intimate. Nothing like what had really been happening. Although Lexie clearly recalled how it had felt, how even then her brain had fired off frantic warning signals that she hadn't fully understood about the unfortunate chemistry Rafe caused to spark into life.

"And could an engagement be in the offing for our other prince?" he read the caption aloud. The small piece went on to answer its own question, speculating that this was just the latest dalliance for a man with more than his share of oats to sow. It asked when the second prince was going to grow up and settle down. It listed Rafe's previous girlfriends and then went on to wonder at the identity of the mystery woman.

A tap sounded at the door and it opened slightly. Rafe nodded for a woman in the palace staff uniform, carrying a silver tray with two coffees, to come in.

He waited till she'd left again. "I didn't know whether you'd had time for your coffee."

"I started one, but I spilt it." She pointed out the stain on the second paper.

Rafe passed her the coffee, made just how she liked it.

"Thank you."

He sat and leaned back in his chair, swiveling to look out the window as he sipped his own coffee.

"What should we do?"

He took his time answering. "I know I said I didn't think that picture would make it to the papers, and clearly I was wrong. But I really don't think anyone's going to recognize you. Your face is largely obscured, and you really didn't look like you. I only recognized you that night because I was there. Looking at this—" he tapped the paper "—if I didn't know it was you, I wouldn't guess it. You're safe."

"But you?"

His frown deepened.

"They've got it all wrong, suggesting it was something it's not. They're tarnishing your reputation, and bringing up all your earlier girlfriends."

"Tarnishing my reputation?" He sat back in his chair and laughed. "My reputation is so blackened a little tarnish isn't going to show. And as for *all* my other girlfriends—" he glanced back at the list "—I'd scarcely have had time for even half of the women mentioned."

"It doesn't make you angry?"

"Why waste the emotion on something I can't change?

Like I said, some other news will come along and this will be forgotten."

"What about Adam and your father?"

"What about them?"

"I thought maybe if I explained it to them?"

Rafe smiled. "To save my reputation?"

"Well, yes." It sounded silly.

The smile softened, and a curious expression lit his eyes. "No," he said slowly. "All you'd do is damage your own. And for no good reason. We both know what that was and wasn't."

She couldn't figure him out. "Why do you let people think the worst of you? You did it with Adelaide and the frog and you're doing it now."

"The frog?"

"Arthur. Back when I was eight. I thought you threw him at me. That Adam had rescued me. I was so upset with you about it, and I'm sorry."

"Lex, it was fourteen years ago. It doesn't matter."

"It must have mattered then."

"Even if it did, it certainly doesn't now."

"I used to call you the Frog Prince."

He laughed, that rumble that started in his chest. "So that's why you kissed me. To see if I'd turn into a prince."

She laughed, too. "Like you weren't already one to start with." Though it really had taken her a while to see that. "I'm sorry, anyway."

"For what?"

"For believing the worst of you."

His smile was gentle. "You're too sweet for this life,

Lex. If you let what other people think get to you they'll hurt you even if they don't mean to."

Just like she cared what he thought about her, and was doubtless going to be hurt by him even though he wouldn't mean to?

Holding her gaze, he folded the paper and pushed it across the desk toward her.

Uncomfortable under his scrutiny, she felt sillier than ever. "So I should just say nothing?"

"'No comment,' particularly when you haven't even been asked for one, is your greatest friend. But the pictures aren't the real question."

She wasn't going to ask.

"Us," he said.

Lexie couldn't hold his gaze for fear of what she might reveal, so she looked out the window at the bright morning. For a moment she let herself entertain thoughts of the possible answers, possible outcomes. But in the end she gave the only answer she could. "Same strategy as for the pictures," she said, pretending nonchalance. That's what he'd want from her. No drama. "Ignore it. I'll be gone soon and we won't even have to see each other. There is no us. That's what we agreed."

"And that's still how you want to play it?"

He gave no hint of the sentiment behind the neutral question, but she was guessing relief. "Unless you can think of a better way that doesn't involve hurting anyone."

"You mean Adam?"

And her. But she didn't say that. "It's going to be bad enough when news of the broken engagement gets out. Can you imagine if anyone gets wind that you and I…"

"That we what?"

He was going to make her say it. "That we slept together."

"Is that all it was?"

What was he playing at? "Of course that's all it was. Just something we apparently needed to get out of our systems."

"And did you? Get me out of your system?"

"Yes." She might be a liar, but she wasn't a fool. And if she admitted that sleeping with Rafe had done nothing to get him out of her system, rather had only shown her a deep pleasure and ecstasy she hadn't known existed, that even now the needy physical part of her wanted him, wanted him just to hold her even, then he'd feel obliged to gently point out that they could never have a future.

She'd save them both that excruciating exchange.

This was the only way to play it. The only way to emerge unscathed.

As dawn began to win out over darkness, Lexie got up. It was no hardship when, after the nightmare yesterday had turned into, she hadn't been sleeping anyway. She made her way through the maze of palace corridors, passing only a handful of quietly observant staff members whose expressions revealed nothing of what they thought, what they knew.

Outside, she took the path through the dew-covered rose gardens, too preoccupied to stop and smell them. The path led her, eventually, to the labyrinth.

A place of meditation and thought. A place to seek answers. She'd walked it once already a few days earlier. That time had been out of curiosity. This time she felt the need for its reputed calming and problem-solving benefits—the labyrinth's famed metaphorical journey within.

She watched the path as she entered the circling waist-high hedges of the labyrinth and listened to the quiet crunch of her own footsteps on the gravel. After the first quarter circle the path turned back on itself and then took her deceptively toward the center. It was only then that she looked up at the spreading oak tree there.

Still and watching her from the bench that encircled the tree sat Rafe. Lexie didn't so much as break her stride and she certainly didn't turn and leave, much as she suddenly wanted to. Instead, she kept putting one foot in front of the other, following the path. She had to keep passing and re-passing in front of his line of sight, near to him and then far. She didn't look to see whether he was watching her, but he was. She didn't need to look to know it. She could feel it.

With all the turning back and circling, it took her a strangely long time to reach him, and then there was nothing else to do but sit beside him. Duke lay at his feet and lifted his head as she sat. "I didn't realize you were here when I started."

"That much was obvious from the doe-in-the-headlights look in your eyes when you first saw me." She heard the smile in his voice.

"I don't want to interrupt this time for you."

"You're no interruption, Lex." Did he know he was the only one who called her that? He reached for one of the hands curled into fists on her lap, straightened her fingers and then enfolded her hand in his.

The sight and sensation of their joined hands pierced something within her. As she made to extricate her hand, his grip tightened. "I thought we weren't going to..."

"What? Hold hands? I thought we weren't going to sleep together again."

"We're not sleeping together again."

"Then I'm holding your hand. There's no one here to see us. And it would be pleasanter if you didn't make a big deal about it. It fits so well in mine."

Lexie didn't answer, didn't argue. It did fit well, like the most natural thing in the world.

She closed her eyes and leaned back and thought of everything that had happened since this man first took her hand on the croquet lawn back home and kissed it. So much, too much, and yet not enough.

She'd thought yesterday's papers were something to worry about. Today's were far worse.

"How did the meeting with your father go?" Yesterday Prince Henri had seen advance copies of today's papers. News of the end of her engagement to Adam had broken like a dam bursting. No one knew where the leak had come from. It didn't really matter now. Speculation was beginning on the Internet that somehow Rafe was involved. He'd told her of his summons to see his father and let her know that he'd be telling his father as much of the truth as he thought he needed to know. She hadn't asked precisely how much that involved.

"He demanded that I marry you. He always does whenever I'm involved in a scandal. He thinks a big royal wedding will go a long way to fixing things."

"Oh." It hurt that he could be so blasé. That suddenly she was just one of his many scandals. "What did you say to him?"

"That I'd live my life according to my own dictates, not his."

"Oh." It was exactly what she'd known he would say. She'd never have married him just to please his father anyway, so there was no reason for the feeling of loss.

"Adam joined in the lecture, too. He's very protective of you."

"I'm sorry."

"Don't be. You were worth it."

Were? Past tense.

His thumb rubbed gently over the back of her hand.

"Did you hear from your mother?" he asked a short while later.

"Yes. I let her know that the rumors were starting and that they weren't totally unfounded." Suddenly pictures were appearing of every public exchange she'd had with Rafe, and somehow they all managed to look charged and intense. Probably because they had been.

"How did she take it?"

"Let's just say that, whatever happens, one of our parents is going to be bitterly disappointed."

"Let me guess. She demanded that you never see me again."

"That's pretty much it."

"And what did you tell her?"

"I thought of you, and of how you'd react if someone told you what to do, and I told her that I was old enough to decide for myself who I saw and who I didn't."

"Good for you."

"And then I kind of spoiled it by telling her that I'm coming home the day after the christening, anyway. I could go sooner, but it would feel like running away. And Adam and your father have both asked me to stay. I'm not sure why. Something to do with Marconis and Wyndhams never backing down from a challenge, and a strong offence being the best form of defense. And they mentioned dignity, too. They kind of lost me, but I said I would stay." Rafe was the only one who hadn't asked her to stay.

Even now he said nothing. Not that she expected a pleading, heartfelt *don't go, stay with me forever* from this man, but a girl was allowed her daydreams. Lexie shook her head. She of all people should have learned her lesson about daydreams and fantasies and fairy tales.

"You've had a miserable time here, haven't you?"

"No, it's—"

"Have you done anything just for you, just for the sheer enjoyment of it?"

"That wasn't the purpose of the trip."

Shaking his head he stood and pulled her up with him. "Come on." He started walking.

"What? Where?"

"If we can't please both of our families then let's

annoy them both. And really give the press something to talk about."

"What do you mean?" He was leading so fast through the labyrinth she was getting dizzy.

"Do you trust me, Lexie?"

"No." She had no idea what he was planning, but was almost certain she wasn't going to like it. And yet she hurried along beside him, her heart beating faster in exhilaration and anticipation.

He laughed, turned back and planted a quick hard kiss on her lips. "Wise woman."

Forty minutes later, Lexie strapped herself into the seat next to Rafe, their shoulders touching.

"Ready?" he asked.

"No." She gripped his hand.

"Too bad." Photographers ran toward them, snapping pictures as the roller coaster of San Philippe's only theme park began to gather speed and then shot them forward. Lexie managed not to scream until they were out of sight.

The photographers were still there, a hungry pack of them, snapping away as the roller coaster eased to a stop. Lexie's hair had come free from her hair tie, helped, she suspected, by Rafe, and must surely look a fright.

Her mother would be appalled.

Lexie laughed at the prospect, suddenly not caring what people thought. Suddenly appreciating Rafe's philosophy.

The photographers followed them, at a distance, almost all day long. Taking pictures of the most mundane of things. Walking, talking, laughing, Rafe winning her a teddy bear in a shooting booth. It was all so clichéd. And all so much fun.

The only privacy they got was when Rafe managed to get a quiet booth in the riverside café where they stopped for dinner, the proprietor fiercely denying entry to anyone with a camera.

At the nightclub he took her to they danced till the small hours of the morning.

By the time Lexie fell into bed—alone—she was exhausted but happy. It was the best day she could remember, well, ever. Even with the repressed pall of sorrow that everything was ending. They'd talked of the present, never the future. Because, she knew, Rafe didn't do futures.

Ten

Amongst a sea of talking and laughing christening guests, Rafe reluctantly took hold of the baby. He was happy to be godfather—Mark and Karen were good friends—but why did people always expect that he'd want to hold their children? Although maybe godfathers ought to want to. Lex would doubtless have an opinion on the subject. Lex, whom he did want to hold, but couldn't and wouldn't because she was leaving tomorrow, going back to her old life. It was for the best.

They'd had yesterday, undoubtedly a mistake given the outcry in the media. But a mistake he couldn't regret. He'd wanted it to last forever, wanted her smiles and her laughter.

He looked into the clear blue and strangely alert eyes of the child in his arms, who appeared, much like Rafe, to be wondering why this strange man was holding her. Karen called to someone across the room and walked away, and Rafe had to stop himself from calling her back.

"If you cry now," he quietly encouraged the child whose name he'd already managed to forget, "your mother will come back for you." In Rafe's experience, that was how this scenario usually played out. Unfortunately, this child didn't know the drill and merely blinked. He was fairly sure she was a girl, though that long gown she, or he, had worn for the cathedral ceremony wasn't necessarily a guarantee of femininity.

Conversation flowed around him, and the baby continued to study him. "I hold you responsible," he said, and the baby smiled. "If it hadn't been for this christening, I could have been in Vienna by now. Or maybe even Argentina." And he wouldn't have entangled his life and emotions with Lexie. Although he couldn't bring himself to regret what they'd shared.

The baby's stare turned accusing.

"Okay," he admitted. "I stayed for her, too. But don't you dare tell anyone."

He heard a bubbling, sexy laugh and followed the sound to Lexie, where she stood talking with Adam and Karen. She wore a silky red wrap dress. He'd been pleased to see her in it. Pleased and turned on, but he ignored the second reaction. She'd at least stopped trying to hide her vibrancy behind fiercely elegant clothes. No point now, he guessed, given that she wasn't marrying his brother. She was leaving. Her hair was pulled into a twist at the back of her head, its lushness contained.

That fact pleased him, too. He admitted to a proprietary attitude to her hair—it featured in so many of his fantasies.

She caught him watching her. Her gaze dipped to the baby in his arms and her eyes widened in surprise. *Yes, Lexie,* he thought, *I do know how to hold a child, it's just not something I do voluntarily.* And Lexie was exactly the sort of woman who'd want children, who'd be a natural, loving mother. Which was why he had to let her go.

He looked around for Karen. Surely he'd done his godfatherly duty and could hand the baby back. And leave. "Okay, kid, where's your mother?" Only now the child had closed its eyes and—he couldn't believe it—gone to sleep in his arms. It was the strangest feeling. He held the warm bundle a little closer.

"You're in trouble now." He heard a soft, smiling voice at his side.

"Meaning?" he asked Lexie, wanting only to hand the baby away so he could fill his arms with this woman instead. Yes, he was in trouble all right.

"I understood you have a policy of never falling asleep with a woman, and I'm figuring that extends to letting them fall asleep in your arms." She spoke quietly, her words winding sensuously around him.

"First time for everything."

She touched her fingertip gently to the sleeping child's cheek.

"You want children?" he asked, even though the answer was obvious in the softness of her smile, in the tenderness and longing that lit her face.

"Someday. Doesn't everyone?" The smile widened with secret thoughts and plans.

"No. Not everyone."

"Like Everest?"

"Exactly." He smiled back, enthralled, held captive by what felt like an almost physical connection to her. The entire roomful of people could fade away and he wouldn't notice. She felt it, too. This wasn't one-sided. Which only made the situation worse.

"But don't you? Want children." She searched his face.

"It's not something I've thought about." And he was terrified that looking at her, children were something he could want. "Here, do you want to hold her?" He nodded at the soundly sleeping little girl. If Lexie was holding the baby, she'd stop looking at him. And the sight of her holding a baby would stop him thinking thoughts he shouldn't. He couldn't possibly lust after a woman holding an infant. It would just be wrong.

"Emma?"

That was her name, of course.

"Yes, please."

He passed the sleeping child to Lexie. They had to stand close, almost chest to chest, only Emma between them, hands bumping and sliding.

"Babies aren't your thing?" Lexie asked, not looking at him, as she took Emma's weight, held her to her chest.

"Not at all." His standard answer came to him. And yet he'd felt the strangest reluctance to let go of the small bundle. The child who had fallen asleep in his arms.

"You'll be a great father. Once you give yourself permission to love," she said. "It doesn't have to be scary."

Oh, but it was.

She couldn't leave soon enough. It was torture seeing her. Seeing her hope, her optimism.

As Karen approached, Rafe took a flute of champagne from a passing waiter. He saw one of his few remaining bachelor friends and headed to talk to him. Preferably about polo or something equally safe, equally shallow.

Lexie rested her hands on the rough stone of the windowsill and looked out through the tall, narrow window. The day room was at the top of the castle's southernmost turret. Rafe had mentioned it once, mentioned its forever views and its isolation. After navigating corridors and climbing endless winding stone stairs, Lexie could see why it was so was so seldom used. But the views over the manicured palace grounds and the rolling countryside beyond were worth the effort. The sky was a clear, bright blue, taunting her. It should be dreary and miserable to match her mood.

The room was just as she'd imagined. A contrast of textures and centuries. Leather couches, shaped to fit the circular space, lined the small room. A plush rug lay in the center of the floor.

She'd escaped the christening, escaped the sound of Rafe's laughter with his friend, to come here. She'd lost track of how long she'd been standing, looking out and trying not to think, when the heavy door opened behind her. She turned as the man she'd been trying not to think about stepped into the room. He paused, clearly not expecting to see her here. "Is the party over?" she asked.

"Still going." He gave a half smile. "I bailed. Thought I'd come up here for a little time-out."

Lexie took a single step away from the window. "You stay," she said. "I was just going."

But as he crossed to her she didn't seem able to move any farther.

"It's so beautiful up here," she said.

"Yes," he said, his gaze never leaving her face. He stopped in front of her and brushed a thumb across her cheek. Did that mean he'd seen the telltale tracks of her tears?

"I'm leaving." She didn't know whether she spoke the words for his benefit or for hers. The only thing she did know was that the prospect of her departure was a dark, yawning chasm. The thought of leaving San Philippe forever. The thought of leaving Rafe. Forever. It weighed almost unbearably on her.

"I know." He lowered his head and placed the gentlest of kisses on each of her cheekbones. And then he pulled her into his arms and she went willingly. He held her tightly to him and she absorbed the sensation of being pressed against him, tried to commit it to memory, tried to detail each part of her that touched him and where and how, the feel of his cheek resting on her head, his arms around her.

She tilted her head up to look at him, to study his face. He returned her scrutiny for the longest time. And then he kissed her. Soft and gentle, the knowledge of her leaving in his kiss. She tasted the faint trace of champagne on his lips.

What started out soft and gentle grew heated and hungry. Breathing hard, Rafe lifted his head. "We shouldn't. *I* shouldn't."

She pulled his head back down. "We should." She smiled against his lips, heedless. "I'm leaving anyway. What can it hurt now?"

"It can hurt you. You deserve better. Someone needs to look out for you, and if you won't protect yourself from me then I have to do it."

"I deserve this. After all you've put me through, I deserve *this*."

But still he backed away.

Lexie pulled the silk ribbon that held the front of her dress in place and the dress fell open. "Don't go."

"That's a low trick, Lex." Rafe stopped dead. "It wouldn't be humanly possible now." He walked slowly back to her. "Have I told you red is my favorite color?" He looked into her eyes as he pushed her dress from her shoulders, smiled as it pooled at her feet, then trailed his fingers in its wake to touch the red of her bra, and then her panties. "Do you know what you do to me?"

"I'm hoping it's something like what you do to me."

As he slid his hands to her waist, and slowly up and round, she trembled beneath his touch. His fingers found the clasp they sought, and her bra whispered to the floor.

She gasped as he knelt before her and pressed a kiss

to the center of her panties. And then he drew the fine lace from her hips, over her thighs.

One more kiss, and another gasp. He trailed more kisses upward, another to her belly, between her breasts, her neck. With her eyes on him he undid his buttons. He discarded his shirt, his pants, his boxers. No pretence, no barriers. Till he stood before her, bathed in golden sunlight, strong and proud and hers.

For now.

Him. Her. Nothing else.

He reached for her hair, ran his fingers through its sun-warmed length, ran his hands over the curve of her shoulders, down her arms till his hands founds hers.

Holding her gaze, he lifted her hands and pressed a kiss to the back of each. Then, lowering his hands, he slid his fingers between hers, stretching them apart. Palms touched, breath mingled.

And then he touched his lips to hers, with a gentleness born of constraint.

She moved. Closed the gap between them till her breasts pressed against his chest and her belly pressed against his erection.

He pulled her closer still, hard against him, deepening the kiss at the same time, and they moved together, legs twining, hands searching, all the while each drinking in the taste of the other.

Kissing, they made it as far as the center of the room and then no farther. Dropping to their knees on the rug, hands and lips had free rein.

Lexie pushed him back and he pulled her with him.

She straddled him and then sheathed herself on him, loving the feel of him in her, under her. Loving him.

He was hers.

For now.

He lifted his hands to her breasts, caressed and kneaded. He pulled her forward so he could take a nipple in his mouth. His hands shifted to her waist, her hips, and he was pushing into her deeper, pulling her onto him harder.

She rode his thrusts, and he drove her higher, further, into darkness and light. And then she was gasping, whimpering. Her eyes flew open, locked on his, all beauty and blind passion, and together they cried out.

Lexie fell forward onto him, her hair curtaining his face, her body pulsing around his.

And he held her tight to him.

In the darkness, Lexie clung to Rafe's hand, keeping close as he led her through the castle's dimly lit halls. They'd made love again and again in the turret room. And then slept. And now, in the small hours, they found their way, stumbling and laughing, through corridors and downstairs.

He stopped outside a door, pushed it open and led her into a room. Lit only by the light of the moon, Lexie could still see it was a bedroom. *Rafe's* bedroom.

Not releasing her hand, he crossed with her to the massive sleigh bed. He lifted his hands to her hair. "We should sleep."

"Yes." They should. She had no idea what time it was, knew only that it was late or very early. But she slipped her hands around his waist, pressed her lips to his. She had this one stolen night with him. She wouldn't waste it. She pulled him unresisting down with her onto the bed, reveled in the weight of him on her and over her.

And after the rug and the couch of the turret room, his broad bed was a novelty. Room to roll and tangle and laugh and touch.

Lexie woke with sunlight warming one side of her face and Rafe's chest warming the other side. His heart beat strong and steady beneath her cheek. His arms rested loosely around her. As she woke fully, she basked in the magic, the beauty, of being with him.

She tilted her face up to see him watching her and then pulled away to see him better.

He let her go, his hands trailing from her.

Instantly, she regretted pulling away. When she'd been lying close, touching, eyes closed, anything had been possible. There had at least been a fragile hope of a glittering future. That they—she and Rafe—might be possible.

Now, lying on her side, she studied him. Rumpled hair, beard-shadowed jaw and a slow, sexy smile, but it was the wariness in his dark eyes that pierced the fragile magic of the morning, that sucked away her happiness.

And she knew in that moment that she should never have come to his room, should never have fallen asleep with him so that they then had to navigate waking up together. The memories of their night together would now forever end with this.

She'd given up her dreams because of him. But not *for* him. She knew not to allow herself to be that stupid. But she hadn't been able to love his brother when her every thought had been of Rafe. When she had felt things for Rafe and wanted things from Rafe that she would never feel or want from Adam.

She was leaving today. And she knew he wouldn't, couldn't, offer her a future. And yet here she lay, wanting precisely that. A future. With Rafe.

Not the man of her dreams, but the man of her realities. The man who understood her and made her laugh and made her want him.

The wariness in his eyes now froze her hopes, her heart. She could almost see the regrets and his questions and fears. Would she want to marry him now, want to have his babies, want to trap him? Already he was formulating words to soften his rejection.

She had wanted, desperately, to make love with him, but not to love him, to fall in love with him. She hadn't wanted that. But heaven help her, looking at him now, feeling already the pain in her heart, she realized that she had fallen anyway. So the answer to those fearful questions in his eyes was—yes, she wanted to marry him and yes, she wanted to have his babies. And most of all she wanted him to love her. But no, she didn't want to trap him.

"Lexie." His voice had the sexiest early-morning rasp.

She touched a finger to his lips. "I don't think you should say anything. I don't want regrets or excuses, and I couldn't bear false promises. I'm here, in your bed, and I know that's breaking all your rules, but it wasn't planned.

"I'm going today, we both knew that, so we both knew last night was just...last night. And this morning is this morning. So don't say anything. Unless of course it's 'make love with me right now.'" She tried to make it a joke. But even though there was only a hollow space where her heart used to be, the rest of her still wanted him. Just once more. And that need had slipped through in her voice.

She saw his hesitation even as he lifted his hand to touch her hair. The warm lips parted beneath her fingertip, but no words came out.

She slipped from the bed.

He made no move to stop her.

At the door to the bathroom she turned back and tried to smile. Giving up, she swallowed past the lump in her throat. "Last night was perfect. Thank you."

Eleven

Rafe stood on the lowest of the palace steps. Cloaked in the royal Marconi calm that revealed nothing of their private thoughts, his father, brother and sister were gathered around Lexie. She hugged each of them in turn, then looked for him. He stepped down. Neither royal protocol nor experience had prepared him to bid farewell to a woman like Lexie. A woman who meant the things Lexie meant to him.

Mere hours ago she had been in his bed. It had killed him, not asking—begging—her to stay, in his bed, in his life. But he'd shattered enough of her dreams. She deserved her fairy tale. Despite his title, he was no one's fairy tale, and never would be.

Dry-eyed, she walked to him. Pale and strong and… the most beautiful woman he'd ever known. A soul-deep beauty, rare and precious. He couldn't stop himself, he touched a hand to her hair, her jaw, tried to commit to memory the feel of her, even though forgetting her was critical to his future happiness. He hadn't been going to embrace her, but she stepped into his arms, and if his life had depended on it, he couldn't have avoided wrapping them around her for the chance of holding her to him one last time.

She was the one to break the contact, stepping away from him. For a moment he saw the question and hope in her eyes. The same look he'd seen when she woke up in his arms this morning.

Then she smiled, and it was the saddest smile he'd ever seen. Clenching his fists, he kept his hands at his sides. "I didn't mean to make you sad, Lex," he said quietly. "If I could take back last night, for your sake, I would. We should have ended with the day before yesterday. That was what I wanted to give you."

If anything, her smile grew both sadder and brighter. "I wouldn't," she answered. "That day was perfect. But last night was even better."

"You'll find a good man. One worthy of you. One who's everything he should be. Better than Adam. Better than me." Someone who loved her for who she was. Someone who could offer her marriage and the family she wanted. Someone who'd treat her with respect and reverence. Not someone who couldn't even wait till they got to the other side of a room but dragged her down to a rug on the floor.

"My only requirement is that he loves me."

"He'd be a fool not to."

"There's no shortage of fools."

She got into the waiting car and he watched it pull away, seeming to pull a piece of him with it.

Lexie's departure was vastly different from her arrival. No eager, waving crowds waited at the airport. A fact for which she was deeply grateful. A handful of photographers loitered at the barriers, doubtless waiting to document the fact that the woman who'd spurned their favorite prince and been spurned in turn by the other one did actually leave their country.

Joseph, the head of security, escorted her across the tarmac and up the stairs to the jet. She knew it was meant as a courtesy. It felt like she was being seen off the premises, that like the press, he wanted to make sure she really did go, that there would be an end to the havoc she'd wrought.

She wanted that end, too, to the havoc of her personal and emotional life, though she knew the pain was only just beginning.

On board she sank onto one of the deep cream couches and did up her seatbelt at the gentle prompting of the hostess. Lexie had deliberately chosen the couch because it didn't face a window. She closed her eyes and waited. Finally the tone of the jet's engines changed and they began to taxi along the runway. She resisted the urge to take one last look at San Philippe as they gathered speed and then became airborne. The wheels locked back up into the undercarriage with a thudding finality.

She'd expected tears, but they never came. All she felt was a great, welling hollowness.

So much for not making a spectacle of herself. She'd done that and so much worse.

She heard a sound in the cabin. The hostess. If only she could be left alone. "I'm fine, thanks," she said. "I don't need anything."

"Or anyone?" a deep, achingly familiar voice asked.

Her eyes flew open and she drank in the sight of Rafe as he smiled down at her and then lowered himself onto the couch beside her. "What are you doing here?" She was almost afraid to ask. "How did you even get here?"

He took her hand, held tight to it. "The second question's easy to answer. I took a leaf out of your book and came by motorbike. I passed you just before the airport."

"And the first question?" She clung to his hand like a lifeline. So much depended on his answer. Hope filled her, but she'd had her hopes dashed before now and the prospect of it happening again terrified her.

"A, I'm not a fool and B, I'm not a martyr."

That was no answer. At least not one she understood. "Meaning?"

"I said only a fool wouldn't love you. And clearly I'm not a fool because I do—love you. I don't know when or how it happened. I wanted you almost from the start, from the time I first saw you in the nightclub, no surprise there. I'd wanted women before, so I didn't think it was anything I couldn't control." He made a derisive sound.

A laugh cut short. "But the wanting that started that night has only grown stronger, become something more than I even believed existed—love." He shrugged, but the grip on her hand tightened. "And the love is well out of my control. I've got no idea how it even happened and only one idea of what to do about it." He ran gentle fingers down a lock of her hair, reverently touched her face.

The hostess appeared, took one look at them and just as quickly disappeared.

"I didn't mean it to happen, Lex, but it did. And till half an hour ago I thought letting you go was the right thing to do, which is when I remembered I'm not a martyr. I'm not willing to sacrifice my happiness while you look for someone worthy of you. I want to be the one you wake up with every morning. Though I know I'm not your fairy tale."

She opened her mouth to argue, but he silenced her with a finger to her lips. "Let me finish, Lex. This isn't easy for me, but I need to say it, need you to hear it." When she nodded, he continued. "I know I'm not the one you wanted to love. And I know there are better men out there than me. But I can't let them have you. At least not without offering myself to you first. I want to marry you, to be yours, to make you mine. I want all the things I never thought I would. Knowing you has changed so much for me, for the better. But it was only the awful prospect of actually losing you that forced me to see it."

He searched her face and then in a sudden movement swooped in, covered her lips with his and kissed her.

And she clung to him, kissed him back, drank in the taste of him, reveled in the feel of him. She didn't have the willpower or even the desire to deny him.

Too soon, he broke the kiss, rested his forehead against hers. His hands cupped her jaw, his fingers threading into her hair. She held him, breathed in his scent, drew it deep within her, resented having to exhale and lose that part of him she'd captured. Her weakness for him was absolute.

He took her hands again, folding strong, sure fingers around hers. "Say you'll have me?"

She was desperate to say yes and yet she couldn't. "Rafe—" she clung to his hands, the contact imperative "—you haven't thought this through. You once said you were trying to protect me from you. But it's you who needs to be protected from me. Think about your father and your country. Think about what the press will say."

"I don't care what anyone other than you says. And, in case you haven't noticed, I'm still waiting for a yes here."

"I care what they say about you. They'll vilify you."

"Not just me." He smiled. "You, too. But not for long. And at least we'll be in it together. I'll get us through it. Trust me, I've had practice. Besides, you haven't seen this morning's papers, have you?"

"No. I couldn't bear it anymore."

"It's not all bad news. Some bright spark in the press corps has realized that my father only ever said he had given permission for his son and Alexia Wyndham Jones to marry. He never said which son. So along with all the photos of you and me together, the press are speculating that this is what Dad, the master manipulator, meant all along, that he was playing them. They're rewriting history to suit themselves. And Dad'll be happy to go along with it."

"He couldn't possibly have had any idea that we'd fall in love."

"So you do love me?" He studied her face.

She paused, unable to deny this man a moment longer. "With all my heart."

"And do you mind if we don't do the big royal wedding thing?"

"I don't mind at all." She was still trying to process what was happening. That Rafe loved her, that he wanted to wake up with her every morning.

"Good." He smiled. "Because my father's not the only wily one. I have it all figured out. The pilot's already changed the flight plan. We're heading to Vegas. And we're getting married. Today. May as well give the press something to get really worked up about. We can be San Philippe's Rebel Royals. And in tricking them and denying them all their royal wedding, we'll have sunk so low that the only way to go will be upward in the public's opinion. And as soon as you have my babies everyone, but me especially, will be happy. All will be forgiven and forgotten."

He lifted her hand, covering it with his other so that it disappeared within his clasp. "Lex, you're a part of me that I hadn't even realized was missing. The best part." Tenderness shone in his dark eyes. He released her hand to cup her face, and she pressed her cheek against the warmth of his palm. "Alexia Wyndham Jones, Lexie, my Lexie. I love you. You are my Everest, my everything."

Finally, finally he kissed her again and she knew despite what he'd said, she had her fairy tale.

* * * * *

A QUEEN FOR
THE TAKING?

KATE HEWITT

CHAPTER ONE

ALESSANDRO DIOMEDI, KING of Maldinia, opened the door to the opulent reception room and gazed resolutely upon the woman intended to be his bride. Liana Aterno, the daughter of the duke of Abruzzo, stood in the centre of the room, her body elegant and straight, her gaze clear and steady and even cold. She looked remarkably composed, considering the situation.

Carefully Sandro closed the door, the final click seeming to sound the end of his freedom. But no, that was being fanciful, for his freedom had surely ended six months ago, when he'd left his life in California to return to Maldinia and accept his place as first in line to the throne. Any tattered remnant of it had gone when he'd buried his father and taken his place as king.

'Good afternoon.' His voice seemed to echo through the large room with its gilt walls and frescoed ceilings, the only furniture a few ornate tables of gold and marble set against the walls. Not exactly the most welcoming of spaces, and for a moment Sandro wished he'd specified to put Lady Liana into a more comfortable chamber.

Although, he acknowledged cynically, considering the nature of their imminent discussion—and probable relationship—perhaps this room was appropriate.

'Good afternoon, Your Highness.' She didn't curtsey,

which he was glad of, because he hated all the osten-
tatious trappings of royalty and obeisance, but she did
bend her head in a gesture of respect so for a moment he
could see the bare, vulnerable nape of her neck. It almost
made him soften. Then she lifted her head and pinned
him with that cold, clear-eyed gaze and he felt his heart
harden once more. He didn't want this. He never would.
But she obviously did.

'You had a pleasant journey?'

'Yes, thank you.'

He took a step into the room, studying her. He supposed she was pretty, if you liked women who were colourless. Her hair was so blonde it appeared almost white,
and she wore it pulled back in a tight chignon, a few
wispy tendrils coming to curl about her small, pearl-
studded ears.

She was slight, petite, and yet she carried herself with
both pride and grace, and wore a modest, high-necked,
long-sleeved dress of pale blue silk belted tightly at the
waist, an understated strand of pearls at her throat. She
had folded her hands at her waist like some pious nun
and stood calmly under his obvious scrutiny, accepting
his inspection with a cool and even haughty confidence.
All of it made him angry.

'You know why you're here.'

'Yes, Your Highness.'

'You can dispense with the titles. Since we are considering marriage, you may call me Alessandro, or Sandro,
whichever you prefer.'

'And which do you prefer?'

'You may call me Sandro.' Her composed compliance
annoyed him, although he knew such a reaction was unreasonable, even unjust. Yet he still felt it, felt the deep-
seated desire to wipe that cool little smile off her face

and replace it with something real. To feel something real himself.

But he'd left real emotions—honesty, understanding, all of it—behind in California. There was no place for them here, even when discussing his marriage.

'Very well,' she answered evenly, yet she didn't call him anything; she simply waited. Annoyance warred with reluctant amusement and even admiration. Did she have more personality than he'd initially assumed, or was she simply that assured of their possible nuptials?

Their marriage was virtually a sealed deal. He'd invited her to Maldinia to begin negotiations, and she'd agreed with an alacrity he'd found far too telling. So the duke's daughter wanted to be a queen. What a surprise. Another woman on a cold-hearted quest for money, power, and fame.

Love, of course, wouldn't enter into it. It never did; he'd learned that lesson too many times already.

Sandro strode farther into the room, his hands shoved into the pockets of his suit trousers. He walked to the window that looked out on the palace's front courtyard, the gold-tipped spikes of the twelve-foot-high fence that surrounded the entire grounds making his throat tighten. *Such a prison.* And one he'd reentered willingly. One he'd returned to with a faint, frail hope in his heart that had blown to so much cold ash when he'd actually seen his father again, after fifteen years.

I had no choice. If I could have, I'd have left you to rot in California, or, better yet, in hell.

Sandro swallowed and turned away.

'Tell me why you're here, Lady Liana.' He wanted to hear it from her own mouth, those tightly pursed lips.

A slight pause, and then she answered, her voice low

and steady. 'To discuss the possibility of a marriage between us.'

'Such a possibility does not distress or concern you,
considering we have never even met before?'

Another pause, even slighter, but Sandro still felt it.
'We have met before, Your Highness. When I was twelve.'

'Twelve.' He turned around to inspect her once again,
but her cold blonde beauty didn't trigger any memories.
Had she possessed such icy composure, as well as a resolute determination to be queen, at twelve years old? It
seemed likely. 'You are to call me Sandro, remember.'

'Of course.'

He almost smiled at that. Was she provoking him on
purpose? He'd rather that than the icy, emotionless composure. Any emotion was better than none.

'Where did we meet?'

'At a birthday party for my father in Milan.'

He didn't remember the event, but that didn't really
surprise him. If she'd been twelve, he would have been
twenty, and about to walk away from his inheritance,
his very self, only to return six months ago, when duty
demanded he reclaim his soul—or sell it. He still wasn't
sure which he'd done. 'And you remembered me?'

For a second, no more, she looked...not disconcerted,
but something close to it. Something distressing. Shadows flickered in her eyes, which, now that he'd taken a
step closer to her, he saw were a rather startling shade
of lavender. She wasn't so colourless, after all. Then she
blinked it back and nodded. 'Yes, I did.'

'I'm sorry to say I don't remember you.'

She shrugged, her shoulders barely twitching. 'I
wouldn't have expected you to. I was little more than
a child.'

He nodded, his gaze still sweeping over her, wondering what thoughts and feelings lurked behind that careful, blank mask of a face. What emotion had shadowed her eyes for just a moment?

Or was he being fanciful, sentimental? He had been before. He'd thought he'd learned the lessons, but perhaps he hadn't.

Liana Aterno had been one of the first names to come up in diplomatic discussions after his father had died, and he'd accepted that he must marry and provide an heir—and soon.

She was related to royalty, had devoted her life to charity work, and her father was prominent in finance and had held various important positions in the European Union—all of which Sandro had to consider, for the sake of his country. She was eminently and irritatingly suitable in every way. The perfect queen consort—and she looked as if she knew it.

'You have not considered other alliances in the meantime?' he asked. 'Other…relationships?' He watched her pale, heart-shaped face, no emotion visible in her eyes, no tightening of her mouth, no tension apparent in her lithe body. The woman reminded him of a statue, something made of cold, lifeless marble.

No, he realised, what she really reminded him of was his mother. An icy, beautiful bitch: emotionless, soulless, caring only about wealth and status and fame. About being queen.

Was that who this woman really was? Or was he being stupidly judgmental and entirely unfair, based on his own sorry experience? It was impossible to tell what she felt from her carefully blank expression, yet he felt a gut-deep revulsion to the fact that she was here at all, that she'd accepted his summons and was prepared to marry a stranger.

Just as he was.

'No,' she said after a moment. 'I have not…' She gave a slight shrug of her shoulders. 'I have devoted myself to charity work.'

Queen or nun. It was a choice women in her elevated position had had to make centuries before, but it seemed archaic now. Absurd.

And yet it was her reality, and very close to his. King or CEO of his own company. Slave or free.

'No one else?' he pressed. 'I have to admit, I am surprised. You're— What? Twenty-eight years old?' She gave a slight nod. 'Surely you've had other offers. Other relationships.'

Her mouth tightened, eyes narrowing slightly. 'As I said, I have devoted myself to charity work.'

'You can devote yourself to charity work and still be in a relationship,' he pointed out. 'Still marry.'

'Indeed, I hope so, Your Highness.'

A noble sentiment, he supposed, but one he didn't trust. Clearly only queen would do for this icy, ambitious woman.

Sandro shook his head slowly. Once he'd dreamed of a marriage, a relationship built on love, filled with passion and humour and joy. Once.

Gazing at her now, he knew she would make an able queen, a wonderful queen—clearly she'd been grooming herself for such a role. And the decision of his marriage was not about desire or choice. It was about duty, a duty he'd wilfully and shamefully ignored for far too long already.

He gave a brisk nod. 'I have obligations in the palace for the rest of this afternoon, but I would like us to have dinner together tonight, if you are amenable.'

She nodded, accepting, unsmiling. 'Of course, Your Highness.'

'We can get to know each other a bit better, perhaps, as well as discuss the practical aspects of this union.'

Another nod, just as swift and emotionless. 'Of course.'

He stared at her hard, wanting her to show some kind of emotion, whether it was uncertainty or hope or simple human interest. He saw nothing in her clear violet gaze, nothing but cool purpose, hard-hearted determination. Suppressing a stab of disappointment, he turned from the room. 'I'll send one of my staff in to see to your needs. Enjoy your stay in the palace of Averne, Lady Liana.'

'Thank you, Your Highness.'

It wasn't until he'd closed the door behind him that he realised she'd never called him Sandro.

Liana let out a long, slow breath and pressed her hands to her middle, relieved that the fluttering had stopped. She felt reassuringly calm now, comfortingly numb. So she'd met Alessandro Diomedi, king of Maldinia. Her future husband.

She crossed to the window and gazed out at the palace courtyard and the ancient buildings of Averne beyond the ornate fence, all framed by a cloudless blue sky. The snow-capped peaks of the Alps were just visible if she craned her neck.

She let out another breath and willed the tension to dissipate from her body. That whole conversation with King Alessandro had been surreal; she'd almost felt as if she'd been floating somewhere up by the ceiling, looking down at these two people, strangers who had never met before, at least not properly. And now they intended to marry each other.

She shook her head slowly, the realisation of what her future would hold still possessing the power to surprise and even unnerve her although it had been several weeks since her parents had suggested she consider Alessandro's suit.

He's a king, Liana, and you should marry. Have children of your own.

She'd never thought to marry, have children. The responsibility and risk were both too great. But she knew it was what her parents wanted, and a convenient marriage, at least, meant a loveless one. A riskless one.

So marry she would, if King Alessandro would have her. She took a deep breath as the flutters started again, reminded herself of the advantages of such a union.

As queen she could continue to devote herself to her charity work, and raise the profile of Hands To Help. Her position would benefit it so much, and she could not turn away from that, just as she could not turn away from her parents' wishes for her life.

She owed them too much.

Really, she told herself, it was perfect. It would give her everything she wanted—everything she would let herself want.

Except it didn't seem the king wanted it. *Her.* She recalled the slightly sneering, incredulous tone, the way he'd looked at her with a kind of weary derision. She didn't please him. Or was it simply marriage that didn't please him?

With a wary unease she recalled his sense of raw, restless power, as if this palace could not contain him, as if his emotions and ideas would bubble over, spill forth.

She wasn't used to that. Her parents were quiet, reserved people, and she had learned to be even more quiet and reserved than they were. To be invisible.

The only time she let herself be heard was when she was giving a public address for Hands To Help. On stage, talking about what the charity did, she had the words to say and the confidence to say them.

But with King Alessandro? With him looking at her as if... Almost as if he didn't even *like* her?

Words had deserted her. She'd cloaked herself in the cool, numbing calm she'd developed over the years, her only way of staying sane. Of surviving, because giving into emotion meant giving into the grief and guilt, and if she did that she knew she'd be lost. She'd drown in the feelings she'd never let herself acknowledge, much less express.

And King Alessandro, of all people, wasn't meant to call them up. This marriage was meant to be *convenient*. Cold. She wouldn't have agreed to it otherwise.

And yet the questions he'd asked her hadn't been either. And the doubt his voicing of them stirred up in her made her insides lurch with panic.

Tell me why you're here, Lady Liana.... Such a possibility does not distress or concern you, considering we have never even met before?

He'd almost sounded as if he *wanted* her to be distressed by the prospect of their marriage.

Perhaps she should have told him that she was.

Except, of course, she wasn't. Wouldn't be. Marriage to King Alessandro made sense. Her parents wanted it. She wanted the visibility for Hands To Help. It was the right choice. It had to be.

And yet just the memory of the king's imposing figure, all restless, rangy muscle and sinewy grace, made her insides quiver and jump. He wore his hair a little too long, ink-black and streaked with silver at the temples, carelessly rumpled as if he'd driven his fingers through it.

His eyes were iron-grey, hard and yet compelling. She'd had to work not to quell under that steely gaze, especially when his mouth had twisted with what had looked—and felt—like derision.

What about her displeased him?

What did he want from her, if not a practical and accepting approach to this marriage?

Liana didn't want to answer that question. She didn't even want to ask it. She had hoped they would be in agreement about this marriage, or as much as they could considering she hadn't wanted to marry at all.

But then perhaps King Alessandro didn't either. Perhaps his seeming resentment was at the situation, rather than his intended bride. Liana's lips formed a grim smile. Two people who had no desire to be married and yet would soon be saying their vows. Well, hopefully they wouldn't actually be seeing all that much of each other.

'Lady Liana?'

She turned to see one of the palace's liveried staff, his face carefully neutral, standing in the doorway. 'Yes?'

'The king requested that I show you to your room, so you may refresh yourself.'

'Thank you.' With a brisk nod she followed the man out of the ornate receiving room and down a long, marble-floored corridor to the east wing of the palace. He took her up a curving marble staircase with an impressive gold bannister, and then down yet another marble corridor until he finally arrived at a suite of rooms.

During the entire journey she'd only seen more staff, liveried and stony faced, giving her the uneasy sense that she was alone in this vast building save for the countless nameless employees. She wondered where the king had gone, or, for that matter, the queen dowager. Surely Sandro's mother, Sophia, intended to receive her?

Although, Liana acknowledged, she couldn't assume anything. The summons to Maldinia's royal palace had come so quickly and suddenly, a letter with Alessandro's royal insignia on top, its few pithy sentences comprising the request for Lady Liana Aterno of Abruzzo to discuss the possibility of marriage. Liana had been in shock; her mother, full of expectation.

This would be so good for you, Liana. You should marry. Why not Alessandro? Why not a king?

Why not, indeed? Her parents were traditional, even old-fashioned. Daughters married, produced heirs. It was perhaps an archaic idea in this modern world, but they clung to it.

And she couldn't let them down in their hopes for her. She owed them that much at least. She owed them so much more.

'These will be your rooms for your stay here, my lady. If you need anything, simply press the bell by the door and someone will come to your attention.'

'Thank you,' Liana murmured, and stepped into the sumptuous set of rooms. After ensuring she had no further requirements, the staff member left with a quiet click of the door. Liana gazed around the huge bedroom, its opulence a far cry from her modest apartment in Milan.

Acres of plush carpet stretched in every direction, and in the centre of the room, on its own dais, stood a magnificent canopied four-poster bed, piled high with silk pillows. The bed faced a huge stone fireplace with elaborate scrollwork, and several deep armchairs in blue patterned silk flanked it. It was a chilly March day and a fire had already been laid and lit, and now crackled cheerfully in the huge hearth.

Slowly Liana walked towards the fireplace and stretched her hands out to the flames. Her hands were icy; they always went cold when she was nervous. And despite her every attempt to convey the opposite to King Alessandro, she *had* been nervous.

She hadn't expected to be, had assumed a marriage such as theirs would be conducted like a corporate merger, their introduction no more than a business meeting. She wasn't naive; she knew what marriage would entail. Alessandro needed an heir.

But she hadn't expected his energy, his emotion. He'd been the opposite of her in every way: restless, quick-tempered, seething with something she didn't understand.

She closed her eyes, wished briefly that she could return to the simple life she'd made for herself working at the foundation, living in Milan, going out on occasion with friends. It probably didn't look like much to most people, but she'd found a soothing enjoyment in those small things. That was all she'd ever wanted, all she'd ever asked for. The safety of routines had calmed and comforted her, and just one meeting with Sandro Diomedi had ruffled up everything inside her.

Swallowing hard, she opened her eyes. *Enough.* Her life was not her own, and hadn't been since she was eight years old. She accepted that as the price she must pay, *should* pay.

But she wouldn't think anymore about that. It was as if there were a door in Liana's mind, and it clanged shut by sheer force of will. She wouldn't think about Chiara.

She turned away from the fire, crossing to the window to gaze out at the bare gardens still caught in the chill of late winter. Strange to think this view would become familiar when she was wed. This palace, this life, would all become part of her normal existence.

As would the king. *Sandro.*

She suppressed a shiver. What would marriage to King

Alessandro look like? She had a feeling it wouldn't look or feel like she'd assumed. Convenient. Safe.

She'd never even had a proper boyfriend, never been kissed except for a few quick, sloppy attempts on a couple dates she'd gone on over the years, pressured by her parents to meet a boy, fall in love, even though she hadn't been interested in either.

But Alessandro would want more than a kiss, and with him she felt it would be neither sloppy nor quick.

She let out a soft huff of laughter, shaking her head at herself. How on earth would she know how Alessandro would kiss?

But you'll find out soon enough.

She swallowed hard, the thought alone enough to make her palms go icy again. She didn't want to think about that, not yet.

She gazed around the bedroom, the afternoon stretching emptily in front of her. She couldn't bear to simply sit and wait in her room; she preferred being busy and active. She'd take a walk through the palace gardens, she decided. The fresh air would be welcome.

She dressed casually but carefully in wool trousers of pale grey and a twin set in mauve cashmere, the kind of bland, conservative clothes she'd chosen for ever.

She styled her hair, leaving it down, and did her discreet make-up and jewellery—pearls, as she always wore. It took her nearly an hour before she was ready, and then as soon as she left her room one of the staff standing to attention in the endless corridor hurried towards her.

'My lady?'

'I'd like to go outside, please. To have a stroll around the gardens if I may.'

'Very good, my lady.'

She followed the man in his blue-and-gold-tasselled

uniform down the corridor and then down several others and finally to a pair of French windows that led to a wide terrace with shallow steps leading to the gardens.

'Would you like an escort—?' he began, but Liana shook her head.

'No, thank you. I'll just walk around by myself.'

She breathed in the fresh, pine-scented mountain air as she took the first twisting path through the carefully clipped box hedges. Even though the palace was in the centre of Maldinia's capital city of Averne, it was very quiet in the gardens, the only sound the rustle of the wind through the still-bare branches of the trees and shrubs.

Liana dug her hands into the pockets of her coat, the chilly wind stinging her cheeks, glad for an afternoon's respite from the tension of meeting with the king. As she walked she examined the flowerbeds, trying to identify certain species although it was difficult with everything barely in blossom.

The sun was starting to sink behind the snow-capped peaks on the horizon when Liana finally turned back to the palace. She needed to get ready for her dinner with the king, and already she felt her brief enjoyment of the gardens replaced by a wary concern over the coming evening.

She could not afford to make a single misstep, and yet as she walked back towards the French windows glinting in the late afternoon sun she realised how little information King Alessandro had given her. Was this dinner a formal occasion with members of state, or something smaller and more casual? Would the queen be dining with them, or other members of the royal family? Liana knew that Alessandro's brother, Leo, and his wife, Alyse, lived in Averne, as did his sister, the princess Alexa.

Her steps slowed as she came up to the terrace; she

found herself approaching the evening with both dread and a tiny, treacherous flicker of anticipation. Sandro's raw, restless energy might disturb her, but it also fascinated her. It was, she knew, a dangerous fascination, and one she needed to get under control if she was going to go ahead with this marriage.

Which she was.

Anything else, at this point, was impossible, involved too much disappointment for too many people.

She forced her worries back along with that fascination as she opened the French windows. As she came inside she stopped short, her breath coming out in a rush, for Alessandro had just emerged from a gilt-panelled door, a frown settled between his dark, straight brows. He glanced up, stilling when he saw her, just as Liana was still.

'Good evening. You've been out for a walk in the gardens?'

She nodded, her mind seeming to have snagged on the sight of him, his rumpled hair, his silvery eyes, his impossibly hard jaw. 'Yes, Your Highness.'

'You're cold.' To her complete shock Alessandro touched her cheek with his fingertips. The touch was so very slight and yet so much more than she'd expected or ever known. Instinctively she jerked back, and she watched as his mouth, which had been curving into a faint smile, thinned into a hard line.

'I'll see you at dinner,' he said flatly. He turned away and strode down the hall.

Drawing a deep breath, she threw back her shoulders, forced herself to turn towards her own suite of rooms and walk with a firm step even as inside she wondered just what would happen tonight—and how she would handle it.

CHAPTER TWO

ALESSANDRO GAZED DISPASSIONATELY at his reflection as he twitched his black tie into place. This afternoon's meeting with Lady Liana had gone about as well as he could have expected, and yet it still left him dissatisfied. Restless, as everything about his royal life did.

This palace held too many painful memories, too many hard lessons. *Don't trust. Don't love. Don't believe that anyone loves you back.*

Every one drilled into him over years of neglect, indifference, and anger.

Sighing, he thrust the thought aside. He might hate returning to the palace, but he'd done it of his own free will. Returned to face his father and take up his kingship because he'd known it was the right thing to do. It was his duty.

And because you, ever naive, thought your father might actually forgive you. Finally love you.

What a blind fool he was.

He wouldn't, Sandro thought as he fastened his cufflinks, be blind about his wife. He knew exactly what he was getting into, just what he was getting from the lovely Lady Liana.

Yet for a moment, when he'd seen Liana coming through the French windows, her hair streaming over her shoulders like pale satin, the fading sunlight touching it with gold, he'd felt his heart lighten rather ridiculously.

She'd looked so different from the coldly composed woman he'd encountered in the formal receiving room. She'd looked alive and vibrant and beautiful, her lavender eyes sparkling, her cheeks pink from the wind.

He'd felt a leap of hope then that she might not be the cold, ambitious queen-in-waiting she'd seemed just hours ago, but then he'd seen that icy self-possession enter her eyes, she'd jerked back when he had, unthinkingly, touched her, and disappointment had settled in him once more, a leaden weight.

It was too late to wish for something else for his marriage, Sandro knew. For his life. When he'd received the phone call from his father—after fifteen years of stony silence on both sides—he'd given up his right to strive or even wish for anything different. He'd been living for himself, freely, selfishly, for too long already. He'd always known, even if he'd acted as if he hadn't, that it couldn't last. Shouldn't.

And so he'd returned and taken up his kingship and all it required…such as a wife. An ambitious, appropriate, perfect wife.

His expression hardening, he turned from his reflection and went in search of the woman who fitted all those soulless requirements.

He found her already waiting in the private dining room he'd requested be prepared for their meal. She stood by the window, straight and proud, dressed in an evening gown of champagne-coloured silk.

Her face went blank as she caught sight of him, and after a second's pause she nodded regally as he closed the door behind him.

Sandro let his gaze sweep over her; the dress was by

no means immodest and yet it still clung to her slight curves. It had a vaguely Grecian style, with pearl-and-diamond clips at each shoulder and a matching pearl-and-diamond pendant nestled in the V between her breasts.

The dress clung to those small yet shapely breasts, nipping in at her waist before swirling out around her legs and ending in a silken puddle at her feet. She looked both innocent and made of ivory, everything about her so cold and perfect, making Sandro want to add a streak of colour to her cheeks or her lips—would her cheeks turn pink as they'd been before if he touched her again?

What if he kissed her?

Was she aware of his thoughts? Did she feel that sudden tension inside her as well? He couldn't tell anything from her blank face, her veiled eyes.

She'd pulled her hair back in a tight coil, emphasising her high cheekbones and delicate bone structure, and he had a mad impulse to jerk the diamond-tipped pins from her hair and see it spill over her shoulders in all of its moon-coloured glory. What would she do, he wondered, if he acted on that urge? How would this ice princess in all her white, silken haughtiness respond if he pulled her into his arms and kissed her quite senseless?

Almost as if she could sense the nature of his thoughts she lifted her chin, her eyes sparking violet challenge. *Good.* Sandro wanted to see emotion crack that icy demeanour; he wanted to sense something real from her, whether it was uncertainty or nervousness, humour or passion.

Passion.

It had been a while since he'd been with a woman, a lot longer since he'd been in a relationship. He felt a kick of lust and was glad for it. Perhaps he would act on it tonight. Perhaps *that* would melt the ice, and he would

find the real woman underneath all that haughtiness…
if she existed at all. He hoped, for both of their sakes,
that she did.

'Did you have a pleasant afternoon?' he asked politely.
He moved to the table that was set for two in front of the
huge fireplace and took the bottle of wine that had been
left open to breathe on the side.

'Yes, thank you.' She remained by the window, utterly
still, watching him.

Sandro lifted the bottle. 'May I pour you a glass?'

A hesitation, and then she nodded. 'Yes, thank you.'

Yes, thank you. He wondered if he could get her to say
it a third time. The woman had perfect manners, perfect
everything, but he didn't want perfection. He wanted
something real and raw and passionate—something he'd
never had with any woman, any *person*, even though he'd
long been looking for it. Searching and striving for it. He
suspected Lady Liana was the last person who could satisfy him in that regard.

He poured them both glasses of red wine, the ruby
liquid glinting in the dancing light thrown from the
flames of the fire. He crossed the room to where she
still stood by the window and handed her the glass, letting his fingers brush hers.

He felt her awareness of that little act, her eyes widening slightly before she took the glass with a murmured
thanks. So far they'd been alone for five minutes and
she'd said thank you three times, and nothing else.

He walked back to the fire, taking a long swallow of
his wine, enjoying the way the velvety liquid coated his
throat and fired his belly. Needing that warmth. 'What
did you think of the gardens? Were they to your liking?'
he asked, turning around to face her. She held the wine

glass in front of her, both hands clasped around it, although she had yet to take a sip.

'Yes, thank you—'

'Yes, thank you,' he mimicked, a sneering, almost cruel tone to his voice. He was reacting out of a deep-seated revulsion to this kind of shallow conversation, this *fakery*. It reminded him of too much disappointment, too much pain. Too many lies. 'Do you say anything else?'

She blinked, but otherwise showed no discomfiture. 'Are you irritated by my manners, Your Highness?'

'You are meant to call me Sandro, but you have yet to do so.'

'I apologise. Your first name does not come easily to me.'

He arched an eyebrow, curious yet also still filled with that edgy restlessness that he knew would lead him to say—or do—things they both might regret.

'And why is that?' he asked, and she lifted her shoulders in a tiny shrug.

'You are the king of Maldinia.'

'It's nothing more than a title.'

Her mouth tightened, eyes flashing before she carefully ironed out her expression, her face smoothing like a blank piece of paper. 'Is that what you truly think?'

No, it wasn't. The crown upon his head—the title before his name—was a leaden weight inside him, dragging him down. It always had been, rife with expectations and disappointment. He'd seen how his father had treated that title, and he had no desire to emulate him. No desire to spiral down that destructive path, and yet he did not know if he possessed the strength to do otherwise. 'What do you think?' he asked.

'I think it is an honour and a privilege.'

'And one you are eager to share.' He heard the sardonic

edge to his words and he knew she did too, even though her expression didn't change, didn't even flicker. Funny, how he knew. How he'd somehow become attuned to this ice princess without even trying.

Or maybe he just knew her type, the kind of woman who would do anything to be queen, who didn't care about love or friendship or any softer emotion. Hadn't he encountered such women before, starting with his own mother? And Teresa had been the same, interested only in his wealth and status. He'd yet to find a woman who didn't care about such things, and he no longer had the freedom to search.

'Of course,' she answered calmly.

'Even though you don't know me.'

She hesitated, and he took another sip of wine, watching her over the rim of his glass. He wondered how far he would have to push her to evoke some response—*any* response. Further than that, clearly, for she didn't answer, merely sipped her own wine, her expression coolly serene.

'It doesn't bother you,' he pressed, 'that we barely know each other? That you are going to pledge your life to a stranger? Your body?'

Awareness flared in her eyes at his provocative remark, and he took a step towards her. He wanted her to admit it did, longed for her to say something real, something about how strange or uncertain or fearful this arrangement was. Something. Anything.

She regarded him for a moment, her expression thoughtful and yet still so shuttered. 'So you asked me earlier,' she remarked. 'And yet I thought that was the point of this evening. To get to know one another.'

'Yet you came to Maldinia prepared to marry me without such a luxury.'

'A fact which seems to provoke you, yet I assume you have been prepared to marry me under the same circumstances?' She was as coolly challenging as he had been, and he felt a flicker of respect, a frisson of interest. At least she'd stopped with her milky thank yous. At least she was being honest, even if he despised such truth.

'I was and still am,' he answered. 'I have a duty to provide an heir.'

The faintest blush touched her cheeks at the mention of heirs and she glanced away. 'So you are acting out of duty, and I am not?'

'What duty insists you marry a king?'

'One it appears you wouldn't understand.'

'Oh, I understand,' he answered, and she pressed her lips together, lifted her chin.

'Do you? Why don't you tell me, then, what you understand?'

He stared at her for a moment, and then decided to answer her with honesty. He doubted he'd get even a flicker of response from her. 'You want a title,' he stated flatly. 'A crown. Wealth and power—'

'And in exchange I will give you my allegiance and service,' she answered back, as unruffled as he'd suspected. 'Children and heirs, God willing. Is it not a fair trade?'

He paused, amazed at her plain speaking, even a little admiring of it. At least she wasn't pretending to him, the way so many others would. He could be thankful for that, at least. 'I suppose it is,' he answered slowly. 'But I would prefer my marriage not to be a trade.'

'And yet it must be, because you are king. That is not my fault.'

'No,' he agreed quietly. 'But even so—'

'You think my reasons for this marriage are less than yours,' Liana finished flatly. 'Less worthy.'

Her astuteness unnerved him. 'I suppose I do. You've admitted what you want, Lady Liana. Money. Power. Fame. Such things seem shallow to me.'

'If I wanted them for my own gratification, I suppose they would be.'

He frowned. 'What else could you possibly want them for?'

She just shook her head. 'What has made you so cynical?'

'Life, Lady Liana. Life.' He glanced away, not wanting to think about what had made him this suspicious, this sure that everyone was just out for something, that people were simply to be manipulated and used. Even your own children.

'In any case, you clearly don't relish the prospect of marriage to me,' she said quietly.

'No, I don't,' he answered after a pause. He turned to meet her clear gaze directly. 'I'm sorry if that offends you.'

'It doesn't offend me,' she answered. 'Surprises me, perhaps.'

'And why is that?'

'Because I had assumed we were in agreement about the nature of this marriage.'

'Which is?' he asked, wanting to hear more despite hating her answers, the reality of their situation.

She blinked, a hint of discomfiture, even uncertainty, in the way she shifted her weight, clutched her wine glass a little more tightly. 'Convenience.'

'Ah, yes. Convenience.' And he supposed it was convenient for her to have a crown. A title. And all the trappings that came with them. 'At least you're honest about it.'

'Why shouldn't I be?'

'Most women who have wanted my title or my money have been a bit more coy about what they really want,' he answered. 'More conniving.'

'You'll find I am neither.'

'How refreshing.'

She simply raised her eyebrows at his caustic tone and Sandro suppressed a sigh. He certainly couldn't fault her honesty. 'Tell me about yourself,' he finally said, and she lifted her shoulders in a tiny shrug.

'What is it you wish to know?'

'Anything. Everything. Where have you been living?'

'In Milan.'

'Ah, yes. Your charity work.'

Ire flashed in her eyes. 'Yes, my charity work.'

'What charity do you support again?'

'Hands To Help.'

'Which is?'

'A foundation that offers support to families with disabled children.'

'What kind of support?'

'Counselling, grants to families in need, practical assistance with the day-to-day.' She spoke confidently, clearly on familiar ground. He saw how her eyes lit up and everything in her suddenly seemed full of energy and determination.

'This charity,' he observed. 'It means a lot to you.'

She nodded, her lips pressed together in a firm line. 'Everything.'

Everything? Her zeal was admirable, yet also surprising, even strange. 'Why is that, Lady Liana?'

She jerked back slightly, as if the question offended her. 'Why shouldn't it?'

'As admirable as it is, I am intrigued. Most people

don't live for their philanthropic causes. I would have thought you simply helped out with various charities as a way to bide your time.'

'Bide my time?'

'Until you married.'

She let out an abrupt laugh, the sound hard and humourless. 'You are as traditional as my parents.'

'Yet you are here.'

'Meaning?'

He spread his hands. 'Not many women, not even the daughters of dukes, would enter a loveless marriage, having barely met the man in question, in this day and age.'

She regarded him coolly. 'Unless, of course, there was something in it for them. Money. Status. A title.'

'Exactly.'

She shook her head. 'And what do you see as being in it for you, Your Highness? I'm curious, considering how reluctant you are to marry.'

His lips curved in a humourless smile. 'Why, all the things you told me, of course. You've detailed your own attributes admirably, Lady Liana. I get a wife who will be the perfect queen. Who will stand by my side and serve my country. And of course, God willing, give me an heir. Preferably two.'

A faint blush touched those porcelain cheeks again, intriguing him. She was twenty-eight years old and yet she blushed like an untouched virgin. Surely she'd had relationships before. Lovers.

And yet in their conversation this afternoon, she'd intimated that she hadn't.

'That still doesn't answer my question,' she said after a moment. 'I understand your need to marry. But why me in particular?'

Sandro shrugged. 'You're a duke's daughter, you have

shown yourself to be philanthropic, your father is an important member of the European Union. You're fertile, I assume?'

The pink in her cheeks deepened. 'There is no reason to think otherwise.'

'I suppose that aspect of unions such as these is always a bit of a risk.'

'And if I couldn't have children?' she asked after a moment. 'Would we divorce?'

Would they? Everything in him railed against that as much as the actual marriage. It was all so expedient, so cold. 'We'll cross that bridge when we come to it.'

'How comforting.'

'I can't pretend to like any of this, Lady Liana. I'd rather have a normal relationship, with a woman who—' He stopped suddenly, realising he was revealing too much. *A woman who chose me. Who loved me for myself, and not because of my money or my crown.* No, he wasn't about to tell this cold-blooded woman any of that.

'A woman who?' she prompted.

'A woman who wasn't interested in my title.'

'Why don't you find one, then?' she asked, and she didn't sound hurt or even peeved, just curious. 'There must be a woman out there who would marry you for your own sake, Your Highness.'

And she clearly wasn't one of them, a fact that he'd known and accepted yet still, when so baldly stated, made him inwardly flinch. 'I have yet to find one,' he answered shortly. 'And you are meant to call me Sandro.'

'Then you must call me Liana.'

'Very well, Liana. It's rather difficult to find a woman who isn't interested in my title. The very fact that I have it attracts the kind of woman who is interested in it.'

'Yet you renounced your inheritance for fifteen years,'

Liana observed. 'Couldn't you have found a woman in California?'

He felt a flash of something close to rage, or perhaps just humiliation. She made it sound as if he was pathetic, unable to find a woman to love him for himself.

And maybe he was—but he didn't like this ice princess knowing about it. Remarking on it.

'The women I met in California were interested in my wealth and status,' he said shortly. He thought of Teresa, then pushed the thought away. He'd tumbled into love with her like a foolish puppy; he wouldn't make that mistake again. He wouldn't have the choice, he acknowledged. His attempt at relationships ended in this room, with this woman, and love had no place in what was between them.

'I'm not interested in your wealth,' Liana said after a moment. 'I have no desire to drape myself with jewels or prance about in designer dresses—or whatever it is these grasping women do.'

There was a surprising hint of humour in her voice, and his interested snagged on it. 'These grasping women?'

'You seem to have met so many, Your— Sandro. I had no idea there were so many cold, ambitious women about, circling like hawks.'

His lips twitched at the image even as a cynical scepticism took its familiar hold. 'So you do not count yourself among the hawks, Liana?'

'I do not, but you might. I am interested in being your queen, Sandro. Not for the wealth or the fame, but for the opportunity it avails me.'

'And what opportunity is that?'

'To promote the charity I've been working for. Hands To Help.'

He stared at her, not bothering to mask his incredulity. Was he really expected to believe such nonsense? 'I know you said that the charity meant everything to you, but, even so, you are willing to marry a complete stranger in order to give it greater visibility?'

She pursed her lips. 'Clearly you find that notion incredible.'

'I do. You are throwing your life away on a good cause.'

'That's what marriage to you will be? Throwing my life away?' She raised her eyebrows, her eyes glinting with violet sparks. 'You don't rate yourself highly, then.'

'I will never love you.' Even if he had once longed for a loving relationship, he knew he would never find it with this woman. Even if she wanted to be queen for the sake of some charity—a notion that still seemed ridiculous— she still wanted to be queen. Wanted his title, not him. Did the reason why really matter?

'I'm not interested in love,' she answered, seeming completely unfazed by his bald statement. 'And since it appears you aren't either, I don't know why our arrangement can't suit us both. You might not want to marry, Your Highness—'

'Sandro.'

'Sandro,' she amended with a brief nod, 'but obviously you have to. I have my own reasons for agreeing to this marriage, as you know. Why can we not come to an amicable arrangement instead of festering with resentment over what neither of us can change?'

'You could change, if you wanted to,' Sandro pointed out. 'As much as you might wish to help this charity of yours, you are not bound by duty in quite the same way as I am.'

Her expression shuttered, and he felt instinctively that

she was hiding something, some secret sorrow. 'No,' she agreed quietly, 'not in quite the same way.'

She held his gaze for a moment that felt suspended, stretching into something else. All of a sudden, with an intensity that caught him by surprise, he felt his body tighten with both awareness and desire. He wanted to know what the shadows in her eyes hid and he wanted to chase them away. He wanted to see them replaced with the light of desire, the blaze of need.

His gaze swept over her elegant form, her slight yet tempting curves draped in champagne-coloured silk, and desire coiled tighter inside him.

An amicable arrangement, indeed. Why not?

She broke the gaze first, taking a sip of wine, and he forced his mind back to more immediate concerns…such as actually getting to know this woman.

'So you live in Milan. Your parents have an apartment there?'

'They do, but I have my own as well.'

'You enjoy city life?'

She shrugged. 'It has proved convenient for my work.'

Her charity work, for which she didn't even get paid. Could she possibly be speaking the truth when she said she was marrying him to promote the charity she supported? It seemed absurd and extreme, yet he had seen the blazing, determined light in her eyes when she spoke of it.

'What has made you so devoted to that particular charity?' he asked and everything in her went tense and still.

'It's a good cause,' she answered after a moment, her expression decidedly wary.

'There are plenty of good causes. What did you say Hands To Help did? Support families with disabled children?'

'Yes.'

A few moments ago she'd been blazing with confidence as she'd spoken about it, but now every word she spoke was offered reluctantly, every movement repressive. She was hiding something, Sandro thought, but he had no idea what it could be.

'And did anything in particular draw you to this charity?' he asked patiently. Getting answers from her now felt akin to drawing blood from a stone.

For a second, no more, she looked conflicted, almost tormented. Her features twisted and her eyes appealed to him with an agony he didn't understand. Then her expression shuttered once more, like a veil being drawn across her face, and she looked away. 'Like I said, it's a good cause.'

And that, Sandro thought bemusedly, was that. Very well. He had plenty of time to discover the secrets his bride-to-be was hiding, should he want to know them. 'And what about before you moved to Milan? You went to university?'

'No. I started working with Hands To Help when I was eighteen.' She shifted restlessly, then pinned a bright smile on her face that Sandro could see straight through.

'What about you, Sandro?' she asked, stumbling only slightly over his name. 'Did you enjoy your university days?'

He thought of those four years at Cambridge, the heady freedom and the bitter disillusionment. Had he enjoyed them? In some respects, yes, but in others he had been too angry and hurt to enjoy anything.

'They served a purpose,' he said after a moment, and she cocked her head.

'Which was?'

'To educate myself.'

'You renounced your title upon your graduation, did you not?'

Tension coiled inside him. That much at least was common knowledge, but he still didn't like talking about it, had no desire for her to dig. They both had secrets, it seemed.

'I did.'

'Why?'

Such a bald question. Who had ever asked him that? No one had dared, and yet this slip of a woman with her violet eyes and carefully blank expression did, and without a tremor. 'It felt necessary at the time.' He spoke repressively, just as she had, and she accepted it, just as he had. Truce.

Yet stupidly, he felt almost disappointed. She wasn't interested in him; of course she wasn't. She'd already said as much. And he didn't want to talk about it, so why did he care?

He didn't. He was just being contrary because even as he accepted the necessity of this marriage, everything in him rebelled against it. Rebelled against entering this prison of a palace, with its hateful memories and endless expectations. Rebelled against marrying a woman he would never love, who would never love him. Would their convenient marriage become as bitter and acrimonious as his parents'? He hoped not, but he didn't know how they would keep themselves from it.

'We should eat,' he said, his voice becoming a bit brusque, and he went to pull out her chair, gesturing for her to come forward.

She did, her dress whispering about her legs as she moved, her head held high, her bearing as straight and proud as always. As she sat down, Sandro breathed in the perfumed scent of her, something subtle and floral, perhaps rosewater.

He glanced down at the back of her neck as she sat, the skin so pale with a sprinkling of fine golden hairs. He had the sudden urge to touch that soft bit of skin, to press his lips to it. He imagined how she would react and his mouth curved in a mocking smile. He wondered again if the ice princess was ice all the way through. He would, he decided, find out before too long. Perhaps they could enjoy that aspect of their marriage, if nothing else.

'What have you been doing in California?' she asked as one of the palace staff came in with their first course, plates of mussels nestled in their shells and steamed in white wine and butter.

'I ran my own IT firm.'

'Did you enjoy it?'

'Very much so.'

'Yet you gave it up to return to Maldinia.'

It had been the most agonising decision he'd ever made, and yet it had been no decision at all. 'I did,' he answered shortly.

She cocked her head, her lavender gaze sweeping thoughtfully over him. 'Are you glad you did?'

'Glad doesn't come into it,' he replied. 'It was simply what I needed to do.'

'Your duty.'

'Yes.'

Sandro pried a mussel from its shell and ate the succulent meat, draining the shell of its juices. Liana, he noticed, had not touched her meal; her mouth was drawn into a prim little line. He arched an eyebrow.

'Are mussels not to your liking?'

'They're delicious, I'm sure.' With dainty precision she pierced a mussel with her fork and attempted, delicately, to wrest it from its shell. Sandro watched, amused, as she wrangled with the mussel and failed. This was a food that required greasy fingers and smacking lips, a wholehearted and messy commitment to the endeavour. He sat back in his chair and waited to see what his bride-to-be would do next.

She took a deep breath, pressed her lips together, and tried again. She stabbed the mussel a bit harder this time, and then pulled her fork back. The utensil came away empty and the mussel flew across her plate, the shell clattering against the porcelain. Sandro's lips twitched.

Liana glanced up, her eyes narrowing. 'You're laughing at me.'

'You need to hold the mussel with your fingers,' he explained, leaning forward, his mouth curving into a mocking smile. 'And that means you might actually get them dirty.'

Her gaze was all cool challenge. 'Or you could provide a knife.'

'But this is so much more interesting.' He took another mussel, holding the shell between his fingers, and prised the meat from inside, then slurped the juice and tossed the empty shell into a bowl provided for that purpose. 'See?' He lounged back in his chair, licking his fingers with deliberate relish. He enjoyed discomfiting Liana. He'd enjoy seeing her getting her fingers dirty and her mouth smeared with butter even more, actually living life inside of merely observing it, but he trusted she would find a way to eat her dinner without putting a single hair out of place. That was the kind of woman she was.

Liana didn't respond, just watched him in that chilly way of hers, as if he was a specimen she was meant to examine. And what conclusions would she draw? He doubted whether she could understand what drove him,

just as he found her so impossibly cold and distant. They
were simply too far apart in their experience of and desire for life to ever see eye to eye on anything, even a
plate of mussels.

'Do you think you'll manage any of them?' he asked,
nodding towards her still-full plate, and her mouth firmed.

Without replying she reached down and held one shell
with the tips of her fingers, stabbing the meat with her
fork. With some effort she managed to wrench the mussel from its shell and put it in her mouth, chewing resolutely. She left the juice.

'Is that what we call compromise?' Sandro asked softly
and she lifted her chin.

'I call it necessity.'

'We'll have to employ both in our marriage.'

'As you would in any marriage, I imagine,' she answered evenly, and he acknowledged the point with a
terse nod.

Liana laid down her fork; clearly she wasn't going to
attempt another mussel. 'What exactly is it you dislike
about me, Your Highness?'

'*Sandro.* My name is Sandro.' She didn't respond and
he drew a breath, decided for honesty. 'You ask what I
dislike about you? Very well. The fact that you decided
on this marriage without even meeting me—save an un-
remarkable acquaintance fifteen years ago—tells me everything I need to know about you. And I like none of it.'

'So you have summed me up and dismissed me, all
because of one decision I have made? The same decision
you have made?'

'I admit it sounds hypocritical, but I had no choice.
You did.'

'And did it not occur to you,' she answered back, her
voice still so irritatingly calm, 'that any woman you ap-

proached regarding this marriage, any woman who accepted, would do so out of similar purpose? Your wife can't win, Sandro, whether it's me or someone else. You are determined to hate your bride, simply because she agreed to marry you.'

Her logic surprised and discomfited him, because he knew she was right. He was acting shamefully, *stupidly*, taking out his frustration on a woman who was only doing what he'd expected and even requested. 'I'm sorry,' he said after a moment. 'I realise I am making this more difficult for both of us, and to no purpose. We must marry.'

'You could choose someone else,' she answered quietly. 'Someone more to your liking.'

He raised an eyebrow, wearily amused. 'Are you suggesting I do?'

'No, but…' She shrugged, spreading her hands. 'I do not wish to be your life sentence.'

'And will I be yours?'

'I have accepted the limitations of this marriage in a way it appears you have not.'

Which made him sound like a hopeless romantic. No, he'd accepted the limitations. He was simply railing against them, which as she'd pointed out was to no purpose. And he'd stop right now.

'Forgive me, Liana. I have been taking out my frustrations on you, and I will not do so any longer. I wish to marry you and no other. You are, as I mentioned before, so very suitable, and I apologise for seeming to hold it against you.' This little speech sounded stiltedly formal, but he did mean it. He'd made his choices. He needed to live with them.

'Apology accepted,' she answered quietly, but with no

real warmth. Could he even blame her? He'd hardly en-
deared himself to her. He wasn't sure he could.

He reached for his wine glass. 'In any case, after the
debacle of my brother's marriage, not to mention my
parents', our country needs the stability of a shock-free
monarchy.'

'Your brother? Prince Leo?'

'You know him?'

'I've met him on several occasions. He's married to
Alyse Barras now.'

'The wedding of the century, apparently. The love
story of the century....' He shook his head, knowing
how his brother must have hated the pretence. 'And it
was all a lie.'

'But they are still together?'

Sandro nodded. 'The irony is, they actually do love
each other. But they didn't fall in love until after their
marriage.'

'So their six-year engagement was—?'

'A sham. And the public isn't likely to forgive that
very easily.'

'It hardly matters, since Leo will no longer be king.'
God, she was cold. 'I suppose not.'

'I only meant,' she clarified, as if she could read his
thoughts, 'that the publicity isn't an issue for them anymore.'

'But it will be for us,' he filled in, 'which is why I have
chosen to be honest about the convenience of our marriage. No one will ever think we're in love.'

'Instead of a fairy tale,' she said, 'we will have a business partnership.'

'I suppose that is as good a way of looking at it as any
other.' Even if the thought of having a marriage like his
parents'—one born of convenience and rooted in little

more than tolerance—made everything in him revolt. If a marriage had no love and perhaps not even any sympathy between the two people involved, how could it not sour? Turn into something despicable and hate-filled?

How could *he* not?

He had no other example.

Taking a deep breath, he pressed a discreet button to summon the wait staff. It was time for the next course. Time to move on. Instead of fighting his fate, like the unhappy, defiant boy he'd once been, he needed to accept it—and that meant deciding just how he could survive a marriage to Lady Liana Aterno.

CHAPTER THREE

LIANA STUDIED SANDRO'S face and wondered what he was thinking. Her husband-to-be was, so far, an unsettling enigma. She didn't understand why everything she did, from being polite to trying to eat mussels without splattering herself with butter, seemed to irritate him, but she knew it did. She saw the way his silvery eyes darkened to storm-grey, his mobile mouth tightening into a firm line.

So he didn't want to marry her. That undeniable truth lodged inside her like a cold, hard stone. She hadn't expected that, but could she really be surprised? He'd spent fifteen years escaping his royal duty. Just because he'd decided finally to honour his commitments didn't mean, as he'd admitted himself, that he relished the prospect.

And yet it was hard not to take his annoyance personally. Not to let it hurt—which was foolish, because this marriage wasn't personal. She didn't want his love or even his affection, but she had, she realised, hoped for agreement. Understanding.

A footman came in and cleared their plates, and Liana was glad to see the last of the mussels. She felt resentment stir inside her at the memory of Sandro's mocking smile. He'd enjoyed seeing her discomfited, would have probably laughed aloud if she'd dropped a mussel in her lap or sent it spinning across the table.

Perhaps she should have dived in and smeared her face and fingers with butter; perhaps he would have liked her better then. But a lifetime of careful, quiet choices had kept her from making a mess of anything, even a plate of mussels. She couldn't change now, not even over something so trivial.

The footman laid their plates down, a main course of lamb garnished with fresh mint.

'At least this shouldn't present you with too much trouble,' Sandro said softly as the door clicked shut. Liana glanced up at him.

She felt irritation flare once more, surprising her, because she usually didn't let herself feel irritated or angry...or anything. Yet this man called feelings up from deep within her, and she didn't even know why or how. She definitely didn't like it. 'You seem to enjoy amusing yourself at my expense.'

'I meant only to tease,' he said quietly. 'I apologise if I've offended you. But you are so very perfect, Lady Liana—and I'd like to see you a little less so.'

Perfect? If only he knew the truth. 'No one is perfect.'

'You come close.'

'That is not, I believe, a compliment.'

His lips twitched, drawing her attention to them. He had such sculpted lips, almost as if they belonged on a statue. She yanked her gaze upwards, but his eyes were no better. Silvery grey and glinting with amusement.

She felt as if a fist had taken hold of her heart, plunged into her belly. Everything quivered, and the sensation was not particularly pleasant. Or perhaps it was *too* pleasant; she felt that same thrill of fascination that had taken hold of her when she'd first met him.

'I would like to see you,' Sandro said, his voice lowering to a husky murmur, 'with your hair cascading over your shoulders. Your lips rosy and parted, your face flushed.'

And as if he could command it by royal decree, she felt herself begin to blush. The image he painted was so suggestive. And it made that fist inside her squeeze her heart once more, made awareness tauten muscles she'd never even known she had.

'Why do you wish to see me like that?' she asked, relieved her voice sounded as calm as always. Almost.

'Because I think you would look even more beautiful then than you already are. You'd look warm and real and alive.'

She drew back, strangely hurt by his words. 'I am quite real already. And alive, thank you very much.'

Sandro's gaze swept over her, assessing, knowing. 'You remind me of a statue.'

A statue? A statue was cold and lifeless, without blood or bone, thought or feeling. And he thought that was what she was?

Wasn't it what she'd been for the past twenty years? The thought was like a hammer blow to the heart. She blinked, tried to keep her face expressionless. Blank, just like the statue he accused her of being. 'Are you trying to be offensive?' she answered, striving to keep her voice mild and not quite managing it.

His honesty shouldn't hurt her, she knew. There was certainly truth in it, and yet… She didn't want to be a statue. Not to this man.

A thought that alarmed her more than anything else.

'Not trying, no,' Sandro answered. 'I suppose it comes naturally.'

'I suppose it does.'

He shook his head slowly. 'Do you ever lose your temper? Shout? Curse?'

'Would you prefer to be marrying a shrew?' she answered evenly and his mouth quirked in a small smile.

'Does anything make you angry?' he asked, and before she could think better of it, she snapped, 'Right now, you do.'

He laughed, a rich chuckle of amusement, the sound spreading over her like chocolate, warming her in a way she didn't even understand. This man was frustrating and even hurting her and yet...

She liked his laugh.

'I am glad for it,' he told her. 'Anger is better than indifference.'

'I have never said I was indifferent.'

'You have shown it in everything you've said or done,' Sandro replied. 'Almost.'

'Almost?'

'You are not quite,' he told her in that murmur of a voice, 'as indifferent as you'd like me to believe—or even to believe yourself.'

She felt her breath bottle in her lungs, catch in her throat. 'I don't know what you mean, Your Highness.'

'Don't you?' He leaned forward, his eyes glinting silver in the candlelight. 'And must I remind you yet again that you are to call me Sandro?'

She felt her blush deepen, every nerve and sinew and sense so agonisingly aware. Feeling this much *hurt*. She was angry and scared and, most of all, she wanted him... just as he knew she did. 'I am not inclined,' she told him, her voice shaking, 'to call you by your first name just now, *Your Highness*.'

'I wonder, under what circumstances would you call me Sandro?'

Her nails dug into her palms. 'I cannot think of any at the moment.'

Sandro's silvery gaze swept over her in lingering assessment. 'I can think of one or two,' he answered lazily, and everything in her lurched at the sudden predatory intentness in his gaze. She felt her heart beat hard in response, her palms go cold and her mouth dry. 'Yes, definitely, one or two,' he murmured, and, throwing his napkin on the table, he rose from the chair.

She looked, Sandro thought, like a trapped rabbit, although perhaps not quite so frightened a creature. Even in her obvious and wary surprise she clung to her control, to her coldness. He had a fierce urge to strip it away from her and see what lay beneath it. An urge he intended to act on now.

Her eyes had widened and she gazed at him unblinkingly, her hands frozen over her plate, the knife and fork clenched between her slender, white-knuckled fingers.

Sandro moved towards her chair with a loose-limbed, predatory intent; he was acting on instinct now, wanting—needing—to strip away her cold haughtiness, chip away at that damned ice until it shattered all around them. She would call him Sandro. She would melt in his arms.

Gently, yet with firm purpose, he uncurled her clenched fingers from around her cutlery, and the knife and fork clattered onto her plate. She didn't resist. Her violet gaze was still fastened on him, her lips slightly parted. Her pulse thundered under his thumb as he took her by the wrist and drew her from the chair to stand before him.

Still she didn't resist, not even as he moved closer to her, nudging his thigh in between her own legs as he lifted his hands to frame her face.

Her skin was cool and unbearably soft, and he brushed his thumb over the fullness of her parted lips, heard her tiny, indrawn grasp, and smiled. He rested his thumb on the soft pad of her lower lip before he slid his hands down to her bare shoulders, her skin like silk under his palms.

He gazed into her eyes, the colour of a bruise, framed by moon-coloured lashes, wide and waiting. Then he bent his head and brushed his mouth across hers, a first kiss that was soft and questioning, and yet she gave no answer.

She remained utterly still, her lips unmoving under his, her hands clenched by her sides. The only movement was the hard beating of her heart that he could feel from where he stood, and Sandro's determination to make her respond crystallised inside him, diamond hard. He deepened the kiss, sliding his tongue into her luscious mouth, the question turning into a demand.

For a woman who was so coldly determined, her mouth tasted incredibly warm and sweet. He wanted more, any sense of purpose be damned, and as he explored the contours of her mouth with his tongue he moved his hands from her shoulders down the silk of her dress to cup the surprising fullness of her breasts. They fitted his hands perfectly, and he brushed his thumbs lightly over the taut peaks. Still she didn't move.

She was like the statue he'd accused her of being, frozen into place, rigid and unyielding. A shaft of both sexual and emotional frustration blazed through him. He wanted—*needed*—her to respond. Physically. Emotionally. He needed something from her, something real and alive, and he would do whatever it took to get it.

Sandro tore his mouth from hers and kissed his way along her jawline, revelling in the silkiness of her skin even as a furious determination took hold of him once more.

Yet as his mouth hovered over the sweet hollow where her jaw met her throat he hesitated, unwilling to continue when she was so unresponsive despite the insistence pulsing through him. He had never forced a woman, not for so much as a kiss, and he wasn't about to start now. Not with his bride. Submission, he thought grimly, was not the same as acceptance. As want.

Then she let out a little gasping shudder and her hand, as if of its own accord, clasped his arm, her nails digging into his skin as she pulled him infinitesimally closer. She tilted her head back just a little to allow him greater access to her throat, her breasts, and triumph surged through him. She wanted this. *Him.*

He moved lower, kissing his way to the V between her breasts where the diamond-and-pearl pendant nestled. He lifted the jewel and licked the warm skin underneath, tasted salt on his tongue and heard her gasp again, her knees buckling as she sat down hard on the table amidst the detritus of their dinner.

Triumph mixed with pure lust and he fastened his hands on her hips, sliding them down to her thighs so he could spread her legs wider. He stood between them, the silken folds of her dress whispering around him as he kissed her like a starving man feasting at a banquet.

He felt her shy response, her tongue touching his before darting away again, and he was utterly enflamed. He slid the straps of her dress from her shoulders, freeing her breasts from their silken prison.

She wore no bra, and desire ripped through him at the sight of her, her head thrown back, her breath coming in gasps as she surrendered herself to his touch, her face flushed and rosy, her lips parted, her body so wonderfully open to him. *This* was how he'd wanted to see her. He bent his head, kissing his way down her throat, his hand cupping her bared breast—

And then the door opened and a waitress gasped an

apology before closing it again quickly, but the moment, Sandro knew, had broken. Shattered into shock and awkwardness and regret.

Liana wrenched herself from his grasp, holding her dress up to her bare front, her lips swollen, her eyes huge and dazed as she stared at him.

He stared back in both challenge and desire, because as much as she might want to deny what had just happened between them, her response had said otherwise. Her response had told him she really was alive and warm and real beneath all that ice, and he was glad.

'Don't—' she finally managed, the single word choked, and Sandro arched an eyebrow.

'It's a little late for that. But obviously, I've stopped.'

'You shouldn't have—'

'Stopped?'

'Started—'

'And why not? We are to be married, aren't we?'

She just shook her head, fumbling as she attempted to slide her arms back into the dress, but she couldn't manage it without ripping the fragile fabric. Sandro came to stand behind her, unzipping the back with one quick tug.

'Don't touch me—'

'I'm helping you dress,' he answered shortly. 'You can't get your arms through the straps otherwise.'

Wordlessly she slid her arms through the straps, and he felt her tremble as he zipped her back up, barely resisting the urge to press his lips to the bared nape of her neck and feel her respond to him again.

Her hair had come undone a bit, a few tousled curls lying against her neck. The back of her dress, he saw, was crumpled and stained from where she'd sat on the table. Just remembering made hot, hard desire surge through him again. She might, for the sake of pride or modesty, play the ice maiden now, but he knew better. He wanted to make her melt again, even as he watched her return to her cold composure, assembling it like armour.

'Thank you,' she muttered and stepped quickly away from him.

'You're welcome.' He surveyed her, noticing the faint pink to her cheeks, the swollen rosiness of her mouth. She would not look at him. 'I'm afraid our meal is quite ruined.'

'I'm not hungry.'

He couldn't resist quipping, 'Not for food, perhaps.'

'Don't.' She dragged her gaze to his, and he was surprised—and slightly discomfited—to see not simple embarrassment in her stormy gaze, but a tortured recrimination that ate at the satisfaction he'd felt at her physical response. He'd seduced her quite ruthlessly, he knew. His kisses and caresses had been a calculated attack against her senses. Her coldness.

But she *had* responded. That had been real. Even if she regretted it now.

He folded his arms. 'Our marriage might be one of convenience, Liana, but that doesn't mean we can't—or shouldn't—desire one another. Frankly I find it a relief.' She shook her head wordlessly, and a different kind of frustration spiked through him. 'What do you see our marriage looking like, then? I need an heir—'

'I *know* that.' She lifted her hands to her hair, fussing with some of the diamond-tipped pins. A few, he saw, had fallen to the floor and silently he bent to scoop them up and then handed them to her. She still wouldn't look at him, just shoved pins into the tangled mass of silvery hair that he now realised was really quite a remarkable colour. Quite beautiful.

'Are you a virgin?' he asked abruptly, and her startled gaze finally met his. She looked almost affronted.

'Of course I am.'

'Of course? You're twenty-eight years old. I'd hardly expect, at that age, for you to save yourself for marriage.'

Colour deepened in her cheeks. 'Well, I did. I'm sorry if that is yet another disappointment for you.' She didn't sound sorry at all, and he almost smiled.

'Hardly a disappointment.' Her response to him hadn't been disappointing at all. 'But I can understand why you might feel awkward or afraid about what happened between—'

'I'm not *afraid*.' Her lips tightened and her eyes flashed. She dropped her hands from her hair and busied herself with straightening her rather ruined dress.

'What, then?' Sandro asked quietly.

Her hands shook briefly before she stilled them, mindlessly smoothing the crumpled silk of her dress. 'I simply wasn't... This isn't...' She took a breath. 'I wasn't expecting this.'

'It should be a happy surprise, then,' Sandro answered. 'At least we desire each other.' She shook her head, the movement violent. 'I still fail to see the problem.'

She drew a breath into her lungs, pressed her hands against her still crumpled dress. 'This marriage was— is—meant to be convenient.'

'Not that convenient,' Sandro answered sharply. 'We were always going to consummate it.'

'I know that!' She took another breath; her cheeks were now bright pink. 'I simply don't... I don't want to *feel*...' She broke off, misery swamping her eyes, her whole body. Sandro had the sudden urge to comfort her, to offer her a hug of affection rather than the calculated caress of moments before.

What on earth was causing her such torment?

Liana felt as if Sandro had taken a hammer to her heart, to her very self, with that kiss. She'd very nearly shattered into a million pieces, and it was only by sheer strength of will that she'd kept herself together.

She'd never been touched like that before, never felt such an overwhelming, aching need for even more. More touches, more kisses, more of Sandro. It had called to a craving inside her she hadn't even known she had. Didn't want.

Because if she opened herself up to wanting anything from Sandro—even *that*—she'd open herself up to pain. To disappointment. To feeling, and she'd cut herself off from all of it for too long to want it now. To risk the fragile security she'd built around her heart, her self.

The point of this marriage, she thought helplessly, was that it wouldn't demand such things of her. It would be safe.

Yet nothing felt safe now. And how could she explain any of it to Sandro without sounding as if she was a freak? A frigid freak?

I'm sorry, Sandro, but I have no desire to enjoy sex with you.

She sounded ridiculous even to herself.

'What is it you don't want to feel, Liana?' he asked and she just stared at him.

This. Him. All of it. What could she tell him? He was clearly waiting for an answer. 'I…I don't want to desire you,' she said, and watched his eyebrows raise, his mouth thin.

'And why is that?'

Because it scares me. You scare me. She'd sound like such a pathetic little mouse, and maybe she was, but she didn't want him knowing it. Knowing how weak and frightened she was, when she'd been trying to seem strong and secure and safe.

Clearly it was nothing more than a facade.

Sandro was still staring at her, his expression narrowed and assessing. He probably couldn't imagine why any woman wouldn't desire him, wouldn't *want* to desire him. She'd read enough gossip websites and trashy tabloids to know Sandro Diomedi, whether he was king of Maldinia or IT billionaire, had plenty of women falling at his feet.

She didn't want to be one of them.

Oh, she'd always known she'd have to do her duty in bed as well as out of it. She might be inexperienced, but she understood that much.

She also knew most people didn't think of it as a duty. She'd read enough novels, seen enough romantic movies to know many people—*most* people—found the physical side of things to be quite pleasurable.

As she just had.

She felt her face heat once more as she remembered how shameless she had been. How good Sandro's mouth had felt on hers, his hands on her body, waking up every deadened nerve and sense inside her—

She looked away from him now, willing the memories to recede. She didn't *want* to wake up. Not like that.

'Liana?' he prompted, and she searched for an answer, something believable. Something that would hurt him, as she'd been hurt first by his derision and incredulity, and then by his desire. A Sandro who reached her with his kiss and caress was far more frightening than one who merely offended her with his scorn.

'Because I don't respect you,' she said, and she felt the electric jolt of shock go through him as if they were connected by a wire.

'Don't *respect*?' He looked shocked, almost winded, and Liana felt a vicious stab of petty satisfaction. He'd shaken up everything inside her, her sense of security and even her sense of self. Let him be the one to look and feel shaken.

Then his expression veiled and he pursed his lips. 'Why don't you respect me?'

'You've shirked your duty for fifteen years, and you need to ask that?'

Colour touched his cheekbones, and she knew she'd touched a nerve, one she hadn't even considered before. But there was truth in what she'd said, what she'd felt. He'd walked away from all he was meant to do, while she'd spent a lifetime trying to earn back her parents' respect for one moment's terrible lapse.

'I didn't realise you were so concerned about my duty.'

'I'm not, but then neither are you,' Liana snapped, amazed at the words—the feeling—coming out of her mouth. Who was this woman who lost her temper, who melted in a man's arms? She felt like a stranger to herself, and she couldn't believe how reckless she'd been with this man...in so many ways. How much he made her feel. Physically. Emotionally. So in the space of a single evening she'd said and done things she never had allowed herself to before.

'You're very honest,' Sandro said softly, his voice a dangerous drawl. 'I appreciate that, if not the sentiment.'

Liana dropped her hand from her mouth, where it had flown at his response. She knew she should apologise, yet somehow she could not find the words, or even the emotion. She wasn't sorry. This man had humiliated and hurt her, used her to prove some terrible point. She might be appallingly innocent by his standards, but she had enough sense to know he'd kissed her not out of simple and straightforward desire, but to prove something. To exhibit his power over her.

And he had. Oh, he had.

But he wouldn't now.

Sandro drew himself up, his mouth as thin and sharp as a blade, his eyes no more than silver slits. 'Clearly we have no more to say to one another.'

'What—?' Shock cut off her voice. Twenty years of trying to be an obedient and dutiful daughter, and she'd wrecked it in a matter of moments. *Why* had she been so impetuous, so stupid?

'I don't think we have any need to see each other again either,' he said, and Liana scrambled to think of something to say, anything to redeem the situation.

'I realise I spoke in haste—'

'And in truth.' He gave an unpleasant smile. 'Trust me, Lady Liana, I do appreciate your honesty. I have lived with far too much dissembling to do otherwise. However, since this is, as we have both agreed, a marriage of convenience, there is no point in attempting to get to know one another or find even one point of sympathy between us. In this case...' he paused, eyeing her coldly '...we will both do our duty.'

Her stomach hollowed out. 'You mean—'

'The wedding will be in six weeks. I'll see you then.' And without another word, the king turned on his heel and left her alone in the room, amidst the scattered dishes and ruined meal, her mind spinning.

Sandro strode from the dining room, fury beating in his blood, his bride-to-be's words ringing in his ears.

You've shirked your duty for fifteen years, and you need to ask that?

She'd cut to the heart of it, hadn't she? The empty heart of him. And even though he knew she was right, it was exactly what he had done, and he hated that she knew. That she'd pointed it out, and that she didn't respect him because of it. Who was she but a woman intent on selling herself for a crown and a title, never mind how she cloaked it with ideas of duty and selfless charity work? How dared she toss her contempt of him in his face?

And yet still her words cut deep, carved themselves into his soul. They held up a mirror to the selfishness of his heart, the inadequacy he felt now, and he couldn't stand it. Couldn't stand the guilt that rushed through him, along with the resentment. He didn't want to be here, didn't want to be king, didn't want any of this, and yet it was his by right. By duty. Even if he didn't deserve it. Even if he felt afraid—*terrified*—that he could not bear the weight of the crown his father hadn't even wanted to give him.

He yanked open the door to the study that had once been his father's and still smelled of his Havana cigars. Sandro opened a window and breathed in the cold night air, tinged even here in the city with the resin of the pines that fringed the capital city. He willed his heart to slow, the remnants of his desire, making his body ache with unfulfilment, to fade.

Briefly he considered whether he should break off his engagement. Find another bride, someone with a little more warmth, a little more heart. Someone who might actually respect him.

And just who would that be, when the truth is and always will be that you walked away from your duty?

That you don't deserve your crown or the respect it commands?

He closed his eyes briefly, pictured his father's face twisted in derision moments before he'd died.

You think I wanted this? You?

And deluded fool that he insisted on being, he actually had. Had hoped, finally, that his father accepted him. Loved him.

Idiot.

Sandro let out a shuddering breath and turned away from the window. He wouldn't call off the wedding, wouldn't try to find a better bride. He was getting about as good a deal as he could hope for.

What kind of woman, after all, agreed to a marriage of convenience? A woman like Liana, like his mother, intent on everything but emotion. And that was fine, really, because he didn't have the energy for emotion either. He didn't even think he believed in love anymore, so why bother searching for it? Wanting it?

Except that need seemed hardwired into his system, and had been ever since he'd been a little boy, desperate for his father's attention, approval, and most of all, love, when all he'd wanted was to use him as a pawn for publicity, so he could pursue his own selfish desires. Desires Sandro had been blinded to until his naive beliefs had been ripped away.

'Sandro?'

Sandro turned around to see his brother, Leo, standing in the doorway of his study. Six months ago Leo had been first in line to the throne, as he had been ever since their father had disinherited Sandro and put Leo forward. Fifteen years of bracing himself for the crown, and then Sandro had unexpectedly returned and set him free. At least that was how Sandro had always viewed it; Leo hadn't protested, and Sandro knew his brother hated the pretence of royal life as much as he had.

Yet he'd made a damn good heir to the throne in his absence, so much so that Sandro had wondered if Leo regretted his return.

He'd chosen not to ask.

Leo was a cabinet minister now, lived in a town house in Averne with his bride Alyse, and was working on passing a bill to provide broadband to the entire country, drag Maldinia into the twenty-first century.

'What is it?' Sandro heard the terse snap of his voice and sighed, rubbing a hand over his face. 'Sorry. It's been a long day.'

'You met with Lady Liana?'

'Yes.'

'Is she suitable?'

Sandro laughed, the sound humourless and harsh. 'Definitely.'

Leo stepped into the room and closed the door. 'You don't sound pleased.'

'Did either of us really wish to marry for duty?'

'Sometimes it can work out,' Leo answered, a hint of a smile in his voice, on his face.

'Sometimes,' Sandro agreed. Things had certainly worked out for his brother. He was in love with his wife and free to pursue his own interests and ambitions as he chose.

'I always thought Liana was nice enough,' Leo offered carefully. 'Although she seemed…sad to me, sometimes.'

'Sad?' Sandro shook his head even as he recalled the shadows in her eyes, the secrets he felt she'd been hiding. Yes, she had seemed sad. She'd also seemed determined, resolute, and as cold and hard as the diamond she'd worn around her neck. The diamond he'd lifted when he'd licked the skin underneath....

Remembering made lust beat along with his fury, and hell if that wasn't an unwholesome mix. Sighing, he pushed away from the window. 'I didn't realise you knew her.'

Leo's smile was wry. 'Father considered an alliance between us, briefly.'

'An alliance? You mean *marriage*?' Sandro turned around to stare at his brother in surprise. Yet how could he really be shocked? Leo had been the future king. And hadn't Liana already shown him just how much she wanted to be queen? For fifteen years—over half her life—he'd been essentially out of the picture. Of course she'd looked at other options.

As had his own brother, his own father.

'So what happened?' he asked Leo, and his brother's smile was crooked and yet clearly full of happiness. Of joy.

'Alyse happened.'

Of course. Sandro had seen the iconic photo himself, when it had been taken over six years ago. Leo had been twenty-four, Alyse eighteen. A single, simple kiss that had rocked the world and changed their lives for ever. And for the better now, thank God.

'Although to be honest,' Leo continued, 'I don't think Liana was ever really interested. It seemed as if she was humouring me, or maybe her parents, who wanted the match.'

Or hedging her bets, perhaps, Sandro thought, just in case the black-sheep heir made a reappearance. 'I'm happy for you, you know,' he said abruptly. 'For you and Alyse.'

'I know you are.'

Yet he heard a coolness in his brother's voice, and he could guess at its source. For fifteen years they hadn't spoken, seen each other, or been in touch in even the paltriest of ways. And this after their childhood, when they'd banded together, two young boys who had had only each other for companionship.

Sandro knew he needed to say something of all that had gone before—and all that hadn't. The silence and separation that had endured for so long was, he knew, his fault. He was the older brother, and the one who had left. Yet the words he knew he should say burned in his chest and tangled in his throat. He couldn't get them out. He didn't know how.

This was what happened when you grew up in a family that had never shown love or emotion or anything real at all. You didn't know how to be real yourself, as much as you craved it—and you feared that which you craved.

And yet Leo had found love. He was real with Alyse. Why, Sandro wondered in frustration, couldn't he be the same?

And in the leaden weight of his heart he knew the answer. Because he was king…and he had a duty that precluded such things.

CHAPTER FOUR

LIANA GAZED AT her reflection in the gold-framed mirror of one of the royal palace's many guest suites. She was in a different one from the last time she'd been here six weeks ago, yet it was just as sumptuous. Then she'd come to Maldinia to discuss marriage; this time she was here for a wedding. Hers.

'You're too thin.' Her mother Gabriella's voice came out sharp with anxiety as she entered the room, closing the door behind her.

'I have lost a little weight in the past few weeks,' Liana said, and heard the instinctive note of apology in her voice. Everything with her parents felt like an apology, a way to say sorry over and over again. Yet she could never say it enough, and her parents never seemed to hear it anyway.

They certainly never talked about it.

'I suppose things have been a bit stressful,' Gabriella allowed. She twitched Liana's short veil over her shoulders and smoothed the satin fabric of the simple white sheath dress she wore.

Her wedding to Sandro was to be a quiet affair in the palace's private chapel, with only family in attendance. After the fairy-tale proportions of Leo and Alyse's ceremony, and the resulting fallout, something quiet and dignified was needed. It suited Liana fine.

She wondered what Sandro thought about it. She hadn't seen him since she'd arrived two days ago, beyond a formal dinner where she'd been introduced to a variety of diplomats and dignitaries. She'd chatted with everyone, curtsied to the queen, who had eyed her coldly, and met Sandro's sister, Alexa, as well as his brother, Leo, and sister-in-law, Alyse.

Everyone—save the queen—had been friendly enough, but it had been Sandro's rather stony silence that had unnerved her. It had occurred to her then in an entirely new and unwelcome way that this man was going to be her *husband*. She would live with him for the rest of her days, bear his children, serve by his side. Stupid of her not to think it all through before, but suddenly it seemed overwhelming, her decision reckless. Was she really going to say vows based on a desire to please her parents? To somehow atone for the past?

No wonder Sandro had been incredulous. And it was too late to change her mind now.

Gabriella put her hands on Liana's shoulders, met her gaze in the mirror. 'You do want this marriage, Liana, don't you?' Liana opened her mouth to say of course she did, because she knew she couldn't say anything else. Not when her mother wanted it so much. Even now, with all the doubts swirling through her mind, she felt that. Believed it.

'Because I know we might seem old-fashioned to you,' Gabriella continued in a rush. 'Asking you to marry a man you've barely met.' Now Liana closed her mouth. It was old-fashioned, but she wasn't going to fight it. Wasn't going to wish for something else.

What was the point? Her parents wanted it, and it was

too late anyway. And in any case, a real marriage, a marriage based on intimacy and love, held no appeal for her.

Neither did a husband who seemed as if he hated her.

And wasn't that her fault? For telling him she didn't respect him? For pushing him away out of her own hurt pride and fear? But perhaps it was better for Sandro to hate her than call up all those feelings and needs. Perhaps antipathy would actually be easier.

'I just want you to be happy,' Gabriella said quietly. 'As your father does.'

And they thought marrying a stranger would make her happy?

No, Liana thought tiredly, they didn't want her to be happy, not really. They wanted to feel as if she had been taken care of, dealt with. Tidied away. They wanted to forget her, because she knew soul deep that every time her parents looked at her they were reminded of Chiara. Of Chiara's death.

Just as she was.

If she married Sandro, at least she'd be out of the way. Easier to forget.

Better for everyone, really.

She drew a breath into her lungs, forced her expression into a smile. 'I am happy, Mother. I will be.'

Her mother nodded, not questioning that statement. Not wanting to know. 'Good,' she said, and kissed Liana's cold cheek.

A few minutes later her mother left for the chapel, leaving Liana alone to face the walk down the aisle by herself. Maldinian tradition dictated that the bride walk by herself, and the groom keep his back to her until she reached his side.

A stupid tradition, probably meant to terrify brides into submission, she thought with a grimace. And would it terrify her? What would the expression on Sandro's face be when he did turn around? Contempt? Disgust? Hatred? *Desire?* She knew she shouldn't even care, but she did.

Ever since she'd first met Sandro, she'd started caring. Feeling. And that alarmed her more than anything.

She closed her eyes, fought against the nerves churning in her stomach and threatening to revolt up her throat. Why had this man woken something inside her she'd thought was not just asleep, but dead? How had he resurrected it?

She longed to go back to the numb safety she'd lived in for so long. For twenty years, since she was eight. Eight years old, pale faced and trembling, staring at the grief-stricken expressions on her parents' faces as she told them the truth.

I was there. It was my fault.

And they had, in their silence, agreed. Of course they had, because it *was* the truth. Chiara's death had been entirely her fault, and that was a truth she could never, ever escape.

This marriage was, in its own way, meant to be more penance. But it wasn't meant to make her *feel.* Want. Need.

Yet in the six weeks since she'd returned from Maldinia, it had. She felt the shift inside herself, an inexorable moving of the tectonic plates of her soul, and it was one she didn't welcome. Ever since Sandro's scathing indictment of her, his assault on her convictions, her body, her whole self, she'd started to feel more. Want more. And she was desperate to stop, to snatch back the numbness, the safety.

'Lady Liana? It's time.'

Woodenly Liana nodded and then followed Paula, the

palace's press secretary, to the small chapel where the service would take place.

'This will be a very quiet affair,' Paula said. 'No cameras or publicity, like before.'

Before, when Alyse and Leo's charade had blown up in their faces, Liana knew, and they'd been exposed as having faked their fairy-tale love story for the entirety of their engagement. This time there was no charade, yet Liana still felt as if everything could explode around her. As if it already had.

'All right, then.' Paula touched her briefly on her shoulder. 'You look lovely. Don't forget to smile.'

Somehow Liana managed to make the corners of her mouth turn up. Paula didn't look all that satisfied by this expression of expectant marital joy, but she nodded and left Liana alone to face the double doors that led to the chapel, the small crowd, and Sandro.

Drawing a deep breath, she straightened her shoulders, lifted her chin. She was doing this for a good reason. Forget her own feelings, which she'd tried to forget for so long anyway. There was a good reason, the best reason, to marry Sandro, to make her life worth something. Her sister.

For a second, no more, she allowed herself to think of Chiara. *Chi-Chi.* Her button eyes, her impish smile, her sudden laugh.

I'm doing this for you, Chi-Chi, she thought, and tears, tears she hadn't let herself cry for twenty years, rose in her eyes. She blinked them back furiously.

Forward.

'Lady Liana?'

Liana turned to see Alyse Barras—now Diomedi— walking towards her, a warm smile on her pretty face. She wore an understated dress of rose silk, with a matching coat and hat. Silk gloves reached up to the elbow on each slender arm. She looked every inch the elegant, confident royal.

Liana had met Alyse briefly at the dinner last night, but they hadn't spoken beyond a few pleasantries.

'I'm sorry we haven't had a chance to talk properly,' Alyse said, extending one hand that Liana took stiffly, still conscious of the tears crowding under her lids. 'I just wanted to tell you I know how you feel. Walking down an aisle alone can be a little frightening. A little lonely.' Her gaze swept over Liana's pale figure in obvious sympathy, and she instinctively stiffened, afraid those treacherous tears would spill right over. If they did, she feared there would be no coming back from it.

'Thank you,' she said, and she knew her voice sounded too cool. It was her only defence against losing it completely in this moment. 'I'm sure I'll manage.'

Alyse blinked, her mouth turning down slightly before she nodded. 'Of course you will. I just wanted to say... I hope we have a chance to get to know one another now that we're both part of this family.' Her smile returned. 'For better or for worse.'

And right now felt like worse. Liana nodded, too wretchedly emotional to respond any further to Alyse's friendly overture.

'Thank you,' she finally managed. 'I should go.'

'Of course.' Alyse nodded and stepped back. 'Of course.'

Two footmen came forward to throw open the doors of the chapel, and with that icy numbness now hastily re-assembled, her chin lifted and her head held high, Liana stepped into her future.

The chapel was as quiet and sombre as if a funeral were taking place rather than a wedding. A handful of guests she didn't know, her parents in the left front row. Sandro's back, broad and resolute, turned towards her. She felt the tears sting her eyes again, her throat tighten and she willed the emotion away.

This was the right thing to do. The only thing she could do. This was her duty to her parents, to the memory of her sister. She was doing it for them, not for herself. *For Chiara....*

She repeated the words inside her head, a desperate chant, an appeal to everything she'd done and been in the twenty years since Chiara's death.

This was her duty. Her atonement. Her absolution. She had no other choice, no other need but to serve her parents and the memory of her sister as best she could.

And as she came down the aisle she finally made herself believe it once more.

Sandro had heard the doors to the chapel open, knew Liana was walking towards him. He fought an urge to turn around, knowing that tradition had Maldinian grooms—royal ones, at least—facing the front until the bride was at their side.

When she was halfway down he gave in and turned around, tradition be damned. He wanted to see Liana, wanted to catch a glimpse of the woman he was about to promise to love, honour, and cherish before he made those binding vows. For the past six weeks he'd been trying *not* to think of her, of the proud contempt he'd seen on her face the last time they'd spoken, when she'd told him with a sneer in her voice that she didn't respect him.

And as shocked as her contemptuous indictment had been, how could he actually be surprised? Hurt? She'd been speaking the truth, after all.

Now as she came down the aisle, her bearing regal

and straight, her chin tilted proudly and her eyes flashing violet ice, he felt the hopes he hadn't even realised
he still had plummet.

She was just as he remembered. Just as composed,
just as soulless and scornful as he'd first feared. And in
about three minutes she would become his wife.

As she joined him at the altar, her dress whispering
against his legs, she lifted her chin another notch, all
haughty pride and cool purpose.

Sandro turned away without so much as a smile and
listened to the archbishop begin with a leaden heart.

An hour later they were man and wife, circulating
through one of the palace's many receiving rooms among
the few dozen guests. They still hadn't spoken to each
other, although Sandro had brushed his lips against Liana's cold ones at the end of the ceremony before she'd
stepped quickly away.

They'd walked down the aisle together, her hand lying
rigidly on his arm, and gone directly to one of the palace's salons for a champagne reception.

Liana, Sandro couldn't help notice, seemed to take to
the role of queen with instant, icy poise. She smiled and
chatted with a reserved dignity that he supposed fitted
her station. She was friendly without being gregarious
or warm or real.

She wasn't, he thought, anything he wanted. But he
had to live with it, with her, and he was determined to
put such thoughts behind him.

He moved through the crowds, chatting with various
people, conscious of Liana by his side, smiling and yet
so still and straight, so proud. She seemed untouchable
and completely indifferent to him, yet even so he found
his mind—and other parts of his body—leaping ahead
to a few hours from now, when they would leave the re-

ception and all the guests behind and retire upstairs to the tower room that was the traditional honeymoon suite.

There wouldn't actually be a honeymoon; he saw no point, and he doubted Liana did either. But tonight... Tonight they would consummate their marriage. The prospect filled him with desire and distaste, hunger and loathing.

He wanted her, he knew, but he didn't want to want her, not when she didn't even respect him. And she obviously didn't want to want him.

Sandro took a long swallow of champagne, and it tasted bitter in his mouth. What a mess.

Liana felt tension thrum through her body as she made a valiant effort to listen to another dignitary talk about Maldinia's growing industry, and how Prince Leo was helping to raise funds for technological improvements.

But her real focus was on the man next to her. Her husband. He listened and chatted and smiled just as she did, but she felt the tension in his body, had seen the chilly expression in his eyes when he'd turned to her, and in the moment before she'd said her vows she had felt panic bubble up inside her. She'd wanted to rip off her veil and run back down the aisle, away from everything. The anxiety and hope in her parents' eyes. The ice in her groom's. And the churning fear and guilt inside herself that she could never escape, no matter how far or fast she ran.

And so she'd stayed and repeated the vows that would bind her to this man for life. She'd promised to love and honour and obey him, traditional vows for a traditional marriage, and she'd wished she'd considered how different it would feel, to fill her mouth full of lies.

She didn't love this man. She hadn't honoured him. And as for obedience...

Sandro placed a hand on her elbow, and despite every intention not to feel anything for him, just that simple touch set sparks racing up her arm, exploding in her heart. She hated how much he affected her. Hated how weak and vulnerable he made her feel, how he made her want things she knew he would never give her.

'We will say our goodbyes in a few minutes,' he said in a low voice, and Liana stiffened.

'Goodbyes? But we're not going anywhere.'

Sandro's mouth curved in a humourless smile. His eyes were as hard as metal. 'We're going to our honeymoon suite, Liana. To go to bed.'

She pulled her arm away from his light touch, realisation icing her veins. Of course. Their wedding night. They would have to consummate their marriage now. It was a duty she'd known she would have to perform, even if she hadn't let herself think too much about it. Now it loomed large and incredibly immediate, incredibly *intimate*, and even as dread pooled in her stomach she couldn't keep a contrary excitement from leaping low in her belly—fear and fascination, desire and dread all mixed together. She hated the maelstrom this man created within her.

'You aren't going to steal away yet, are you?' Alyse approached them, Leo by her side. 'I haven't even had a chance to talk with Liana yet, not properly.'

Liana offered a sick smile, her mind still on the night ahead, alone with Sandro.

'You'll have plenty of opportunity later,' Sandro answered, his fingers closing once more over Liana's elbow. 'But for now I want my bride to myself.' He smiled as he said it, but to Liana it felt like the smile of a predator, intent on devouring its prey.

And that was how intimacy with Sandro felt. Like

being devoured. Like losing herself, everything she'd ever clung to.

Alyse glanced uncertainly at Sandro before turning back to Liana. 'We'll have to have a proper chat soon,' she said, and Liana nodded jerkily.

'Yes, I look forward to getting to know both of you,' she said with as much warmth as she could inject into her voice, although she feared it wasn't all that much. 'You both seem very happy in your marriage.'

'And you will be in yours, Queen Liana,' Leo said quietly, 'if you just give Sandro some time to get used to the idea.'

Liana watched as he slipped his hand into his wife's, his fingers squeezing hers gently. Something in her ached at the sight of that small yet meaningful touch. When had she last been touched like that?

It had been years. Decades. She'd found it so hard to give and receive affection after Chiara's death. For a second she could almost feel her sister's skinny arms hook around her neck as she pressed her cheek next to hers. She could feel her silky hair, her warm breath as she whispered in her ear. She'd always had secrets, Chiara, silly secrets. She'd whisper her nonsense in Liana's ear and then giggle, squeezing her tight.

Liana swallowed and looked away. She couldn't think of Chiara now or she'd fall apart completely. And she didn't want to think about the yearning that had opened up inside her, an overwhelming desire for the kind of intimacy she'd closed herself off from for so long. To give and receive. To know and be known. To love and be loved.

None of it possible, not with this man. Her husband.

She might be leaving this room for her wedding night, but that kind of intimacy, with love as its sure foundation, was not something she was about to experience. Something she didn't *want* to experience, even if everything in her protested otherwise.

Love opened you up to all sorts of pain. It *hurt*.

But she didn't even need to worry about that, because right now she and Sandro were just going to have sex. Emotionless sex.

They spent the next few minutes saying their goodbyes; her mother hugged her tightly and whispered that she hoped she would be happy. Liana murmured back nonsense about how she already was and saw the tension that bracketed her mother's eyes lessen just a little. Her father didn't hug her; he never had, not since Chiara had died. She didn't blame him.

A quarter of an hour later she left the reception with Sandro; neither of them spoke as they walked down several long, opulent corridors and then up the wide front staircase of the palace, down another corridor, up another staircase, and finally to the turret room that was kept for newlyweds.

Sandro opened the door first, ushering her in, and Liana didn't look at him as she walked into the room. She took in the huge stone fireplace, the windows open to the early evening sky, the enormous four-poster bed piled high with silken pillows and seeming almost to pulse with expectation.

She resisted the urge to wipe her damp palms against the narrow skirt of her wedding gown and walked to the window instead, taking in several needed lungfuls of mountain air. The sun was just starting to sink behind the timbered houses of Averne's Old Town, the Alps fringing the horizon, their snowy peaks thrusting towards a violet sky. It was all incredibly beautiful, and yet also chilly and remote. As chilly and remote as she felt, shrinking further and further into herself, away from the reality—the intimacy—of what was about to happen between them.

Behind her she heard the door click shut.

'Would you like to change?' Sandro asked. He sounded formal and surprisingly polite. Liana didn't turn from the window.

'I don't believe I have anything to change into.'

'There's a nightdress on the bed.'

She turned then and saw the silk-and-lace confection spread out on the coverlet. It looked horribly revealing, ridiculously romantic. 'I don't see much point in that.'

Sandro huffed a hard laugh. 'I didn't think you would.'

She finally forced herself to look at him. 'There's no point in pretending, is there?'

'Is that what it would be?' He lounged against the doorway; while she'd been gazing out of the window he'd shed his formal coat and undone his white tie. His hair was ruffled, his eyes sleepy, and she could see the dark glint of a five o'clock shadow on his chiselled jaw, the hint of chest hair from the top opened buttons of his shirt. He looked dissolute and dangerous and...*sexy*.

The word popped into her head of its own accord. She didn't want to think of her husband as sexy. She didn't want to feel that irresistible magnetic pull towards him that already had her swaying slightly where she stood. She didn't want to feel so *much*. If she felt this, she'd feel so much more. She would drown in all the feelings she'd suppressed for so long.

'You weren't pretending the last time I kissed you,' Sandro said softly, and to Liana it sounded like a taunt.

'You're as proud as a polecat about that,' she answered. Sandro began to stroll towards her.

'Why fight me, Liana? Why resist me? We're married. We must consummate our marriage. Why don't we at least let this aspect of our union bring us pleasure?'

'Because nothing else about it will?' she filled in, her tone sharp, and Sandro just shrugged.

'We've both admitted as much, haven't we?'

Yes, she supposed they had, so there was no reason for her to feel so insulted. So *hurt*. Yet as Sandro kept moving towards her with a predator's prowl, she knew she did.

He stopped in front of her, close enough so she could feel the heat of him, and he could see her tremble. She stared blindly ahead, unable to look at him, to see what emotion flickered in his eyes. Pity? Contempt? Desire? She wanted none of it, even as her body still ached and yearned.

Sandro lifted one hand and laid it on her shoulder; she could feel the warmth of his palm from underneath the thin silk of her gown. He smoothed his hand down the length of her arm, the movement studied, almost clinical, as if he was touching a statue. And she felt like a statue just as he'd accused her of being: lifeless, unmoving, even as her blood heated and her heart lurched. Sandro sighed.

'Why don't you take a bath?' he said, turning away. 'Relax for a little while. If you don't want to wear that nightgown, there are robes in the bathroom that will cover you from chin to toe.'

She watched out of the corner of her eye as he moved to the fireplace, his fingers deftly undoing the remaining studs of his shirt. He shrugged out of it, the firelight burnishing the bronzed skin of his sculpted shoulders, and Liana yanked her gaze away.

On shaky, jelly-like legs she walked to the bathroom, her dress whispering around her as she moved, and closed the door. Locked it. And let out a shuddering breath that ended on something halfway to a sob.

CHAPTER FIVE

SANDRO LEANED BACK in the chair by the fire and gazed moodily at the flames flickering in the huge hearth. Resentment warred with guilt inside him as he listened to Liana move in the bathroom, turning on taps. Taking off her clothes. Would she be able to get that slinky dress off by herself? He knew she wouldn't ask for help.

Ever since they'd entered this room with all of its sensual expectation she'd become icier than ever. It angered him, her purposeful coldness, as if she couldn't stand even to be near him and wanted him to know it, but he still couldn't keep a small stab of pity from piercing his resentment. She was a virgin; even if she would never admit it, she had to be a little nervous. He needed to make allowances.

The desire he'd felt for her still coiled low in his belly but even so he didn't relish the prospect of making love to his wife. Of course there would be no love about it, which was neither new nor a surprise. He shouldn't even want it, not when he knew what kind of woman Liana really was.

He had no illusions about how she would handle their wedding night. Lie stiff and straight as a board on that sumptuous bed, scrunch her eyes tight, and think of her marital duty. Just the thought of it—of her like that—was enough to turn his flickering desire into ash.

Distantly Sandro realised the sounds from the bathroom had stopped, and he knew she must be stuck in that dress. He rose from the chair, dressed only in his trousers, and rapped on the bathroom door.

'Liana? Do you need help getting out of your gown?' Silence. He almost smiled, imagining how she was wrestling with admitting she did, and yet not wanting to accept anything from him. Certainly not wanting him to unzip her. 'I'll close my eyes,' he said dryly, half joking, 'if you want me to help you unzip it.'

'It's not a zipper.' Her voice sounded muffled, subdued. 'It's about a hundred tiny buttons.'

And before he could stop himself, Sandro was envisioning all those little buttons following the elegant length of her spine, picturing his fingers popping them open one by one and revealing the ivory skin of her back underneath. Desire leapt to life once more.

'Then you most certainly need help,' he said, and after a second's pause he heard the sound of the door unlocking and she opened it, her head bowed, a few tendrils of hair falling forward and hiding her face.

Wordlessly she turned around and presented him with her narrow, rigid back, the buttons going from her neck to her tailbone, each one a tiny pearl.

Sandro didn't speak as he started at the top and began to unbutton the gown. The buttons were tiny, and it wasn't easy. It wasn't a matter of a moment either, and he didn't close his eyes as he undid each one, the tender skin of her neck and shoulders appearing slowly underneath his fingers as the silk fell away in a sensual slide.

His fingers brushed her skin—she felt both icy and soft—and he felt her give a tiny shudder, although whether

she was reacting out of desire or disgust he didn't know.
He sensed she felt both, that she was as conflicted as he
was—probably more—about wanting him. The realisation sent a sudden shaft of sympathy through him and he
stilled, his fingers splayed on her bared back. He felt her
stiffen beneath him.

'If you'd rather,' he said softly, 'we can wait.'

'Wait?' Her voice was no more than a breath, her back
still rigid, her head bowed.

'To consummate our marriage.'

'Until when?'

'Until we're both more comfortable with each other.'

She let out a little huff of laughter, the sound as cynical
as anything he'd ever heard. 'And when will that be, do
you think, Your Highness? I'd rather just get it over with.'

What a delightful turn of phrase, he thought sardoni-
cally. Her skin had warmed under his palm but when he
spread his fingers a little wider he felt how cold she still
was. Cold all the way through. 'You're right, of course,'
he answered flatly. 'We might as well get it over with.'

She didn't answer, and he finished unbuttoning the
dress in silence. She held her hands up to her front to
keep it in place, and Sandro could see the top curve of her
bottom, encased enticingly in sheer tights, as she stepped
back into the bathroom. She closed the door, and with a
grim smile he listened to her lock it once more.

Liana lay in the bath until the water grew cold and the
insistent throb of her body's response to Sandro started
to subside—except it didn't.

She'd never been touched so intimately as when he'd
unbuttoned her dress. She realised this probably made
her seem pathetic to a man like him, a man who was so
sensual and passionate, who had probably had a dozen—a

hundred—lovers. As for her? She'd had so little physical affection in her life that even a casual brush of a hand had everything in her jolting with shocked awareness.

And now the feeling of his fingers on her back, the whisper of skin on skin, so intimate, so *tender*, an assault so much softer and gentler than that life-altering kiss they'd had six weeks ago and yet still so unbearably powerful, had made that awakened need inside her blaze hotter, harder, its demand one she was afraid she could not ignore.

The water was chilly now, and reluctantly she rose from the tub, and swathed herself in the robe that covered her just as Sandro had promised but which she knew he could peel away in seconds.

She took time brushing and blow-drying her hair, stared at her pale face and wide eyes, and then pinched her cheeks for colour. No more reasons to stay in here, to stall.

Taking a deep breath, she opened the bathroom door.

Sandro was facing the window, one arm braced against its frame, wearing only a pair of black silk pyjama bottoms, and the breath rushed from Liana's lungs as she gazed at him, the firelight flickering over his powerful shoulders and trim hips, his hair as dark as ink and his skin like bronze. He looked darkly powerful and almost frightening in his latent sensuality, his blatant masculinity. Just his presence seemed to steal all the breath from her body, all the thoughts from her head.

She straightened her spine, took a deep breath. 'I'm ready.'

'Are you?' His voice was a low, sardonic drawl as he turned around, swept her from head to toe in one swiftly assessing gaze. 'You look terrified.'

'Well, I can't say I'm looking forward to this,' Liana

answered, keeping her voice tart even though her words were, at least in part, no more than lies. 'But I'll do my duty.'

'I thought you'd say something like that.'

'Then perhaps you're getting to know me, after all.'

'Unfortunately, I think I am.'

She flinched, unable to keep herself from it, and Sandro shook his head. 'I'm sorry. That was uncalled for.'

'But you meant it.'

'I only meant…' He let out a long, low breath. 'I just wish things could be different.'

That she was different, he meant. Well, sometimes she wished she were different too. She wished being close to someone—being vulnerable, intimate, *exposed*—wasn't scary. Terrifying.

Was that what Sandro wanted? That kind of…closeness? The thought caused a blaze of yearning to set her senses afire. Because part of her wanted that too, but she had no idea how to go about it. How to overcome her fear.

'Well, then,' she finally said, every muscle tensed and expectant. A smile twitched at his lips even though she still sensed that restless, rangy energy from him.

'Do you actually think I'm going to pounce on you right this second? Deflower you like some debauched lord and his maiden?'

'I hope you'll have a bit more finesse than that.'

'Thank you for that vote of confidence.' He strolled towards her with graceful, loose-limbed purpose that had Liana tensing all the more.

He stood in front of her, his gaze sweeping over her so that already she felt ridiculously exposed, even though she wore the bathrobe that covered her completely.

'You're as tense as a bow.' Sandro touched the back

of her neck, his fingers massaging the muscles knotted there. 'Why don't you relax, just a little?'

Her fingers clenched convulsively on the sash of her robe. Relaxation felt like an impossibility. 'And how am I supposed to do that when I know—' She stopped abruptly, not wanting to admit so much, or really anything at all.

Sandro's dark eyebrows drew together in a frown as he searched her face. 'When you know what?'

'That you don't like me,' she forced out, her voice small and suffocated, her face averted from his. 'That you don't even respect me or hold me in any regard at all.'

Sandro didn't answer, just let his gaze rove over her, searching for something he didn't seem to find because he finally sighed, shrugged his powerful shoulders. 'And you feel the same way about me.'

'I—' She stopped, licked her lips. She should tell him that she'd only told him she didn't respect him to hurt him and hide herself, because she'd hated how vulnerable she'd felt. And yet somehow the words wouldn't come.

'I think it's best,' Sandro said quietly, 'if we put our personal feelings aside. The last time we were alone together, I kissed you.' He spoke calmly, rationally, and yet just that simple statement of fact caused Liana's heart to thud even harder and a treacherous, hectic flush to spread over her whole body. 'You responded,' he continued, and she closed her eyes, the memory of his kiss washing over her in a hot tide. 'And I responded to you. Regardless of how different we are, and how little regard we have for each other's personal priorities or convictions, we are physically attracted to one another, Liana.'

He rested his hands lightly on her shoulders, and she felt the warmth of his palms even through the thick terry cloth of her robe. 'It might seem repellent to you, to be attracted to someone you don't respect, but *this* is the only point of sympathy it appears we have between us.'

And with his hands still on her shoulders he bent his head and brushed his lips across hers. That first taste of him was like a cool drink of water in the middle of a burning desert. And her life *had* been a desert, a barren wasteland of loneliness and yearning for something she hadn't realised she'd missed until he'd first touched her.

Her mouth opened instinctively under his, her hands coming up to clutch the warm, bare skin of his shoulders, needing the contact and the comfort, the closeness. Needing him.

His lips hovered over hers for a moment, almost as if he was surprised by the suddenness of her response, the silent *yes* she couldn't keep her body from saying. Then he deepened the kiss, his tongue sweeping into the softness of her mouth, claiming and exploring her with a staggering intimacy that felt strangely, unbearably sweet.

It felt *important*, to be touched like this. To feel warm hands on her body, gentle, caressing, accepting her in a way she'd never felt accepted before. Not since she'd lost Chiara, since she'd let her go.

She'd never understood how much she needed this in the years since then, the touch of a human being, the reminder that she was real and alive, flesh and blood and bone, emotion and want and need. She was so much more than what she'd ever let herself be, and she felt it all now in an overwhelming, endless rush as Sandro kissed her.

And then he stopped, pulling back just a little to smile down at her with what seemed terribly like smugness. 'Well, then,' he said softly, and she heard satisfaction and perhaps even triumph in his voice, and with humiliation scorching through her she pulled away.

Of course he didn't accept her. Didn't like her, didn't

respect her. Didn't even know her. And she didn't want
him to, not really, so with all that between them, how
could she respond to him this way? How could she crave
the exposing intimacy she hated and feared?

Numbness was so much easier. So much safer. She
might have lived her life in a vacuum, but at least it had
been safe.

She tried to pull back from Sandro's light grasp and
he frowned.

'What's wrong?'

'I don't—'

'Want to want me?' he filled in, his voice hardening,
and Liana didn't answer, just focused on keeping some
last shred of control, of dignity, intact. *Blink. Breathe.
Don't cry.*

'But you do want me, Liana,' Sandro said softly. 'You
want me very much. And even if you try to deny it, I'll
know. I'll feel your response in your lips that open to
mine, in your hands that reach for me, in your body that
responds to me.' He brushed his hand against her breast,
his thumb finding the revealingly taut peak even underneath her heavy robe. 'You see? I'll always know.'

'I know that,' she choked. 'I'm not denying anything.'
She turned her face with all of its naked emotion away
from him.

'No,' he agreed, his voice as hard as iron now, as hard
as his gunmetal-grey eyes. 'You're not denying it. You're
just resisting it with every fibre of your being. Resisting
me.' She let out a shudder, and he shook his head. 'Why,
Liana? You agreed to this marriage, as I did. Why can't
we find this pleasurable at least?'

'Because…' Because she wasn't strong enough. She'd
open herself up to him just a little and a tidal wave of
emotion would rush through her. She wouldn't be able

to hold it back and it would devastate her. She knew it instinctively, knew that giving in just a little to Sandro would crack her right open, shatter her into pieces. She'd never come together again.

How could she explain all of that?

And yet even so, she knew she had to stop fighting him, stop this futile resistance, because what purpose did it really serve? She was married to this man. She had known they would consummate this marriage. She just hadn't expected to feel so much.

'Liana,' Sandro said, and he sounded so tired. Weary of this, of her.

'I'm sorry,' she said quietly. 'I'll...I'll try better.'

'Try better?' He raised his eyebrows. 'You don't need to prove yourself to me, Liana.'

Didn't she? Hadn't she been proving herself to her parents, to everyone, for so long she didn't know how to do anything else? How to just *be*?

She dragged in a deep breath. 'Let's...start over.' She forced herself to meet his narrowed gaze, even to smile although she felt her lips tremble, and the tears she'd kept at bay for so long threatened once more to spill.

When had she become so emotionally fragile? Why did this man call up such feelings in her? She wanted to be strong again. She wanted to be safe.

She wanted to get this awful, exposing encounter over with.

'Start over,' Sandro repeated. 'I'm wondering just how far we need to go back.'

'Not that far.' She made her smile brighter, more determined. She could do this. They'd get over this, and life would be safe again. 'You're right. I...I do want you.' The words were like rocks in her mouth; she nearly choked on them. Willing her hands to be steady, she undid the sash of her robe, shrugged it off, and stood before him naked.

Sandro's gaze widened, and Liana felt herself flush, a rosy stain covering her whole body that could not be hidden. And she longed to hide it, hide her whole self, mind and body and heart, yet she forced herself to stand there, chin tilted proudly, back straight. Proud and yet accepting.

Sandro shook his head, and her heart swooped inside her. 'This isn't starting over,' he said quietly. 'This is you just gritting your teeth a bit more and putting a game face on.'

'No—' she said, and with desperation driving her, a desperate need to get this all finished with so she could hide once more, she crossed to him and, pressing her naked body against his, she kissed him.

Sandro felt the softness of her breasts brush his bare chest, her lips hard and demanding on his, a supplication his libido responded to with instant acceptance. Instinctively his arms came up and he pulled her closer, fitted her against the throb of his arousal and claimed the kiss as his own.

She tasted so sweet, and her body was so soft and pliant against his. Too pliant. He inwardly cursed.

He didn't want this. Liana might be submitting to him, but it was an awful, insulting submission. He wanted her want, needed her not just to acknowledge her desire of him, but to embrace it, *him*, even if just physically. Emotionally they might be poles apart, but couldn't they at least have this?

Almost roughly, his own hands shaking, he pushed her away from him and shook his head.

'No. Not like this.'

Her eyes widened. 'Why not?'

He stared at her for a moment, wondering just what was going on behind that beautiful, blank face. Except she wasn't quite so blank right now. Her eyes were filled with panic, and her breath came in uneven, frantic gasps.

This wasn't the understandable shy reticence of a virgin, or even the haughty acceptance of the ice queen he'd thought she was. This was, he realised with a sudden jolt of shock, pure *fear*.

'Liana...' He put his hands on her shoulders and felt a shudder rack her body. 'Did you have a bad experience?' he asked quietly. 'With a man? Is that why you're afraid of me? Of physical intimacy?'

She whirled away, snatched up her robe, and pushed her arms into the billowing sleeves. 'I'm not afraid.'

'You're certainly giving a good impression, then.' He folded his arms, a cold certainty settling inside him. Something had happened to her. It all made sense: her extreme devotion to her charity work, her lack of relationships, her fear of natural desire. 'Were you...abused? Raped?'

She whirled back round to face him, a look of shocked disbelief on her face. *'No!'*

'Most women wouldn't fight a natural, healthy desire for a man, Liana. A man who has admitted he wants you. Why do you?'

'Because...' She licked her lips. 'Because I wasn't expecting it,' she finally said and he raised his eyebrows.

'You weren't expecting us to find the physical side of things pleasant? Why not?'

She shrugged. 'Nothing about this marriage or our meeting suggested we would.'

'The kiss we shared six weeks ago didn't clue you in?'

he asked, a gentle hint of humour entering his voice, surprising even him.

She blushed. He liked it when she blushed, liked how
it lit up her face and her eyes, her whole self. It gave him
hope. 'Before that, I mean,' she muttered.

'All right, fine. You weren't expecting it. But now
it's here between us, and you're still fighting it. Why?'

She hesitated, her gaze lowered, before she lifted her
face and pinned him with a clear, violet stare. 'Because
I agreed to this marriage because it was convenient, and
I didn't want anything else. I didn't want love or even
affection. I didn't want to get to know you beyond a…a
friendly kind of agreement. I thought that's how you
would think of this marriage too, and so far nothing—'
her breath hitched, her face now fiery '—nothing has
been like I expected!'

He didn't know whether to laugh or groan. 'But you're
still not telling me why you don't want those things,' Sandro finally said quietly. 'Why you don't want love or affection.' And while her admission didn't surprise him,
he suspected the reason for it was different from what
he'd thought. She wasn't cold. She was hiding.

She stared at him mutinously, and then her lower lip
trembled. It made him, suddenly and fiercely, want to
take her in his arms and kiss that wobbling lip. Kiss the
tears that shimmered in her eyes, tears he knew instinctively she wouldn't let fall. Then the moment passed and
her expression became remote once more. 'I just don't.'

'Still not an answer, Liana.'

'Well, it's the only one I have to give you.'

'So you don't want to tell me.'

'Why should I?' she demanded. 'We barely know each
other. You don't—'

'Like you?' he filled in. 'That might have been true

initially, but how can I ever get to like you, or even know you, if you hide yourself from me? Because that's what the whole ice-princess act is, isn't it? A way to hide yourself.' He'd never felt more sure of anything. Her coldness was an act, a mask, and he felt more determined than ever to make it slip, to have it drop away completely.

'Oh, this is ridiculous.' She bit her lip and looked away. 'I don't know why you can't just toss me on the bed and have your wicked way with me.'

He let out a choked laugh of disbelief. Liana, it seemed, had read a few romance novels. 'You'd really prefer that?'

'Yes.' Her eyes turned the colour of a stormy sea and she shook her head. 'I want to want that,' she said, her voice filled with frustration, and he thought he understood.

She wanted something different now. Well, so did he. He wanted to know this contrary bride of his, understand her in a way he certainly didn't now. But he was getting a glimpse of the woman underneath the ice, a woman with pain and secrets and a surprising humour and warmth. A woman he could live with, maybe even love.

Unless of course he was being fanciful. Unless he was fooling himself just as he had with Teresa, with his father, believing the best of everyone because he so wanted to love and be loved.

But surely he'd developed a little discernment over the years?

'I'm not going to throw you on that bed, Liana,' he said, 'and have my way with you, wicked or otherwise. When we have sex—and it won't be tonight—it will be pleasurable for both of us. It will involve a level of give and take, of vulnerability and acceptance I don't think you're capable of right now.'

She didn't answer, just flashed those stormy eyes at

him, so Sandro smiled and took a step closer to her. 'But I will sleep with you in that bed. I'll lie next to you and put my arms around you and feel your softness against me. I think that will be enough for tonight.' He watched her eyes widen with alarm. 'More than enough,' he said, and he tugged on the sash of her robe so it fell open and she walked unwillingly towards him.

'What are you doing—?'

'You can't sleep in that bulky thing.' He slid it from her shoulders, smoothing the silk of her skin under his palms. 'But if you want to wear that frothy nightgown, go ahead.'

Her chin jutting out in determination, she yanked the nightgown from the bed and put it on. It was made mostly of lace, clinging to her body, and Sandro's palms itched to touch her again.

'Now what?' she demanded, crossing her arms over her breasts.

'Now to bed,' Sandro said, and he pulled her to the bed, lay down, and drew her into his arms. She went unresistingly, yet he felt the tension in every muscle of her body. She was lying there like a wooden board.

He stroked her hair, her shoulder, her hip, keeping his touch gentle yet sure, staying away from the places he longed to touch. The fullness of her breasts, the juncture of her thighs.

If he was trying to relax her, it wasn't working. Liana quivered under his touch, but it was a quiver of tension rather than desire. Again, Sandro wondered just what had made his wife this way.

And he knew he wanted to find out. It would, he suspected, be a long, patient process.

He continued to slide his fingers along her skin even as his groin ached with unfulfilled desire. He wanted her, wanted her in a way he hadn't let himself before. He'd fought against this marriage, against this woman, because he'd assumed she was the same as the other conniving women he'd known. His mother. Teresa.

But he suspected now—hell, knew—that his wife wasn't like that. There was too much fear and vulnerability in that violet gaze, too much sorrow in her resistance. She fought against feeling because she was afraid, and he wanted to know why. He wanted to know what fears she hid, and he wanted to help her overcome them. He wanted, he realised with a certainty born not of anger or rebellion but of warmth and fledgling affection, to melt his icy wife.

CHAPTER SIX

LIANA STIRRED SLOWLY to wakefulness as morning sunshine poured into the room like liquid gold. It had taken her hours to get to sleep last night, hours of lying tense and angry and afraid, because this was so not what she'd expected from her marriage. What she'd wanted.

Yet it seemed it was what she'd wanted, after all, for with every gentle stroke of Sandro's fingers she felt something in her soften. Yearn. And even though her body still thrummed with tension, the desire to curl into the heat and strength of him, to feel safe in an entirely new way, grew steadily like a flame at her core.

And yet she resisted. She fought, because fear was a powerful thing. And her mind raced, recalling their conversations, Sandro's awful questions.

Were you abused? Raped?

He wasn't even close, and yet she was hiding something. Too many things. Guilt and grief and what felt like the loss of her own soul, all in the matter of a moment when she'd failed to act. When she'd shown just what kind of person she really was. He'd seen that, even if he didn't understand the source, and she could never tell him.

Could she? Could she change that much? She didn't know if she could, or how she would begin. With each stroke of Sandro's fingers she felt the answer. *Slowly. Slowly.*

And eventually she felt her body relax of its own accord, and her breath came out in a slow sigh of surrender. She didn't curl into him or move at all, but she did sleep.

And she woke with Sandro's hand curved round her waist, his fingers splayed across her belly. Nothing sexual about the touch, but it still felt unbearably intimate. She still felt a plunging desire for him to move his hand, higher or lower, it didn't matter which, just *touch* her.

And then Sandro stirred, and everything in her tensed once more. He rose on one elbow, brushed the hair from her eyes, his fingers lingering on her cheek.

'Good morning.'

She nodded, unable to speak past the sudden tightness in her throat. 'Sleep well?' Sandro asked, and she heard that hint of humour in his voice that had surprised her last night. She'd seen this man cold and angry and resentful, but she hadn't seen him smile too much. Had only heard him laugh once.

And when he softened like this, it made her soften too, and she didn't know what would happen then.

'Yes.' She cleared her throat, inched away from him. 'Eventually.'

'I slept remarkably well.' He brushed another tendril of hair away from her cheek, tucked it behind her ear, his fingers lingering.

Liana resisted the urge to lean into that little caress. 'What are we going to do today?'

'We have a few engagements.' Smiling, Sandro sat up in bed, raking his hair with his hands, so even though she was trying to avoid looking at him Liana found her gaze drawn irresistibly to his perfectly sculpted pectoral muscles, the taut curve of his biceps. Her husband was beautiful—and fit.

'What engagements?' she asked, forcing her brain back into gear.

'A brunch with my delightful mother as well as my sister and my brother and his wife. An appearance on the balcony for the adoring crowds.'

He spoke with a cynicism she didn't really understand, although she could probably guess at. 'You don't like being royal,' she said, 'do you?'

He sighed and dropped his hands. 'Not particularly. But hadn't you already figured that out, since I shirked my royal duty for fifteen years?' His gaze met hers then, and instead of anger she saw recrimination. She recognised it, because she'd felt it so often herself.

'I shouldn't have said that,' she said quietly. 'I'm sorry.'

'Why, Liana.' He touched her chin with his fingers, tilting her face so their gazes met once more. 'I don't think you've ever apologised to me before. Not sincerely.'

'I am sorry,' she answered. Her chin tingled where he touched her. 'I was just trying to hurt you, so I said the first thing that came to mind.'

'Well, there was truth in it, wasn't there?' His voice came out bitter and he dropped his hand from her face. 'I did shirk my duty. I ran away.'

And she knew all too well how guilt over a mistake, a wrong choice, ate and ate at you until there was nothing left. Until your only recourse was to cut yourself off from everything because numbness was better than pain. Was that how Sandro felt? Did they actually have something—something so fundamental to their selves—in common?

'But you came back,' she said quietly. 'You've made it better.'

'Trying to.' He threw off the covers and rose from

the bed. 'But we should get ready. We have a full day ahead of us.'

He was pulling away from her, she knew. They'd had a surprising moment of closeness there, a closeness that had intrigued her rather than frightened her. And now it was Sandro was who shuttering his expression, and she felt a frustration that was foreign to her because she was usually the one who was pulling away. Hiding herself.

So maybe this was why Sandro had been feeling so frustrated. It was hard to be on the receiving end of someone's reticence—especially when you actually wanted something else. Something more.

'Where are we meant to get ready?' she asked. 'I've only got my wedding dress or this nightgown here.'

Sandro pushed a discreet button hidden in the woodwork of the wall. 'One of your staff will show you to your room,' he said and turned away.

A few minutes later a shy young woman named Maria came to the honeymoon suite and showed Liana her own bedroom, a room, judging from its frilly, feminine décor, Sandro clearly wouldn't share.

So this was what a marriage of convenience looked like, Liana thought, and wondered why she didn't feel happier. Safer. She'd have her own space. Sandro would leave her alone. All things she'd wanted.

Yet in that moment, standing amidst the fussy little tables and pink canopied bed, she wasn't quite so sure she wanted them anymore. They didn't feel as comforting as she'd expected.

Maybe she was just tired. Feeling more vulnerable from everything she and Sandro had said and shared last night. The memory of his hands gently stroking her from shoulder to thigh still had the power to make her quiver.

Enough. It was time to do the work she'd come here

to do, to be queen. To remember her duty to her parents, to her sister, to everything she'd made her life about.

And not think about Sandro, and the confusion of her marriage.

An hour later she was showered and dressed in a modest dress of lavender silk, high necked and belted at the waist. She'd pulled her hair back into its usual tight chignon and then frowned at her reflection, remembering what Sandro had said.

I would like to see you with your hair cascading over your shoulders. Your lips rosy and parted, your face flushed.

For a second she thought about undoing her hair. Putting some blusher on her cheeks. Then her frown deepened and she turned away from the mirror. She looked fine.

Downstairs, the royal family had assembled in an opulent dining room for the official brunch. And it felt official, far from a family meal. A dozen footmen were stationed around the room, and the dishes were all gold plate.

The queen dowager glided into the room, her eyes narrowed, her mouth pursed, everything about her haughty and distant.

Was that how Sandro saw her? Icy and remote, even arrogant? Liana felt herself inwardly cringe. She'd never considered how others saw her; she'd just not wanted to be seen. Really seen. The woman underneath the ice. The girl still trying to make herself invisible, to apologise for her existence.

Sophia went to the head of the table and Sandro moved to the other end. A footman showed Liana her place, on the side, and for a second she hesitated.

As queen, her place was where Sophia now sat, eyeing everyone coldly. Clearly the queen dowager did not want to give up her rights and privileges as monarch, and Liana wasn't about to make a fuss about where she sat at the table. She never made a fuss.

And yet somehow it hurt, because she realised she wanted Sandro to notice where she sat. Notice her, and put her in her rightful place.

He didn't even look at her, and Liana didn't think she was imagining the triumph glittering in her mother-in-law's eyes as she sat down.

Sandro excused himself directly after the brunch, and Liana hadn't had so much as two words of conversation with him. They were meant to appear on the palace balcony at four o'clock, and she had a meeting with her secretary—someone already appointed and whom she hadn't met—at three.

And until then? She'd wander around the palace and wonder yet again just what she was doing here. What had brought her to this place.

Most of the palace's ground floor was made up of formal receiving rooms much like the one she'd first met Sandro in. Liana wandered through them, sunlight dappling the marble floors. As she stood in the centre of one room, feeling as lost and lonely as she ever had and annoyed that she did, she heard a voice from behind her.

'Hello.'

She turned to see Alyse standing in the doorway, looking lovely and vibrant and full of purpose. She'd changed from her more formal outfit for brunch, and now wore a pair of jeans and a cashmere sweater in bright pink. Liana suddenly felt absurd and matronly in her high-necked dress and tightly coiled hair. She fiddled with the pearls at her throat, managed a smile.

'Hello.'

'Did you have a good night?' A blush touched Alyse's cheeks. 'Sorry. I didn't mean that— Well.' She laughed and stepped into the room. 'I was only asking if you'd slept well.'

'Very well, thank you,' Liana answered automatically, and Alyse cocked her head.

'You look tired,' she said, her voice filled with sympathy. 'It's so overwhelming, isn't it—marrying into royalty?'

'It's been a lot to take in,' Liana answered carefully. She didn't want to admit just how overwhelming it had been, and how uncertain and unfulfilled she felt now.

'At least you don't have the press to deal with,' Alyse said with a little laugh. 'That was the hardest part for me. All those cameras, all those reporters looking for a hole in our story, and of course they found one.'

'Was that very hard?'

Alyse made a face. 'Well, I certainly didn't like facing down all those sneering reporters, but the hardest part was how it affected Leo and me.'

Curious now, Liana took an inadvertent step towards her sister-in-law. 'And how did it?'

'Not well. Everything was so fragile between us then. It wasn't ready to be tested in such a way.' She gave Liana a smile. 'Fortunately we survived it.'

'And you love each other now.' Alyse's smile was radiant, the joy in her voice audible, and Liana felt a sharp shaft of jealousy. She'd never wanted what Alyse and Leo had before, never let herself want it. Yet now the yearning that had been skirting her soul seemed to swamp it completely.

She swallowed past the huge lump that had formed in her throat and forced a smile. 'I'm so happy for you.' And she was, even if she was also jealous. Even if she was realising she wanted something more than she could ever expect from Sandro, or even herself.

'It might not be for me to say this,' Alyse said quietly, laying a hand on Liana's arm, 'but Leo and Sandro—they haven't had easy lives, royal though they may be.'

'What do you mean?'

'Their relationship with their parents...' Alyse sighed and shook her head. 'It wasn't healthy or loving. Far from it.'

Liana just nodded. She couldn't exactly say her relationship with her parents was healthy, even if she loved them. She wasn't sure if they loved her. If they could, anymore, and she could hardly blame them.

'Sophia doesn't seem like the most cuddly person I've ever met,' she said, and Alyse gave a wry smile back.

'No, and neither was the king. And yet I think both Leo and Sandro wanted their love, even if they wouldn't admit it. They might not trust love, they might even be afraid of it, but they want it.'

'Leo did,' Liana corrected.

'And I think Sandro does too. Give him a chance, Liana. That's all I'm really saying.'

And again Liana could just nod. Sandro might want love, but he didn't want *her* love. Did he? Or could he change? Could *she*?

She still didn't know if she wanted to change, much less whether she had the courage to try. She'd entered this marriage for a lot of reasons, and none of them had been love. She'd never even let herself think about love.

She'd been skating on the surface of her life, and now the ice below was starting to crack—and what was beneath it? What would happen when it shattered and she fell? She couldn't bear to find out, and yet she had a horrible feeling she would whether she wanted to or not.

But would Sandro be there to catch her? Would he even want to?

'Thank you for telling me all this,' she said, turning back to Alyse. 'It's very helpful.'

'Of course. And you must come have dinner with us one night, you and Sandro. Escape from the palace for a bit.'

After Alyse had gone she went to meet her private secretary, an efficient young woman named Christina. Liana sat and listened while Christina outlined all her potential engagements: cutting ribbons at openings of hospitals and schools, attending events and galas, choosing a wardrobe created by Maldinian fashion designers.

'Are there many?' she asked. 'Maldinia is a small country, after all.'

'A few,' Christina said confidently. 'But of course, your stylist will go over that with you.'

'All right.' Already Liana felt overwhelmed. She hadn't considered any of this. 'I'd like to support a charity I've been working with for many years,' she began, and Christina nodded quickly.

'Of course, Hands To Help. Perhaps a fundraiser in the palace?'

'Oh, yes, that would be wonderful.' She felt her heart lighten at the thought. 'I can contact them—'

'I believe they've already been contacted by King Alessandro,' Christina said. 'It was his idea.'

'It...was?' Liana blinked in surprise. Sandro had seemed sceptical and even mystified about her charity work, yet he'd thought to arrange a fundraiser? Her heart lightened all the more, so it felt like a balloon on a string, soaring straight up. 'Where is the king? Do you know?'

Christina glanced at her watch. 'I imagine he's getting ready for your appearance together in twenty minutes.'

She pulled out a pager and pressed a few numbers. 'I'll page your stylist.'

Just minutes later Liana was primped and made up for the appearance on the balcony. Sandro strode into the room, looking as handsome as ever in his royal dress, but also hassled. Liana's heart, so light moments ago, began a free fall. She hated that her mood might hinge on his look, that such a small thing—the lack of a greeting or a glance—could affect it.

And yet it did. Despite all her attempts to remain removed, remote, here she was, yearning. Disappointed.

'Ready?' he said, barely looking at her, and then with his hand on her lower back they stepped out onto the ornate balcony overlooking the palace courtyard, now filled with joyous Maldinians.

The cheer that rose from the crowd reverberated right through her, made her blink in surprise. She'd never felt so much...*approval.*

'I think they want us to kiss,' Sandro murmured, and belatedly Liana realised they were chanting *'Baccialo!'*

Sandro slid his hand along her jaw, turned her to face him. His fingers wrapped around the nape of her neck, warm and sure, as he drew her unresistingly towards him. His lips brushed hers, soft, hard, warm, cool—she felt it all in that moment as her head fell back and her hands came up to press against his chest.

The roar of the crowd thundered in her ears, matching her galloping pulse as Sandro's mouth moved over hers and everything inside her cracked open.

She wanted to be kissed like this. Loved like this. She was tired of hiding away, of staying safe.

Sandro stepped away with a smile. 'That ought to do it.'

Liana blinked the world back into focus and felt everything in her that had cracked open scuttle for shelter. That kiss had been for the crowds, not for her. It hadn't meant anything.

Their marriage was still as convenient as it ever had been…and she wished it weren't.

As soon as they left the balcony Sandro disappeared again and Liana went to meet with her stylist and go over her wardrobe choices.

'A queen should have a certain modest style,' the stylist explained as she flipped through pages of designs, 'but also be contemporary. The public should feel you can relate to them.'

Liana glanced down at her chaste, high-necked dress. 'So what I'm wearing…?'

'Is beautiful,' the stylist, Demi, said quickly. 'So elegant and classic. But perhaps something a little…fresher?'

'Yes, I suppose I could update my look a little bit,' Liana said slowly. She'd been dressing, for the most part, like a businesswoman facing menopause, not a young woman in her twenties. A young woman with everything ahead of her.

But she'd never actually felt as if she had anything ahead of her before, and she didn't know if she did now.

She had a quiet supper in her bedroom, as Sophia was dining out and Alyse and Leo had gone back to their town house. Sandro was working through dinner, and it wasn't until it was coming on ten o'clock that she finally went to find him.

She had no idea what she'd say, what she wanted to say. He was leaving her alone, just as she'd hoped and wanted. How could she tell him she actually wanted something different now, especially when she wasn't sure herself what that was?

She wandered through the downstairs, directed by footmen to his private study in the back of the palace. With nerves fluttering in her tummy and her heart starting to thud, she knocked on the door.

'Come in.'

Liana pushed open the door and stepped into a wood-panelled room with deep leather club chairs and a huge mahogany desk. Sandro sat behind it, one hand driven through his hair as he glanced up from the papers scattered on his desk.

'Liana—' Surprise flared silver in his eyes and he straightened, dropping his hand. 'I'm sorry. It's late. I've been trying to clear my desk but it never seems to happen.'

'A king has a lot of work to do, I suppose,' she answered with a small smile. Sandro might have avoided his royal duty for most of his adult life, but he was certainly attending to it now.

'What have you been doing today? You had some appointments?'

She nodded. 'With my private secretary and stylist. I've never had a staff before.'

'And is it to your liking?'

'I don't know whether it is or not. It's overwhelming, I suppose. My style is meant to be fresher, apparently.'

'Fresher? It makes you sound like a lettuce.'

'It does, doesn't it?' She smiled, enjoying this little banter. 'I know I've dressed a bit—conservatively.'

He glanced at the lavender dress she still wore. 'And why do you think that is?'

'I suppose I've never wanted to draw attention to myself.'

He nodded slowly, accepting, and Liana fiddled with

the belt at her waist, uncomfortable with even this little honesty. 'Are you—are you coming to bed?'

He gazed at her seriously. 'Do you want me to?'

Yes. And no. She didn't know what she wanted anymore. She'd had such clear purpose in her life...until now. Until she suddenly wanted more, more of him, more of feeling, more of life. Yet she couldn't articulate all that now to Sandro.

He sat back, his hands laced over his middle as he let his gaze sweep over her. 'You're still scared. Of me.'

'Not of you—'

'Of marriage. Of—intimacy.'

She swallowed hard, the sound audible. 'Yes.' It was more than she'd ever admitted before.

'Well, you can breathe easy, Liana. We won't make love tonight.'

Make love. And didn't that conjure all sorts of images in her head? Images that made her dizzy, desires that dried her throat and made everything inside her ache. 'When—?' she asked, her voice only a little shaky, and he smiled.

'Soon, I think. Perhaps on our honeymoon.'

'Honeymoon?' They weren't meant to have a honeymoon. What was the point, when your marriage was about convenience?

'Well, honeymoon might be overstating it a bit. I have to go to California, wrap up some business. I want you to go with me.'

Her cheeks warmed, her blood heated. Everything inside her melted. *He wanted her.* Was it foolish to feel so gratified? So...thrilled?

'Is that all right?' Sandro asked quietly. 'Do you want to go with me, Liana?'

A week ago, a day ago, she would have prevaricated.

Protected herself. She'd never admitted want to herself, much less to another person. Now she nodded. 'Yes,' she said. 'I want to go with you.'

CHAPTER SEVEN

SANDRO SAT ACROSS from Liana on the royal jet and picked a strawberry dipped in chocolate from the silver platter between them. He held it out to her, a mischievous smile playing about his mouth. They were halfway across the Atlantic and he was determined to begin what he suspected would be the very enjoyable process of melting his wife.

It was already working; last night she'd lain in his arms and it had only taken her an hour to relax. He'd watched her face soften in sleep, those tightly pursed lips part on a sigh. Her lashes had fluttered and brushed against her porcelain-pale cheeks. He'd stroked her cheek, amazed at its softness, at the softness he felt in himself towards this woman he'd thought was so hard. So icy and cold.

Yet even as he'd held her and stroked her cheek, he'd wondered. Doubted, because God only knew his judgment had been off before. He'd thought the best of his parents, of the one woman he'd let into his heart. He'd insisted on it, even when everything said otherwise.

Was he doing the same now? Desperate, even now, to love and be loved? Because Liana might lie in his arms, but she didn't always look as if she wanted to be there. One minute she was kissing him with a sudden, sweet passion that had taken him by surprise on the balcony and the next she was cool and remote, all chilly indifference.

Which was the real woman?

Now Liana eyed the chocolate strawberry askance. 'You have a thing about messy food.'

'They tend to be aphrodisiacal.'

'Aphro— *Oh*.' Her cheeks pinked, and he grinned.

'Try one.'

'I don't—'

'You don't like strawberries? Or chocolate? I can't believe it.'

'I've never had one before.'

'A strawberry?'

'Not one dipped in chocolate.' Her blush deepened and she looked away. 'Sometimes I think I must seem ridiculous to you.'

Surprise made him falter. He dropped his hand, still holding the strawberry, the chocolate smearing his fingers. 'Nothing about you is ridiculous, Liana.'

'I know I haven't experienced much of life.'

'And why is that?'

She paused, pressed her lips together. 'I don't know.'

But he thought she did. She must at least have a good guess. No need to press her now, though. Instead he held out the strawberry once more. 'Try it.'

She hesitated, her lips still pursed, everything in her resisting. Then he saw the moment when she made the decision to be different, and with a little shrug and a smile she reached for it. He drew back, his eyes glinting challenge. 'Open your mouth.'

Her eyes widened and for a second he thought he'd pushed too far. Too hard. But she did as he said, parting her lips so he could hold the strawberry out to her. He felt his groin harden and ache as she touched the tip of her pink tongue to the chocolate and licked.

'Mmm.' She sounded so sweetly innocent and yet as seductive as a siren as she gazed at him with eyes as wide and clear as lakes. He could drown in them. He was drowning, lost in this moment as she licked the chocolate again. 'I don't think I knew what I've been missing,' she said huskily, and he knew she wasn't just talking about a single, simple strawberry.

'Liana...' His voice was a groan as she bit into the strawberry, juice trickling down her chin, chocolate smearing her lush lips.

She ate it in two bites, and then Sandro could hold back no longer. He reached for her, dragging his hands through her hair as he brought her face to his and kissed her strawberry-sweet lips.

She tasted better, sweeter than any strawberry. And he wanted her more than he'd wanted anything or anyone before in his life. He kissed her deeply, as if he was drawing the essence of her right out of her mouth and into himself. Wanting and needing to feel her closer than a kiss, with his hands spanning her waist he drew her onto his lap, fitted her legs around him so she pressed snugly against his arousal and he flexed his hips against hers, craving that exquisite friction.

'Now, that's better,' he murmured and she let out a choked laugh.

'Sandro—' She broke off, her head buried in his neck, and Sandro stilled.

He was moving too fast. He'd forgotten, in the sweet spell of that kiss, that she was a virgin. Untouched. Inexperienced.

Sandro closed his eyes and willed the tide of his desire

back. Even so it misted his mind with a red haze. Gently he eased her off his lap.

'Sorry. Lost my head a bit there.'

'It's okay,' she murmured, but her face was still buried in his neck.

Sandro leaned back against the sofa cushions and tried, without success, to will away the ache in his groin.

'Sex doesn't scare me, you know,' she said suddenly, and he suppressed a smile.

'I'm very glad to hear it.'

'It's just…' She licked her lips, sending a shaft of lust burrowing deep into him. *Painful.* 'Everything else does. About…being with someone.'

'What do you mean?'

'Intimacy. Like you said. Sharing things. Being— vulnerable.'

He smiled, tried to draw her into that smile, into something shared. 'None of it is a walk in the park, is it?'

'You mean it scares you too?'

'Sometimes.' He was the one to glance away now. 'I'm not exactly an expert in all this myself, you know, Liana.'

'But you've had loads of relationships, according to the media anyway.'

'Don't believe everything you read.'

Her eyebrows rose, two pale arcs. 'It's not true?'

He shifted in his seat, uncomfortable to impart so much, yet knowing he could only be honest with this woman. His wife. 'I've had quite a few…sexual relationships, I admit. They didn't mean anything to me.'

'That's more than I've had,' she said with a soft laugh that wobbled at the end, a telling note.

He felt a sudden stab of surprising regret for all the pointless encounters he'd had, all attempts to stave off the loneliness and need he'd felt deep inside. The need that was, amazingly, starting to be met by this woman.

'Have you ever…loved anyone?' Liana asked softly. 'I mean, a woman? A romantic… Well, you know.'

'Yes.' Sandro paused, pictured Teresa. What had drawn him to her originally? She'd been so different from everything about his former life, he supposed. A California girl, with sun-kissed hair and bright blue eyes, always ready to laugh, always up for a good time. It had taken him nearly a year to realise Teresa only wanted a good time. With his money. His status. She wasn't interested in the man he really was, didn't want to do the whole 'for better or for worse' thing. At least, not for worse.

'Sandro?' Liana's soft voice interrupted the bleakness of his thoughts. 'You must have loved her very much.'

'Why do you say that?'

'Because your face is like a thundercloud.'

He shook his head. 'I thought I loved her.'

'Is there really a difference?'

He sighed. 'Maybe not. Sometimes disillusionment is worse than heartbreak.'

'How were you disillusioned?'

He shrugged, half amazed he was telling her all of this. 'I thought she loved me for me. But I discovered she was really only interested in my money and status, and not so much me, or being faithful to me.' He'd caught her in bed with the landscaping guy, of all people. She hadn't even been sorry.

Liana pressed her lips together. 'So that's why you're so suspicious.'

'Suspicious?'

'Of me.'

He hesitated then, because as much as he'd been enjoying their conversation and this new, startling intimacy, her words reminded him that she had agreed to marry him for exactly those reasons. Money. Power. A title.

Nothing had really changed, except maybe in his own sentimental mind.

He pushed the thought away; he wanted, for once, to enjoy the simple pleasure of being with a woman. With his wife. 'Have another strawberry,' he said, and held another one out to her parted lips.

Liana licked the last of the chocolate from her lips, every sense on impossible overload. She'd never felt so much—the sweetness of the strawberry, the seductive promise of his kiss, the alarming honesty of their conversation that left her feeling bare and yet bizarrely, beautifully light, as if she'd slipped the first tiny bit of a burden she'd been carrying so long she'd forgotten it was weighing her down. Crippling her.

This was why people fell in love, she supposed. This was what the magazines and romance novels hinted at—and yet she didn't even love Sandro. How could she, when she barely knew him?

And yet he was her husband, and he'd held her all night long and kissed her as if he couldn't get enough. She'd had more with him already than she'd ever had before, and if that made her pathetic, fine. She was pathetic. But for the first time in her life she could almost glimpse happiness.

But could he? Could they have something other than a marriage of convenience, even if they wanted it? Her own emotions and desires were a confused tangle, and she had no idea what Sandro's were. What he thought. What he felt. She didn't want to ask.

'What are you thinking about?' Sandro asked as he popped a strawberry into his own mouth.

'Lots of things.'

'You're all sunlight and shadows, smiling one minute, frowning the next.'

'Am I?' She laughed a little, tried for some more of this hard honesty. 'I guess I'm trying to figure out what I think. What I feel.'

'Maybe,' Sandro suggested softly, 'you should stop thinking so much. Just run with it.'

She nodded. Yes, that seemed like a good idea. Stop analysing. Stop worrying. Just…feel.

She'd spent half a lifetime trying not to feel, and now that was all she wanted to do. She laughed aloud, the sound soft and trembling, and Sandro smiled.

'Good idea?' he asked and she nodded again.

'Yes,' she answered with a smile. 'Good idea.'

They arrived in Los Angeles tired and jet-lagged, but Liana was still euphoric. This was a new place, a new day. A new life.

A limo was waiting for them at the airport, and Liana kept her nose nearly pressed on the glass as they drove through the city to Sandro's beachside villa in Santa Monica.

'I've never been to the US before, you know,' she said as she took in the impressive elegance of Rodeo Drive, the iconic Hollywood sign high above them.

'Consider yourself a tourist. I have some work to do, but we can do the sights.'

'What are the sights?'

'The usual museums and theme parks. The beach. I'd like to take you to a spa resort out in Palm Desert and pamper you to death.'

She let out a little laugh as a thrill ran through her. 'That sounds like a pretty good way to go.'

'I don't think you've ever been pampered,' Sandro said quietly. 'Spoiled.'

'Who would want to be spoiled?'

'I mean…' He shrugged, spread his hands. 'Treated. Indulged. Given an experience just to enjoy and savour.'

No, she'd never had any of those things, not remotely. 'Well, good thing I'm with you, then,' she said lightly. 'Pamper away.'

Sandro smiled and let it drop; she knew he knew there were things she wasn't saying, things she was afraid to say. And would she ever tell him? She thought of his fingers stroking her back, her hip, softening her. *Slowly, slowly.*

The limo pulled up to Sandro's gated mansion and they spent the next hour walking through it. He showed her the voice-controlled plasma-screen television, the shower stall big enough for two people that was activated by simply placing your palm on the wall.

'This place is like something out of James Bond,' she said with a laugh. 'I had no idea you were a gadget guy.'

'I worked in IT.'

'And Leo does too, doesn't he? I remember someone saying at our reception that he's drafting an IT bill.'

'He is.' Sandro's expression seemed to still, everything in him turn wary. 'He's worked hard in my absence.'

She heard the note of recrimination in his voice that she'd sensed before and she wanted to ask him about it. Wanted to know if he struggled with guilt the way she did. But the sun was so bright and they'd been having so much fun exploring his house that she didn't want to weigh down the lightness of the moment.

And, she knew, she was a coward.

They had lunch out on the private beach in front of the house, although Liana's body clock was insisting it was some impossible, other time. She stretched her legs out on the sun-warmed sand and gazed out at the Pacific, started to fall halfway asleep.

Or maybe it was all the way asleep, because she startled to wakefulness when Sandro scooped her up in his arms.

'Time for bed, I think,' he murmured, and carried her across the sand and into the house. She sank onto the silk sheets of his king-size bed and felt the mattress dip as Sandro lay next to her, his arm still around her.

He drew her against him so her head rested on his shoulder, the steady thud of his heart under her cheek. Liana let out a little breathy sigh of contentment. How had she gone without this all of her life?

She must have fallen asleep, because she awoke in the middle of the night, the room drenched in darkness save for a sliver of moonlight that bisected the floor. The space in the bed next to her yawned emptily.

Liana shook her hair out of her face and glanced around the bedroom, but Sandro was nowhere to be seen. On bare feet she padded through the upstairs looking for him, wondering where he'd gone—and why he'd left her in the middle of the night.

She finally found him downstairs in his study, dressed only in a pair of black silk pyjama bottoms, just as he had been on their wedding night. He had his laptop in front of him and papers were scattered across his desk. He worked so hard, she thought with a twist of guilty regret. She'd accused him of neglecting his royal duty, of being someone she couldn't respect, but she was beginning to see just how far from the truth that accusation had been.

'Can't sleep?' she asked softly and he glanced up, the frown that had settled between his brows smoothed away for a moment.

'My body clock is completely out of sync. I thought I might as well get some work done.'

'What are you working on?'

'Just tying up some loose ends with DT.'

'DT?'

'Diomedi Technology.'

She came into the room, driven by a new and deeper curiosity to know this man. To understand him. 'You founded it, didn't you? When you...moved?'

The smile he gave her was twisted, a little bitter. 'You mean when I abandoned my royal duty to pursue my own pleasures?'

She winced. 'Don't, Sandro.'

'It's true, though.'

'I'm not sure it is.'

'And how do you figure that, Liana?' His voice held a hard edge but she had a feeling for once it wasn't for her. He was angry with himself for leaving, for somehow failing. She knew because she understood that feeling too well. The churning guilt and regret for doing the wrong thing or, in her case, nothing at all.

Briefly she closed her eyes, willed the memory of Chiara's desperate gaze away, at least for this moment. Her sister's face, she knew, would haunt her for the rest of her life.

'I think there's always more to the story than there first appears,' she said quietly, coming to perch on the edge of his desk. 'You told me leaving felt necessary at the time, but you didn't tell me why.'

He glanced down at the papers on his desk. 'I didn't think we had that sort of relationship.'

Her breath hitched and she willed it to even out again. 'We didn't. But—but maybe we do now. Or at least, we're trying to.'

He glanced up at her then, everything about him inscrutable. Fathomless. 'Are we?'

Liana stared back at him, words on her lips and fear in her heart. This was the moment when she should show her hand, she knew. Her heart. Tell him that in the few days since they'd been married she'd started to change. He'd changed her, and now she wanted things she'd never let herself want. Affection. Friendship. *Love.*

The words were there and they trembled on her lips but then the fear of exposing so much want and need made her swallow them and offer a rather watery smile instead.

'You tell me.'

Wrong answer, she knew. A coward's answer. Sandro looked away. 'I don't know, Liana. I don't know what secrets you're hiding, or why you've, as you said yourself, experienced so little of life. It's almost as if you've kept yourself from it, from enjoying or feeling anything, and I won't know why or understand you until you tell me.' He glanced back at her then, his expression settled into resolute lines. 'But I'm not even sure you really want that. You told me you married me because of the opportunities being queen would give this charity of yours. Has that changed?'

She swallowed. 'No, not exactly.' Sandro's expression tightened and he started shuffling his papers into piles. 'But I've changed, Sandro, at least a little. I want to get to know you. And I hope you want to know me.' And that, Liana thought with a weary wryness, was about as honest as she could make herself be right now.

Sandro gazed at her thoughtfully. 'And how do you propose we do that?'

'Get to know one another, you mean?' She licked her lips, saw Sandro's gaze drop to her mouth, and felt warmth curling low in her belly. 'Well…as we have been doing. Talking. Spending time with one another.'

'We can talk all you like, but until you tell me whatever it is you're keeping from me, I don't think much is going to change.'

'But I told you I've already changed,' she said quietly. 'A little, at least. You've changed me.'

'Have I?' Sandro asked softly. He was still staring at her mouth and Liana felt a heavy languor begin to steal through her veins, making her feel almost drunk, reckless in a way she so rarely was. 'I can think of another way we could get to know one another,' she whispered.

He arched an eyebrow, heat flaring in his eyes, turning them to molten silver. 'And what would that be?'

'This.' She leaned forward, her heart thudding hard, and brushed her lips across his.

His mouth was cool and soft, his lips only barely parted, and he didn't respond as she'd expected him to, pulling her in his arms and taking control. No, he was waiting to see what she would do. How far she would go.

Emboldened, Liana touched her tongue to the corner of Sandro's mouth, heard his groan, felt it in the soft rush of breath against her own lips. Desire bit deeper, and she brought her hands up to his shoulders, steadying herself on the edge of his desk as she kissed him again, slid her tongue into his mouth with a surge of pure sexual excitement she thrilled to feel.

'Liana…' Sandro's hands tangled in her hair as he fastened his mouth more securely on hers, taking the kiss from her and making it his. Theirs.

And what a kiss it was. Liana could easily count the number of times she'd been kissed, half of them by Sandro, but this kiss was something else entirely. This kiss was shared, a giving and a taking and most of all an admission. A spilling of secrets, a confession of desire.

It felt like the most honest thing she'd ever done.

And then it was more than a kiss as Sandro swept all his papers aside and hauled her across the desk. She came willingly, sliding onto his lap, her legs on either side of him as she felt the hard, insistent press of his arousal against her and pleasure spiked deep inside.

Sandro deepened the kiss, his hands moving over her, cupping her breasts, the thin cotton of her sundress already too much between them. In that moment she wasn't afraid of her own feelings, the strength of her own desire—and his. She just wanted more.

Recklessly Liana pulled the dress over her head and tossed it to the floor. Sandro's gaze darkened with heat and then she unclasped her bra and sent it flying too. She was wearing only her panties, and even that felt like too much clothing.

'You're so beautiful,' he whispered huskily as his hands roved over her. 'Your skin is like marble.'

A small smile twitched her lips. 'Like a statue?'

He glanced up at her, his hands now cupping her breasts, his thumbs brushing over their taut peaks. 'Like Venus de Milo.' And then he put his mouth to her breasts and if she were a statue she came alive under him, writhing and gasping as he teased her with his tongue and lips.

She tangled her hands in his hair, arching her back and pressing against him, gasping aloud when he flexed his hips upwards and she felt the promise of what was to come, of what it would feel like to have him inside her, to be part of him. She wanted it now.

Sandro let out a shaky groan. 'Not here, Liana. Let me take you to bed—'

'Why do we need a bed?' she murmured and she slid

his hands up his bare chest, fingers spreading across hot skin and hard muscle.

'Your first time—'

'Are there rules about a woman's first time? Does it have to be on a bed, with roses and violins?'

He let out a shaky laugh. 'I don't have any roses at the moment—'

'I don't actually like roses.' She pressed against him, muscles she hadn't known she had tightening, quivering. 'Or violins.'

'Even so—'

'I want this.' She might not be able to be honest about everything yet, but she could be honest about this. About this real, rushing desire she felt. 'I want you. And I want you here, now, just like this.'

He eased away from her, but only to hold her face in his palms and search her expression. She stared back, firm in her purpose, clear-headed even in the midst of the haze of sexual desire. 'You want me,' he said slowly, almost wonderingly, and she leaned forward so her breasts brushed his chest and her lips touched his.

'I want you,' she whispered against his mouth, and then she kissed him again, another honest kiss, deeper this time, drawing everything from him even as she gave it back.

She'd never grow tired of this, she thought hazily as Sandro kissed his way down her body and her head fell back. She'd never have enough of this, of him. Her breath came out in short gasps as his fingers skimmed the waistband of her panties and then with one swift tug tore the thin cotton and tossed them aside, along with his own pyjama bottoms.

The sudden feel of his fingers against her most sen-

sitive flesh made her let out a surprised cry, and all her
muscles clenched as Sandro slid his fingers inside her.

She dropped her head on his shoulder, her fingernails
biting into his back as he moved his hand with such delicious certainty and a wave of pleasure so intense and
fierce it almost hurt crashed over her.

'*Sandro.*' Her breath came out in a shudder. 'Why
didn't I know about this?'

'Because you didn't let yourself,' he murmured, and as
his hand kept moving her hips moved of their own accord,
her body falling into a rhythm as natural as breathing.

'I—I want you,' she gasped, each word coming out
on a pant. 'I want you inside me.'

'It could hurt a little, your first—'

'Shut up about my first time,' she cut him off on a
gasp, angling her hips so she was poised over him. She
met his hot gaze as she sank slowly onto him, her eyes
widening as she felt herself open and stretch. Her hands
gripped his shoulders, and his hands were fastened to her
hips, their bodies joined in every way. 'Nothing about
this hurts.'

That wasn't quite true. Nothing hurt, but the feel of
him inside her was certainly eye-opening. *Intense.* And
wonderful. Intimate in a way she'd always been afraid
to be. To feel.

She never wanted to go back to numbness again.

Sandro's gaze stayed on hers as he began to move,
his hands on her hips guiding her to match his rhythm.

'Okay?' he murmured and she laughed, throwing her
head back as pleasure began shooting sparks deep inside her, jolts of sensation that made speech almost impossible.

'More than okay,' she answered when she trusted her
voice. 'Wonderful.'

And then words failed her as sensation took over, and Sandro's body moved so deeply inside hers she felt as if he touched her soul.

Maybe he did, because when the feelings finally took over, swamping her completely so her voice split the still air with one jagged cry of pleasure, she knew she'd never felt as close to a human being before, or ever.

And it felt more than wonderful. It felt as if he'd brought her back to life.

CHAPTER EIGHT

THEY HAD FIVE days in California, five days of seeing the sights and enjoying each other's company and each other's bodies. Making love.

That was what it felt like to Sandro, what it *was*. He was falling in love with his wife, with the warm woman who had broken through the coldness and the ice.

Looking at her as they strolled down the pier in Santa Monica, Sandro could hardly believe Liana was the same coolly composed woman he'd met two months ago. She wore a sundress in daffodil yellow, her pale hair streaming about her shoulders, her eyes sparkling and her cheeks flushed. She looked incandescent.

Her step slowed as she glanced at him, her brow wrinkling. 'You're giving me a funny look.'

'Am I?'

'Do I have ice cream on my face or something?' She'd been eating a chocolate ice cream with the relish usually exhibited by a small child, and every long lick had desire arrowing inside him and making him long to drag her back to his house and make love to her in yet another room. So far they'd christened his study, his bedroom, the shower, the beach, and the front hall when they'd been in too much of a rush to get any farther inside. At this rate, Santa Monica pier would be next, and damn the crowds.

'I'm just enjoying watching you eat your ice cream.'

'Is it really that fascinating?' She laughed and Sandro felt himself go hard as she took another lick, her pink tongue swiping at the chocolate with a beguiling innocence.

'Trust me, it is.'

She faltered midlick as she took in the hotness of his gaze, and then with an impish little smile she leaned forward and gave him a chocolatey kiss. 'That's to tide you over till later.'

'How much later?'

'I want to walk to the end of the pier.'

Sandro groaned and took her arm. 'You're going to kill me, woman.'

'You'll die with a smile on your face, though.'

'Or else a grimace of agony because you're too busy enjoying your ice cream to satisfy your husband.'

She arched her eyebrows in mock innocence. 'I believe I satisfied my husband twice today already, and it's not even noon. I think you might need to talk to a doctor.'

'I might,' he agreed. 'Or maybe you just need to stop eating ice cream in front of me.' And then because he couldn't keep himself from it any longer, he pulled her towards him and kissed her again, deeper this time, more than just something to tide him over until he could get her alone.

The ice-cream cone dangled from Liana's fingers and then fell to the pier with a splat as she kissed him back, looping her arms around his neck to draw his body against her pliant softness, and he very nearly lost his head as everything in him ached to finish what they'd started right there, amidst the rollerbladers and sun-worshippers.

And Liana must have agreed with him, because she

kept kissing him, with all the enthusiasm he could ever want from a woman.

A woman he was falling in love with, and damn if he didn't want to stop.

A flashbulb going off made him ease back. The paparazzi hadn't bothered them too much since they'd arrived in LA; there were enough famous people in this town to make Sandro, thankfully, just another celebrity. But having his hands all over his wife in public was front-page fodder for sure.

'Sorry,' he said, and eased back. 'That's going to be in the papers, I'm afraid.'

'I don't care,' Liana answered blithely. 'We're married, after all.' She glanced down at their feet. 'But you'd better buy me another ice cream.'

'Not a chance.' Sandro tugged her by the hand back down the pier. 'I won't be answerable for my actions if I do.'

Several hours later they were lying in his bed—they'd made it there eventually, after christening another room of his beach house, this time the kitchen—legs and hands entwined, the mellow afternoon sunlight slanting over them.

And as much as Sandro never wanted any of it to end, he knew it had to.

'I've finished up with DT,' he said, sliding a hand along the smooth tautness of Liana's belly. 'We should return to Maldinia tomorrow.'

'Tomorrow?' He heard the dismay in her voice and then she sighed in acceptance, putting her hand over his and lacing her fingers through his. 'It went by so fast. I don't think I've ever enjoyed myself so much.'

'Me neither. But duty calls.' He heard the slightly sardonic note enter his voice, as it always did when he talked about his royal life, and he knew Liana heard it too.

She twisted towards him, her expression intent and earnest, her bare breasts brushing his chest. An interesting combination, and one that made Sandro want to kiss her again. And more.

'Why do you hate being king?' she asked, and he felt as if she'd just touched him with a branding iron. Pain, white-hot, lanced through him. Desire fled.

'Why do you think I hate being king?' he answered, glad his voice stayed even.

'Maybe hate is too strong a word. But whenever you talk about it—about Maldinia and the monarchy—you get this...*tone* to your voice. As if you can't stand it.'

He started to shift away from her, sliding his fingers from her own, but she tugged him back, or at least stayed him for a moment. 'Don't, Sandro,' she said quietly. 'I'm not trying to offend you or make you angry. I just want to know you.'

'I think you've known me pretty well this week, wouldn't you say?'

Her expression clouded, her eyes the colour of bruises. 'But that's just sex.'

'Just sex? I'm offended.'

'All right, fine. Amazing sex, but still, I want to know more than your body, as fantastic as that is.'

He stared at her then, saw the shadows in her eyes, the uncertain curve of her mouth. 'Do you really, Liana?' he asked quietly. 'We've had a wonderful time this past week, I'll be the first to admit it. But we haven't talked about anything really personal and I think you've liked it that way.'

Her lips trembled before she firmed them into a line and nodded. 'Maybe I do. I'm a private person, Sandro, I admit that. There are—things I don't like talking about. But I still want to get to know you. Understand you.'

'So I bare my soul while you get to keep yours hidden? Doesn't sound like much of a fair trade to me.'

'No, it doesn't.' She was silent for a moment, nibbling her lip, clearly wrestling with herself. Sandro just waited. He had no idea what she was going to say or suggest, and he felt a wariness leap to life inside him because she might accuse her of keeping things back, but he knew he was too.

About his family. His father. Himself.

'How about this,' she finally said, and she managed to sound both resolute and wavering at the same time. It made Sandro want to gather her up in his arms and kiss her worries away, as well as his own. That would be far more enjoyable than talking. 'We ask each other questions.'

He frowned, still wary. 'Questions?'

'Sounds simple, doesn't it?' she agreed with a wry smile that tugged at his heart. And other places. 'What I mean is we take turns. You ask me a question and I have to answer it. Then I get to ask you a question and you have to answer it.' She eyed him mischievously, although he could still tell this was big for her. And for him. Honesty, intimacy? He might crave it but that didn't make it easy. 'I'll even,' she added, 'let you go first.'

Sandro took a deep breath, let it out slowly. He nodded. 'Okay.'

'Okay. Ask me the first question.' Liana scrambled into a seated position, her legs crossed, her expression alert. She was completely naked and Sandro didn't know whether he wanted to ask her a question or haul her into his arms. No, actually he did.

Sex would be easier. Safer. And far more pleasurable.

But he'd accused Liana of holding things back and he'd be both a coward and a hypocrite now if he was the one to pull away. He drew another deep breath and sifted through all the things he'd wondered about his wife. 'Why have you devoted your life to Hands To Help?'

She inhaled sharply, just once, and then let it out slowly. 'Because my sister had epilepsy.'

Surprise flashed through him. 'You've never mentioned—'

She held up one slender palm. 'Nope, sorry. My turn now.'

'Okay.' He braced himself for the question he knew she would ask, the question she'd asked before. *Why do you hate being king?* And how would he answer that? Nothing about that answer was simple. Nothing about it was something he wanted to say.

'Why did you choose California?' she asked, and his jaw nearly dropped. She was gazing at him steadily and he knew with a sudden certainty that she was going easy on him. Because she knew how hard he'd found her first question. And yet he'd cut right to the quick with his own. He felt a surge of feeling for this woman who had shown him in so many ways just how strong and deep and wonderful she was.

'I chose California because I wanted to go into IT and it was a good place for start-up businesses. Also, for the weather.'

She smiled, just slightly, and he felt herself tense for his next question. 'What's your sister's name?' he asked, and to his surprise and recrimination her eyes filled with tears. He'd meant it to be an easy question, but obviously it wasn't.

'Chiara.' She drew a clogged breath. 'I called her Chi-Chi.'

The past tense jumped out at him and he realised what

a moron he was. He should have realised her sister was
no longer alive. 'What—?'

She shook her head. 'My turn.' She blinked rapidly
until the tears receded, although Sandro would have
rather they'd fallen. When, he wondered, had Liana last
cried? He had a feeling it had been a long, long time ago.

'What made you renounce your inheritance?'

It felt necessary at the time. That was what he'd told
her before. He could say the same now, but it wasn't really much of an answer. He gazed at her steadily, saw
the remnant of old sorrow in her eyes even as she gazed
unblinkingly back. 'Because I thought I'd lose myself—
my soul—if I stayed.'

'Why—?'

'Fair's fair. My turn now.'

'All right.'

He saw her brace herself, everything in her tensing
for his next question. 'How did your sister die?' he asked
softly.

For a second, no more, her features twisted in a torment that made him want to lean forward to embrace
her, comfort her, but then her expression blanked again
and she said quietly, 'She choked during an epileptic fit
when she was four years old.'

This time he didn't keep himself from reaching for
her. 'God, Liana. I'm sorry.' No wonder she devoted herself to her damned charity, to supporting the families of
children like Chiara. She remained in his arms, stiff and
unyielding as he stroked her hair, her shoulder. 'How old
were you when it happened?'

'Eight.' She drew a shuddering breath. 'But that's two
questions from you, so I get two now.'

'We could stop—'

'Not a chance.' She eased back, dabbed at her eyes with one hand before she stiffened her shoulders, gave him a look of stony determination.

'Why did you feel as if you'd lose yourself, your soul, if you stayed in Maldinia?'

They were drawing the big guns now, Sandro thought wryly. Asking and admitting things that made them both very uncomfortable. Terribly vulnerable. 'Because I couldn't stand all the hypocrisy.'

'What hypocrisy?'

'It's my turn now—'

'No.' She shook her head, her pale hair flying over her shoulders. 'I get two questions in a row, remember.'

'Damn.' He smiled wryly, sighed. 'The hypocrisy of my parents as well as myself.'

'What—?'

'Nope.' He shook his head now. 'My turn.'

She closed her eyes, and he felt as if she was summoning strength. 'Go ahead.'

'What was your favourite subject in school?'

Her eyes flew open and she stared at him in surprise, before a small smile tugged at her mouth. 'Art. What was yours?'

'Computers.'

They stared at each other for a long moment, the only sound their breathing, the rustle of covers underneath their naked bodies. 'Do you want to stop?' Liana asked softly, and he realised he didn't. He wanted to tell everything to this woman, bare his soul and his heart along with his body. And he wanted her to do it too, and, more importantly, to want to. He wanted that intimacy. That vulnerability. That trust, that love.

And he hoped to God that Liana wanted it too.

* * *

Liana held her breath while Sandro's gaze roved over her and then he smiled and shook his head.

'No, let's keep going. My turn to ask now.'

She nodded, steeling herself. It was almost a relief to answer his questions, like lancing a wound or easing an intense pressure. But it also hurt, and while he might have given her a break with the last question she didn't think he would now.

'Why didn't you go to university?'

'Because I wanted to start working with Hands To Help as soon as I could.' That one, at least, was easy, even if it most likely made him think she was a bit obsessive about her charity. That was because he didn't know the whole truth about Chiara; he hadn't asked. And she wasn't, she acknowledged, going to admit it unless he did.

Now her turn. She eyed him, his body relaxed and so incredibly beautiful as he lay stretched out across from her, unashamedly naked, the late afternoon sunlight glinting off his burnished skin, the perfect tautness of his muscled body. 'How were your parents hypocrites?'

He didn't say anything for a long moment, his gaze drawn and thoughtful, and finally Liana prompted him softly. 'Sandro?'

'It's not just a one-sentence answer.'

'We didn't make a rule about answers having to only be one sentence.'

'But it's easier, isn't it?' He glanced up at her, eyes glinting even as his mouth twisted with something like bitterness. 'We're both revealing as little information as we can.'

She couldn't deny that. 'So we start small,' she said with a shrug. 'No one said this had to be a complete confessional.'

'My parents were hypocrites because they only pretended that they loved us when there was a camera or reporter around. When it mattered.'

'Why—?'

'Nope. My turn.' So he was sticking with a one-sentence answer. She gave a little shrug of assent and waited, wondering just what he would ask her next. 'What do you fantasise about doing with me that we haven't done already?'

Shock had her jaw dropping even as heat blazed through her at his heavy-lidded look. 'Umm...' Her mind was blank, spinning. 'Going to the cinema?'

He let out a low, throaty chuckle. 'I see I'm going to have to rephrase that question.'

Her cheeks warmed. She might have been unabashed with him in the bedroom—or whatever room it happened to be—but talking about it felt different. More revealing somehow. 'My turn,' she said, her voice nearly a croak as she willed her blush to fade. She was suddenly, achingly conscious that they were both naked. That they'd just made love but already she wanted to again. And so, it seemed, judging from his words as well as the proud evidence of his body, did Sandro.

'What's your question, Liana?' Sandro asked in a growl. 'Because the way you're looking at me, I'm not going to give you the time to ask me.'

'Sorry.' She jerked her gaze up to his face, tried to order her dazed thoughts. 'Umm... How were you a hypocrite?'

'Because I bought into their lies and when I realised that's what they were I kept it going.' He tossed the words away carelessly, but they made Liana want to ask more. Understand more.

'My turn now,' Sandro said, his voice a growl of sexual

intent. 'Now I'll rephrase my last question. What do you fantasise about doing with me *sexually* that we haven't already done?'

Just the question, in that husky murmur of his, made her breasts ache and her core throb. 'We've already done a lot....'

'Are you saying there isn't something?' Sandro asked silkily, his tone suggesting that he knew otherwise.

'No, not exactly....'

'Then what? Play by the rules, Liana. Answer the question.'

She pressed her hands to her face. 'This is embarrassing.'

'Why?'

'I—I don't know.'

'I think you do.'

'Fine, if you know so much, you tell me what I fantasise about.'

He laughed softly. 'I don't think so. You're not going to get off that easily.' His mouth curved in a wicked smile. 'No pun intended. But I will tell you what I fantasise about.'

'Okay,' she breathed, and Sandro leaned forward, all predatory power and sexual intent.

'I fantasise about tasting you.' Liana inhaled sharply and felt her insides turn liquid. 'And I don't mean your mouth.'

She let out a wobbly laugh. 'I might be inexperienced, but I didn't think that's what you meant.'

'I want to taste you, Liana. I want to feel you tremble against me while I do.'

She closed her eyes, images, amazing, explicit images, blitzing through her brain, making it impossible to think. To respond. And yet the words came of themselves and with her eyes still closed she heard herself whisper, 'I want that too.'

And then Sandro was reaching for her and kissing her, his mouth hard and hot and yet so very sweet. His hands slid down her body as his tongue delved deep and Liana tangled her fingers in his hair, drawing him closer, needing him more.

But then he began to move his mouth down her body and she knew where he was going, knew what he wanted—and what she wanted. Everything in her seemed to still and hang suspended, waiting, yearning—

And then her breath came out in a sudden gasp of pleasure as he spread her thighs and put his mouth to her, his tongue flicking against the sensitive folds, everything in her exposed and open and vulnerable.

It was exquisite. Unbearable. *Too much.* Too much pleasure, too much openness, too much feeling. She felt his breath against her heated, tender skin and she let out a choked gasp, felt tears start in her eyes. Tears that felt like the overflow of emotion in her soul.

'*Sandro...*'

He lifted his head slightly. 'Do you want me to stop?'

'*No—*'

And then he tasted her again, deeper still, his mouth moving over her so surely, and her thighs clenched, her hands fisting in his hair as she cried out her climax and tears trickled down her cheeks. She felt as if she'd been broken and put together again; as if Sandro had reconstructed her.

He rested his cheek against her tummy as her heart rate slowed and she wiped the tears from her face with trembling fingers.

Gently he reached up and took her hands from her face, wiping the remaining tears away with his thumbs.

'I'm sorry,' she whispered.

'Sorry? What on earth for?'

'For crying—'

'I don't mind your tears, Liana.' He kissed her navel. 'You're amazing,' he said softly and she let out a shaky laugh.

'I feel as weak as a kitten.'

'Amazing,' he repeated, and Liana had a sudden, overwhelming urge to tell him she loved him, but she kept the words back. Despite what they'd just done, it felt like too much too soon.

So instead she decided to admit to her fantasy and pay him in kind.

Gently she pushed at his shoulder and he lifted his head, his chin resting on her tummy, to gaze at her, his expression sleepy and hooded. 'It's your turn now,' she said, and that sleepy gaze became suddenly alert.

'My turn?'

She pushed him again and with a smile he rolled over onto his back, everything about him masculine, magnificent, *hers*. 'Fair's fair,' she said and, with a blaze of sensual anticipation and ancient, feminine power, she straddled his thighs, bent her head so her mouth brushed his navel—and then moved lower.

CHAPTER NINE

LIANA GAZED AT her reflection and tried to still the nervous fluttering in her stomach. They'd been back in Maldinia for a week, and tonight was the fundraiser for Hands To Help.

In the week since they'd returned from California, they'd continued exploring the sexual side of their relationship with joyous abandon. The nights were pleasure-filled, and the days...?

Liana wasn't so sure about the days. They'd both been busy with royal duties, but there had still been time to spend just with each other—if they had wanted to. Sandro, however, hadn't sought her out. They certainly hadn't had any more question-and-answer sessions, and the most honest either of them seemed to be was with their bodies. Not their words. Not their hearts.

It was ironic, really, that she wanted that now. She'd entered this marriage because she'd believed it would be convenient, that it *wouldn't* involve her heart. She hadn't wanted love or intimacy or any of it—and now she did.

Now she did so much, and Sandro was the one pulling away. She'd felt his emotional withdrawal from the moment they'd stepped off the royal jet. At first she'd thought he was just preoccupied with work; he'd spent the entire fourteen-hour flight from LA working in his study on the plane. But after a week of incredible sex and virtually no conversation, she knew work couldn't be the only reason.

She'd gone over what Sandro had told her about himself many times, yet those few terse sentences hardly gave anything away.

My parents were hypocrites because they only pretended that they loved us when there was a camera or reporter around. When it mattered.

Because I bought into their lies and when I realised that's what they were I kept it going.

What did it mean, he kept it going? And what, really, did his parents' lack of love have to do with being king? Unless he simply found the whole atmosphere of the palace too toxic to endure. Liana had to admit she always felt herself tense when the queen dowager was around. But to walk away from everything he'd known and been for fifteen whole years? There had to be more to his story, just as there was more to hers.

And even if she wanted to admit more to Sandro, he didn't seem willing or interested to hear it. He'd been perfectly polite, of course, even friendly, and at night he made her body sing. But they'd been teetering on the edge of a far deeper intimacy and since returning here Sandro had taken a few definite, determined steps back.

Which shouldn't, Liana told herself, make her feel restless. Anxious. Why couldn't she accept what they had and deem it enough? It was more than she'd ever had before, more than she'd ever let herself want.

And yet it wasn't enough. Not when she'd had a glimpse—a taste—of just how much more they could have.

Taking a deep breath, she forced her thoughts away from such pointless musings and inspected her reflection once more. She wore an emerald-green evening gown, a bold choice for her, and she'd selected it with the help of Demi, her stylist. She wondered what Sandro would think of the asymmetrical cut, with one shoulder left bare. She worn her hair up, but loosely, unlike the more severe chignons she used to favour. To finish the outfit she'd chosen diamond chandelier earrings and a matching necklace that had belonged to her mother.

She took a deep breath and turned away from the mirror. The maid, Rosa, who had helped her dress, smiled encouragingly. 'You look lovely, Your Highness.'

'Thank you, Rosa.'

Rosa handed her a matching wrap of emerald satin and Liana draped it over one arm before leaving her suite of rooms. The dress whispered against her legs as she walked down the corridor, her heart thudding harder with every step that took her towards Sandro. What would he think of her gown? And what would he think of *her*? Tonight was such an important night for her, finally bringing more visibility to Hands To Help, and yet in this moment she cared more about what Sandro thought than anything else. She wanted that intimacy back again, that closeness that didn't come from sex—as amazing as that was—but from simply being with one another. Talking and laughing in a way they hadn't since returning from California.

Sandro was waiting at the bottom of the palace's sweeping staircase as Liana came down. He looked dark and dangerous and utterly devastating in black tie, his hair brushed back, his eyes glittering like shards of silver.

He stilled as she approached, his expression going utterly blank as his gaze swept her from head to toe, making Liana wonder just what he thought. It was the first time she'd worn a formal gown since their marriage.

'You look beautiful,' he said quietly, and pleasure flared through her at the obvious sincerity of those simple words. 'That colour suits you.'

'Thank you,' she murmured. 'You do amazing things to a tuxedo.'

His mouth quirked in a smile and his eyes lightened to the colour of a dawn mist as he took her arm. 'I'd like to do amazing things to you,' he whispered as he drew her down the last few steps.

'And I'd like you to do them,' she answered back. 'I have a few amazing things up my sleeve as well.'

Sandro grinned, and even as familiar heat flared inside her Liana knew it wasn't enough. Sex wasn't enough, never would be. But now was surely not the time for a heart-to-heart. Perhaps later tonight they would talk again. Learn each other again.

Sandro's grin faded and Liana stilled, wondering what had changed, when he addressed a member of the palace staff, who came hurrying forward.

'Your Highness?'

'Please bring the crown jewels to my study. The emerald parure, I think.'

'Very good, Your Highness.'

'The crown jewels?' Liana repeated, and touched the chandelier necklace around her throat. 'But—'

'What you're wearing is very lovely,' Sandro said as he led her towards his study, one hand warm and firm on the small of her back. 'But there is a piece from the royal collection that would suit you—and that dress—perfectly. Do you mind?'

'Mind?' She shook her head. 'No, of course not.'

'Here you are, Your Highness.' The footman brought in a mahogany case inlaid with ivory, and placed it on the desk before handing Sandro the keys.

'Thank you,' Sandro murmured, and the man left as he unlocked the case and lifted the lid. Liana gasped at the sight of the glittering jewels within, and Sandro turned to her with a glint in his eye. 'Lovely, aren't they?' he murmured. 'Supposedly once owned by Napoleon.'

'For Josephine?'

'His empress. And you are my queen.'

His queen. Liana thrilled to the words, to their implication. She was his, heart and soul, whether he knew it or not. Whether he wanted it or not. Yet in this moment she felt only happiness as he lifted the heavy necklace from its velvet bed, the diamond-encrusted emeralds catching the light and twinkling as if lit with a fire from within. 'May I?' Sandro asked softly, and wordlessly she nodded, holding her breath as she felt his fingers, warm and sure, on the back of her neck.

Goosebumps rose on her flesh as he unclasped her diamond necklace and slid it from her, his fingers brushing the tender skin of her neck, the hollow of her throat. Liana bit her lip to keep a shudder of pure longing from escaping her. He reduced her to want so effortlessly, and yet she felt his own response, the strength of his own need as his fingers rested against her throat, his breath hitching slightly as it fanned the nape of her neck. She eased back against him, leaning against his chest, and his hands came around her shoulders, cradling her. For a perfect moment she felt completely at peace, wonderfully loved. He brushed his lips against her neck and then he steadied her again, before putting the emerald-and-diamond necklace around her throat, the stones heavy against her skin and warm from his hands.

He clasped the necklace and then rested his hands on her shoulders again, his fingers curling around her, seeming to reach right inside. 'Liana…' he began, his voice an ache, a caress, and everything in her longed to know what he was thinking. Feeling. And what he was going to say.

But he didn't say anything, just slid his hands from her shoulders and reached for the other pieces of the parure: earrings, bracelet, and a tiara.

'I've never actually worn a tiara,' Liana said as he placed it on her loose updo. 'Does it look ridiculous? As if…as if I'm trying to be a princess?'

'You're not a princess,' Sandro reminded her. 'You are a queen.'

Liana touched the stones, wanting once again to tell him she loved him. Had he been about to tell her the same thing? She didn't know whether she dared to hope, and she didn't say anything, just put on the earrings and bracelet.

'Thank you,' she said, when she was wearing all of the jewels. 'They're amazing.'

'You're amazing. They look beautiful on you. A true queen.'

She met his eyes, smiling, only to have her smile wobble and then slip completely from her face as she saw the frown settle between Sandro's brows, the darkness steal into his eyes. He might call her a true queen, but she didn't know then whether he wanted to be her king.

Sandro watched Liana from across the crowded ballroom where the fundraiser for Hands To Help was being held; she was talking to several dignitaries, a flute of champagne in one slender hand, her body resplendent, like an emerald flame, in that amazing dress, the light from the crystal chandeliers catching the strands of gold and silver in her moon-coloured hair. She looked beautiful, captivating, and every inch the consummate queen.

Sandro saw several men cast her covert, admiring

glances, and he felt his insides clench with a potent mix of jealousy, desire, and love.

He loved her. He hadn't told her, hadn't even wanted to tell her, not just because he didn't know if she loved him, but because he didn't trust his own feelings. His own self.

Hadn't he been wrong before? And while their time in California had been sweet, and their nights together since then even sweeter, he still didn't know if it was real.

Well, sex was real. Real and raw and powerful. But love? Could he love her after so short a time? What had happened to the icy, reserved woman he'd first met? Had she really changed—and had he?

Restlessly, Sandro shifted and took a sip of champagne. Watching Liana now, he felt a new and unwelcome realisation sweep over him. Here she was in her element; she was queen. He saw the sparkle in her eyes as she talked about Hands To Help, the regal bearing of her beautiful body. This, he thought, made her come alive in a way he hadn't seen before, even when she'd been in his arms. This was why she'd agreed to marry him in the first place, what gave her her whole reason for being.

To be queen.

And while that shouldn't bother him, he knew it did. Because while Liana made a beautiful and perfect queen, he didn't feel like her match.

He didn't deserve to be king.

If I could have, I'd have left you to rot in California, or, better yet, in hell.

So many months after his father's death, his savage nearly last words still had the power to hurt him. To make him question himself, just as he had so many years before. His father hadn't called him back from California because he'd wanted a reconciliation, as Sandro had so naively believed.

No, his father had asked him because he was desperate. Because the media mess of Leo and Alyse's marriage had seemed irredeemable. Sandro was the second choice.

He hadn't realised any of that until his father had died, three weeks after he'd called him in California. The former king had known he was terminally ill, had wanted to get the succession sorted out before his death.

Had really wanted Leo.

Sandro's gaze moved from his wife to his brother, chatting with a group of IT businessmen, Alyse by his side. Would Leo make a better king than him?

Sandro was sure of it.

And yet from the moment he'd returned Leo hadn't offered a single word of protest. He'd stepped aside gracefully, had accepted his position as cabinet minister with a nod and a smile. Leo, Sandro had to assume, was relieved. And why shouldn't he be?

Neither of them had wanted to follow in their father's footsteps. Neither of them had wanted the awful burden of royal duty.

And yet here they were.

One of the footmen flanking the room rang a bell, and Sandro watched as the crowd fell silent and with a shyly assured smile Liana went to the front of the room. Sandro watched her, felt a surge of admiration and love, and yet washed over it all was desperation. Because she was too good for him. Because he didn't believe she could really love him, a man who had shirked his duty for so long. A man who was second best.

'Thank you all so much for coming,' Liana said, her voice clear and musical. Sandro felt as if he could listen to her for ever. And everyone else must have too because the room went utterly silent as she spoke about Hands To Help's mission and what it meant to her.

She didn't, Sandro realised with a flicker of surprise, talk about her sister.

But he could hear the passion in her voice, the utter sincerity, and he knew everyone else could too. And when she was done the room broke out into an applause that was not merely polite, but spontaneous and sincere.

Sandro's gut twisted. How could this amazing woman love him?

She moved through the crowd, chatting with various guests, but he saw her gaze rove restlessly over the clusters of people and knew she was looking for him.

He came forward, smiling as he took her by the hand. 'Well done. You spoke beautifully, Liana.'

Pink touched her cheeks and her eyes sparkled. How had he ever thought she was a statue? Or icy and cold? In this moment she looked real, warm, vibrant, and glorious. He almost told her he loved her right then.

Almost.

But he didn't, because along with his other sins he was a coward. He didn't want to hear the silence he feared would be the answer back…just as it had been before.

Liana felt Sandro's preoccupation as they left the fundraiser and headed for their suite in the private family wing of the palace. It was past midnight and all around them the palace was dark and hushed, only a few sleepy footmen on duty.

'I think it went well tonight, don't you?' Liana said as they turned down the corridor that housed their suite of rooms.

'Very well.' His lips curved in a smile but his voice was toneless, and she had no idea what he was thinking. Feeling.

'Thank you for organising it,' she said, hating that she felt awkward, even if just a little. 'It was very thoughtful.'

'It was the least I could do.'

Sandro opened the door to his bedroom, the bedroom they'd shared since returning from California even though Liana had her own adjoining room.

Uncertainly she stepped in behind him, because she couldn't decipher his mood at all and she was getting so very tired of wondering. Worrying.

'Sandro—'

Before she could say another word she was in his arms, her back pressed against the door as he kissed her with a raw, rough intensity she hadn't felt before. It was a kiss of passion but it felt like grief. Even so it ignited everything inside her and she kissed him back, matching him even though part of her cried out that whatever was wrong between them, it couldn't be solved by sex.

Maybe Sandro disagreed. Or maybe sex was all he wanted, for he slid his hands down her satin-clad legs before sliding the material up to her hips. Heat flared as he pressed his hand against her, the thin silk of her panties the only barrier between them.

She put her hands on either side of his face, tried to get him to look at her. 'Sandro, what is it?' she whispered even as an insistent, pleasurable ache had started between her thighs, urged on by the press of his hand. 'What's wrong?'

'Nothing's wrong,' he answered, his voice thick with desire. 'I just need you, Liana. I want you. Now.' He hoisted her leg up and wrapped it around his hip, and as he kissed her again Liana closed her eyes, let the sensation wash over her.

She wanted him too, and while she wanted his honesty

more, she understood he needed this. Needed her. And maybe that could be enough, at least for now.

He buried his head in the curve of his neck, a shudder racking his body as he moved against her. Liana put her arms around him, drawing him even closer, and then he was inside her, and it felt as deep and overwhelming and as wonderful as always.

She met him thrust for thrust, gasping out his name, her head thrown back against the door, and afterwards as their hearts raced against each other and the sweat cooled on their skin Sandro whispered against her throat.

'I love you.'

Everything in Liana stilled, and she felt a fragile happiness emerge from the tumult of her emotions like the first bloom of spring, tender and new.

She smoothed his hair away from his face and kissed his lips. 'I love you too.'

Neither of them spoke, and even as they remained in each other's arms Liana wondered why that confession of love—something she'd longed for—made her feel sadder than ever.

CHAPTER TEN

SANDRO STARED UNSEEINGLY down at the various letters he'd been given by his secretary to sign. The words blurred in front of him and wearily he rubbed his eyes. He'd been working in his study all day, reviewing fiscal plans and budget cuts in preparation for a meeting with his cabinet tomorrow.

He could see Leo's mark on everything he read, from the proposal to extend broadband to most of the country—something his brother felt passionately about, just as he did—to the necessary budget cuts in the palace. Leo clearly would rather go without a few luxuries than cut anything that affected his people.

He would have made a good king, Sandro thought, not for the first time. If the press hadn't uncovered the whole marriage masquerade debacle, his brother would have been a great king. And he *would* have been king, because Sandro would have stayed in California. He wouldn't have come back. Wouldn't have married Liana.

Wouldn't have had any of it.

Sighing, he rubbed his temples, felt the beginnings of a headache.

A quick knock sounded and then Leo opened the door, closing it behind him.

'I'm heading home, but I just wanted to make sure you didn't need me for anything?'

'No, I think I'm ready for tomorrow.' He tapped the papers in front of him. 'I can see you've done a lot of good work here, Leo.'

Leo shrugged. 'Just doing my job.'

Sandro nodded, even as he felt that tension and awful uncertainty ratchet up inside him. And it had been Leo's job, for fifteen years. A hell of a long time. 'You did it well.'

'Thank you,' Leo answered, and Sandro heard the repressive note in his brother's voice, felt a pang of sorrow. Once, they'd been close, two small boys banding together. Now he felt a distance yawn between them and he had no idea how to close it.

He stared down at the papers again, wished he knew the words to say, and had the courage to say.

'Sandro?' Leo asked for a moment. 'Is everything all right…between you and Liana?'

'Between me and Liana?' Sandro's voice came out sharp. 'Why do you ask?'

Leo shrugged. 'Because I know you married for convenience, and yet I've seen the way you look at each other. Something's going on.'

'We're married, Leo. Of course something is going on.'

'Do you love her?'

Sandro felt his throat go tight. 'That's between Liana and me, isn't it?'

'Sorry. I don't mean to be nosy.' Leo sighed. 'I just want you to be happy.'

'And since you've just fallen in love you want everyone else to as well.'

'Something like that, I suppose.'

'Don't worry about Liana and me, Leo. We're fine.' Sandro spoke with a firmness he didn't really feel, because they weren't fine. Not exactly. Ever since returning to Maldinia, he'd felt the emotional distance yawn between them. Physically things were amazing, exciting. But emotionally? He might have been honest and vulnerable and all that in California, but here? Where the memories mocked him? When the fear that he didn't deserve any of this, couldn't live up to it, suffocated him?

No, not so emotionally available now. Here. Even if, in a moment of weakness, he'd told her he loved her.

'Okay,' Leo said after a moment. 'Well. Goodnight.'

'Goodnight.'

It was early evening and a purple twilight was settling over the palace and its gardens as Sandro left his study a few minutes after Leo. He and Liana had a dinner engagement that evening, something official and most likely boring at the Italian embassy.

But before he got ready for it, he wanted to see Liana. Talk to her…although he had no idea what he was going to say.

He found her in the pretty, feminine little room she used as her own study, going over her schedule with her private secretary. Sandro watched them for a moment, two heads bent together, smiling and chatting as they reviewed certain points.

Liana was in her element, and that was brought home to him no more so than when she looked up and smiled her welcome.

'I've just been going over my schedule—it looks like a very busy week!'

'Does it?' The secretary, Christina, excused herself, and Sandro closed the door, leaning against it. 'So what are you doing?'

'Well...' Liana glanced down at the typewritten sheet. 'On Monday I'm visiting the paediatric ward of the hospital here in Averne. Tuesday is a lunch for primary care-givers of disabled and elderly. Wednesday I'm meeting with a primary school, and Thursday I'm officially open-ing a new playground in the city's public gardens.' She looked up, eyes sparkling. 'I know I'm not inventing a cure for cancer or anything, but I like feeling so useful.'

'Surely you felt useful before, when you worked for Hands To Help.'

'Yes, I did,' Liana answered after a moment. 'Of course I did. But sometimes...' She trailed off, and, in-trigued, Sandro stepped closer.

'Sometimes?'

Liana gave a little shrug. 'Sometimes it hurt, working there. It reminded me of—of my sister.'

'Do you miss her?' he asked quietly and she blinked rapidly, needlessly straightening the papers in front of her.

'Every day.'

'It must be hard. I didn't think many people actually died from epilepsy.'

'They don't.'

'So Chiara was just one of the unlucky ones?'

And for some reason this remark made her stiffen as if she'd suddenly turned to wood. 'Yes,' she said, and her voice was toneless. 'She was unlucky.'

Sandro stared at her, saw how the happiness and ex-citement had drained from her, and felt guilt needle him. Damn it, he'd done that. He shouldn't have asked those questions, and yet he'd just been trying to get to know her all over again. Get closer.

Yet you keep your secrets to yourself.

'I'm sorry I've been a bit—distant lately,' he said abruptly, and Liana looked up, startled.

'At least you noticed.'

'And you have too, I assume?'

'Yes.' Her voice was soft, sad. 'I know we've been— Well, the nights have been—' She laughed a little, shook her head. 'You know what I mean.'

'I certainly do.'

'But we haven't talked, really. Not since California.'

Not since they'd sat across from each other on his bed, naked not just with their bodies but with their souls. He sighed. 'Returning to this palace always brings back some bad memories for me. It's hard to combat them.'

'What memories, Sandro?'

He dragged his hand across his eyes as words burned in his chest, caught in his throat. How much to admit? To confess? 'A lot of memories.' She just waited, and he dropped his hand. 'Memories of my father always telling me how he was counting on me,' he said, his voice expressionless now. 'Counting on me to be a good king. Just like him.'

'Just like him?' Liana repeated softly, a slight frown curving her mouth downwards. She knew, just as the whole world did, that his father hadn't been a good king at all. He'd been dissolute, uninterested in his people, a spendthrift, a scoundrel, an arrogant and adulterous *ass*.

And Sandro had idolised him.

'He was my hero, growing up,' he said, and then laughed. 'Which sounds ridiculous, because you know as well as I do there was nothing heroic about him.'

'But you were a child.'

'I believed that until I was eighteen.' He winced just saying it aloud. 'I insisted on believing it, even when boys at boarding school taunted me with the truth, even when

I saw the newspaper headlines blaring about his affairs, his reckless spending.' He shook his head. 'I convinced myself they were jealous or just stirring up trouble. I insisted on believing he was a good man, even when everything showed me otherwise.'

'That's not something to be ashamed of, Sandro,' Liana said quietly. 'Believing the best of someone, someone you love.'

'But that's it, isn't it? Because I was so desperate to love him, and believe he loved me back. I wanted to impress him with how good I could be—as good as he was. I wanted to believe the reason I hardly ever saw him was because he was so busy with his important duties, not because he didn't give a damn. Not because he'd rather screw and spend his way through Europe than spend one unnecessary moment with his son.' He broke off, nearly panting, the old rage and hurt coursing through him so hard and fast he felt as if he couldn't breathe.

And he felt so ashamed—ashamed that it still made him angry, still hurt. Ashamed that Liana knew.

She rose from her desk and he stiffened as she put her arms around him, drew his head to her shoulder as if he was still that desperate, deluded, and disappointed child.

And maybe he was.

'Oh, Sandro.' She was silent for a moment, stroking his hair, and he closed his eyes, revelling in her acceptance, her comfort even as he acknowledged that he didn't deserve it. 'What was the final straw, then?' she asked and he stiffened.

'The final—'

'What was the thing that made you leave?'

He drew a shuddering breath. 'I found out the truth about him when I was eighteen, at university. It was the first time I'd really had any freedom, and everything about it made me start to wonder. Doubt.'

She nodded slowly. 'I know how that feels.'

'And then one afternoon my father's private secretary called me up and asked me to issue a statement that he'd been visiting me that week when he hadn't. It didn't make any sense to me, but I did it. I started really doubting then, though, and the next time I was home I asked my father why he'd wanted me to do that.' He was silent for a moment, recalling the look of impatience on his father's face. 'He'd been with a mistress, some pretty young thing my mother was annoyed about, and he knew there would be a big media fuss if the tabloids got wind of it. He told me all of this so matter-of-factly, without so much as a flicker of guilt or remorse, and I suppose that's when the scales really fell from my eyes.' Sandro let out a long, weary sigh. 'But I didn't actually leave until three years later. Three years of going along with it all, corroborating his stupid stories, lying to the press, to him, to myself, about everything.'

Liana's gaze was wide and dark. 'And then?'

'And then...' He'd told more to this woman than he had to anyone else, and yet he still felt reluctant to reveal all. Reveal himself, and his own weaknesses. 'And then I just couldn't take it anymore. I hated who I'd become. So I told him I was renouncing my inheritance, that I wanted to start my own business and live my own life.' It sounded so selfish, even now, after all these years. 'The funny thing is,' Sandro made himself continue, 'I didn't really mean it.'

He saw surprise flash across Liana's face. 'You didn't?'

'No, I was just—testing him, I suppose. Pushing him. Because I expected him to beg me to stay, admit he loved me and it was all a mistake and— I don't even know.'

He let out a ragged huff of laughter as he raked his hand through his hair. 'How stupid can you be, eh?'

'I don't call that stupid,' Liana said quietly. 'Desperate, maybe.'

'Fine. I was desperate. Desperate and deluded right to the end, because of course he didn't do any of that. He just laughed in my face and told me to go right ahead. He had another son who would do just as well.'

And so he'd gone, proud and defiant and so desperately hurting. He'd gone, and he'd stayed away for fifteen years, only to come back because he'd thought his father had finally seen the light. Would finally admit he was sorry, he'd been wrong, he really did love him.

Blah. Blah. Blah. None of that, of course, had happened. But he'd told Liana enough, and he didn't feel like admitting to that.

'I'm sorry,' Liana whispered, and brushed a kiss across his lips. 'For all of it.'

'So am I.' He kissed her back, needing her touch, her sweetness. Needing to forget all the hurt and anger and disappointment he'd just raked up with his words.

And she did make him forget it; in Liana's arms he didn't feel like the sad, needy boy desperate for love. He didn't feel like a man racked by remorse and guilt for turning his back on his duty. He didn't feel like a king who didn't deserve his crown.

He just felt like a man, a man this amazing, wonderful, vibrant woman loved.

And that was all he wanted to be.

That night Liana lay in bed with Sandro's arm stretched out across her stomach and felt as if the first of the past's ghosts had been banished.

But what about hers?

She recalled Sandro's innocent question, so gently posed. *So Chiara was just one of the unlucky ones?*

She hadn't told Sandro the truth about that. About her. Chiara had been unlucky because she'd had a sister who had gone blank and still and unmoving when she'd needed her most. She'd had Liana.

And while part of her craved to tell Sandro the truth, to have him know and accept her wholeheartedly, the rest of her was too afraid because there were no guarantees. No promises that Sandro would accept her, would love her, if he knew how badly she'd failed someone she'd loved.

Her parents hadn't. Her father hadn't spoken to her for months after Chiara's death; even now he never quite looked at her when they talked. And he never showed her any affection. They'd never been the most demonstrative family—Chiara had cornered the market on that—but since her little sister's death her father hadn't touched her at all. Not one kiss or hug or even brush of the hand.

And could she really blame him?

She was a hypocrite, Liana knew, for wanting Sandro's secrets, his pain and shame and fear, and keeping all of hers back. If she'd been able to accept and love him, why couldn't he do the same for her?

Because your secrets are worse, your sins greater.

And yet not telling him—keeping that essential part of her back—felt like a cancer gnawing at all of her certainties, eating her heart.

How could she keep something so crucial from him?

CHAPTER ELEVEN

SANDRO ATTEMPTED TO listen as one of his cabinet ministers talked, his voice reminding him of the buzzing of a bumblebee that flung itself against the window of one of the palace's meeting rooms. He'd been closeted in here with his cabinet for nearly three hours and he'd barely been able to hear a word that had been said.

All because of Liana.

Ever since he'd unburdened himself to her he'd felt as if they were closer than ever. He loved her more than ever, for simply loving him. And that fact—that they actually loved each other—felt like an incredible blessing, a miracle.

A wonder and a joy.

And yet occasionally, when he glimpsed the shadows in her eyes, the way she'd suddenly turn away, he'd still feel as if she was keeping something from him. Hiding part of herself, but he didn't want to press. Demand answers she might not be ready to give. They had time, after all. Their love was new, perhaps fragile. He wasn't ready to test it in that way.

They had time.

'Your Highness?'

With effort Sandro jerked his gaze back to his expectant cabinet and attempted to focus on the discussion of domestic policy that had been taking up the better part of the afternoon.

'Yes?'

The minister of economic policy cleared his throat. 'We were just going to take a look at the budget Prince Leo proposed....'

Sandro glanced down at the painstakingly and laboriously made list of figures he'd assumed his ministers had put together. Not just Leo.

'Leo drafted this budget?' he asked, heard how sharp his voice sounded. 'When?'

He saw several ministers glance at Leo sitting on the other end of the table and an unease that had been skirting the fringes of his mind for months now suddenly swooped down and grabbed him by the throat. He felt as if he couldn't breathe.

'A few years back, when—' one of the ministers began, glancing uncertainly at Leo, whose face was expressionless, his body still.

'Years,' Sandro repeated, his mind spinning. Years ago, when Leo had thought he would be king.

He turned to stare at his brother, who gazed evenly back. 'I didn't realise you had taken such an interest, Leo,' he murmured. His father would have been alive, of course, and reigning as king. Leo would have been waiting, no more than a reluctant placeholder. Or so Sandro had thought.

But perhaps his brother hadn't been so reluctant, after all.

'I took an interest in all government policy,' Leo answered, and Sandro couldn't tell a thing from his tone. 'Naturally I wanted to be prepared.'

'For when you would become king,' Sandro clarified,

and he felt a silent tension ripple its way around the room, felt it in Leo's body as well as his own.

'Yes.'

The air felt charged, electric. Why hadn't Leo told him this before? Why had he kept it from him, like some damn secret he was the only one who didn't know?

'Perhaps we ought to review your proposals,' Sandro said after a moment. 'I'd be interested in knowing just what they are.'

Something flickered across Leo's face, something sad, almost like grief. 'Of course,' he said. 'I'll have my assistant put all the relevant paperwork in your study.'

They held each other's gaze for a moment longer, a moment that felt taut with tension, almost hostile. Then Sandro broke first, reaching for another sheaf of papers as the meeting went on.

Three hours later Sandro sat in his father's study, dazed by what he had learned and read. What he had never known, even if he should have. Guessed, or at least wondered about.

For fifteen years Leo had thought he would be king. Sandro had been utterly out of the picture, disinherited, as good as forgotten, and Leo would have been preparing for his own kingship, planning on it. And then Sandro had swept in and taken it away without so much as a passing thought for his brother.

He sank onto a chair in his study, his head in his hands. He'd spent the past few hours reading all of Leo's proposals, well-thought-out multi-year plans for industry, economic policy, energy efficiency. After his father's outdated and uninterested reign, Leo had been poised to take Maldinia in a whole new and exciting direction.

Until Sandro had returned and taken it all away from him.

Sandro's mind spun with realisations, with new understanding about the nature of the coolness between him and the brother he'd once loved more than any other person. The brother who had hero-worshipped him as a child. The brother who he had left because he'd been so angry and hurt by his father's contempt and rejection.

The brother, he thought hollowly, who would make an excellent king.

Better than he would.

Why had Leo never told him of his ambitions, his plans? When Sandro had returned, Leo had not made a single protest. He'd stepped aside so quickly Sandro had assumed he'd been relieved to be done of his duty. He'd projected his own feelings onto Leo without ever really considering how his brother might have changed over the past decade and a half.

Yet the uncertainty had always been there, lingering. The fear that Leo would make a better king than he would—deserved to be king more than he did—had always taunted him from the dark corners of his heart and mind.

And now?

Now, Sandro thought numbly, he should step aside and let his brother rule as he'd been intending to for so long. As he deserved to. The cabinet would surely approve; their respect and admiration for Leo and his proposals had been evident in every word they'd spoken this afternoon.

And if Leo were king…Sandro would be free, as he'd claimed he always wanted. He could return to California, take up the reins of his IT firm once more. Be his own man. Live his own life.

Why did the thought make his stomach sour and his fists clench?

He knew why; of course he did. Because of Liana. Liana had married him to become queen. No matter what feelings had since grown between them since then, he could not escape that truth. He couldn't escape the hard reality that their marriage was that of a king and queen, based on convenience and duty. Not a man and woman deeply in love, as much as he might still wish for it. As much as it had felt like that, for the past few weeks.

Weeks. They'd only had weeks together, little more than a handful of days. Put that against fifteen years of Leo working for the monarchy and there was no question. No contest.

A knock sounded on the door and Sandro jerked his head up, blinking the room back into focus. 'Come in.'

'Sandro?' Leo stood in the doorway.

Sandro stared at his brother and felt a pressure build in his chest. Everything inside him felt so tight and aching he could barely force the words out. 'Why didn't you tell me?'

Quietly Leo closed the door, leaned against it. 'Tell you what, exactly?'

'How hard you've been working these past fifteen years—'

Leo raised an eyebrow. 'Did you think I'd been slacking off?'

'No, but—' Sandro raked his hands through his hair, shook his head. 'I thought— I thought— I don't know what I thought.'

'Exactly,' Leo answered, and with a jolt Sandro realised that underneath his brother's unruffled attitude was a deep, latent anger—an anger he was now giving voice to, even as his tone remained steady. 'You didn't think. You haven't thought about me or what I've been doing when you were away for fifteen years, Sandro, and you didn't think about me when you returned.'

Sandro stared at Leo, felt a hot rush of shame sweep over him. 'That's not true, Leo. I did think of you.'

'In passing?' The cynicism in his brother's voice tore at him. 'A moment here or there? You didn't even say goodbye.'

Sandro glanced down. No more excuses. 'I'm sorry,' he said quietly. 'I should have. I should have done it all differently.'

'So why did you leave, out of curiosity?' Leo asked after a moment. 'Did it all just get a bit much for you?'

'I suppose you could say that. I felt— I honestly felt as if I'd lose my soul if I stayed another minute. All the lies, Leo, all the pretending. I couldn't stand it.'

'Neither could I.'

'I know.' Sandro dragged in a breath. 'And I'm sorry if it felt as if I were dumping you in it. But when Father disinherited me— Well, I had no choice then. I had no place here.'

Leo's expression tightened. 'He only disinherited you because you told him you were leaving.'

'I was bluffing,' Sandro confessed flatly. He felt that familiar ache in his chest. 'I was trying to make him admit— Oh, God, I don't even know what. That he needed me. Loved me.' He blinked hard and set his jaw. 'Stupid, I know.'

He couldn't look at Leo, didn't want to see the pity or scorn on his brother's face. 'Not stupid,' Leo said after a moment. 'Naive, maybe, in believing there was anything good in him. He was the most selfish man I ever knew.'

'And I can't believe I didn't see that until I was eighteen years old. You saw through him from the first, didn' you? And I insisted on believing he was a good man. That he loved me.'

Leo shrugged. 'I was always more cynical than you.'

'I am sorry,' Sandro said again, and he felt his regret and remorse with every fibre of his being. He hoped his brother did too. 'I should have reached out to you. Explained. And when I came back I should have asked if you still wanted to be king—'

'It's not a game of pass the parcel, Sandro. Father chose you to be king. He never really wanted me.'

Sandro shook his head. 'That's not true. It was me he didn't want.'

Leo let out a hard bark of laughter. 'Oh? How do you reckon that?'

'He told me. When I threatened to leave. He said he didn't care, I should go right ahead, because he had another son who would do just as well.'

Leo stared at him for a long moment. 'He never acted as if he thought I would,' he finally said. 'He was always telling me how I was second choice, second best, and he only put up with me at all because you were out of the picture.'

Sandro shook his head slowly. 'What a bastard.'

'I know.'

They sat in silence for a moment, but it lacked the tension and hostility of a few moments before. It felt more like grief.

'Even when I came back,' Sandro finally said, the words painful to admit even though he knew Leo needed to hear them, 'he said he'd still rather have you as his heir. It was only because of the media fallout with Alyse that he summoned me.'

'He was just looking for an excuse to get you back.'

'I don't know.' Sandro sat back in his chair, weary and

heartsick at the thought of how their father had manipulated them for so long. Hurt them with his casual cruelty. 'It's all so pointless. Why did he want us both to feel like a second choice? What good would it do?'

'Because he was a weak man and he wanted us to be weak. Strength scared him. If one of us was actually a decent king, his own legacy would look even worse.'

'Maybe so.' They were both silent for a moment, and then, a new heaviness inside him, Sandro spoke again. 'And you would be a good king, Leo, no matter what our father thought.'

Leo just shrugged. 'I would have done my duty, just as you will.'

'I wish I'd known—'

'Do you, really?' There was no anger in Leo's voice, just a certain shrewdness. 'Because you never asked.'

'I know.' His own weakness shamed him. He hadn't asked because he hadn't really wanted to know, no matter what he said now. Hadn't wanted to consider that not only did he not deserve his title, but his brother did. 'I've been ashamed of myself, Leo. For running away all those years ago. For not being strong enough to stay. What kind of king acts like that?'

Leo was silent for a long moment. 'Sometimes it's stronger to go.'

'It didn't feel like strength to me.'

'You did what you needed to do, Sandro. There's no point raking yourself over the coals now. The past is finished.'

'It's not finished,' Sandro said quietly. 'Not yet.'

Leo frowned. 'What do you mean?'

He met his brother's gaze squarely. 'You should be king.'

Leo narrowed his eyes. 'Sandro—'

'I shouldn't have come back,' he continued steadily, as if Leo hadn't even spoken. 'If I hadn't, you'd be king now. All those plans, all those proposals—you'd have put them into place.'

Leo just shrugged again, but Sandro saw a certain tautness to his brother's mouth, a hardness in his eyes. He was right; his brother still wanted to be king. Still *should* be king. 'Tell me, Leo, that there isn't at least a part of you that wants what you deserve. What you'd been preparing for, for half of your life. It's only natural—'

'Fine. Yes.' Leo bit off the words and spat them out. 'I'll admit it. A *part*. It's hard to let go of certain expectations of what you think your life is going to look like. I thought I'd be king, and I wanted to be a damn good one after Father. Then in the matter of a moment it was snatched away from me. I won't pretend that didn't sting a little, Sandro.'

'More than a little.'

'Fine. Yes. What does it matter now?'

'It matters now,' Sandro said quietly, 'because I should abdicate. Let you take the throne as planned.'

Leo's eyebrows shot up. 'Don't be ridiculous—'

'I've only been king for six months. A blip on the radar. The people here don't even know me, except as the brother who ran away.' His smile twisted. 'The prodigal son. I don't know why I didn't see it before. I suppose I was too blinded by my own misery. But it makes sense, Leo. You know it does.'

'I don't know anything of the sort.' Leo's jaw bunched. 'Stop talking nonsense, Sandro.'

'It isn't nonsense—'

'Do you *want* to abdicate?'

He heard curiosity in his brother's voice, but also a certain eagerness, even if Leo would insist otherwise

with every breath in his body. Sandro knew better, and
he kept his face blank, his voice toneless, as he gave the
only answer he could. 'Of course I do. It's the right thing
to do. You'd make a better king, and I never wanted to
be king anyway. You know that, Leo.' He felt as if the
words were tearing great strips off his soul, pieces from
his heart, and yet he knew it was the only thing he could
say. Could do, even if it meant losing Liana. His brother
deserved his rightful place.

And he deserved his.

Woodenly he rose from the desk. 'It shouldn't take
long to put it into motion.'

'Sandro, wait. Don't do anything rash—'

'It's not rash. It's obvious to me, Leo. And to you, I
think.'

He turned, saw his brother shaking his head, but there
was a light in his eyes neither of them could deny. He
wanted this. Of course he did.

Smiling, Sandro put a hand on Leo's shoulder. 'I'm
happy for you,' he said, and then he left the room.

Liana gazed in the mirror, smoothed a strand of hair away
from her forehead and checked that her dress—a full-
skirted evening gown in a silvery pink—looked all right.

She heard the door to her bedroom open and saw with
a light heart that it was Sandro.

'I was wondering where you were. We're due at the
Museum of Fine Art in an hour for the opening of the
new wing.' Sandro didn't answer, and she smoothed the
skirt of her evening gown. 'I don't know about this dress.
Do I look too much like Cinderella?'

'An apt comparison.'

She laughed lightly and shook her head. 'How's that?'

'She found her prince, didn't she? At the ball. And then she lost him again.'

For the first time since he'd entered the room Liana registered his tone: cool and flat. She turned to face him with a frown. 'What's wrong, Sandro?'

He lifted one shoulder in a shrug. 'Nothing's wrong.'

Confusion deepened into unease. Alarm. 'You're acting rather strange.'

'I had an eye-opening cabinet meeting today.'

'Oh?' Liana eyed him warily, noting the almost eerie stillness of his body, the blankness of his face. She hadn't seen him look like this in weeks...since they'd first been strangers to one another, talking marriage. 'Eye-opening?' she repeated cautiously. 'Why don't you tell me about it?'

'The details don't matter,' he dismissed. 'But it's made me realise—' He stopped suddenly, and for a moment the blankness of his face was broken by a look of such anguish that Liana started forward, her hands outstretched.

'Sandro, what is it? What's wrong?'

'I'm planning to abdicate, Liana.'

Sandro watched the shock rush over Liana, making her eyes widen, her face go pale. She looked, he thought heavily, horrified.

'Abdicating?' she finally repeated, her voice little more than a whisper. 'But...why?'

He felt emotions catch in his chest, words lodge in his throat and tangle on his tongue. So far her reaction was far from hopeful. She looked shell-shocked. Devastated. And all because she wouldn't be queen. 'Does it really matter?'

'Of course it matters.'

'Why?' The one word was raw, torn from him. He

stared at her, willing her expression to clear, for her to say it didn't matter, after all. She'd follow him anywhere. She'd love him without a throne or a title or a crown. But why should she say that? She obviously didn't feel it.

She didn't say anything. She just stared at him helplessly, her face pale and shocked as she shook her head slowly. 'Because, Sandro, you're *king*. And I'm your wife.'

'My queen.'

'Yes, your queen! You can't just leave that behind—'

'But I did before, as you've reminded me—'

'I've reminded you? When was the last time I've mentioned that?'

'You haven't forgotten.'

'I don't have amnesia! It's not something you can just forget.'

'Exactly.'

'Why are you thinking of this?' Liana asked, her voice wavering, her expression still dazed. 'It seems so sudden—'

'And unwelcome, obviously.' There could be no mistaking her disappointment, her distress at learning he might no longer be king. And she would no longer be queen.

'Of course it's unwelcome,' Liana said, and Sandro's last frail hope withered to ash. 'We were just starting to build a life here, a life I thought you were happy with—'

'Being king is not my life. It's not *me*.' The words, he knew, had been in his heart, burning in his chest for his whole life. Hadn't he wanted his parents, his friends, *anyone* to see that he was more than this title, this role? Hadn't he wanted just one person in his life to see him as something other than future king, heir apparent?

And obviously Liana didn't. He hated that he'd put

himself out there again. 'But obviously,' he continued, his voice cold and lifeless now, 'you don't feel the same.'

Liana went even paler, even stiller. 'What do you mean?'

'Our marriage doesn't have much point now, does it?' he asked, his mouth forming a horrible parody of a smile. 'If I'm not king, you're not queen.'

Something flashed across her face but he couldn't tell what it was. 'True,' she said, her voice expressionless. She'd assembled her features into a mask, the Madonna face he recognised from when they'd first met, icy and composed. Sandro hated seeing her like that again, when he'd seen her so vibrant and beautiful and alive. So real with him...except perhaps none of it had been real, after all, or at least not real enough.

'And if our marriage has no point,' he forced himself to continue, 'then there's no point to being married.'

He didn't see so much as a flicker on her face. *Damn it,* he thought, *say something. Fight for me. For us.* Here he was, pushing as he always did, practically begging. *Accept me. Love me.* And of course she didn't.

She just remained silent, staring and still. No response at all. Even so Sandro ached to go to her, take her in his arms. Kiss her into responding to him, just as he had when they'd first met. He wanted to demand that she admit the days they had were real, and they could have more. That she could love him even if he weren't king.

Still Liana didn't speak, and with a sound that was somewhere between a sneer and a sob Sandro stalked out of the room.

Liana stood there, unmoving and silent as the door clicked shut. He'd left. In a matter of moments—not much more than a minute—her entire life, all her hope and happiness, had been destroyed.

Just as before.

Just as when Chiara had choked to death and she'd watched and done nothing. Been unable to do anything, and that appalling lack of action would haunt her for all of her days.

And had she learned nothing in the past twenty years? Once again she'd let her own stunned silence damn her. She had seen from Sandro's expression that he wanted something from her—but what? As she'd stared at him, his expression so horribly blank, she'd had no idea what it was. And while her mind spun and her body remained still, he walked out of her room.

Out of her life.

As if the realisation had kick-started her, she suddenly jerked to life, strode to the door, and wrenched it open. Sandro was halfway down the hallway, his bearing straight and proud as he walked away from her.

'Stop right there, Sandro.'

He stiffened, stilled, then slowly turned around. 'I don't think we have anything more to say to each other.'

'You don't *think*?' Liana repeated in disbelief. She grabbed handfuls of her frothy dress as she strode towards him, full of sudden, consuming rage. 'You just drop that bombshell on me and walk out of my life with hardly a word, and you think that's *it*?' Her voice shook and tears started in her eyes, although she didn't know whether they were of anger or grief. 'You told me you *loved* me, Sandro. Was that a lie?'

'You told me the same,' he answered coolly.

She stared at him for a moment, trying to fathom what had brought him to this decision. 'I think I get it,' she finally said slowly. 'This is another ultimatum.'

'Another—'

'Just like with your father.'

'Don't—'

'Don't what? Don't tell the truth? You threatened to leave once before, Sandro, with your father all those years ago. You wanted him to admit he loved you and he didn't. He disappointed you and so you left, and now you're doing the same to me, threatening me—'

'It wasn't a *threat*.'

'Maybe you don't think it was. Maybe you are seriously considering abdicating. But you didn't come to me as a husband, Sandro. As a—a lover and a friend. You didn't sit me down and tell me what was on your mind, in your heart, and what I might think about it. No, you just walk in and drop your damned bomb and then leave before the debris has even cleared.'

'Your response was obvious—'

'Oh, really? Because as I recall I didn't say much of anything. I was still processing it all and you decided that meant I couldn't love you if you weren't king. You jumped to so many damn conclusions you made my head spin.' And her heart break.

Sandro folded his arms. 'You made your reasons for our marriage clear, Liana. You wanted to be queen—'

'You're going to throw that at me? After everything we've said and done and felt?' She shook her head, her throat too thick with tears to speak. Finally she got some words out. 'Damn you, Sandro. Damn you for only thinking about your feelings and not mine.'

A muscle flickered in his jaw. 'So you're denying it?'

'Denying what?'

'That you married me to become queen—'

'No, of course not. That is why I chose to marry you. There were a lot of messed-up reasons behind that choice, but what I am trying to say—what I thought you knew—is that I've *changed*. As I thought you had changed, except maybe you didn't because I thought you were a cold-hearted bastard when I met you, and you certainly seem like one now.' He blinked, said nothing, and the floodgates of Liana's soul burst open. She drew in a wet, revealing breath.

'I never told you about Chiara's death.'

He blinked again, clearly surprised, maybe discomfited. 'You told me she choked—'

'Yes, she had a seizure and she choked on her own vomit. But what I didn't tell you was that I was there. The only one there. My parents were away and our nanny was busy. I was alone in the room with her and I watched her choke and I couldn't move to help her. Couldn't even speak. I panicked, Sandro, so badly that it caused my sister's death. I could have run to her, could have called for help, and instead I was frozen to the floor with shock and fear.' She felt her chest go tight and her vision tunnel as in her mind's eye Chiara's desperate face stared up at her in mute appeal. And she'd simply stood there, wringing her hands. 'By the time I finally got myself to move, it was too late.' She'd run to her, turned her over. Cleared out her mouth with her own scrabbling fingers, sobbing her sister's name. And Chiara had just stared lifelessly back. *Too late.*

Liana drew in another ragged breath. 'I as good as killed her, Sandro, and I'll live with that for my whole life.' She realised, distantly, that tears were running down her face but she didn't care. Didn't wipe them away. 'And when you delivered your awful ultimatum, I froze again. Didn't speak. Didn't move. But damn if I'm going to lose my soul again, Sandro, because I didn't have the courage or the presence of mind to do something.'

She stepped closer to him, close enough to poke him in the chest. 'I love you. You love me. At least I hope you do, after what I just told you—'

He shook his head, his own eyes bright. 'Do you really think something like that would make me change my mind?'

'I don't know. It changed my parents' minds. At least, it felt like that. We've never recovered. I never recovered, because I spent the past twenty years living my life as an apology and cloaking myself in numbness because feeling meant feeling all the guilt and shame and fear, and I couldn't do that and survive.'

'Liana—' Sandro's face was twisted with anguish, but she wasn't done.

'So we love each other, then, and I might not know much about love but I do know that when you love someone, you believe the best of them. You don't wait for them to let you down. You don't set up situations so they fail. Maybe you've been looking for love for most of your life, Sandro, since you didn't get it from your parents. Guess what? I didn't get it either. My father has barely looked at me since Chiara died. But even I know enough to realise that you don't find love when you act like it's going to disappoint you. When you don't trust it or the person who is meant to love you for five minutes of honest conversation.' She shook her head, empty now, so terribly empty. 'You think I disappointed you by not saying something when you wanted me to. Well, you know what, Sandro? *You* disappointed *me*.'

And with another hopeless shake of her head, she turned and walked back down the hall, away from him.

CHAPTER TWELVE

HE'D SCREWED UP. Big time. It was nearing midnight and Sandro sat in his study, gazing broodingly into space.

Every word Liana had spoken was true.

He had given her an ultimatum, been testing her and the truth of her feelings. It had been an arrogant and appalling thing to do, and, worst of all, he'd been so self-righteous about it.

And while he hadn't had the courage to be honest with her, she'd possessed more than enough to be honest with him. He thought of what she'd admitted about her sister and felt tears sting his eyes.

He was such a bastard.

It had taken him all of ten seconds to realise just how wrong he was, but ten seconds was too long because Liana had already locked her bedroom door, and she wouldn't answer it when he hammered on it and asked her—begged her—to let him in.

He'd hated feeling as if he was begging for love or just simple affection from his parents, hated how as a child he'd always tried to get his father to notice him. But he didn't care now how desperate or foolish or pathetic he looked. He'd go down on his knees to beg his wife to forgive him. He just wanted to be given the chance.

He heard the door to his study open and lurched forwards, hoping against all the odds that it was Liana.

It wasn't. It was Leo.

'Sandro,' he said, unsmiling. 'What the hell did you do?'

'What do you mean?'

'Half the palace could hear Liana shouting at you. And she doesn't shout.'

'I told her I was abdicating.'

Leo stared at him for a long moment. 'Sandro,' he finally said, 'you are a damned idiot.'

Sandro tried to smile, but it felt as if his face were cracking apart. 'I know.'

Leo stepped forward. 'And so am I.'

'What do you mean?'

'I don't want you to abdicate, Sandro. I don't want to be king.'

Sandro shook his head. 'I saw it in your eyes—'

Leo shook his head impatiently. 'Oh, screw that. Yes, as I told you before, there is a part of me that feels hard done by. Disappointed. I'll get over it, Sandro. I'm a big boy. So are you. And you have spent the past six months working yourself to the bloody bone to prove what a good king you are. A great king. You're the only one who doesn't think so.'

'No, I don't,' Sandro said in a low voice. He closed his eyes briefly. It was the first time he'd admitted it out loud.

'And why is that? Why don't you think you'll make— *you are*—a good king?'

Sandro didn't answer for a long moment. Admitting so much to anyone, especially Leo, who had once idolised him, was painful. 'Because,' he finally said in a low voice, 'I shirked my duty, didn't I? I ran away.'

'And you came back.'

'After fifteen years—'

'So? Is there a time limit? And running away—if you really want to call it that—seemed like your only choice back then.' Leo's voice roughened with emotion. 'I believe that, Sandro, even if I've acted like I didn't because I was hurt. I know you wouldn't have left me like that unless you felt you had to.'

Sandro felt his eyes fill. 'I wouldn't have,' he said, his voice choked as he blinked hard. 'I swear to you, Leo, I wouldn't have.'

They stared at each other, faces full of emotion, the air thick with both regret and forgiveness.

Finally Leo smiled, and Sandro did too. 'Well, then,' he said. 'You see?'

Sandro dragged a hand over his eyes. 'I'm not sure I see anything.'

'Leave behind the bitterness and anger, Sandro. Forget about how Mother and Father raised us, how they treated the monarchy. Usher in a new kingdom, begin a new era. You can do it.'

'And what about you?'

'Like I said, I'll get over it. And to be honest, I'm a little relieved. I admit, when you first came back, I was shocked. Hurt too, if I'm honest, because after fifteen years of working myself to the bone to prove myself to our father, he cast me aside at the first opportunity. But I've already promised myself not to live steeped in bitterness or regret, Sandro, and in their own way things have worked out for the best. I'm happy not to be in the spotlight. So is Alyse. We've spent a hell of a long time there, and it wasn't very pleasant.'

'And what of your ambitions? Your plans?'

With a wry smile Leo gestured to the papers scattered

across the desk. 'Feel free to use them. And consult me anytime. My fees are quite reasonable.'

Sandro felt something unfurl inside him, a kind of fragile, incredulous hope. 'I don't know,' he said and Leo just smiled.

'No one does, do they? No one knows what's going to work, what's going to happen. But you have my support, and Alyse's, and the cabinet's.' He paused. 'And you have Liana's, but you might have to grovel a bit to get it back.'

To his amazement Sandro felt a small smile quirk his mouth. 'There's no might about it,' he answered. 'That's a definite.'

'So what are you waiting for?'

'She won't see me.'

'She's angry and hurt. Give her a little time.'

Sandro nodded, even though he didn't want to give her time. Didn't want to wait. He wanted to break her door down and demand that she listen to him. Tell her what an ass he'd been and how much he loved her.

He just needed to find a way to make her listen.

Liana stood in her bedroom with its spindly chairs and feminine décor and stared out of the window at the gardens now in full, glorious spring. The roses were just beginning to unfurl, their petals silky and fragrant. Everything was coming to life, and she felt as if she was dead inside.

She had barely slept last night, had tossed and turned and tormented herself with all the what-ifs. What if she'd said something when Sandro had wanted her to? What if she'd let him back in when he'd knocked on her door and asked her to talk to him?

But she couldn't talk; she felt too empty and grief-stricken for words. She'd given Sandro everything. *Ev-*

erything. And he hadn't loved her enough to wait five minutes—five *seconds*—to explain. Say something. Do something.

And what had he done but judge her and jump to conclusions? Was that what love was?

If so, she was better off without it. Without him.

Even if her heart felt like some raw, wounded thing, pulsing painfully inside her. It would heal. She would. She didn't want to go back to numbness, but maybe she'd go back a *little.* Feel a little less. Eventually.

And as for her marriage? Sandro was right; if he wasn't king, she didn't need to be queen. They certainly didn't need to stay married for convenience's sake. He didn't need an heir, after all, and maybe he wanted to return to his life in California. Maybe he didn't want her anymore. Maybe her confession about Chiara had made him despise her.

Yet the thought of actually divorcing was too awful to contemplate. Maybe they would simply live as strangers, seeing as little of each other as possible, just as she'd envisioned a lifetime ago. Just as she'd *wanted.*

The thought was almost laughable, ridiculous; she certainly didn't want it now. But after the debacle of their confrontation last night, she wasn't sure how they could go on.

Behind her she heard the door open and she drew a shuddering breath. She'd asked Rosa to bring her breakfast to her room because she couldn't face seeing everyone—much less Sandro—in the dining room.

'Liana.'

Everything in her tensed at the sound of Sandro's voice. She turned, saw he was carrying her breakfast tray. She shook her head.

'Don't, Sandro.' Although she wasn't sure what she

was asking him not to do. *Don't break my heart, fragile thing that it is, again.*

'Don't what?' he asked quietly. 'Don't say I'm sorry?'

She drew a shuddering breath. 'Are you?'

'Unbelievably so. More than I've ever been, for anything, in my life.'

She shook her head. It wasn't that simple, that easy. 'Why did you do that to me?'

'Because I'm a stupid, selfish idiot.'

'I'm serious, Sandro.'

'So am I.' With a sad smile he put the breakfast tray down on the table by her bed. He gestured at one of the silver dishes on the tray. 'Strawberries. No chocolate, though.'

Liana just folded her arms. 'I want answers, Sandro.'

'And I'll tell you. You know how you thought you looked like Cinderella last night?'

She eyed him warily; she had no idea where he was going with this. 'Yes....'

'You are Cinderella, Liana. You came to the castle to marry a prince, except in this case the said prince was a king and he wasn't all that charming. He was kind of an ass, actually.'

A smile twitched at her mouth even though she still felt heavy inside. 'Was he? Why?'

'Because he was so consumed with how frustrated he felt and all the things he wanted out of life that he didn't have and how no one loved him. Pathetic, whingy little so-and-so, really.'

'I think you might be being a little hard on him.'

'No, he definitely was. He never thought about what other people might be feeling, especially his Cinderella.'

Her mouth curved again in a tremulous smile, almost

of its own volition. 'I wouldn't say he was *quite* that self-absorbed.'

'He was worse,' Sandro answered. 'Cinderella couldn't find that pointy glass slipper because it was stuck up his ass.'

She let out a sudden, startled laugh. '*Sandro*—'

'He had no idea what he was doing or how much he was hurting people.' He took a step towards her, a sad, whimsical smile on his face. 'Seriously, Liana, he was a mess.'

'And what happened?'

'Cinderella woke him up with a good old slap. Yanked her shoe out and made him realise just how self-important and stupid he was being—about a lot of things. Her. His family. His past. Himself.'

'And?' she asked softly.

'And he only hopes he can still make it right.' He took another step towards her, and he was close enough to touch. She almost did. 'I hope I can make it right, Liana, by telling you how wrong I've been. How unbelievably, unbearably stupid and selfish.' The smile he gave her was shaky, vulnerable, and it made her yearn. She shook her head, not ready to surrender even though another part of her ached to.

'You hurt me, Sandro.'

'I know. I was so afraid of being pushed away again. Rejected. And instead I did exactly what you said. I set up a situation where I'd force you to fail, because it was better than feeling like a failure myself. I'm so sorry.'

Liana felt the burn of tears beneath her lids. 'I forgive you.'

'Enough to take me back?'

She wanted him back. Wanted his arms around her,

her head on his shoulder, the steady thud of his heart against her cheek. 'You can't ever do that again.'

'I won't.'

'I know we'll argue, Sandro, I'm not saying we can't disagree or get angry or annoyed or what have you. But you can't—you can't set me up like that. Make me feel like a failure.' Her throat clogged and she blinked hard. 'Because I've felt like that before, and I don't ever want to feel it again.'

'Oh, Liana. Sweetheart.' He took her in his arms then, and she went, pressing her cheek against his shoulder just as she'd longed to. 'I'm sorry for what you endured with your sister,' he whispered, and the first tears started to spill.

'It was my fault.'

'No, it wasn't.'

'Didn't you listen—?'

'I listened, Liana. And I heard a woman who has been torturing herself for two decades about something that was an accident. You were eight years old, Liana, and you were in shock. Where was that nanny anyway?'

'I don't know.'

'If anyone should feel guilty—'

'But I should have done something. I could have—'

'Did you love your sister?'

'More than anything—'

'Then how can you blame yourself for something that was out of your control? If you could have saved her, you would have. The fact that you didn't meant you weren't able to. You didn't know how. You panicked, you froze, yes, but you were *eight*, Liana, a child. And someone else should have been there.'

She shook her head, her tears falling freely now. 'It's not that easy.'

'No, it isn't. But if you can forgive me, then you can forgive yourself. For your own sake, Liana, as well as mine. Because I love you so very much and I can't stand the thought of this guilt eating away at you until there's nothing left.' He eased back from her, gazed down at her with eyes that shone silver. 'I love you. I love your strength and your grace and even your composure that terrified and annoyed me in turns when we first met. I love how you've stepped so beautifully into being a queen my country—our country—is starting to love, just as I love you.'

His words dazed her so much she could hardly speak. Finally she fastened on to the one thing that seemed least important, least overwhelming. 'But I'm not queen any-more.'

'Yes, you are.' The smile he gave her now was crooked and he reached out to brush at her damp cheeks. 'I'm not going to abdicate. I spoke to Leo, and he talked some sense into me. I realised I was thinking of it because I've felt so much guilt and regret about leaving. Running away. And then I was about to do it again.' He shook his head, his thumbs tracing the lines of her cheekbones, wiping away her tears. 'Do you think you're willing to stay married to such a slow learner? A slow learner who loves you quite desperately?'

'Of course I am.' Liana's lips trembled as she tried to smile. 'I'm a bit of a slow learner, myself. I love you, Sandro, but it scared me for a long time, to feel that much, never mind admitting it. But I do love you. So very much.'

He framed her face with his hands, brought her closer to him so her forehead rested against his. They stayed that way for a moment, neither of them speaking, every-thing in Liana aching with emotion and a new, deeper happiness than she'd ever felt before. A happiness based on total honesty, deep and abiding love.

'We're quite a pair, aren't we?' he murmured. 'Wanting love and being afraid of it at the same time.'

She pressed one hand to his cheek, revelling in the feel of him, and the fact that he was here, that he'd come back and he loved her. 'Love *is* pretty scary,' she said, a smile in her voice, and Sandro nodded, his forehead bumping against hers.

'Terrifying, frankly.'

She let out a shaky laugh and put her arms around him. 'Definitely terrifying. But I do love you, Sandro.'

'And I love you.' He kissed her gently on the lips, a promise and a seal. 'And since it seems that we're both slow learners, it will take us a long time to figure this love out. I think,' he continued as he drew her closer and deepened the kiss, 'it will take the rest of our lives.'

EPILOGUE

One year later

LIANA SMOOTHED THE satin skirt of the gown, admired the admittedly over-the-top ruffles of lace that fell to the floor.

She turned to Sandro with a smile and a shake of her head. 'I can't believe you wore this.'

'If I'd been a little more self-aware at the time, I'm sure I would have been mortified.'

'Well, you were only three months old,' she teased. 'Isabella seems to like it, at any rate.'

'She's a smart girl.'

They both gazed down at their daughter, Isabella Chiara Alexa Diomedi, her eyes already turning the silver-grey of her father's, her dimpled smile reminding Liana with a bittersweet joy of her sister.

With a smile for her daughter, Liana scooped her up and held her against her shoulder, breathed in her warm baby scent.

'Careful,' Sandro warned. 'You just fed her and she likes to give a little bit of that back.' He gave a mock grimace. 'I should know. The palace dry-cleaning bill has skyrocketed since this little one's arrival.'

'I don't mind.'

There was nothing she minded about taking care of her daughter. She was just so happy, so incredulously grateful, to have the opportunity. Isabella's birth had been, in its own way, a healing; no one could replace Chiara, but her daughter's birth had eased the long-held grief of losing her sister.

A gentle knock sounded on the door, and then her mother poked her head in. 'May I come in?'

Liana felt herself tense. Her parents had arrived last night for Isabella's christening; she hadn't actually seen them save for a few formal functions since her wedding. And as usual when she saw her mother, she felt the familiar rush of guilt and regret, tempered now by Sandro's love and her daughter's presence, but still there. Already she could hear the note of apology creep into her voice.

'Of course, Mother. We're just getting Isabella ready for the ceremony.'

Gabriella Aterno stepped into the room, her features looking fragile and faded as always, her smile hesitant and somehow sad.

Sandro stepped forward. 'Would you like to hold her?'

'Oh—may I?'

'Of course,' Liana said, and, with her heart full of too many emotions to name, she handed her daughter to her mother.

Gabriella looked down into Isabella's tiny, impish face and let out a ragged little laugh. 'She has Chiara's dimples.'

Liana felt a flash of shock; her mother had not mentioned Chiara once since her sister's funeral. Twenty-one years of silence.

'She does,' she agreed quietly. 'And her smile.'

'Perhaps she'll have her dark curls.' Gently Gabriella fingered Isabella's wispy, dark hair. 'You two were al-

ways so different in looks. No one would have thought
you were sisters, save for the way you loved each other.'
She looked up then, her eyes shining with tears, the grief
naked in her face, and Liana knew how much just those
few sentences had cost her.

'Oh, Mother,' she whispered. She swallowed past the
tightness in her throat. 'I'm so sorry—'

'I'm sorry Chiara isn't here to see her niece,' Gabriella
said. 'But I like to think she still sees, from somewhere.'

'Me too.' Liana blinked hard, focused on her daughter
in her mother's arms, and said what had been burning inside her for too many years. 'I'm sorry I didn't save her.'

Gabriella jerked her head up, her eyes wide with
shock. 'Save her? Liana, you were eight years old.'

'I know, but I was there.' Liana blinked hard, but it was
too late. The tears came anyway. 'I saw— I *watched*—'

'And you've blamed yourself all this time,' Gabriella
said softly. 'Oh, my dear.'

'Of course I blamed myself,' Liana answered, batting
uselessly at the tears that trickled down her cheeks. 'And
you blamed me too, Mother, and Father as well. I'm not
angry—I understand why—' She choked on the words,
felt Sandro's comforting hand on her shoulder, and she
pressed her cheek against it, closed her eyes against the
rush of pain and tried to will the tears back.

'Liana, my dear, we blamed ourselves,' Gabriella confessed, her voice trembling with emotion. 'Of course we
did—we were her parents. She was our responsibility,
not yours.'

Liana opened her eyes, stared at her mother's grief-
stricken face. 'But you never said anything,' she whispered. 'Father hasn't even so much as hugged me since—'

'We didn't like to talk about it,' Gabriella told her. 'As

I'm sure you realised. Not because of you, though, but because of us. We felt so wretchedly guilty. I still do.'

'Oh, Mother, no—' Impulsively and yet instinctively Liana went to put her arms around Gabriella, the baby between them.

'All three of us have been consumed by guilt, it seems,' Gabriella said with a sniff. 'And I know your father and I didn't handle it properly back then, or ever. We should have been there for you, spoken to you about it, helped you to grieve. We were too wrapped up in our own pain, and I'm sorry for that.' She shook her head slowly, her eyes still bright with tears. 'I'm sorry I didn't realise how much you blamed yourself. I just assumed—' Her mother drew in a quick breath. 'Assumed you blamed me.'

Liana shook her head. 'No, never.'

They were both silent for a moment, struggling with these new revelations and the emotions they called up. In Gabriella's arms Isabella stirred, gurgled, and then gave her grandmother a big, drooly smile.

Gabriella let out a choked cry of surprise and joy. She turned to Liana with a tear trickling down one pale cheek. 'Then maybe this is a new start for all of us, Liana,' she said, her voice wavering, and Liana nodded and smiled.

She knew there was more to be said, to be confessed and explained and forgiven, but for now she revelled in the second chance they'd all been granted. A second chance at happiness, at love, at life itself.

Gabriella handed the baby back to Sandro and slipped down to the chapel where the christening would be held. Liana gazed at her husband and daughter and felt her heart might burst with so much feeling. She felt so much now, all the emotions she'd denied herself for so long. Joy and wonder, grief and sorrow. She wouldn't keep herself from feeling any of it ever again.

'I couldn't have imagined any of this before I met you,' she said softly. 'Talking to my mother so honestly. Having a husband and child of my own. Loving someone as much as I love you. You've changed me, Sandro.'

'And you've changed me. Thank God.' He smiled wryly and then, with the expertise of a father of a baby, he shifted Isabella to his other shoulder and drew Liana towards him for a kiss. 'This really is the beginning, Liana,' he said softly as he kissed her again. 'Of everything.'

* * * * *